RISE OF THE EXILED LADY

BOOKS BY MICHAEL J ALLEN

<u>Blood Phoenix:</u>
1. ASHES OF RAGING WATER
2. RULED BY TAINTED BLOOD
3. VENGEFUL ARE THE DROWNED
4. RISE OF THE EXILED LADY
5. RAZING THE LAST BASTION

<u>Scion (Original):</u>
1. SCION OF CONQUERED EARTH
2. STOLEN LIVES
3. HIJACKED
4. UNCHAINED

<u>Bittergate:</u>
1. MURDER IN WIZARD'S WOOD
2. THE WIZARD'S BANE
3. FORGE OF WAR
4. SCYTHE OF ILLUSIONS

<u>Guns of Underhill:</u>
1. FEY WEST

<u>Dumpstermancer:</u>
1. DISCARDED
2. DUPLICITY

<u>Delirious Scribbles:</u>
(SHORT STORIES)

- WYRM'S WARNING
- SCRAPING BOTTOM
- CRIMINAL JUSTICE
- DREAMS OF TREASURE
- DESPERATE
- THE BOTTOM LINE

COMING SOON:

<u>Binarai Online:</u>
1. STORM REFUGE
2. ROGUE PLANET
3. POWER BREAK

<u>Wayman Chronicles:</u>
1. CROSSWAYS

<u>Guns of Underhill:</u>
2. METTLE KINGDOM

<u>Dumpstermancer:</u>
3. DECOY

<u>Scion Rising (Remaster)</u>

RISE OF THE EXILED LADY

BLOOD PHOENIX CHRONICLES: BOOK FOUR

MICHAEL J ALLEN

Delirious
Scribbles Ink

Delirious Scribbles Ink, Inc.

Copyright

This is a work of fiction. Names, characters, places and incidents are a product of the author's imagination or are used fictitiously. Locales, businesses, companies, events, institutions, and public names are sometimes used under fair use licensing for atmospheric purposes only and are not representative of their namesake. Any resemblance to actual people—living, dead or in between—is completely coincidental.

Copyright © 2019 by Michael J. Allen.

All rights reserved. No part of this publication may be reproduced, distributed or transmitted in any form or by any means, including photocopying, recording, or other electronic or mechanical methods, without the prior written permission of the publisher, except in the case of brief quotations embodied in critical reviews and certain other noncommercial uses permitted by copyright law. For permission requests, write to the publisher, addressed "Attention: Permissions Coordinator," at the address below.

Delirious Scribbles Ink, Inc.
4519 Woodruff Road
Suite 4, #108
Columbus, Georgia 31904
www.deliriousscribblesink.com

Interior Layout ©2022 Delirious Scribbles Ink, Inc.
Cover Design ©2022 Delirious Scribbles Ink, Inc.
Cover Art ©2019 Andrea Fodor

ISBN 978-1-944357-14-6 (intl. tr. pbk.)
ISBN 978-1-944357-18-4 (hc.)
ISBN 978-1-944357-09-2 (epub)
ISBN 978-1-944357-76-4 (large print)

Printed in the United States of America
10 9 8 7 6 5 4 3 2 1
Rise of the Exiled Lady / Michael J. Allen. — 1st ed.

For Dave, yet another inspiring author friend who challenges me to be better, nicer and much, much taller.

For B, B & E, J, S & J, and L.

Delirious Scribbles Readers Group

Like free stories?

How about curated deals for Science Fiction and Fantasy books?

Get your first benefit—a FREE story sent right to you—by becoming a member of the Delirious Scribbles Readers Group.

Begin your journey, just scan this image with your phone camera!

Content Advisory

In order to provide my readers the best possible experience as well as be responsive to reader requests, I've created a reader-curated content advisory on my website. If you are sensitive to certain kinds of fictional representations, please check this book's listings before reading.

I hope you enjoy this story...

— Michael J Allen

To visit the advisory, just scan this image with your phone camera.

Chapter One

Legions of Strife

Vitae

Scurith rushed into the faerie glade, entering along the cobbled path through blood-soaked mud. He lowered his grey and tan furred canid form in a hasty bow. "Master, more Sidhe are coming. For your plan to succeed, we must depart before witnesses arrive."

I turned to the faithful thrall who'd sold me out at my request. "Quite right."

Rage and adrenaline eased slowly.

My trap had succeeded perfectly. It was in the Sidhe's nature to betray one another. They expected it. After Aquaylae's betrayal, I knew there was little chance of reclaiming my Champion blades from within Creation. The two elven knights pinned to their knees before me had died too many times, failed too many times to risk one-on-one combat in the mortal realms.

So, I played to their expectations. I'd fabricated a drama with myself as the fool, but it was I left laughing in the end.

My hands massaged the grips of the Seelie and Unseelie Champion blades. Both swords responded to my touch, wriggling to fit the hands of my newest and most superior body yet.

"I very much wish to slay you. Nevertheless, I am willing to be merciful on one condition. As we are low on time, I give you five seconds to oath your cooperation. Swear service unto me in releasing Mare from this blade, and you shall not share the fate of Mariena and Vusolaryn."

"Master, we must hurry. They will not cooperate. Slay them and let us be away."

"Will either of you submit to reason?" I asked.

Dolumii spat in my face.

A growl escaped the trollman holding him.

Gherrian closed his eyes. "I am disinclined."

Scurith whined, ears pressed flat to his head. "Master, if too many arrive, we will not be able to slay them before they are able to report what you've done here."

Irritation flashed through me. My fingers tightened around the swords. "Fine. We'll take Dolumii and Gherrian with us."

"Begging your pardon, Master, but I thought the plan was to slay all witnesses," Scurith said.

I let my cruel intentions play out along raspberry-painted lips. "I'd like to play with them before...well, let's not spoil the surprise."

The coyll bowed, gesturing to my enforcers. The hulking, black-washed mortal corpses my mortal thrall had animated with troll DNA collected the glade's many bodies—living and dead— while the winged, reanimated children's corpses flew overwatch.

As they did so, I transmogrified into pure life plasma. Stepping carefully through the battlefield, being mindful to control my essence lest it burn or stain the ground, I drew all of the spilled Sidhe blood into my body. I absorbed the powerful essence, keeping it separate from my own. Even so, a nova of magic exploded up my legs the moment my essence touched Mariena's spilled blood.

My lips curled.

I'd spoken true. This newest body infused via rebirth with the essence of two powerful knights felt nigh unstoppable in a way none of my previous rebirth experiments had been. Being reborn with the essence of two Nephilim, first children of the Fallen themselves, would make me the greatest shield in history—the Hand of God in Creation.

And with this kind of power, I will wrest Mare from the Champion blade.

I drew in Vusolaryn as I had his rival and stepped through the Arch opened to my palace, leaving behind an immaculate glade and a mystery served up to confound the Sidhe.

Just desserts on a silver platter.

Ignis

Ignis struggled to draw essence around his soul, focusing on dwarfism instead of his customary form. The valve in the stone basin's bottom restricted the flow, but he knew how it worked. He knew essence waited in the reservoir beneath.

Like a flame struggling to catch on an oil lamp's dry wick, his body flickered and faded only to grow to life in the end. His smile blossomed the moment lips formed to hold it.

Quayla beat me.

His center of gravity settled, and he knew by feel that his new body was female. Mahogany locks hung nearly enough to curtain proud bronze breasts. In his new compact body, his dark-walled cage left plenty of room to move. He shifted muscular hips to get a feel for his new flesh.

An angry face, bending left and right trying to see Ignis, appeared beyond the heat-stained square window. "What the hell happened? Why isn't Quayla here?"

Ignis's body flashed to pure flame without a thought, riding the surge of fury through a full body transmog. He raised himself to float where he could meet his enemy's eyes. "I know full well you are watching us, so you know exactly what happened, Dunham. She beat me fair and square, so you can take your questions and shove them up your ass with a hot poker."

A massive weight pressed down on Ignis. Had he still been in a human body, bones would've splintered, but compressing flame only created stars. The pressure eased. Dunham's face disappeared. He returned ahead of a sudden wash of agony. Every atom of Ignis felt as if it were being torn in half.

"I ordered you to feel pain when you even thought such comments," Dunham snarled.

He did at that.

"Why aren't you suffering for your insolence? Tell me the truth."

Despite not having lungs, Ignis's breath left him as Dunham's fingers throttled Ignis's stolen heart.

"I am."

The simple phrase was the literal truth, so no more agony worsened Ignis's ordeal.

"If you don't want to die—"

"Screw off, Dunham. You can't afford to kill any more of us. Besides, I obeyed you to the letter."

Dunham darkened.

Ignis's pain intensified.

The Anseelie Queen appeared over Dunham's shoulder. Her delicate fingers drew him away.

"Where the hell have you been?" Dunham demanded.

For the barest fraction of a split second, fury tightened her eyes. Her face relaxed into a smile. "Little angel's room."

Ignis's pain waned as Dunham's attention shifted away. "You're suppose—"

The anger returned to transform her face into something terrifying—angel to demon in a blink. "I am not actually your assistant, Dunham, quite the opposite in fact. I have a war to wage, one my general isn't tending properly. Since your attention isn't on what's important, that leaves me to take care of business, doesn't it?"

Dunham glanced over his shoulder at Ignis, his face that of a teen called out for rebelliousness. He raised the burning ruby of Ignis's former heart into view and squeezed.

Pain lanced through the fire phoenix again. He dropped to the floor of his cage, curled into a tight, agonized ball.

You wait, Dunham. Just wait.

Dunham

Dunham turned his back on Viviane, marching to the control console. Her fingers slapped down on his shoulder like a vice.

"What do you think you're doing?" She asked. "I'm talking to you."

"I'm sending the Terra to take care of Quayla."

"No, you are not."

Dunham darkened, gesturing toward the nearby windows. "I know where she is. I know she's beat to hell. I'm sending the Terra to finish her off, didn't you say we needed her?"

"Vitae has slain Mariena and Vusolaryn. Local Seelie and Unseelie will be in chaos. Now is the time to slay as many of them as we can."

"No!" Red rage ignited along Dunham's skin. "I want Quayla!"

Viviane' s palm slammed into his face, turning rage molten. Magical energy rushed through him until eldritch magic coalesced into green power and throbbed between his fingers.

She hit him again. "Don't challenge me, boy. Even with Summus's essence you are no match for me."

Dunham glowered at her. It had been at least a century since he'd last tried to prove himself her equal. None of those attempts had ended well. Still, he hadn't wielded the power of a divine phoenix on those occasions.

Divine phoenixes replaced archangels like Michael. Shouldn't Summus's power more than match the strength of a fallen angel?

Except, Viviane wasn't just any fallen angel. She had reigned as one of the Dark Trinity. She'd been a Principality of Hell, one of Lucifer's three chosen captains—the Lady of Water. She had eons of experience fighting and surviving creatures far more powerful than Dunham.

He eased the magic back into his core.

"Good." Viviane smiled. "Now dispatch Terra to Sugarloaf Mills mall. Have her clean up the Sidhe at Medieval Times."

Dunham matched her smile. "Of course, mother."

Viviane' s eyes narrowed. Warning filled her voice. "Dunham, this is too important. Whatever you're thinking, don't do it."

"My thoughts dwell only upon sending the Terra to eliminate your enemies. That is what you want, isn't it?"

"If you're speaking specifically of my enemy Sidhe at the Sugarloaf Mills mall, then yes."

"Whom else would I be speaking of?"

Her face hardened. "No one else if you know what's good for you."

Dunham folded his hands behind his back. "Have you had any luck obtaining a new source of life, air or water essence?"

Her expression remained suspicious, but she allowed the change of topic. "I may have a way to gain us another water phoenix. As for life, Vitae is playing right into my hands."

"If you can get us another water phoenix to help keep Summus contained, what are you waiting for?"

Viviane watched him for several moments in tense silence. She arrived at some conclusion without her eyes giving away its contents. "Some things must follow other things. There is no other way."

She marched across the room, descending the spiral stair

toward her apartments. Dunham gave her fifteen minutes to change her mind or return. When she remained absent, he flicked the intercom open. "Terra, I have a mission for you. You will go to your home, slay Quayla, and proceed to the Sugarloaf Mills mall to exterminate a Sidhe enclave."

Terrance

Terrance stepped off of the stone base of his cage. Runes glowed around its circular depression and climbed into lines along the standing stone behind. None of them blazed half as strong as the mulch and fury at his core.

Dunham had slain Caelum.

The mortal had Destroyed the immortal soul of a phoenix with callous disregard for just how special Caelum had been. The air phoenix had been Terrance's brother, a delight to their whole Shield. He'd been created by the Creator Himself to protect Dunham's people from the Sidhe and the Fae Kissed they recruited.

Only the oaths forced upon Terrance through his stolen egg kept the earth phoenix from bringing the entire building down on Dunham's head.

"You mustn't dally," Dunham said. "I'm not sure how long either quarry will remain in position."

Little sister is not your quarry mortal. Something I hope she makes a distinct point in proving.

Terrance inclined his head. "I shall endeavor to serve with all alacrity, *Master*."

"Do we have a problem, Terra?"

"I do not believe we share a problem, but I believe we both face significant troubles in the near future."

Dunham's expression tightened. "Get out of my face, and complete your mission as ordered."

Terrance strode away, descending the spiral stair headed to the elevator and the thirteenth floor locker room for clothes. The modular wall slats that closed off the Sidhe's apartments were in place when Terrance exited the hidden door behind Dunham's office desk. He crossed a lushly-decorated reception area dotted with Celtic and Pict artifacts. A blonde receptionist behind one end of a long mahogany desk eyed Terrance's nakedness, showing her dimples. Terrance ignored her, exiting double glass doors to the elevator banks.

The elevator doors opened the moment he touched the call button. Viviane stood in the car, eyes locked on Terrance's own. She stepped forward, wrapping a robe around the earth phoenix.

"Dunham ordered you to assault Quayla and then head to the Sugarloaf Mills mall, correct?"

Terrance nodded.

"You will proceed to the Sugarloaf Mills Mall first."

I had every intention of doing so.

"If the information Dunham provided is correct, going to Sugarloaf Mills first may allow Quayla to slip away once more."

Viviane' s face hardened. "So be it."

"Dunham may take exception. He's already slain one of us in a fit of pique."

"Yes." She sobered. "That was most unfortunate."

Magma backed Terrance's voice. "Because it hampered your plans or because he Destroyed an immortal soul?"

"Affirming both won't make you feel better, phoenix."

"No."

"You needn't fear for your own safety. He won't do that again. He cannot afford to lose another of you."

Terrance peered into the fathomless depths of the fallen angel's eyes. "I do not believe you are as certain as you sound. Besides, Dunham will have a car waiting for me."

"I've already taken care of the driver."

Terrance inclined his head, resisting the urge to smile.

Excellent news since I had not yet puzzled out the best way to deal with the waiting mortal.

The elevator doors opened up allowing Terrance to traverse halls filled with curious onlookers. He entered the locker room, showered, dressed and continued on to the waiting car.

Quayla

I helped Atlanta Detective Sabrina Foxner load the four stone basins back into her car. She'd reclaimed them from a warehouse where Vitae imprisoned captured Sidhe. None of us had known about our Shieldheart's activities, not even our Watcher Anima. According to Bradley—a formerly enthralled medical examiner—Vitae's experiments to remake himself with Sidhe essence began within the simple, warded walls.

The all but forgotten horrors left rotting in cages soured my stomach even after the fact. After everything I'd survived in the past few weeks, nausea topped all I could feel.

I set the last basin into Sabrina's car. I licked my lips, the itch behind my eyes threatening a flood of despondency.

Caelum's nest. What am I going to do with it now?

Sabrina squeezed my hand. "Are you sure you're all right?"

I met her stormy blue eyes. Sabrina was a hardened warrior, a former homicide detective, but anguish filled her expression.

One word slipped from me voiced by a church mouse. "No?"

She embraced me. My arms wrapped around her solid, muscular frame. I squeezed her to hold myself together. In less than a month, my whole world had been destroyed.

I released her just as my body started to respond to hers. Such a response would've been unwelcome to the homosexual police detective, and I refused to risk alienating her just because my newest body didn't wish to behave. "Thank you, Sabrina, but I have to go."

"Get in the car."

"No. As soon as you're gone, I'm flying out of here."

"In broad daylight? No. Besides, you're a wreck."

"Thanks." A sad smile curled my mouth. "I think at this point, after that fight, the cat's out of the bag."

"Get in the car, Buckler. You need sleep. I'll drive you to Savannah while you rest."

I shook my head. Her acquaintance with me had already gotten her into hot water several times. I didn't want to cause my mortal ally any more grief.

"Don't make me handcuff you again."

I smirked. Her attempts to handcuff me hadn't gone well, but I couldn't help my response. "Guess I know who thinks she's the top."

Frustration undercut her voice. "Buckler."

I got into the car. Exhaustion took me before we'd driven half a mile.

Bradley

Bradley Sky, former junior assistant medical examiner and formerly enthralled slave, hid his face in both hands.

He'd done it.

He'd brought back to life dead children centuries gone.

He'd desecrated corpses to create monsters in service to the biggest monster of all, Master Vitae.

The science had been thrilling. The prospect of contributing to a supernatural war, to rubbing shoulders with fantasy creatures out of novel and Dungeons and Dragons campaigns had been a living dream—until it became nightmare.

I never should've talked Quayla into letting me come back here.

Bradley had wanted to help her...him...whatever. She really was one of the good guys, fighting against evil on every side but still determined to protect humanity in all of its various horribleness.

Vitae's voice cracked through the former laundry room turned underground lab like unexpected thunder. "Thrall!"

Bradley sniffed, rubbing his eyes on a sleeve before turning with a sappy grin glued to his face. "Master, you've returned."

Dammit.

Vitae had died and changed bodies once more. The new one seemed more real. It was definitely more beautiful. The phoenix wrapped his arms around Bradley in a rush. No longer magically enthralled, dopamine no longer shot through Bradley's body at his Master's—

Really should be Mistress's

—pleasure.

Bradley's body didn't even respond to the beautiful woman embracing him. Beautiful or not, there was nothing attractive about the monster wrapped around him.

He dropped his eyes, but he couldn't keep the cracks out of his voice. "How may I serve you, Master?"

Vitae released him. "You already have. We've had a major victory, and while your contribution was minimal, I am feeling magnanimous. How can I reward you? What do mortals desire? A chamber slave? Riches?"

"A day off to rest?"

Vitae frowned. "That is all?"

"Mortals need rest, Great Master. You've asked much of me, and while I'm thrilled to have served, rest is the only thing I can think about right now."

"Perhaps you should invest some of the troll marrow into your own body." Vitae brightened. "Better, I can gift you a few ounces of my essence to restore your body."

Lightning hit Bradley, a little late after the thunder crack but amazing nonetheless. He hid the surge of delight washing through him. "I'd really just rather have a day to rest in my home, Master. Water my plants. See friends. Pay my rent. That sort of thing."

"Take two then, but use the time to transfer your belongings back here. You've earned a place with my other servants."

Slaves.

"Master is too generous."

"I am at that." Vitae continued deeper into the lab toward the essence chambers and his faerie prison.

Chapter Two

Whispered Alliances

Quayla

Sabrina shook me awake. We parked on an old cobblestone road, a river on one side and a line of fudge shops just outside the window.

"River Street," Sabrina grinned. "I might have a fudge addiction."

I smiled, clutching my chest with the hand holding the angel statuette. "We have something in common? The world may come to an end."

She shot me a dirty look. "I figured you could use the river to get going faster."

"Trying to get rid of me? Want all the fudge to yourself?"

"Well, you aren't exactly my type."

"Supernaturally handsome?"

Sabrina shook her head. "Supernatural at all seems a bit out of my wheelhouse."

Warmth blossomed at her expression. "You're learning, Detective, but you might also be selling yourself short."

"If you say so."

I extended the statuette. "Take this. Ani may be able to help you deal with anything that arises, and if nothing else, she can relay information between us."

"Shield Quayla, I don't think that is a good idea," Anima said. "Begging your pardon, Detective."

I flashed a grin skyward. It probably wasn't the right direction exactly, but I knew my friend and Watcher would see anyway. "Well, unless you're going to risk trouble by manifesting, I guess you can't stop me."

"She might be right," Sabrina tapped her phone where it hung off the dashboard. "Besides, you know we have these magic boxes that let us communicate over vast distances."

I gave her a frank look. "Sabrina, I have to turn into pure water and cross the Atlantic under my own power. I'm not sure I'll be able to reform such complicated electronics in a functional state. This way, you have Ani's guidance and I know I can reach you."

"I'm not some rookie, you know," Sabrina said. "I don't need some supernatural dispatcher looking over my shoulder...no offense, Anima."

I shrugged, jumped out of the car and headed for the nearest candy store. A machine in the shop's center wrapped and delivered salt water taffy to a huge bin. Cashiers offered me pralines and said taffy while counters held candies of all kinds and fudge slabs in a dozen flavors. I lamented my inability to buy a little of everything. Despite the name, I had my doubts that salt water taffy would survive actual salt water.

I came away with a small slab of peanut butter fudge. Sabrina turned her nose up when I offered, focusing on a double slab of dark chocolate with walnuts.

Purist.

Eating so much of the rich, heavy treat left me unable to taste the last few bites, but I definitely needed the calories. Not only did I need to cross the Atlantic in a hurry, but I needed to fill my new nest. There was no way to separate enough concentrated essence for a rebirth and not die in the process, but I'd be swimming in my element so it made sense to get a start.

Sabrina lingered in the fudge shop, possibly unwilling to see me leave. I pushed away the thought. Her attitude was so different from when she'd been hunting me, but seeing anything else in it beyond her desire for more samples was delusional optimism.

I ducked into the backseat, intent to pull one down to give me covert access to the trunk. The detective's sedan didn't allow me direct access. I was forced to open the trunk and, despite onlookers, climb inside. Transmogrifying to my liquid form lit the interior enough to find one of the empty nests.

A sob locked my breath in my throat at seeing Caelum's nest.

I am so sorry I failed you, Caelum.

Dunham had killed my brother after he'd failed to defeat me. The mortal's fury might have had some root in Caelum's other actions, but I couldn't shake guilt from yet another mistake that had cost lives.

Immortal rather than mortal this time, but still my fault.

Anima was watching—that was her job—and in the end, I was really the only one of her shields still at large. I braced myself for pain and her unavoidable outrage.

Karambit blades cut away my body from the waist down. The world blurred and spun, but I held onto consciousness long enough to concentrate my essence and shift it into the other empty basin.

Anima's sweet alto scolded me from the statuette in the front seat. Vertigo and the buzzing in my ears spared me the particulars, but I got the overall gist.

I'm sorry, Ani, but if I'm going to stop more people from dying, I need to accept some personal sacrifices.

Transmogrifying with my lower half sealed against bleeding out and a long shirt to cover nakedness, I opened the unlatched trunk. Sabrina thankfully wasn't in view as I dragged myself out by my arms. Several people gawked—though not the former witnesses. One teenager already taking pictures with his phone snapped a photo with a disgusted expression.

I ignored them and checked for oncoming traffic before crossing the painfully uneven cobbles by virtue of a swinging motion. I threw myself in the Savannah River and let myself sink.

Someone dove in after me, but it wasn't Sabrina, and I'd already changed into pure essence. Aquakinesis pushed my body out toward sea, absorbing water to replenish my overall mass.

Such a large amount of new water wasn't a good substitute for essence. It would be sluggish in a fight, but I didn't expect to do more than swim and gobble the occasional slow-swimming fish. The water would merge with my essence over time, growing into what I needed while providing just enough help to speed me toward my former home—the place my mistake had murdered hundreds and brought about the series of events that had Killed Caelum.

I held back tears, concentrating on my flight down river.

I had a long way to go and too little time to get there.

Viviane

Once Terra was pointed in the proper direction and on her way, Viviane set out for the earth phoenix's home. Her conversation with Quayla hadn't gone well. She'd expected the kindred phoenix to jump at the chance of fulfilling her destiny with Viviane's help.

She hadn't.

None of those mortals ever turned me down.

She'd even refused after Viviane threatened to stop covering up all of the faerie incursions. The rebellious young phoenix was willing to let humanity learn about Faery rather than work with a so-called enemy.

A smirk lit Viviane's face.

She'd truly have been the best choice, but there are others left to enlist. She'll prove an interesting adversary. It's been too long since I faced a good one head on.

Viviane returned to Dunham's chambers to ensure he hadn't done anything else stupid. As Viviane had told Quayla, the boy was getting out of hand. Infusing himself with Divine essence had given him a false sense of superiority.

Of course, he also thinks he's the only one drawing power from Summus.

Arthur had fallen to hubris too.

Come to think of it, they all did in the end.

She crested the spiral stair to an empty apartment—excepting the imprisoned phoenixes. She crossed to the five standing stones backed up against a center stone. The basins held the nests of Atlanta's shields, allowing the contained essence to feed a pentagram of power holding Summuseraphi captive on the central stone.

Dunham had augmented the old spell with modern countermeasures on the off chance of mistakes. She hadn't made any. She knew the spell containing the phoenixes as if she'd invented it herself. Still, the boy had outdone himself.

Beads filled with toxins and plagues curtained the life phoenix's cage within a thin layer of protective plastic. The Vitae had yet to occupy the prison, but she intended that to change in the near future. Two vacuum chamber bell jars capped places to hold Quayla and the unfortunately Destroyed Caelum.

I always liked him.

A similar arrangement filled not with vacuum but a self-sealing chemical kept the earth phoenix from affecting escape. Another cage of hafnium carbide laced with coolant tubes feeding a steam generator to power Circlestone's campus kept the now-diminutive fire phoenix.

Only Ignis and Summus remained incarcerated.

Without the full five phoenixes to fuel the containment spells, keeping Summus in place consumed more essence than normal—enough that the amounts she'd laid aside in advance dwindled.

She'd had to raise the payout for phoenix essence in all of the outposts of her Goblin Markets. Even so and even considering the world-wide war she'd arranged, the exceedingly rare substance became more and more difficult to come by.

She opened the Arch to her private island of Faery—the only place Viviane was allowed to enter even though she was outlawed from the whole.

We're all outlaws or else we wouldn't be stuck in this shadow mockery of Creation.

The Fallen hadn't been meant to escape their prison, but they'd been created to serve Creation. With service had come understanding. Millenia of trial and cooperation eventually provided escape. They learned to enter Creation only to find their honored position filled with mortal monkeys and their loyal brethren supplanted by the phoenixes.

And instead of continuing our cooperation, we fell to fighting.

Stepping across the threshold from Creation to Faery was like slipping into a soothing mountainside mineral spring. Every inch of her skin tingled with pleasure and refreshment as she strode onto the tan lines of a deserted island drawn in crayon.

Her sanctuary had actually been a creation of some mortal child—a seventh son of a seventh son much more powerful than Dunham ever could've imagined becoming. He'd believed in the drawing so much that he'd created it in the only place it could be created—Faery. Viviane had confiscated it the moment she'd found it, and surprisingly, her sisters hadn't lodged a protest.

Because unlike the rest of Faery, my island is only connected to Creation. At least, it was when I took it over.

"Viviane."

Viviane turned, cold washing through her to discover her sister standing beneath the orange scribbled sun. "Mab."

Lucifer's other chosen wore overlapping sashes of dark raspberry and icy blue, evergreen and white. Her exile—shortly after the Dark Trinity rebranded themselves as faeries to facilitate approaching increasingly superstitious mortals—had forced Mab to take the mantle of Winter for dark age mortals.

The duty probably hasn't been too big of a stretch. Isn't winter Earth's slumber?

Mab had cooperated with Viviane and the Lord of Air to interfere with Creation's winter season just as Viviane had helped Titania and His Majesty inflict mudslides and plagues upon many a poor village.

Besides, it probably gave her more time in His Majesty's...good graces.

"We need to speak."

Viviane's pulse raced to a sprint.

Is this it? Is this what I've been working toward?

Viviane's serene smile covered her tumultuous emotions. "What brings the Lady of Earth to my little sanctuary?"

"You are banned from Faery."

Sudden panic flashed through Viviane.

Have they found the ways I've built into this place?

"But I'm willing to overlook your crimes—"

Viviane snorted. "That's a bit pot and kettle, don't you think? We're all criminals, if you'll remember."

Mab darkened and the scribbled ground shook. "You are exiled!"

"From a prison full of criminals."

"You deserved it!"

Viviane rolled her eyes. The argument had been trod so many times both high road and low had been worn to thinnest stone.

Mab purpled. "You never should've interfered. I had everything exactly the way I wanted. With my son Mordred on the throne, we'd have been able to recruit thousands to our cause."

"Mordred was a spoiled brat. He threw around too much magic. The shields were moving in."

"So, you gave that mortal your Champion blade? He wasn't even bound to you!"

"Exactly, a charismatic mortal champion without a shred of faerie 'taint' to attract the shields. He'd have built a kingdom to rival heaven. Once the people adored him, I'd have brought him around and had our thousands of converts—a principality of Faery in Creation itself," Viviane darkened. "Instead, you both moved against me and killed Arthur before I could bring it to pass."

"So, you threw a tantrum to spoil our fun, saving that child."

"Dunham will do what Arthur never got a chance to do."

Mab laughed. "He's no Arthur. He's a power-hungry madman."

Viviane opened her mouth to throw their plans in Mab's face only to stop as her scheme poised on her tongue to leap. She folded her arms. "What do you want, Mab?"

"Despite Titania's and my people openly killing each other in Creation and no Divine One to be found, someone is keeping things quiet from the mortals."

Viviane shrugged. "Don't look to me. You took all my subjects, remember?"

"So, you're not recruiting the witnesses?"

"To what end?"

"Maybe to backstab us when we're weak."

"Mortals against you or Titania? They'd lose and I'd be a laughingstock, no thanks."

"So, you have no hidden strength?"

"All you left me was Dunham, and you know about him."

Mab frowned.

"Why?" Viviane asked, holding her breathing as even as she could manage.

"My son Vusolaryn is missing. I think Titania is moving against me. If I'm right, an ally of your power might tip the balance—if you have any strength to add to the fight."

Viviane feigned shock. "Laryn is missing? What happened?"

"I don't know...yet."

"I am sorry, Mab, but I don't know where he is. Has your Champion found nothing?"

"My Champion is missing too."

Yes, hidden behind Vitae's wards…with a little help.

"If it came to a real war, would you oath service to me?"

Viviane laughed. "I oath service to the Morning Star alone."

"Perhaps I misspoke," Mab gestured around them. "I'd be more inclined to forget this little rebellion if I knew you'd side with me in a fight."

"You've both known about this place for over a century. It was created with access to Creation alone. Would you really deprive me of this little spot of peace, sister, just to blackmail me into helping you?"

Mab smiled.

"And what's to keep me from joining Titania instead?"

The smile faded from Mab's face.

Viviane shook her head. "Either way, I'm still exiled. I could only help fight from within Creation—unless I was restored to my throne."

"Never!"

"It's been nice seeing you, Mab. Come by for some sweet tea some ti—oh, right. I'm not allowed within Faery, but you're not allowed direct access to Creation, are you?"

Mab purpled once more.

"Guess we kind of need this place if you want to keep trying to recruit me," Viviane said. "Good bye, sister."

Viviane turned her back, striding across dark blue squiggles to a pool of actual water. She descended into her bower, knowing Mab wouldn't follow to Viviane's admittedly weakened place of power.

Bradley

Bradley's plants were dead when he arrived. A notice on his door demanded his rent and a late fee, claiming possession of deliveries left at his door as hostage.

He hadn't been able to pay his landlord from captivity since the man refused to take electronic payments. Even checks had to be addressed to cash.

Probably cheating on his taxes.

Bradley took the envelope he'd readied before becoming enthralled down as payment, retrieving several deliveries of gaming miniatures, a new Dungeons and Dragon supplement he'd preordered, and the Arch collars he sent himself.

He'd lost his phone ages ago, but since it was a Google Fi phone, he logged onto his computer to review any messages. There were several from his gaming group asking where Bradley'd gone and when they'd continue their campaign. Another four from the government center demanded he call back in regard to an investigation likely more real than the robocalls threatening him with nebulous legal action.

Where do I start?

Part of him wanted to go down to the medical examiner's office and see what had happened with Doctor Mercer in the end. It was possible the investigation revolved around the human piece of shit Vitae's essence forced to confess.

Guilt flashed through Bradley. He'd done the right thing, but he'd enslaved the man in order to do it.

Of course, the calls could be tied into whatever that cop Quayla knew was investigating.

Bradley decided to see his friends one last time before he risked going to jail. He called up the four other members of his gaming group, inviting them over. He met some friction about the short notice, but Bradley explained that he was short on time and what he had in mind would more than make up for giving up their evening plans.

The short, plump figure of Tommy, his other doctor friend, was first to arrive. He carried a collapsible plastic crate of gaming books propped under one arm. A Publix bag filled with snacks crowded into the top next to a massive crown royal bag filled with dice.

"Where've you been, Bradley?" Tommy asked without preamble.

"I'll tell you when everyone's here."

Tommy snorted and sidled over to his normal spot at the dining room table. Knuckles wrapped shave and a haircut against Bradley's door. He opened it to let in the long-haired and often smarmy Eric.

"Damn, I thought it would be nice to see you again, Brad."

Bradley cringed inwardly at the running joke. "Let me guess, it causes you physical pain?"

Eric pantomimed shooting him and squeezed through the doorway. "Tommy, you brought a date...oh, never mind, you just gained weight."

Bradley sighed and closed the door. He'd barely got it latched when another knock vibrated the cheap wood under his fingers. Opening the door revealed the bearded grin of Billy and his beautiful wife Rebecca. She didn't play, but she painted the most incredible miniatures. Since that meant less work for Bradley, he never objected to her sitting at a side table, painting the session away.

Besides, I'm not going to make waves. What I wouldn't do to find a beautiful woman who's supportive of my interests.

Billy turned his back on Bradley to drag a heavily-laden cart inside. He wasn't running the game, but Billy seldom went anywhere without bringing along some elaborately-constructed dice tower to shame all dice towers, including Billy's own previous constructions.

From the looks of the box, the new one was a fully built, multilevel fortress that would take up half the dining table—even with the leaves put in to expand it.

Rebecca smiled at Bradley as she passed. "We've missed you. Everything all right?"

"Just some trouble at work. If you wouldn't mind sitting at the table, I'll bring everyone up to date when Dave gets here."

She smiled, shrugged and helped Billy free his second cart from where it had caught a wheel on the door jam. Dave came to the rescue before she could.

The professional musician smiled the moment he came into view, looking more respectable, almost corporate, compared to the incorrigible Eric.

"All right, we're all here, spill," Tommy said.

"Once we're all settled."

"You might want to start," Billy said. "This will take about a half hour to get set up."

Bradley rolled his eyes. "Maybe wait then, until I've told you what's going on?"

Billy's exuberance flashed away and back so fast it had to have faster-than-light engines.

Bradley approached the table of his friends, assorted gaming paraphernalia scattered around their places. "I, uh, I've been...Tommy, remember the cat?"

All eyes shifted to Tommy.

He seemed to shrink at their combined attention. "I thought I wasn't supposed to talk about that."

"They're never going to believe me if you don't back me up."

"I don't know anything beyond you finding some weird stray."

Bradley took a deep breath. He spread his hands to indicate the various books and miniatures. "It's all real. I've been the prisoner of an honest to God phoenix working alongside real fantasy creatures."

"Bullshit," Eric said.

He gestured to Tommy. "I reanimated a dead alley cat using marrow taken from a troll bone that came into my office."

"Morgue," Eric said.

Tommy's color drained. "Is that what that was?"

Billy shook his head. "You two are putting us on."

Tommy's head shook back and forth so fast it looked like he was mixing paint.

"I don't understand," Rebecca said.

"Fantasy creatures are real, really real...and well, they're not very nice." Bradley drew in a long breath. "Even the good guys can go bad. I found a way to detect magic, and I followed it to..."

Bradley related everything that had happened since Detective Foxner had delivered the troll bone weapon. His friends made faces. They objected. They accused him of telling tall tales. He kept talking until he ran out of words.

"Why are you telling us this?" Dave asked.

"I think I've found a way to help Quayla, not just by reanimating dead bodies with troll marrow." Bradley hesitated, knowing he was about to jump without a parachute while trying to drag his friends from the plane. "I think I can infuse us with a combination of ingredients that would allow us to help Quayla protect Atlanta."

Eric scowled.

Tommy was already shaking his head.

Billy beamed. "You can give us superpowers? Like magic and Hulk strength and immortality?"

"I think so."

"Even if this wasn't bullshit, I'm too pretty to want to look like a troll," Eric said.

"I think I have a way to deal with that," Bradley said. "Maybe even make you prettier."

"You think?" Rebecca asked. "You don't know?"

"Not yet. I'll test this before I give it to you, but...I don't think I can do this alone. You're my friends, and—"

"And you want to turn us into monsters first," Tommy snarled.

"Hey, settle down," Billy stood, gesturing for calm. "How many times have we talked about what we'd do with superpowers? I can't believe you guys wouldn't at least give Bradley a chance to deliver."

"Billy, this could go wrong in so many ways," Rebecca said.

Billy shrugged. "I could get hit by a runaway ambulance tomorrow, but if I had some of that troll DNA, I could walk away from it too."

Bradley flopped into his chair. "Look, I understand if you don't want to participate. I just figure this is so important, I wanted people I can trust by my side."

"You're out of your damned mind," Eric rose, collecting his things. "Been sucking on formaldehyde too much. Real or not, I'm out."

"No," Tommy said. "Bradley, even if what you're talking about is real, you're talking about human experimentation. We could lose our licenses."

"It's fine. I understand," Bradley tried to smile. He'd had plenty of practice hiding his feelings surviving Vitae's moods. He'd hoped his friends would jump at the chance to be real heroes. He understood, but he couldn't help feeling deflated.

"So," Dave asked. "Can we game now?"

"Yeah," Bradley said. "Let me get the stuff."

Eric refused to look at Bradley, grabbing a nearby remote and flipping on Bradley's television.

"This was the scene in Dekalb earlier today."

Tommy's voice brightened. "Hey, that's Valerie."

Dave groaned.

"Turn it up," Tommy said.

Bradley glanced at the television.

A huge she-hulk of stone and crystal battled a small army of elves, goblins and an ogre. Human witches threw fire and lighting at the woman. A spear ran through her guts. She broke it off, flipping backward to transform into a massive stone phoenix and then back into she-hulk human shape once more.

Bradley pointed. "See, I was telling the truth!"

"As of the time of this broadcast," Valerie said. "We've had no word from the Georgia Film commission if this is some new production or just an independent event—possibly a LARB."

Valerie turned to face someone off camera. She smiled at her viewers. "Pardon me, a LARP."

"She says it's a movie," Eric said.

"Or a LARP," Tommy grinned.

"With those kinds of special effects in a raw feed?" Bradley asked.

"Bradley's telling the truth," Billy took Rebecca's hand and adopted a Russian accent. "How about it, honey? Want to be my sexy Natasha?"

Chapter Three

Critical Mass

Terrance

Terrance's driver pulled to an abrupt stop in the Sugarloaf Mills parking lot, cursing to scandalize even a merchant marine.

The Earth phoenix straightened, leaning over enough to give himself a clear view out the front windshield. The dinner show castle and attached shopping mall rested in the center of an expansive medieval village. The construction wasn't a historically accurate medieval village, but a sugar-coated, gingerbread version perpetuated in modern computer role playing games and fantasy novels.

Healthy peasants in colorful fantasy garb ambled along perfectly cobbled streets dotted by trees whose roots didn't push cobbles out of place. Lush grass and softly rolling knolls cradled the clean, colorful buildings surrounded by lush, ancient trees nonindigenous to the surrounding countryside.

Elves and goblins, sprites and pixies wandered the village alongside the human villagers. Tiger-striped dragons the size of Great Danes—Amazonian Fire Drakes—meandered amid perfectly white horses not the least bit startled by predators under hoof.

Separate castes walked side by side without hiding their eyes. The only signs of class deference seemed to be the slightly inclined heads whenever a human encountered a sorcerer or enchantress.

Terrance frowned.

This might be a bit more difficult than Dunham advertised.

He watched several more moments, searching every moving creature for the powerful Sidhe responsible for the presence of Faery inside Creation's borders.

"Is all of that real?"

Terrance sighed. "I fear a great deal of those people are real mortals, some Fae Kissed and others enthralled to play their part."

"How're you going to tell them apart?"

That is a better question than you might think. If I had a full Shield to call upon or even a divine, there might be a chance to unravel this knot.

Dunham had ordered Terrance to exterminate the Sidhe cell. There was no way to tell if Dunham had known the true state of affairs or purposefully sent Terrance into the treacherous situation to gauge the earth phoenix's abilities.

"You will want to retreat a safe distance." Terrance opened the door, stepping into sweltering Atlanta humidity. "This is unlikely to go smoothly."

Terrance had already armored his bones in preparation for a fight, but it seemed his standard defenses were woefully inadequate. If the so-called fantasy creatures wandering the rogue slice of Faery were simulacrum or thralls—which Terrance doubted—then he might be able to persuade the Sidhe involved to surrender through brute force.

It's well that Caelum's comparisons between myself and the Hulk are ill-founded.

He reached into mother earth around him, stretching his will as far as it would reach. He transmogrified his essence beneath a triple thick armor of interlocking quartz and granite plates ranging in size from saucers to dimes. He drew all of the trace amounts of iron he could through the asphalt beneath his feet and consolidated it with all the iron resident in his body.

Under normal circumstances, he'd have collected iron after a death to use against faeries. Having been immediately caged, Terrance had enjoyed only limited opportunities to draw iron from Georgia's red clay.

Iron-clawed battle gloves grew out of his forearms, obsidian and quartz spikes lining the cestus ready to impale and slash flesh.

He pushed his will into earth and asphalt and stomped a foot, willing the ground to shake. The initial shake drew eyes as he amplified his voice to rumble like a mountain avalanche. "By the Undying Light, I demand all Sidhe surrender, assembling for judgement at the border of this village."

Faces darkened, no longer the happy fantasy villagers.

"Fae Kissed must surrender the boons offered them by the Sidhe and kneel in supplication to their Creator to beg absolution."

Anger turned to fury.

Much as Terrance had feared, the entire village populace charged him. Villagers seized makeshift weapons and raced toward him in a riotous mob. Sidhe drew blades and cudgels from their person, following the charge with sufficient leisure to allow the humans first blood.

"This is your last warning," Terrance said. "Any who do not immediately surrender will face summary judgement."

No one stopped.

Arrows filled the sky, bronze and stone tips bombarding his body with the sound of rain on a tin roof.

Terrance's words rumbled the ground. "So be it."

Massive slabs of asphalt ripped out of the ground. They slapped together with ear-shattering booms, smashing Terrance's attackers like bugs between the pages of a great book.

Unfolding the asphalt took energy best reserved for the battle to come, but displaying the smashed bodies to reinforce the attackers' fragility slowed the assault.

Three-story tall ogres charged out of the castle. Long quivers filled with spears and javelin clattered from leather thongs around their waists. Goblins raised axes or swords, cheering the humans into the teeth of Terrance's defense. Several cut down mortals who turned tail at the last moment.

Terrance loped forward, a growl on his lips. Enthralled or not, mortals were under his protection and he would save them—even from their own cataclysmic desires.

Stone spikes speared out of the ground only to have Terrance's punches send their sharp pinnacles rocketing into the charging faeries.

Pixies and sprites dive-bombed over him, dropping explosive vials of fire and poison, acid and tar.

Terrance yanked two unbroken ground spikes from the parking lot, turning toward the next flight of attackers to smash the stones together. Will corralled the stray stones, joining them with other jagged fragments shooting through the air. The barrage holed wings, impaled airborne faeries and knocked the lesser Sidhe from the sky.

Two ogres charged as three others dropped back to hurl their ammunition. Several enchantresses and sorcerers gathered in threes along the back lines, blazing energy zigzagging between their hands as it built up power.

Terrance dodged an ogre fist, tripping the ogre with a sudden wall of asphalt in time to block the second's two-fisted haymaker with the first ogre's head. Terrance darted in close, noxious body odor and putrid breath nearly knocking him back into full retreat. He backhanded the ogre's throat, impaling and slashing the creature's neck only to be deluged in blood.

The other ogre leapt onto both Terrance and the downed ogre's head. Terrance threw himself left over the downed ogre's torso, snapping open jewel wings from his back to lift him clear of the blow.

A spear slammed into his chest a feather's breadth from his heart. Another pierced him and another. Terrance backflipped from the barrage, transmogrifying into his true form and then back into a winged human.

Eldritch magic blasted him before he could recover. Another blast hit him from the side.

Terrance willed their power to ground, but the blows cost him moments.

Laced ogre hands drove Terrance into the ground, then rose to do it again.

Terrance yanked an arch of stone and asphalt over his body as a shield. The protection only lasted a single blow, but allowed Terrance to escape from the ogre's reach into a horde of slavering goblins. Swords and daggers hammered at him from every angle.

Pain lanced up one leg, taint and sickness following a moment later. Terrance grabbed the offending half-elf and tore the troll-bone stiletto from his knee.

Two javelins drove through his armor and into Terrance's shoulder. Another two impaled his guts. Lightning slammed into his body, wrapping him in a corona as it grounded harmlessly off his armor.

Think.

Terrance shattered bones and crushed goblin skulls. He hurled bodies into one another and lifted shrieking Sidhe into place as living shields. Chunks of asphalt smashed attackers or launched them airborne. Iron-tipped cestus gutted elves, obsidian sliced throats and quartz spikes impaled skulls.

Earth essence ran like a mudslide from wound to wound, fill-ing, patching and healing injuries as fast as Terrance could adapt.

He fought the Sidhe for everything he was worth, sending them to the Creator's judgement by the score.

Another ogre slammed a hand filled with javelins into Terrance, driving a dozen spikes into his essence. Terrance fought to heal the wounds. He yanked spears from his body.

A magical blast lanced into a hole left behind by one spear.

Terrance reeled.

Another magical barrage slammed into him.

An arrow slammed through his wing and into the armor of Terrance's shoulder.

The head exploded a moment later, blasting Terrance's arm from his body. Another armor-piercing explosive arrow cost him a leg.

Terrance transmogrified, taking phoenix shape and struggling to fly free. Eldritch bolts hit him like a meteor storm, accompanied by explosive arrows from an elf too plain and clumsy to be a true Sidhe.

Terrance died in a firestorm of Sidhe magic and explosive ordinance, dying moments accompanied by his enemy's cheers.

Anima

Anima watched Terrance fight, amazed at the earth phoenix's prowess against overwhelming odds. She yearned to help him, but Quayla was too far to bring back, and Vitae couldn't be trusted.

Her Shieldheart didn't despise Terrance like he did Aquaylae, but the life phoenix's reason had fallen under the sway of Sidhe taint.

Monitoring Quayla's fights with both poor, lost Caelum and Ignis also included her in Dunham's orders for the captured phoenixes to slay those still at large.

Sending Vitae to Terrance's rescue carried the genuine likelihood of making matters even worse than they already were.

As such, Anima was forced to watch as Terrance fought his heart out only to fall in the end.

Travel faster, Quayla. We need you.

Vitae

A special cage designed not of iron but of carbon something my thrall guaranteed as unbreakable imprisoned Gherrian and Dolumii much like an iron maiden of old. I'd insisted on the addition of short, cold iron spikes that neither the knights nor I could touch without extreme pain and illness. Cylinders that encased their arms had been the only exception to the spikes. Nylon and carbon held the arms of both elven knights, allowing for an intravenous feed on one arm. A modified dialysis machine tapped into the other, providing a means for slow, steady harvesting of their essence without draining them dry.

It took effort not to show my teeth as I cranked one of the long iron spikes further along its threads and into Dolumii's side. "How do I get her out!?"

Dolumii spat at me, but with little strength and less saliva.

Another three cranks pushed the sharp iron tip into his torso. "Release her!"

A word barely escaped him. "No."

"Do you not understand, Sidhe? The only reason you're alive is to free her from your blade. If you won't cooperate you will die. Your patrons are gone. It will be a final death."

"You're ignorant for a know-it-all," Gherrian rasped.

I left Dolumii to his pain long enough to ensure Gherrian shared it. The two insufferable knights had offered insults and derision rather than real help until my rage needed a target.

Their Champion swords found their way into my hands before I'd consciously willed it. The hilts writhed beneath my grip, fitting to my slender fingers.

"Perhaps, but I know one way to ensure you are not reborn."

Scurith sprinted into the room, turning to bow without slowing properly. His paw-like feet slid across the tile. Despite desperate scrabbling, he lost footing and collided with an industrial metal table with a thunk and a whimper. The coyll shook his head, one eye rolling freely in its socket rather than returning to a normal position.

"I'm busy here, Scurith."

Scurith shook his head again, small ears flapping against his head. "Apologies, many apologies, Master, but the oracle senses an incursion of some kind."

I withdrew the iron digging into the elves' sides, shifting my fingers to plasma essence. I caressed their wounds, closing them to keep the damage from stealing my playthings.

"Excuse me, gentlemen. More of your cousins wish to contribute to my campaign."

"Better hurry then," Dolumii rasped. "You wouldn't want Aquaylae to beat you to the kill...again."

Waterfalls filled my ears, clearing as a possibility resolved in my thoughts. "I can only hope Aquaylae appears so I might be done with her once and for all."

A pained chuckle escaped Gherrian. "I do not think she will give you True Death, Vitae. She's too noble for that."

An ocean roared, waves of fury crashing over me.

I mastered myself.

They're trying to enrage me into killing them. That's not a mistake I intend to make. Once they've helped free Mare, with my queen at my side and enhanced with Sidhe essence, I'll have the most powerful Shield in Creation.

I turned my back on them and hurried up to the main hotel, ascended one of two grand, curving stairs to look down from the second-floor railing onto my double-sized oracle. A night sky's worth of stars dusted the map of Atlanta, marking all of my seeds as well as those few remaining from my former shieldmates.

Nausea washed through me.

I scoured the pool until a blinking star drew my attention toward downtown Atlanta. A small circle expanded in the silent oracle, displaying the interior of a mortal court room.

Thank you for little, Anima. I cannot believe I actually miss having you able to speak to us...well, me.

Snatching up fighting canes from an umbrella stand, I lunged toward one of the grand stairs curving down to ground level. I paused to consider. I yearned to take my Champion blades, yearned for the feel of them in my grip.

No. I won't risk them again until Mare is free.

Scurith had my Mercedes just out front by time I reached the doors. The coyote-like humanoid faerie ducked out of my way, shutting the door as I leapt inside. A glance confirmed an SUV filled with bulky enforcers waiting for my lead.

German craftsmanship sped me through Atlanta traffic in luxury. I pulled up to the courthouse, gesturing for one of my trollmen to guard my car.

A quick jog brought me up stone steps toward the ornate courthouse. The building stretched left and right, large enough to contain dozens of rooms which might match the one my silent oracle displayed.

Focus. I've grown soft, spoiled. This is the old way...the better way.

A rush of screaming mortals directed me to the Sidhe disturbance nearly the moment I entered the courthouse. I waded through panicked wafers covered in blood.

One heavy wooden door lay on the tiled hallway, blown off of its hinges while its brother stubbornly clung on to one twisted hinge. Laughter from two distinct voices echoed into the hallway accompanied by sobbing and pained groans. The first laugh hit my ears like a high-pitched giggle of a toddler. The second voice cackled in madness clear without coming into view of its source.

I stepped into the doorway, essence already forming glistening blades at the ends of my batons. A giggling pixie half the height of my weapon rolled back and forth, consumed by mirth from within an inset window sill high enough to escape the reach of splattered blood.

A woman in a once-orange jumpsuit stood in the court-room's heart. Blood coated her arms, damped her long stringy brown hair and painted her from the thighs down. She held a deputy's leg in two hands, eyes closed as she twisted the limb and listened to bones break over and over beneath a bloody grin.

"In the name of the Undying Light, I command you to surrender, faerie. As for you, mortal, you will surrender your boon and beg me for absolution."

"I'm not mortal, not anymore." She cackled at me. Her grin fell away. "You look like my sister. I hate my sister! She abandoned me!"

The mad woman charged.

I stepped into her charge. Both batons slashed into her path to quarter her on her own momentum.

They bounced off of her jumpsuit as she slammed into me. Claws raked my face. She jerked a handful of hair and opened a bloody mouth to bite my neck.

I transmogrified, slipping out of her grip. Another shift of blood to flesh allowed me to bring reshaped scythe blades down on her back.

They didn't impale her.

I glanced up toward a pixie that shouldn't have been able to grant the kind of invulnerability protecting the woman. The faerie had fled, leaving its Fae Kissed to buy its freedom.

The woman swept my legs, clawed hands tearing cloth and flesh from my thighs. Filthy nails anchored in my flesh, jerking my hip toward her mouth. Trollmen seized her limbs, struggling to tear her off of me.

Another transmogrification allowed me to slip her grip. She ripped the arm off one, bringing the bloody stump to her lips only to gag on what she found inside. Claws tore the head off a second trollman and disemboweled the third with inhuman speed.

Mortal police appeared in the doorway. They assessed the carnal house in a moment and opened fire at the woman. She raced toward them, bullets stopping short at her jumpsuit. She grabbed the first by head and jaw, twisting his head off with monstrous strength. She opened her mouth to catch blood spurting from his neck, seemingly growing larger and stronger from his essence.

The other officer emptied his pistol, then hit her with a Taser.

She dropped the first, licking her lips and turning blood red eyes at him. "Your fear is delectable, kine."

Kine? Ah.

I shifted to extend bloody wings into view. "Bow to your Master, blood feaster."

She froze, mortal's neck less than an inch from her fangs. "Are-are you the bl-blood god?"

I had no idea what she was talking about, but whatever it was had kept her from slaying the mortal in her claws. I strode forward. "Come forward, child, drink of my holy essence."

She dropped the guard onto the remains of his partners, stumbling across uneven and slick footing of dismembered bodies to reach me.

I stood before her without flinching.

She grabbed my shoulder and head, hesitating.

I bent my neck to accommodate her, yet still she held back. "Drink!"

She sank fangs into my neck and sucked at my essence. My body transmogrified from blood to shimmering gold and red plasma. Will transformed the essence within her into a burning weapon. She screeched, releasing my throat while she clawed at her own.

Whatever the Sidhe had gifted the mortal woman gave her the power to survive my burning essence. So, as with the street preacher, I took back the life I'd granted along with her own.

She died a shriveled husk writhing on the floor.

Without a divine to ensure her destruction, I tapped my magic. Eldritch fire splayed from my hands, incinerating her with so much heat it melted tiles and ignited bodies and benches.

By time her destruction had been assured, the room was an inferno. I turned to the trollmen cowering away from me. "Bring a hose or extinguisher and put this out."

For the first time in memory, my trollmen refused a command. All the will I could muster failed to bring them forward to combat the fire. More mortal authorities arrived. They vanished only to return with the very firefighting implements I'd demanded of my enforcers.

My fire burned on, unwilling to be banked my mortal means.

Faerie Fire.

Exhausted as I was from unleashing all of my magic to finish the would-be vampire, I had no choice but to fight my own magic. The Seelie magic I'd unleashed would burn down Atlanta, leaving me no choice but to call upon Unseelie magic to stop my magical conflagration.

Exhaustion seemed too small a word for the state in which vanquishing my own power left me. Every muscle ached and a hollowness worse than any hunger tried to devour my core.

A microphone met me on the courthouse steps. "Why did you stop that murder and the fire? Who? What are you?"

News vans and reporters encircled the building behind a police line that I'd trudged through. I looked down at myself to realize my form still pure life plasma. Summuseraphi hadn't bothered to come to any call and he'd blocked all calls to my old friend Vilicangelus. There were no Divine Ones to rewrite reality and the countless mortals beyond the cameras.

I transmogrified back into my human shape, but left my red and gold wings shimmering for the world to see. "I am Vitae, Atlanta's Shield against the Sidhe. The tragedy I've averted inside is exactly the kind of thing we've tried to protect you from."

"You've hidden the truth from mankind?"

"Yes."

"Who gave you the right?" another reporter demanded.

Irritation flashed through me. "He who created you ordered that we not disclose the existence of Faery or its denizens."

"How long have you been watching us?"

"All your days." I said.

"Let me get this straight," the second reporter said. "You've been hiding from us for millions of years, show up looking like some kind of succubus and then expect us just to take your word that you're the good guys and fairies are dangerous?"

Irritation shifted to anger. "If you wish to live, mortal, I suggest you choose to trust His vassals."

"That a threat?"

"Nay. That is a fact."

Reporters latched onto my answer, asking a thousand more questions I hadn't the energy to entertain. I transformed into my native form and flew into the sky, a majestic phoenix fit for the evening news.

Chapter Four

Dire Choices

Bradley

Bradley swallowed, peering into the earnest brown eyes watching him from within the golden fur coat. He stroked the stiff, greying fur of the eleven-year-old Golden Retriever rescued from imminent euthanasia.

Du—the animal wagged its tail in long, weary swishes.

It's the animal. I can't think his name or I won't be able to get through this.

The animal watched him, trust, loyalty and affection in his old face. Bradley had rescued him from a kill shelter—whether Duke knew of his imminent death or not, the dog didn't seem to care. All he cared about was earning the affection of his new master.

A cruel, horrible Master not much different from Vitae.

Bradley gulped.

Duke had been slated for death. Even without the impending needle, he'd lived out all but the last of his months. Bradley wasn't being cruel. He was giving Du—the animal another chance at life.

Besides, I have to test this serum.

Bradley checked two trollmen close at hand. His previous

experiments had required strong, decisive killing. The soft, loyal, golden animal—

Stop that. This has to be done.

Duke sat patiently waiting for whatever came next.

Bradley gestured for the dog to stay, turning his back to retrieve a large syringe filled with gleaming silver liquid. Early versions of simple serum hadn't gone well on the few unbitten rodents fetched for him by grendlings. When the thick concoction of swirling red, green and violet had worked, its effects had worn off quickly.

The newest iterations weren't miracles of bartender mixology. He'd spent countless nights fueled by stimulants and Vitae's essence splitting genes, testing and finally hybridized the ones he wanted. He bound the desirable genes to an otherwise benign virus that would rewrite sections of the animal's DNA.

Bradley knelt down beside the animal and gently took hold of a fatty section of skin.

"Steady boy, this might pinch a little."

Duke's huge tongue ran across Bradley's cheek.

Bradley closed his eyes to keep the tears from escaping. Everything he was doing was for the greater good. In order to empower his gaming group, he'd isolated the nature and beauty from a Seelie elf, the regeneration of an Unseelie troll, the strength of a half-ogre and lastly the inborn speed and agility of an Anseelie coyll. Each origin creature also offered magical resistances and strengths Bradley could include but not fully isolate. He'd combined the virus with an infusion of Vitae's pure essence to give the treated creature a well of life energy to spare the subject's body from devouring itself trying to fuel the transformation.

The silver concoction contained the ability to turn Bradley and his gaming group into super soldiers capable of helping Quayla save Atlanta.

Though few in actual number when considered on a global scale, news of faeries and faerie incidents ran around the clock. Criminals empowered by Sidhe magic filled the news. The world was going to hell on both local and global scales, and Quayla needed help keeping it all together.

A National Guard battalion had cordoned off Atlanta, inspecting all shipments entering the metropolitan area in an attempt to quarantine the city. TCPs—traffic control points—within Atlanta allowed National Guard to check for contraband, known criminals and otherwise make their presence known. Armed Humvees patrolled neighborhoods in a show of force meant to assert and maintain the peace.

News stories had shown Atlanta PD's pitiful attempts to stop people that had traded with the Sidhe for superhero powers. Some of the super vigilantes even stayed—so far—on the good guys side of things.

This is the lesser evil. It will give us those abilities without having to sell our souls.

The National Guard was working hand in hand with Atlanta's new SNat Crimes division to combat the problem, adding muscle to otherwise outgunned police.

Duke licked Bradley again.

Well, the others won't sell their souls anyway.

"I'm sorry, Duke."

He adjusted his grip, getting ready to shake the skin to help ease the large needle in between the dog's skin and fat.

I've got it right this time. Duke will thank me.

The needle slid into the dog's skin. The Golden Retriever didn't so much as whine as the needle pushed deeper under his pelt. Bradley's thumb tensed.

The serum would revitalize the old dog, make him stronger, more beautiful, unable to die. It might enhance the canine's nose, make him run faster, maybe even fly.

All Bradley had to do was depress the plunger.

He pulled the needle back out of Duke's skin, pinched the fat on his own gut before he thought better of it, and injected the serum into his body.

Duke licked Bradley's cheek once more just as fire exploded in

Bradley's guts. Pain and magic burned its way out through his limbs, searing skin to the tips of his extremities.

Vitae

Scurith raced into my chamber without even knocking.

I opened my mouth to reprimand him when his body language and rapid breath registered.

"Master. The oracle...someone...I can't believe it."

I rose, setting aside a copy of *Beowulf*. "What is it?"

The coyll pointed a furred hand. "Wyldfae are invading your sanctum...your other sanctum."

Rather than ask for clarification, I rushed from my study to the balcony railing above the oracle pool. A bubble of action zoomed in a section of Atlanta's reflection. Stunted, two-headed giants known as etune fanned out from an elven knight armored and liveried every bit as well as Dolumii or Gherrian.

The sword in the knight's fist bore an eerie resemblance to the historical descriptions of Excalibur.

Another Champion blade?

"Scurith, who is that knight?"

The coyll stuttered a response. "I-I'm not sure, Master. It c-could be Sir Jahriss, but none have seen him in centuries."

"Sir Jahriss?"

"The Anseelie Champion."

My eyes flit to where the elf's outstretched blade directed the assault on my former sanctuary. Heat flared beneath my jaw. The unmitigated gall that any Sidhe should prance into my domain and attempt to despoil my former home ground my gizzard like a mill stone.

Hurried steps took me back through my study to where the other two Champion blades hung. My fingers stopped an inch from Dolumii's hilt. The challenge of facing down another

Champion blade warranted I take two of my own. At the same time, I could not risk losing Dolumii's sword once more.

Not until Mare is free.

Leaving the Champion blades to their mounts, I descended to the armory with my fighting batons. Adding two captured elven swords provided more than sufficient armament. I surveyed the captured armor, choosing an unattractive but powerful set combining plates and chainmail upon leather suspiciously similar to the human skin I'd discovered binding several old spell tomes.

My touch allowed me to transmogrify the object, shifting it over my body in liquid form to provide a perfect fit. Taking advantage of its transitional state, I altered the colors to black etched with crimson, silver and gold.

"You're a fearsome and mighty warrior, Master."

"Thank you, Scurith."

"Shall I call your enforcers to arms?" Scurith asked.

I shook my head, getting a feeling for the blades and transmogrifying one to alter its balance more to my liking. "They would not arrive in time. I can handle these knaves."

The dwarf-modified elevator provided access to the rooftop garden still under construction. It also allowed me to launch from atop my hotel in phoenix form. Soaring out in the open felt wrong in many ways, but the tickle of wind on pinions large and fine thrilled the bird of prey in me.

I soared across Atlanta, unconcerned by mortal witnesses or means of security monitoring. I was a king on the wing, soaring over my domain with my majesty on display.

As much as I enjoyed the flight, the upcoming conflict required I turn my attention from joy to battle readiness. Three etune guarded an arch on my balcony.

Folding my wings, I dove with a battle screech.

All three etune turned toward my cry, gripping spiked bone clubs. Two stepped forward, choking up right and left in preparation to hit me out of the park.

I rolled around their strikes. Talons shredded the third, tearing both heads from his torso with a trail of blood and severed spine. A backward leap turned into a transmogrifying flip allowing duel sweeping slices across the torso of both turning etune.

The left etune dropped his club and grabbed his midsection. The right snarled through pain, slamming his club to shatter balcony stones when I sidestepped his attack. He recovered faster than I expected, making me dance a bit to land a thrust into his gut.

I didn't see the other etune coming. Defensively seizing his middle caused me to count him out of the fight prematurely. He fell backward as if overcome by the pain only to hit me with two knee-shattering kicks.

The blow catapulted me against the railing, useless legs crumpling to slam my head against the rail. Summoning will and essence with my dizzied senses took too long.

An etune club and a nasty stomp hit me from either side just as flesh turned to essence. Cruel laughter relished my pain as they prepared for another blow. My wings swept in as an after the fact shield, or so the etune seemed to think. The feather-shaped essence slapped against their muscled arms with the sound of flopping salmon.

Feathers turned to tendrils, anchoring in their flesh like barb maggots. Their life flooded into me, repairing and energizing me as they shriveled through a thousand years of aging.

I rose restored, keeping my wings as essence but shifting them to shimmering life plasma.

A slow clap brought my attention to the elven knight. Etune lined up on both of his sides. "So nice of you to come to our summons, Shieldheart. I must also thank you for the demonstration of your abilities."

"Education is very important." A blizzard of gleaming magical stars rocketed across the balcony from my hands, my own charge hot on their blazing tails.

A display of magic and swordsmanship deflected the assault from the knight, but didn't protect the lesser Sidhe. He met my charge with a lunging thrust. I beat his blade away, riposting with the second sword. He caught my second strike in the V of a sword-breaking dagger, snapping it and stabbing with his weapon. I dodged the thrust, parried his slice and twirled my wrist to remove the sword from his hand. He stepped back, drawing the sword back before I could finish the disarm.

I ducked left, winging the broken sword at him and filling the newly-empty hand with a bolt of eldritch fire.

He lunged.

I hurled a scythe of magic and swept my sword at him in a downward slice.

The elf ducked low, sliding under both strikes. He hooked his legs through mine, rolled hard to steal my footing and brought his sword down in a chop.

The blade cut through my torso, nearly halving me at an angle.

I kicked at him, transmogrifying from flesh to energy.

His dagger pierced my thigh, sending a ripple of counter magic through me that kept me from shifting to liquid or energy.

My wing caught him as he rose for another chop to my torso, hard-edged feathers cutting a deep furrow across his daintily-clad chest. A blast of power knocked him from me, buying enough time to yank the dagger free and transmogrify.

He managed his feet, lifting his sword in a flourishing salute. "You're a worthy foe, Shieldheart. Are you sure you wouldn't rather serve the winning side?"

"I am far more than capable of defeating a mere Champion of a dethroned Sidhe."

"Oh, simple bird, I am no Champion." He smirked. The sword's resemblance to Excalibur faded away. "And fortunately for you this is no Champion blade."

He charged once more.

A flurry of slices and strikes put me to my heels. When a hitch in his assault allowed me to drive a counter hard at him, his offhand thrust a fist of lightning into my liquid chest.

Jerks and spasms shot through me, though he lost the hand in the process. I'd have thought the lost hand of great concern but it didn't distract him from slicing his blade through my throat.

Staying together through the blow took power and concentration, both in short supply while being electrocuted. I brought my wings together, scissoring through him at the armpits.

We both fell back.

I cannot speak for his efforts to remain a single entity, but my own demanded my attention.

Just fortunate I got rid of the dagger so I was essence rather than flesh.

Turning over to hand and knees with a single hand holding my throat, I struggled to my feet.

A slow clap brought my attention around to a beautiful woman disguised to look like my newest body. A scent of fresh rain, flowers and taint identified her in an instant.

"Aquaylae," I growled.

She smirked. "No, Vitae. Viviane, the Lady of Water."

I drew my fighting batons, forming crescent moons of edged essence and launched myself at her. She slid out of the way without mussing her hair.

"I'm here to talk, Shieldheart."

"I do not consort with Lucifer's whores. You're a blight on Creation and you need to be Destroyed."

She snorted. "You're one to talk."

I lunged again, this time spinning to the side in a whirl of slashing edges she couldn't possibly avoid.

She avoided them, the flat of her hand slapping the back of my head with giant's strength. The blow flung me forward, sliding across the ground on my face. "Enough, Vitae. I wish to offer you a boon."

"You have nothing I desire, wretch." I regained my feet, pausing to assess the exiled Fallen for a weakness.

"I know how to release Mare."

A blizzard of white noise plunged me drowning into Antarctica's waters. Rage tried to fight the cold, but she extinguished it with her next declaration.

"And once back in her egg, I know how to quicken her hatching."

"Liar."

She shook her head. "Not in this case."

I charged, spinning left, hurling one baton end over end to the right. An extra half whirl let me jog hard directly at her and extend a flurry of essence tendrils directly at her core.

An ocean wave slammed into me out of nowhere, driving me back ass over teakettle only to land on dry ground.

Heat bolstered her accusations. "You are not strong enough to best me, Vitae, but you are strong enough to be of service to me."

"I'd rather meet True Death."

"You'd rather consign Mare to eternal torture than work with me to destroy Seelie and Unseelie invaders? Even though all I ask of you is that you do the duty you were Created to perform?"

"You're a liar and one of Lucifer's temptresses. Nothing you say can be trusted. Mariena and Vusolaryn claimed themselves unable to free Mare. Dolumii and Gherrian parrot their claims."

"Those children employ Swords of Judgement not meant for their use," Viviane drew a sword matching every historical account of Excalibur. "I was given a Sword of Judgement and the gifts to use it by the Most High Himself."

"Your sword does not imprison Mare."

"No, but if you bring me Mab's sword, I can free your love."

"Why would you do such a thing? You are our enemy."

"Aquaylae isn't up to the job, and this region needs a compe-tent water phoenix."

There was nothing I could say to disagree. Viviane spoke my heart on the matter and offered the return of my heart of hearts. "This smacks of a trap. Restoring Mare to my Shield would strengthen your adversaries."

She grinned. "It would strengthen my sisters' adversary. I am but a twice-exiled fallen angel. I have no kingdom. Those that were my children are no longer allowed my guidance."

"Half-truths and evasions."

"Think what you will. All I ask in return for Mare's salvation is that you allow me to inform you of Sidhe within Creation in violation of the Articles of Ararat."

Another thought spurred my tongue. "Which puts to sword's point the question of your presence within Creation yourself. How is it you stand upon Creation's soil in violation of those Articles?"

"I am not Sidhe, Shieldheart, nor am I a sovereign of Sidhe kind."

It seemed a technicality at best. The Articles of Ararat restricted the Queens of the Sidhe from entering Creation on penalty of God's direct wrath. Since the Creator's hand left Viviane unsmited, either she'd hidden from the All Seeing or indeed had some license to dwell within Creation.

"The enemy of my enemy is my friend, Vitae. Cooperate with me on exterminating the Seelie and Unseelie in Creation and I will combine my strength with yours to free Mare from Mab's Sword." Viviane's mouth quirked up in a half grin. "Work with me in good faith, and I will lead you through quickening Mare from her egg back into your arms."

Truly the fruit of Eden could not have held more temptation. The Lady of Water knew seduction better than any succubus birthed from her loins. She offered the key to my shackles in reward for performance of my duty.

"It is said you hold my shields captive, even my divine."

"I do not, though I am allied with he who does."

"If you freed them, we would be able to better thwart the Sidhe in Atlanta."

"They would Destroy you, Vitae. They do not understand the sacrifices you are making on their behalf."

Hardly surprising.

"Mare alone would rally to your side, see your greatness."

Uncertainly spilled words from my lips. "I do not know."

Viviane shrugged. "It makes no difference to me. If you haven't the strength to do what needs done, surely Aquaylae will bargain to regain her brother shields—though it means your True Death and Mare's eternal torment."

Inferno answered back her accusations. "I am strong enough for anything, whore!"

"You're not strong enough to face me. I daresay you are too weak to face even one of your former shields."

"I am supreme!"

"Are you?" Viviane asked. "Quayla slew both Caelum and Ignis when they assaulted her."

"Aquaylae! Her proper name is Aquaylae."

A subtle smile lit Viviane's eyes. "Quayla escaped Dunham when Summuseraphi cannot. She escaped me too. Perhaps it is best you decline. I need a strong phoenix capable of performing her duty without falling to hubris."

I launched myself at Viviane. Her Champion blade answered back every stroke of both my swords. It absorbed spell fire and lightning. I threw all at her and scored nary a scratch.

"I suppose I was wrong. Quayla will be the better choice after all," Viviane said. "Go home and marshal your strength, Vitae. How embarrassing would it be for you to fall to a phoenix little Quayla bested?"

I transmogrified into plasma, employing all of my magic for strength and speed. My swords flashed too fast for an eye to follow.

Bracers of some kind deflected my every blow. She lifted a hand to cover her yawn. I roared my outrage and raised both blades to strike her down. Her hand swept from in front of her mouth, trailing mist. I dodged the unarmed blow and ducked in to slay her.

The watery comet's tail flashed solid only half a gasp before it sliced my head from my shoulders.

Chapter Five

Shaking Foundations

Ignis

A flare of energy behind Ignis signaled the rebirth of another phoenix. Only the proximity allowed him to feel essence combining to form another of his Shield.

Please let it be Terrance.

Ignis didn't wish his brother ill, but any other phoenix meant either Vitae or Quayla falling into Dunham's clutches. A furious roar lifted Ignis's lips into a smile. Whatever happened, it hadn't gone Dunham's way.

A phantom fist wrapped around Ignis's body. Neither squeezing nor pain followed. The dark walls of his cage lifted away, leaving only the magical barrier caging Ignis to keep Dunham's throat unmarked.

Behind Dunham, a big screen television replayed Terrance's dying moments on the network news. Dunham's grip on Ignis's egg faded as an age-old dread solidified to crush Ignis's chest.

Pandora's amphora is shattered. The world knows.

"You will go and finish what your Terra started. Slaughter them all, faerie and human alike, but don't burn the place to the ground."

"Why not?"

"Your Vitae went inside and hasn't come out. I want him, alive."

"I thought you wanted us to kill Vitae and Quayla."

"When your Vitae entered, he wore a new body. Whatever's going on, he's being reborn somewhere else."

Good for you, Vitae.

"So, you want him alive because death means him slipping your trap again."

"Exactly." Dunham glanced past Summus to a murky glass jar. "I'd send Terra with you, but he needs time to recuperate."

Ignis glanced at the dim pentagram lines.

You're low on essence and you can't risk Terrance needing what you have for another rebirth.

"I doubt I have enough essence to be reborn."

"That may be true—through no fault but your own, but after reviewing your fight with Quayla, I'm forced to wonder if you truly wish to abandon all control in her fate."

I thought I'd been circumspect in leading Quayla's thinking, but perhaps you are shrewder than I thought.

"Survive to fight another day or you abandon Quayla and join Caelum."

Ignis's brother's name on Dunham's lips ignited a volcano of sudden fury. Ignis leapt for Dunham's throat, taloned fingers missing by a feather's thickness.

Ignis's body locked in place, falling like a statue to the foot of a wall of white light. Dunham re-appeared a moment later, reclaiming the space he'd surrendered in hasty retreat.

Even had Ignis retained motor function, he'd have been just as stunned. Dunham had slipped into the spirit realm, defending himself with a barrier of Undying Light.

Ignis flicked his gaze to Summus's ragged, emaciated form.

"Yes, I've been feasting on your Divine One's essence." Dunham clasped hands behind his back. "I could have let you at my throat and still rendered you helpless."

I believe him, but where does that leave us?

Ignis glanced at the television only to gasp in shock as Vitae addressed the cameras with his wings on display. Everything about the sight filled Ignis with dread, but nothing so much as Vitae's resemblance to Viviane.

Pressure eased on Ignis's skin. He found Dunham staring at the television as stunned as Ignis felt.

Interesting. Dare I test if I can reach his throat again?

Pressure wrapped around Ignis the moment after the thought appeared. Pain dug into him from a double-dozen angles. He yelped, legs buckling to spill him to the floor.

"You failed that test, Ignis."

Ignis forced his face up to meet Dunham's sneer.

Did I mortal? Or did I catch you blindsided?

"There seems little risk in burning the Sidhe at Medieval Times now, wouldn't you agree?"

"Whatever, just get going." Dunham said. "I have an appointment I don't want to miss."

Dunham

Dunham arrived at Mercedes-Benz Stadium with time enough to survey his preparation. Uncertain Christians filled the stadium to capacity. What with miracles and horrors seemingly cropping up on every street corner, and the Sidhe having been revealed, packing the place had been no effort at all.

Anseelie knight Jahriss preened in a mirror nearby, dressed in a suit which cost more than most sports cars.

Dunham scowled. "I still don't understand why glamour didn't suffice."

"You think you're the only mortal with a natural sensitivity to magic?" Viviane asked. "The suit and makeup won't set off anyone's instincts. Besides, what do you care?"

"You taught me not to be wasteful."

"And yet you murdered Caelum and insist on going through with this...dog and pony show."

"This show will drive the final nail into Atlanta's so-called faithful. The after effects will spread from here throughout the south and then across the world."

"The world's a little busy with the Seelie and Unseelie Courts at the moment, just like we should be."

"Mab approached you. It sounds as if you've thinned the Courts enough."

"Mab has, but Titania hasn't. Both are now able to recruit Fae Kissed far more readily, strengthening their forces."

Dunham searched Viviane's expression. A tightness around her eyes spoke of genuine worry. Revealing Faery to humanity had been part of her plan, but not so soon.

Maybe I should reach out to my military contacts, leveraging the National Guard to thin out the other courts for her.

"You ready, Jahriss?" Dunham asked.

The Anseelie smiled. "I'll have them doubting their faith and throwing accusations at each other long before you make your entrance."

"See that you do." Dunham turned back to Viviane. "Is your agent ready?"

"Yes, Vitae will be distracted."

"Good." Dunham spun, marching for the stage set up in the stadium's center. He wore his best suit with a blazing yellow power tie. He felt like a billion dollars. He felt ready to gut Christianity and leave it on the floor to bleed out.

Two centuries and the moment is finally here.

A nervous-looking man with a balding pate in an untucked dress shirt stepped out of the shadows. "Excuse me, Dunham?"

"What can I do for you Pastor Rueben?"

"I...I'm concerned by something at my host church."

Dunham fought not to smile. "I'm not clergy, Pastor."

"I know, but I don't want to accuse them without proof,

certainly not without someone to corroborate what I think I've discovered."

"I don't really think it's my place—"

"I know, and normally I wouldn't ask, but we're broke. Is there any way I could persuade you to hire a private detective to take a look into what I've found?"

Dunham clapped a hand on the smaller man's shoulder. "Of course, Pastor. I'm sure it's nothing, but I'll be happy to hire a professional to see your fears addressed."

"Thank you."

He squeezed the pastor's shoulder and continued. A spring lightened his steps. The lambs were ready for slaughter.

Let's get bloody.

A small elevator lifted Dunham into the stage set up at the stadium's center. He rose onto the third and topmost tier of the foreshortened ziggurat-style pyramid. A choir filled all four sides, just high enough for all but the very short to be able to see his tier. Handicapped and infirmed had been granted seating on the lowest tier, close enough to bear witness to what was to come.

Dunham allowed himself a chuckle as he stepped off the elevator. He turned on his belt pack, lifted his arms and then his voice. "Good afternoon, people of faith!"

A small cheer raised the volume, but softened once more at his gesture for quiet. "My name is Dunham Heffernan, and it is my pleasure to bring you all together in these strange times. The renowned evangelist Sebastian Jahriss will begin in just a minute, but I wanted to take this opportunity to give credit where credit is due.

"Many people call me a self-made man, but that isn't true. You, people of faith, made me the man I am today. Once upon a time, I was but a drowning boy, but I've risen from those humble travails to the man you see today. Yes, it took years and hard work, but I've managed to claim my due. Today, I'm thrilled to have the opportunity to help you, people of faith, reap all the rewards you and your forebears have sown over the years."

Jahriss rose onto the stage as the crowds cheered.

They shook hands and traded places.

Dunham turned off his microphone. "They're all yours."

Jahriss grinned and turned toward the crowd.

The elevator lowered Dunham into the stage.

Jahriss lifted his voice to be heard. "Sin!"

A hush fell.

"I am a sinner." Jahriss said. "So are you. So-called saints falling short of God's glory by harboring secret sins. We will reap the consequence of sin, answer for our jealousies and our lies...unless..."

Jahriss let the word hang long after Dunham had stepped off the elevator and headed to his private room. He stepped inside to see Jahriss on the monitors.

"In these end times, you have only fleeting moments to repent," Jahriss said.

Dunham smiled at his watch.

Yeah, about thirty-two minutes and thirty-seven seconds.

Detective Foxner

Sabrina Foxner relived the horrifying scene over and over in her mind as she drove down the interstate.

Quayla climbed out of the sedan's trunk missing half of her body. The water phoenix hobbled her way to the water's edge and threw herself in. A stranger dove in after her, trying to save the apparently suicidal cripple while Sabrina herself stood by, too shocked to move.

On one hand, she knew that Quayla was a supernatural creature made of water. Once in the river, she could probably rebuild her bodym if not all at once, a little at a time.

Probably why she left so much of herself in the basin.

On the other hand, Sabrina had witnessed the pain gunshots

caused the phoenix—even when she tried to hide the pain from Sabrina. Tearing, sawing, cutting or otherwise leaving behind half of her body had to have been accompanied by mind-breaking agony.

Maybe she's already broken.

Sabrina shook the thought away. She'd seen Quayla in action, and while a bit sloppy because of her invulnerability, Quayla was neither insane nor stupid.

"Do they do that kind of thing often?" Sabrina asked. "Cut themselves in half?"

Anima didn't answer, though the bronze statuette had changed position when Sabrina wasn't looking so that it now glared over folded arms from the sedan's dashboard.

"Anima?"

"No."

"Did I do something to offend you?" Sabrina asked.

"No, Detective, but you should not have access to the angel network."

"I get that, but this is the only way I know how to communicate with you, and I am trying to understand this hole I've fallen down."

"Lewis Carroll reference? You are well read?"

Sabrina shrugged. "I saw the Johnny Depp movie."

"Oh."

"So, do they?"

"No."

"Look, Anima—you know what, do you have another name you'd rather be called? It's weird calling you Anima."

Anima's voice broke. "Caelum called me Ani-doll."

Sabrina fidgeted, glancing out to a dead deer on the side of the highway, which probably felt less awkward than she did. "Could I just call you Ani?"

"Yes," Anima sniffed.

"All right, Ani, I know you don't want to talk to me like this, but Quayla wanted us to be able to talk."

"She probably didn't want me to feel alone," Anima said. "She's kind like that even though you thought her a heartless animal killer."

Heat prickled the underneath of Sabrina's arms. "Hey, I had good reasons to think that, and she did break into that shelter."

"To protect the animals."

The heat moved up into Sabrina's voice. "I didn't know that. I didn't know there were...goblins—"

"Grendlings."

"Whatever! I didn't know there were any other parties present, so I focused my investigation on the suspect I had. Besides, I knew she was lying to me."

"You are correct. She omitted several things you were not supposed to know, though with greater pleasure than perhaps appropriate."

"And that's why she set my instincts off."

"If you say so, Detective."

"You could call me Foxner since we're going to be working together, or even Sabrina if you wanted."

The voice beyond the statue didn't answer.

"Anima?"

The response didn't come at once. "Yes?"

"Am I disturbing you?"

The soft, girlish voice broke. "No, Dete—Sabrina, it's just I don't know what to do."

"What are you supposed to be doing?" Sabrina asked.

Anima's voice went from broken to shattered. "I'm a W-Watcher. I'm s-supposed to monitor the s-sentry net, re-report Sidhe act-tivity, and c-coordinate between m-my shields and divine."

"Right?"

"B-but they're all g-gone. V-Vitae's gone r-rogue. Dunham's s-somehow imprisoned I-Ignis, Summus and T-Terrance. Q-Quay-la's out of r-reach. I can't c-contact Vilicangelus and Dunham m-mur...Dunham m-murdered C-Caelum."

Sabrina stiffened. "Dunham Heffernan?"

"Y-yes. How d-did you know?"

"Not a lot of Dunham's around Atlanta."

"Oh. Right."

Anima sounded so small. Sabrina's heart went out to her. She knew how to deal with murderers and killers, but she had no idea how to help the young voice sobbing behind the angel statue.

"Dunham murdered Caelum? I don't understand, how is that bad? Okay, I understand how it's bad, but he was a phoenix, right?"

Anima dissolved into hard enough sobs that Sabrina imagined the other woman's whole body shaking with their force.

"Dunham k-killed C-Caelum when he...when he didn't have any ess-essence left. H-he trapped C-Caelum in his egg, then...then he...."

Sabrina couldn't help herself. Even driving, she leaned toward the statue while Anima wailed and hiccupped.

The rest came out in a rushed blur of words. "He threw Caelum's egg off the building!"

Sabrina didn't understand, but the Watcher's grief filled Sabrina's stomach with frozen razor wire.

Her reaction can only mean one thing, this Caelum is really dead. How often can that sort of thing even happen for one of them? They're phoenixes.

Sabrina wanted to reach out to Anima, to offer her comfort somehow, but over the angel network there wasn't a way to hold the distraught woman.

An impotent whisper escaped Sabrina. "I'm sorry."

"I'm...I'm just s-so alone. I don't kn-know what to do. I-I'm s-so scared...."

That I understand.

"Are you in danger?"

"N-No, but poor Q-Quayla...."

"What about Quayla?"

Anima sniffed. "She's lost so much. Her Shield is gone. Vitae stole her nest, m-murdered D-Dylan. Her egg's shattered."

Sabrina frowned. There was too much she didn't understand about her new partner. She'd been plunged into a supernatural world with strange rules and unknown players.

It's a long drive back. Maybe when she calms down, I'll ask.

"I'm sorry, Detective. I'm burdening you and you can't even really understand. Quayla's been through so much, lost so much, but she's still out there fighting...doing her job alone and in constant danger of True Death. She needs help and there's nothing I can do for her."

The world spun like a top doing figure eights. All moisture drained from Sabrina's mouth to leave her gut a writhing nest of vipers. She tightened her hands around the wheel, knuckles turning white as she held onto her emotions in a panicked vice grip.

"Detect—Sabrina? Your vitals are fluctuating wildly. Are you in distress?"

Sabrina sucked on her tongue, unable to moisten her lips. Focus on asphalt kept nightmares caged where they belonged.

"Sabrina?"

Several long minutes passed fighting off the ache low in her belly. When she finally found her voice, her first few words took so much effort to eject they launched in a shout. "Quayla isn't—" Sabrina softened her volume unable to ease the steel from her voice. "Quayla isn't alone. We won't abandon her. We won't...I won't leave her to face all this without backup. Tell me everything I need to know."

Over the hours of boring highway, Anima spun tale after tale. Sabrina's bullshit meter tapped out early on and started flashing out of order long before the innocent voice stopped. Normally, Sabrina might've entertained the idea that Anima used her innocent voice to tell whoppers, but she was speaking through a statue with no visible speakers.

Traffic ahead of her started to pile up. Frustration raised Sabrina's temper. "Great, some idiot on their phone caused a wreck and now everyone has to gawk."

"Actually, there is no accident," Anima said. "There seems to be some kind of military roadblock being erected ahead of you."

Dunham

Twenty minutes' meditation had to suffice Dunham's needs. Shape change magic had never come easy. Viviane blamed his failings on the strength of his self-image, but whatever the reason, he couldn't fail this time.

And I won't.

An unpainted, oak double-door frame stood at one end of the room. Runes burned into the wood waited for his magic. A chain of blood bags acquired from the local children's hospital wreathed the frame glaring accusations at him.

He turned his back on the would-be Arch. A floor-to-ceiling mirror reflected his nakedness, willing but unable to reflect the true man in its surface.

What kind of creature would you display if you could?

He'd done dark things to reach that moment. True, Viviane had molded him from childhood, but he'd held the reins in adulthood. The bargain with the devil's handmaid had been made in childhood, but he'd reaffirmed it down the years. He'd murdered and cheated. He'd swindled and betrayed.

A lifetime of hard choices and dark deeds paraded through his memory. Dunham pushed them away. Shapeshifting required focus and a clear mind.

A topaz and silver egg dropped from his fingers to the street below. A devil-may-care smile flashed from Dunham's lips.

I killed a phoenix, killed Caelum.

He'd heard no end of grief on that count, but Viviane's ire hadn't compared to his own inner regret. He'd had to kill

Caelum. He had to do what needed to be done to prevent the whole thing spinning out of his control.

But I lost control of my temper too.

He'd had to follow through once he'd given his word.

Maybe I should've chosen my motivators more circumspectly.

Dunham pushed regret away. He couldn't change what had been done, but once Quayla and her human confederates had been punished he could—nothing. The Sidhe were running amuck. His caged phoenixes would kill him the moment they had the chance.

And in some ways, I've earned that death.

Dunham wasn't an atheist. He'd been raised by a fallen angel, so denying the existence of God was an impossible vanity. A small, nasty little voice whispered forebodings. Viviane claimed that heaven mandated man be left to deal with man—free will and all that. Still, there had to be consequences for what he had planned —the sin he intended to commit on God's people.

It'll be fine. He'll have His hands full with the Sidhe running amuck. Besides, I'm just showing them their true reflections in a way they'll actually listen.

"Worse case, I help Viviane gets her throne and beg for a small wing of the castle."

Dunham pushed away his worries. He'd chosen his path. He'd follow the plan come hell or lightning from heaven.

He centered himself and drew on his magic. Power spread from his core, filling his limbs cell by tingling cell. He tapped the essence drawn out of Summuseraphi, amplifying the energies pulsing through him.

Dunham focused on the image in his mind, pushed with all of his will and unleashed the magic to run wild.

He grew half again his height, chest and shoulders broadening to match. Sweeping, white, feathered wings unfolded from his back. Muscles swelled and rippled.

Unwilling to leave a single detail open to chance, he embraced the methodologies of his captors. White and gold robes rippled out of his skin. Golden circlets cuffed biceps and forehead. Sandals wrapped up his legs.

Dunham gasped, both from power expended and the man—no angel in the mirror. His reflection resembled a cross between Summuseraphi and a Greek hero. The new face was chiseled as much as the body and nothing like his own.

He flexed the wings, trying to get a feel for how they differed from raven and eagle wings. Unwilling to tempt heaven's wrath just to practice, he'd planned ahead in case the new body flew differently.

He cast a levitation spell, floating just off the ground. Even choosing a room with twelve-foot ceilings and plenty of room, there wasn't enough to truly fly. A few wing beats pushed Dunham over to the Arch.

The magic for opening doorways in Creation was laughably simple, but he performed the spell in conjunction with a lightning storm evocation.

The moment the Arch opened, Dunham filled it with lightning and leapt through on the bolts' tails.

Chapter Six

Object Lessons

Ignis

Ignis launched into the sky from Dunham's balcony, a bone caught in his throat as he remembered Caelum. He winged northeast in phoenix form on Dunham's bidding but also to do his duty.

For years, he'd held himself back, held his temper, damped his fire to ease cleanup. The faeries were out in the open. Mortals knew they existed. Since Ignis couldn't teach one particular mortal the perils of embracing the Sidhe, he intended to teach the home audience.

He streaked out of the sky like a flaming comet, catching every eye he could before executing a superhero landing in honor of Caelum. He rose still aflame, wings stretched down so his primary pinions dragged the asphalt. Two thin lines of fire bracketed his burning footprints.

Camera crews engaged in b-roll filming or supporting anchors interviewing the villagers turned toward him.

Asphalt typically hit boiling point and melted when faced with a regular inferno, but Ignis burned much, much hotter. He strode through the growing blaze, raising his voice to shake the heavens.

"By the Undying Light, I condemn this settlement in the name of the Most High." Ignis tapped his immortal soul. The orange, red and yellow flames of his essence flared to a blazing white of burning magnesium. "All ye who embrace the Sidhe and their creatures of darkness will face the fire of the All Mighty!"

Summus might have taken objection, but Vilicangelus had guided Ignis in learning this higher evolution. Few fire phoenixes ever dared use their souls as fuel to burn with the intensity of a Divine One, but with Atlanta's divine out of commission and the faerie out of hiding, someone needed to put the Fear of God into the populace.

"Consort not with the darkness, lest you be consumed when it is judged."

Ignis broke into a run, burning asphalt lapping at his heels. Faeries poured out of the village toward him. Arrows filled the sky. Ogres emerged, hurling spears and javelins.

Their missiles poofed into clouds of ash the moment they entered within ten feet of him.

Fae Kissed appeared dressed as sorcerers and enchantresses, playing up to the watching cameras.

Ignis leapt into the air as the first faeries reached him.

His wings slapped forward then jerked apart, sending a widening cone of intense white flames rolling over parking lot then faerie grassland for a thousand feet. Asphalt and quaint village buildings vanished in flame and ash like tissue paper tossed upon a bonfire.

A brazen anchor dragged his cameraman toward Ignis in a roundabout arc, intent to get in close for the first soundbite. Heat reddened then crisped his perfect skin long before he got into range, forcing the camera man to abandon his melting camera and pull the anchor away from incineration.

The Fae Kissed darkened, hurrying to trios. Power coalesced between them, building up for a concentrated blast.

"Lay down thy boons, foolish mortals. Surrender thy will and beg the All Mighty for forgiveness. Hear ye your only chance for absolution!"

They unleashed their spells at him.

"On your head be it."

Ignis waded through their blasts. Heat washing off of him fed the wildfire inferno razing the fantasy island of Sidhe power. He transmogrified into his true form, hovering over the conflagration. Wings swept the air, drawing flames up from the fires burning all around him. He drew in the fire, growing larger and larger. More fire swept into his range as he grew. He gathered it all until his wings stretched fifty feet in both directions.

Ignis raised his eyes toward heaven and unleashed a savage cry. He hit the ground in the blackened center, managing his transmog back to human form in time to crash to a superhero landing.

Fire exploded in every direction, rolling over the ground in a blinding white omnidirectional firestorm consuming everything in its path.

He rose, dusted off his diminutive form and strode to the nearest surviving camera.

The college student with the pawnshop video recorder froze in horror, equipment on even though terror vapor locked her.

Ignis looked into the camera and smiled. "I am Ignis, Shield of the Undying Light. As protector of humanity, I give you this warning. The Sidhe are not your friends." He stopped, turning his head to regard the destruction before turning his smile feral. "Any who willingly associate with the faeries are playing with fire."

Colonel O'Curran

Colonel Ronald O'Curran marched into the Atlanta Police precinct. Making nice with local law enforcement tended to be the worst part of the job. He didn't have a grudge against the police like a lot of people did. His father had been a small-town sheriff—one of the few good ones, though he admitted his memories contained some bias.

The National Guard weren't Army Light. They weren't thugs at the beck and call of tin-plated mayors, town councilmen or overly self-important Sheriffs. They had a mission.

In the light of recent events, particularly the rampage of several death row convicts hopped up on supernatural power, his battalion needed to reestablish order in a panic-madden metropolis. Atlanta was a huge, sprawling powder keg on the edge of exploding.

I'm not finished getting my men into place. I need to be focused on that, not kowtowing to some new local policing experiment.

O'Curran restrained the sigh from escape.

Orders are orders.

His march ended at the desk sergeant. The black woman manning the desk juggled a crowd of citizens, two phones and cops coming in and out with only slightly-frazzled aplomb.

She's ex-military, guarantee it.

He took position in the line waiting to chew her ear. Once she'd thinned the crowd and turned eyes on him, he snapped to attention and saluted. The desk sergeant bolted up straight, arm coming part way to a full salute.

O'Curran smirked. "I thought so."

A soft laugh accompanied her back into her seat. "You got me. What can I do for you Colonel?"

"I'm supposed to meet with the head of SNat Crimes," O'Curran said. "I'm a few minutes early, but if he's got the time now, I've got a city to calm."

"Tell me about it." She sighed, shifting her body enough to keep her attention on him while typing into her computer. "I've sent her a message, sir. I'm sorry I don't have time to offer you a cup of coffee."

"Understood. Duty first, right solider?" O'Curran stepped out of the line. "Thanks for the thought just the same."

He found a spot along a nearby wall and waited for the SNat Crimes liaison. Most of what he overheard seemed the regular every day sort of law enforcement challenges. A big screen TV over the waiting area displayed the exotic woman who'd claimed to be a phoenix and some sort of protector in front of the county courthouse.

The founding fathers had made headspace for militia, but something about her struck O'Curran as both insufferable and vigilante. He'd probably suffer in the court of public opinion, but once the basic deployment was in place, he'd have to see about reining her in. Orders designated her as a full ambassador and the hotel where she lived as embassy soil.

She hadn't been granted diplomatic immunity, if only because she'd refused to receive the US envoys that had attempted to establish contact. Another so-called shield had also made quite the impact on the press. The small fire woman struck O'Curran as a showboat, but she at least had her nose in a position that wasn't approaching vertical.

The desk sergeant caught O'Curran's attention, signaling him toward a tall, slender woman with an all-too-cute blonde pixie cut who'd dressed like she wanted to be FBI. Rather than search for him, she grabbed a shorter woman by the arm.

She lowered her voice, but not enough to keep her words from everyone in the immediate area. "I heard you went AWOL with that Buckler woman and blamed it on getting drugged by a bunch of hoodlums. Couldn't catch her so you thought you'd punish her with your bedroom skills?"

The smaller detective snatched her arm away, voice lower and far more dangerous than the first. "Fuck off, Mary."

"There's an opening in homicide now that I'm heading Supernatural Crimes," Mary said. "You used to be a hotshot around here, Sabrina. Maybe they'll take pity and let you do real police work again."

Sabrina darkened. "You haven't the first damned clue what you've gotten yourself into."

"Sure, I do, the fast track out of this hell hole. You're just jealous."

O'Curran expected Sabrina to let the other woman have it. He'd have silently applauded her if she had, but instead her expression softened. "I'm serious, Mary. The Sidhe are dangerous. You need to be careful."

Mary scoffed, eyes rolling as her lips reloaded for another vicious salvo. O'Curran closed the distance, stepping inside Mary's personal bubble and snapped a salute she didn't deserve, but that offered Sabrina a screen behind which to disappear. "Lieutenant Colonel O'Curran, I haven't been given your name yet, but I'm given to understand you're the head of SNat Crimes."

Anger flashed through Mary's expression. Eyes darted around O'Curran's arm, trying to lock onto the other detective once more.

"We have a meeting," O'Curran said.

"Yes, of course. Captain Mary Gamete," Mary extended a hand. "Come with me, Lieutenant, and I'll explain what I need from you."

"Colonel," O'Curran corrected. "And this is a courtesy meeting, Ms. Gamete. My battalions will be offering you support when it is called for—assuming we have the manpower to do so."

"That's not acceptable," Mary said.

To one side, the desk sergeant's mouth turned into an O as she silently drew in breath while shaking her head.

O'Curran's raised his brows, waiting for the clunk of her heel stomping linoleum.

"Your men are to be at SNat's disposal."

O'Curran pointed at her. "*Atlanta* Police."

She eyed him warily.

He pointed at himself. "*National* Guard."

A tirade gathered on her lips.

He leaned close. "Just who do you think the little fish is here, Ms. Gamete? Think about it while I secure the city. Good day."

Dunham

Levitation magic gave Dunham the time he needed to get a better feel for his new wings. A scream punctuated the stadium, cutting off Jahriss mid-sermon. The scream echoed a thousand times as more people noticed Dunham's light-haloed shape.

Far below, Jahriss pointed. "Creator's Mercy."

Dunham swept a quick circuit around the stadium ceiling, drawing every eye, only to stop high above the stage. He waited, hovering in place with the occasional wing flap as directional microphones zeroed in onto him. Cameras filled the stadium screens with his image.

"Behold and tremble, for I bring word from on high."

The crowd quieted.

"Hear, ye sinners, those who've daydreamed and played with phones while an anointed champion laid your sins bare."

Dunham spun, orienting on the congregation from Catholic Shrine of the Immaculate Conception.

"Judgement has come. Your lofty spires have been cast down, made low as the sin in your hearts and unfaithful congregations."

A sweep of wing jetted him over another congregation. "Your pastor uses his pulpit to seduce the young, mired in fornications while his deacons line their pockets."

Another quick flight crossed the stadium. "Your priest wields his followers like a cudgel, persecuting homosexuals in guilt for harboring the same unholy desires."

Dunham shifted back and forth, picking a church and accusing its people. A murmur rose as churchgoers corroborated

Dunham's accusations and accused each other of sins both true and false.

He returned to the center position, tapping into Divine essence until his glow resembled a sun. Slow flaps lowered him until his expanding aura touched the crowd. "Your sins have angered the Most High."

No doubt true enough.

"Hell's been unleashed in Atlanta to punish the wicked."

And everyone else.

"He has abandoned you for your willfulness and stiff-necked sins."

Didn't say which he.

"You will burn for your hypocrisy. You will drown in your own sinful desires...." Dunham held still in the silence, preparing the healing spell. "There may yet be one path to redemption. One chance. Embrace the Repentant Lady, the Fallen Angel exiled from her brethren for turning her heart back to the Truth."

He waited out a three count.

"If you can earn her favor, perhaps you can escape judgement."

In complete contradiction to everything the Bible teaches you.

Dunham smiled, unleashing the healing spell backed by Summuseraphi's power into the congregated infirm.

And here's a miracle to lead you into the depth of your hypocrisies.

Dunham cloaked himself in glamour and fled through the Arch on the brink of collapse.

Vitae

I landed on the new sanctum's roof and descended toward my suite. Laughter drew me out of the stairwell onto the servants' living area. A group of my minions clustered around a gigantic wall-spanning television. An emaciated, smudged little girl just into her adolescence sat in an interview chair with her hands in her lap. Tears drew lines down grimy cheeks.

The well-dressed woman interviewing the girl leaned forward, setting a hand on the girl's. "It's all right Theophany, I understand this is hard for you."

"T-they murder us, the ph-phoenixes..."

"These so-called," the reporter made air quotes. "Shields?"

Theophany nodded. "Yes. We're starving to d-death, Liv, exiled for crimes our...our ancestors c-committed."

As if you haven't repeated their sins.

"Do you want some food?" Liv looked around. "Can we get some food in here?"

"Thank you, but no," Theophany said. "We were created to serve. Sharing our power with mortals sustains us, but the...the..."

Liv made air quotes again. "Shields?"

Theophany gasped back a sob and nodded.

"How does sharing your power feed your kind?"

"We're symbiotes. A relationship with a human gives the human some of our power and gives us what we need to thrive...what we need to rejoin your world."

Liv looked at the camera. "You're refugees, exiled by a despotic regime and just looking for a way to earn a home with your gifts."

Theophany slapped hands over her face, nodding behind her hands. "But Vitae and his kind just want us to languish and die."

"Damn right I want you to die, lying Sidhe!" I hurled an eldritch bolt at the television. Power blackened one corner of the screen. Energy crackled across the television, wreathing it as it fell from its mounts.

Anger and fear watched me from countless Sidhe faces.

"Why are you in here watching this?" I stomped toward the nearest Wyldfae, sending them scurrying for the corners. "Why aren't you out there, stopping the Seelie and Unseelie from destroying my city?"

A familiar female voice filled the room. "I am Ignis, Shield of the Undying Light. As protector of humanity, I give you this warning. The Sidhe are not your friends."

Ignis?

I turned to find a diminutive, burning female shape survey what looked like the aftermath of a nuclear bomb.

Scurith entered. "Pardon me, Master—"

Ignis showed her teeth. "Any who willingly associate with the faeries are playing with fire."

"She doesn't carry the same presence you did during your interview," Scurith said. "But she's terrifyingly eloquent."

My eyes slid from video replays of Ignis's carnage played over and over in slow motion to the grey and tan coyll. His fur flattened to his skin a split second ahead of his ears. He lowered to all fours, tail tucked tight between his legs.

"If this is an example of the kind of protection offered by these so-called shields, is it any wonder why Theophany and her people fear for their lives from hiding?" Liv asked.

I barely turned in time before the firestorm of rage poured out of my hands into the television. My roar echoed off the walls. Violet fire splashed off the large screen, following the contour of the room to plunge all of it in a purple inferno.

I chased Scurith down in the stairwell, snatching the cowering morsel up in my hands. "You want to see terrifying eloquence? Do you, slave? Find me an incursion!"

I hurled the coyll. It yelped when it hit a floor below, managed a clumsy bow and limped out the nearest door with hooded eyes.

Dunham

Dunham surveyed the ballroom. The normally cordial brunch he put on for Atlanta's religious leaders resembled a reunion of retired WWE wrestlers. Pastors and priests, rabbis and ministers warred in islands over forgotten plates of free food.

Fingers stabbed.

Longtime friends hurled insults and venomous slurs.

Accusations flew back and forth from both the betrayers and betrayed.

It took all of Dunham's control not to clap his hands and laugh like a giddy toddler.

Dunham donned his boardroom countenance and crossed to the podium. The microphone made his deep voice boom like Zeus on high. "Gentlemen. This is a place of mutual respect."

"Respect?" One pastor 's finger shook toward his neighbor. "He stole our tithes for his gambling addiction."

"I did no such thing," the accused said. "You're just too enthralled by a spirit of drunkenness."

"Money?" A rabbi demanded. "While you're wrapped up in your greed, this...this...priest is sleeping with my wife and half the wives in my flock."

Dunham blinked.

Viviane hadn't mentioned fabricating that particular situation.

I thought the priest was supposed to be accused of—

"If I were you," another priest said. "I'd be more worried what else he did while he was fornicating with your wife."

"What are you accusing me of, pedophile?" the first priest said.

"Pornographer!"

There it is.

"No wonder God smote your church, Adulterer!" the rabbi said.

"Thief!"

"Embezzler!"

Dunham opened his mouth to twist the knife.

"Serial killer!"

He remained silent, brows rising.

Once he'd recovered, he turned to a pale pastor, addressing her while strategically not turning off his microphone. "No wonder that angel showed up and made those accusations."

The room's attention turned toward Dunham. He held up his hands, feigning embarrassment. "Hey, don't look at me. I believed all of those angel's accusations were bogus...initially."

The room exploded once more.

Quayla

I surfaced off the eastern coast of England in the waters north-northwest of Canterbury. Bobbing in the water, I waited in the rain for night to fade into impending dawn. It'd been a long swim across the Atlantic, but the time in my element had washed away a lot of my pain and fear. I was well fed and my overall mass was greater than it had been that morning at Howell Mill.

I waited in the water, floating in cold water that matched my own interior temperature. After the long aquakinesis-enhanced swim, I wanted to fly the last few miles to Hedingham rather than walk.

Have to wait until the sun rises or my true form will be too visible.

Worries returned with the surface world. I had no idea what was going on in Atlanta. I had to trust Vitae to do his duty. Even if he did the job like a swaggering sociopath, he would protect our Prefecture until my return.

The amulet intermixed with the essence at my neck could allow me to check in with Anima, but I wanted to reach my destination first. I wanted to at least be able to report that in this one small task I'd been successful.

The sun rose slowly, illuminating a storm-darkened morning. I sighed.

My feathered form would show up like a beacon against the

dark skies, forcing my hand. I reached my senses into the surrounding waters and pushed the water between me and my destination down my body and away. I sped through the water, diving once to gobble a slow-moving black bream before stepping out onto a rocky shore.

I transmogrified.

Spare weeks before, transmoging had taken effort and concentration. Technically, the change still did, but it came easier, so much easier, than it had at Howell Mill.

A lot's changed. Me especially.

I gathered my jacket around me and trudged up the walk. My initial entrance into the rainy weather seemed a warm bath compared to the cold sea, but cold rain and wind stole warmth from the skewed perspective. In some ways, I missed the extra fat layers of a female body, but my male biology generated more heat and faster.

Cold and wet, I was a whole lot less miserable than I'd have been female—especially with long hair.

Of course, as a woman I could've probably smiled my way into a ride.

A car stopped beside me on the wrong side of the road. An attractive woman rolled down her window. "Need a ride, luv?"

I smiled, trying to remember the accent I'd tried so hard to convert to southern after being reassigned. "If it wouldn't be too much trouble, ma'am."

"Ma'am?" Her frown shadowed a lovely face. "American?"

"I'm living in the states, but I was born near Hedingham. That's where I'm headed."

"Hop in. I'm not going the whole way, but it'll keep you out of the rain for a time."

"You have my thanks." I rounded the car and got in, drawing some of the water out of my clothes and into my body to minimize the mess I made of her seat.

"No umbrella?"

I shook my head. "Just didn't think about it."

"Suppose I should've asked before I offered a ride, but you aren't one of those Sidhe, are you?"

Ocean cold stole the warmth offered by the car's heater. "What? N-No."

"Suppose you wouldn't tell me if you were. You can keep your bargains if you are. I have all I want."

The car resumed its trek. I learned a lot about her job, her students, even a little local gossip. What I didn't learn was how she knew about the Sidhe.

My suspicious reflection in the side window glowered back accusations. I'd barely survived fighting Ignis. Stealth hadn't been high on my priorities.

She let me off in Colchester. Before I continued on westward, I sought a newspaper stand. The front page told me all I needed to know, but I bought it anyway for more information.

The world knew.

I'd failed in my duty, and mortals around the world suffered because of it. Passersby couldn't see the tears running down my face in the rain, but I felt their judgement. I felt His judgement.

Another stupid, selfish mistake, but this time it won't cost hundreds of lives. Millions are going to die.

An ache in my chest drew me home. Finding Vilicangelus after the fact wouldn't help.

It was too late.

I'd destroyed Creation.

No. I'm not giving up. I'm here to find Vilicangelus and that's just what I'm going to do.

Chapter Seven

Unraveling Deceit

Detective Foxner

Sabrina pulled off Sandy Plains into a residential subdivision. Small houses with manicured lawns edged a maze of roadways curved for the sake of the builder's amusement rather than any logical reason.

The GPS led her to a pink house with white shutters and an overly complicated landscaping scheme. A neighborhood watch sign with a sub sign naming the resident watch captain stood next to the curb—the only stray element in the sculptured yard.

Great.

Sabrina was forced to park a house away from the complainant by the overflow of newer cars parked at the house across from the watch captain.

Probably wants to bitch about the noise or something.

Neighborhood watches definitely served their purpose. The problem was that the kinds of people who wanted to captain such organizations tended to be extreme busybodies. She checked the database, finding exactly what she'd expected. The woman already exiting the front door in a pink housecoat and slippers had a list of complaints to her name longer than some rap sheets.

With everything going on, listening to this woman complain is going to be like scraping my own nails on a chalkboard. Why can't I be out doing something important with Quayla?

A shiver of arousal shot through her body.

Sabrina frowned.

Before she could puzzle out the sudden wetness between her thighs for the male phoenix, the watch captain knocked on her window. "Are you the police?"

Sabrina took a deep cleansing breath, pushing her door open slowly to force the woman to back away. She picked up her tablet as she exited her car. It'd been years since she'd had to take a robbery report herself. So long, that report had been on paper.

Detectives were normally reserved for large burglary rings, fencing operations, and house burglary sprees. Unfortunately, the everyday uniforms weren't available to deal with little miss neighborhood watch captain. They were spread thin working backup for the new SNat Crimes division.

Not any of them have half a clue what they're dealing with.

Mary had transferred into Supernatural Crimes the moment the positions opened.

No doubt thinks it'll be the fast track to another promotion.

"If you're not the police, and you're not a resident's guest, I'm going to have to ask you to leave. We don't allow solicitors in—"

"Good afternoon, ma'am," Sabrina tried to add a little emotion to the flat monotone without much success as she handed over a business card. "My name is Detective Foxner. Are you a Ms. Ricia?"

The woman high-pitched nasal voice barked like an angry chihuahua. "That's *Missus* Ricia, with a hard C sound."

Foxner typed a few letters on the tablet with the accompanying stylus. "I understand you wish to report a theft."

Mrs. Ricia puffed herself up. "Yes, I do."

Sabrina barely restrained a groan.

"Stanley Houston has been stealing things all over the neighborhood." Mrs. Ricia pointed across the street. "Electronics, jewelry...," she lowered her voice, "...lady's unmentionables."

"Have you or your neighbors reported these thefts?"

"That's what I'm doing now."

"Mrs. Ricia, you can't report a theft unless the items stolen were your personal property."

"None of the others are home from work yet."

Sabrina's brows rose. "Then how do you know your neighbors are being burgled?"

She shoved a smart phone into Sabrina's view. Social media posts showed pictures of closed house doors each tagged with #NoSelfie. More pictures showed electronics, open jewelry boxes and indeed women's' lingerie drawers labeled with the same hashtag.

Sabrina licked her lips.

I bet Quayla doesn't have to deal with th—what the fuck?

A small orgasm rippled through Sabrina's body.

"Are you all right, detective? You're suddenly looking flush."

"F-Fine." Sabrina cleared her throat. "Do you have any evidence other than these posted pictures?"

Mrs. Ricia turned toward the house across the street. "Just watch for a minute."

Sabrina watched, focused not on the perfectly normal house but the sudden physical reactions she'd had. She hadn't had a lover in a long time, but even when she'd been in a relationship, she'd never had spontaneous reactions like the one she'd just had.

Besides, I swore off men. Why would thinking about Quayla—"

Another tremor of sensation gripped low in her body then rippled up and down her every nerve.

"There, see?" Mrs. Ricia snapped.

The garage door on the opposite side of the street opened to reveal folding tables lined up along every wall stacked with televisions, stereos, game systems and computers. Various jewelry overflowed from an unlidded Tupperware bin like pirate booty.

Sabrina's dispassionate but breathy reply shuddered a little. "There's nothing illegal about someone hoarding things in—"

A gate between the houses opened for no apparent reason. A television appeared on an open space on one table. A shift in the jewelry box accompanied clinking metal, several thick gold rope chains and a string of pearls appearing.

Sabrina sprinted across the street as the garage door rolled down. She thrust a leg across the door's safety sensor, reversing its motion as the door into the house opened. "Freeze! Police."

"Shit," no one said.

The sound of flesh slapping flesh followed a moment later.

Sabrina took a gamble. "I can see you, Mister Houston, come out from behind the glamour."

A grind of tiny rocks on concrete gave Sabrina her only warning. She dropped low, sweeping her leg out the direction she'd heard the noise. Her leg slammed into something fleshy and solid. Another body hit the ground with an oof of expelled breath. A bat sprang into view and rolled across the concrete.

Sabrina grabbed blindly for an invisible limb. Fingers wrapped around an ankle. A shoe slammed into her face. Heat, pain and a sickening crunch sent her backward onto her ass. Sabrina blinked rapidly, trying to clear the tears accompanying the broken nose. She held her gun low in both hands to prevent it being taken, ignoring the salty blood gushing down her face.

Bloody shoe prints appeared in rapid order, stopping the moment invisible Stanley Houston's run took him onto grass.

Sabrina holstered her gun. She pressed her jacket to her face despite the pain.

"You let him get away," Mrs. Ricia said.

Sabrina's bark made her sound like she was a New Jersey Yankee. "Did you see him?"

"Well, no."

"Do you have a towel?" Sabrina asked.

"Blood stains are very hard to get out."

Sabrina glared at Mrs. Ricia, opening her trunk and snatching a clean oil rag from a half unused bundle. Movement in her peripheral vision caught Mrs. Ricia stepping into the open garage.

"Get away from there."

Ricia snatched a once white, lace-edged negligee from a basket of clothes. "This is from my wedding night."

Sabrina rushed across the street, snatching Mrs. Ricia's arm with a bloody hand not holding the rag to her face.

"Let go of me, Detective. You're ruining my housecoat."

"You're contaminating a crime scene!"

"That pervert stole my—"

"Missus Ricia," Sabrina snapped. "Go back into your home and wait for me there. If you do not do as I instruct, I'll cite you for obstructing an officer in the course of her duty and tampering with a crime scene."

The Neighborhood Watch captain brandished a finger. "I didn't do anything wrong. I'm only—"

"Trespassing in a man's garage in full view of a police detective."

Unlike Stanley Houston.

Mrs. Ricia huffed, stomping across the street to her house like an angry toddler.

<If I had a wolf's nose, I could track the bastard down.>

Though I can't imagine how much breaking a wolf nose would hurt.

Sabrina returned to her car and reached for her radio. She paused, turning instead to the disgusted looking bronze angel statuette. "Anima?"

"Yes, Detective?"

"I just got my nose broken by an invisible suspect."

"I am sorry for your pain."

"Right, thanks, but my question is, was that glamour?"

"I imagine it was something similar."

"How do I get rid of it?"

"In your case, do you have any iron filings?"

"No," Sabrina said. "Thanks for the insight though."

"I still do not think you should be using this channel."

"Yeah, I know. I'm still trying to find a better answer."

Anima went silent for several moments. "I appreciate your consideration, Sabrina."

Sabrina called in for backup, held the oil rag to her face and fumed. She picked up her cell phone and dialed Miri. The oddball forensics tech answered on the second ring.

"Roger's gay bar and truck stop, Muffy the buffer speaking."

"Miri?"

"Hello, Sabrina. What can I do for you?"

"If I gave you an address, is there any way you could come out here with some iron filings?"

"Why?"

Sabrina hesitated. "Um, so I can catch a guy hiding behind faerie magic?"

"I'll be right there."

"I haven't told you where I am yet."

Miri laughed. "Ah, the wonders of GPS."

Vitae

A battle cry echoed off the walls around my nest before the rest of my body finished forming. I leapt out of my basin the moment legs formed, soiling my Persian rug with a trail of bloody essence.

A lumbering ogre smashed me between two cars, Priuses of all things. This cannot be countenanced.

Yanking both Champion blades from their pegs, I charged the door of my suite.

My reflection brought me up short.

An elven madman clutched the elven artifacts. Long red curls matched calves blood coated from wading through a battlefield. Except for the ears and lack of woad, I resembled a naked berserker from Celtic tales.

I am not a barbarian. I will not act like it.

The Lady of Water was a Fallen angel with eons of experience manipulating men. She'd manipulated me into attacking her with her offers and passive aggressive accusations. Furious at being so casually slain, I'd let Viviane's insults get under my skin and sought out a major incursion in a fit of pique.

A burning need to storm the druid's fortress with my troops, slay them both and free the other shields occluded almost all other thoughts.

That's what she wants.

She'd come only because I had chosen to prepare my headquarters before storming hers. She wanted me to attack, both before she slew me and again at the Circlestone building.

Her druid wanted me in his collection.

I would not be so foolish.

Not like Aquaylae.

Ignis and Terrance had been caught on wafer news channels.

As sloppy and careless as Aquaylae was about revealing my Shield to mortal scrutiny, there'd been no news of her. Had I not already freed her from the chains of infatuation with the unworthy wafer she'd spent so much time fornicating, I'd have thought her absence was due to her disappearance into her lusts.

My agents had been unable to find whisper or word of the lazy shield. I'd commanded the search include local dens of debauchery, but their failure combined with Viviane's suggestion that Aquaylae would make a superior confederate led to an obvious conclusion.

Viviane had already captured the incompetent water phoenix. True, she'd tried to occlude the fact with a partially successful gambit—holding Aquaylae up as superior to incense me.

Champion blades returned to their proper places, I dressed once more in suits celebrating the height of English fashion. The heavy clothing wasn't as flexible as the elven robes and it was easily thrice as warm. Neither concern outweighed that so long as I remained male, I would dress as a proper gentleman.

"Scurith!"

It didn't matter if the coyll's sharp ears picked up my voice or not. The other slaves would pass the word if they wished to avoid execution.

"Master, you cal—" Scurith's ears twitched forward and his nose seized several rapid sniffs. "Master, how may I serve you?"

"I've lost my robes at that last incursion site. Send someone to reclaim them with all haste. A winged troll-child."

"A kyrie, Master?"

My brows knit. "Kyrie?"

"Your wafer thrall named the winged enforcers kyrie, something about them being flying and dead but not having a Valhalla to take dead warriors back to."

The nonsense sounded like my thrall. Still, for a queer little wafer, he'd given good service again and again. He'd worked countless hours with only occasional complaints regarding rest or sustenance. In fact, if more wafers served as he did, mortality might not have proven so pathetic.

Perhaps I should breed him.

"Yes, Scurith. Send a pair of kyrie."

Scurith bowed his way out of the room.

"Scurith?"

The coyll stopped in the open doorway. "Master?"

"Send a half dozen elves to watch the oracle. Assign them each six trollmen and four kyrie to put down any incursions that occur."

Scurith opened his maw, but rather than speak objections, he bowed once more. "Yes, Master. At once."

"Instruct them to notify me of any force too large for their squad to thwart and capture."

Scurith's shoulders eased. "Very wise, Master. I shall deliver your instructions."

Business done for the moment, I took the measure of my new body. More power awaited my command, but the balance I'd felt before slaying Mariena and Vusolaryn seemed a hair off.

The former was of greatest import. I brought Dolumii's sword to Mare's suite, bowing to her egg as if we were attending a ball. Sitting cross-legged on her floor, I settled both the blade and egg in my lap. Sliding the edge along my palm provided the sword an offering of blood and power. A sweep of hand bound egg and weapon together via my blood.

I willed it to release Mare into her egg. The totality of my new, enhanced strength rampaged down my limbs into both artifacts, commanding the blade to the single service.

The sword's embedded faces moaned in torment, a subtle thumbing of the sword's metaphysical nose at my efforts.

I summoned Scurith to bring captives.

I sacrificed two score, absorbing their strength to help overpower the sword's resistance.

I failed...once and again a hundred times once.

Scurith brought casks of essence from the torturous apparatus that maintained the lives of Knights Dolumii and Gherrian while it drained their blood.

With strength fled and temper towering in impotent weakness, I returned Mare's egg to its bed.

Viviane's offer flashed through my thoughts. When I pushed it away, I could almost hear her accusing me of being too weak.

No. I'll just have to become even more powerful.

Detective Foxner

Backup arrived before Miri did. Sabrina took advantage of her position to guard the suspect's house and send them beating the bushes. Fortunately, Stanley Houston had a record for petty theft, so she was able to give the uniformed officers a basic description.

Miri arrived in an eye-searingly neon orange vintage Volkswagen Thing wallpapered in fandom decals and bumper stickers.

A chrome Decepticon ornament replaced the Volkswagen symbol on its grill. Her license plate read: KHANGRL.

Miri got out of the car, handing two small plastic cylinders to Sabrina the moment she stepped close enough. "That looks like it hurts."

"No, shit. What was your first guess?"

"The swelling along the bridge of your nose and discoloration beneath your eyes."

Sabrina turned the containers in her hand. Both held iron filings, though of different sizes.

"So, where's your fairy-dusted perp?"

<If I had a wolf nose, I'd know that, wouldn't I?>

"Lost him, and I'm not exactly equipped to track him by scent."

"Guess not. Do you think he'll return to his house?"

"He's confident he's invisible. I tried to bluff him, but he figured out I was lying."

"Then you'll want to spread some of those across the threshold of each door he could use. The iron should react badly with the fairy magic and we should be able to see him."

"How do you know stuff like that?"

"Fantasy novels and Dungeons & Dragons?" Miri frowned. "That is why you asked me to bring the iron filings, right? Because you knew it would interfere with his spell?"

"Of course, I did." Sabrina handed Miri one of the containers. "Go around back and dust his back door while I get the two up front."

Sabrina almost skipped dusting the door leading from the garage to the house, but considering the amount of iron filings and her throbbing nose, she decided to cover all of her bases.

In total contradiction of expectations, Stanley Houston eased the door leading through his garage open ever so slowly, a smug leer pointed at Sabrina.

She drew her weapon. "Freeze, Houston."

He froze for a moment. A sly grin spread across his face,

making his long face turn ratish. He tiptoed around the tables, behind several televisions.

Sabrina kept still, following him out of the corner of her eye.

He appeared with a swirling blue bowling ball. Houston crept closer, rearing back to slam the ball into Sabrina's head. At the last moment, Sabrina slammed a foot into his chest.

Houston fell backward, slamming into a folding table and falling to the floor in an avalanche of hopefully heavy and uncomfortable electronics.

Miri appeared in response to the commotion.

"Help me unbury him."

The two women excavated Stanley Houston. Sabrina put him on his face, cuffing him behind his back. Miri handed over a Miranda card, but instead of taking it, Sabrina yanked up Houston's shirt.

An emerald mark had been burned into his lower torso. It was different from the mark Quayla had shown her, but something told Sabrina that it meant the same thing. A few iron filings caused the mark to flare up and ugly green-grey veins to shoot away through Houston's skin.

"What did you just do?" Miri asked.

"This is the mark of a Sidhe Court. Since it doesn't match the Unseelie mark I was shown, I'm guessing this one is Seelie."

Miri's eyes widened behind her thick glasses. "By the gods, someone showed you what a real Unseelie rune looks like?"

"Yeah."

"What does it mean?"

"It means this bastard made a deal with the Sidhe."

Miri's mouth crooked sideward. "Um, what does that mean for what comes next?"

Sabrina took in a deep breath. "Nothing except we warn the guys watching holding. It's not like the supernatural is our jurisdiction."

"You sure we shouldn't hand him over to that Vitae lady I saw on the television?" Miri asked.

"No." Sabrina snapped. "She's bad news too."

"Wish there was more I could do than sit around tech ops."

"Maybe there is." Sabrina gave Miri a long hard look. "So, theoretically, if I wanted to set up two-way communications with a ghost in my apartment, do you think you could figure out some kind of solution?"

Miri cocked her head. She smiled. "Yeah, I think I can fix up something for that."

Chapter Eight

Homecoming

Bradley

A sharper pain than the incorporeal fangs nibbling his skin stabbed Bradley. "Get up, *wafer*. Master wants you."

He groaned, struggling to sit up. Everything hurt and even on the floor the world spun.

Duke licked his face.

The grendling kicked Duke. "Out of the way, mutt."

The dog yelped, whimpering away with his tail tucked.

The grendling slashed a claw across Bradley's face. "Master wants you, you lazy—"

Bradley backhanded the grendling, sending the diminutive faerie fifteen feet into the nearest wall. Bradley's arm tingled and his stomach snarled, but he sat on the floor and stared.

Duke slunk up to him, lay behind Bradley, wrapping around to set his nose on Bradley's leg.

Bradley scratched Duke's ears absently.

The grendling struggled to its feet, pulling a wicked, curved trollbone dagger taken from some huge troll's ribcage. "You'll suffer for that, wafer."

The bottom of Bradley's shoe intercepted the grendling, catapulting the faerie across the room to make a second dent.

Bradley sprang to his feet in far too fast a rush. He scrambled around the other lab equipment to the nearest reflective surface. His warped reflection wore highwater pants and a shirt too short for the long arms in its sleeves. He hadn't become a muscled behemoth like the other enforcers, but the dented walls belied his meek frame.

"Great Gygax." Bradley ran a hand through his hair, coming back with a fistful of red locks.

Cold washed through him.

Ginger fingers tested the hair still on his head, only to have it all come free. Panic shot through him. It wasn't that Bradley was particularly fond of his hair or all the work it took to tame the unruly curls, but losing all his hair wasn't a sign of health.

Like Blake Hedison in Delirious.

Bradley's thin mustache wiped away like a strawberry milkshake. He cringed and checked his eyebrows. For whatever reason, they remained anchored to his face.

"Thrall!"

Bradley whirled so fast that he actually went around twice.

Master Vitae's gorgeous body thundering into the room caused his own to stir. Having already outgrown his pants, the sensation wasn't pleasant.

"I summoned you."

Bradley tensed for the pain that had accompanied Vitae's displeasure while he'd been enthralled. It didn't come. He looked down into Vitae's eyes.

"Apologies, Master."

Vitae's eyes narrowed. "What have you done to yourself?"

Excuses and explanations rampaged through his thoughts, pillaging grey matter for something that wouldn't result in punishment. "Laundry accident. Shrank my clothes and caused an allergic reaction. I was trying to make myself presentable."

Vitae's gaze intensified. Tingles spread out of Bradley's eyes, enveloped his head and shot down his body. "When I call, you obey even if that brings you to my presence naked."

A barely audible voice echoed Vitae's words. Bradley dropped his eyes. "Yes, Master. What can I do for you?"

Vitae's finger brought Bradley's eyes back up. "I require more child corpses. You will procure them."

Fury spiked through Bradley. Pain ignited his fingertips.

Like hell I will.

Vitae cocked his head ever so slightly. "Problem, slave?"

Bradley curled his lips and stared into the middle distance between their faces. "No, Master. I will find some way to acquire you more child corpses."

"Good. Be about it." Vitae spun on his heels, hips sashaying a delicious path toward the door. "At least your screw up got rid of that ridiculous mustache. Fix your hair. I won't have lazy slobs in my employ."

The door closed behind Vitae.

Bradley mocked her soundlessly. "Fix your hair."

He paced the room, fury bubbling from his gut like it'd become a lava-filled caldera. He wasn't going to dig up children. He wasn't going to desecrate more.

"And employees get paid, you obnoxious snob." He slammed a fist through a table full of beakers.

The obnoxious grendling struggled to its feet, crawling to its lost knife. "I saw that, slave. Master Vitae will flay your skin for such insolence."

Bradley whirled, fury doubling. He brandished a finger. "I've had about enough of you."

A blue bolt of magic wove a haphazard path across the room and slammed into the grendling. The little faerie collapsed, a look of shock in his glazed eyes.

"Great Gygax! I can cast magic missile!"

Quayla

The town of Hedingham had grown a lot in the one hundred and fifty-nine years since I'd seen it. A sign on the outskirts bore a population number of almost five thousand, easily twenty-fold the number that had dwelt in Hedingham during my previous residence. Once a collection of buildings strung together by cobblestone and dirt byways, the town had transmogrified into paved streets and side by side lines of two-story buildings.

I walked its streets, expecting without good reason to recognize someone or once more hear cries for my death. One block near town's center called to me. I crossed to the empty space, seeing the remains of attempts to build upon the ground or grow the space into some kind of a park.

The whole square remained dead, cursed by one of the Fae Kissed that had burned before the villagers got to me.

A ghostly platform with long burned-away wood flickered and crackled. A woman mad with pain and old-fashioned insanity cackled Sidhe curses.

"You can see her too." An old woman reminiscent of Mrs. Cox shifted brown eyes magnified by Coke bottle glasses between me and the cursing soul.

"Roma forebears?"

The woman's cackle echoed the soul frozen in anger. "You have the sight too, my boy?"

"She ever stop cursing?"

"Not in the seventy-seven years I've lived here."

"I'm surprised no one has helped her move on."

"You're the only one who's even seen her besides me."

No time like the present.

A shiver ran through me the moment my foot stepped within the barren square. The burning woman fell quiet, eyes turning to watch my approach. Hatred hissed through her teeth. "You."

I stopped at the foot of the ghostly platform, unwilling to stand atop it once more. "What about me?"

"They'd never have found me if not for you." Fingers swept through something like a peasant warding gesture, except the moment she thrust her hand forward, taint spread into my flesh. "Share my curse, turncoat."

The laugh escaped me before I thought better of it. "Generally, when I die, my soul is reborn, not stu—"

She threw her head back and laughed. "Death will hunt you, take those you love, destroy all you protect. You will know only misery and pain so long as my magic lingers."

"Then let's see about cleaning up you and your magic."

She brandished a burned finger. "Oh, no. You will not so easily slip my vengeance. My earth magic will survive until world's end."

Spreading taint sent a chill up my spine. "You won't."

I stepped onto the platform. Every footfall echoed on boards long rotted to dust. Back to the post, flames licking at my soul, I focused on my essence.

The other soul writhed and shrieked, flailed and spat like a furious cat, occupying the same space as I did. Taint filled me. Flames flared up, cooking my limbs.

If Ignis couldn't kill me, no two-hundred-year-old campfire is going to prevail.

I pushed my essence into the fire. The flames danced out of the way. It didn't shrink. Will pushed more of my power against the ancient bonfire to no avail. My essence and the phantom flames would not occupy the same space. No amount of effort could force the water to smother the fire.

The witch cackled triumphantly. "You cannot win. I will be a blight, a curse to remind these people of their sins forever."

I stepped away from the post, surveying the scene.

The unrepentant soul sneered at me, lost in hatred and anger. Her claims suggested she'd been an earth witch before the Sidhe offered her power, possibly the child of another Fae Kissed.

If my mistake hadn't revealed her, would I have faced her? Would I have failed as I did with Emma?

Vilicangelus's words whispered out of memory. *<No matter where your journey takes you, follow your heart. The one given you is precious.>*

Tears welled up in my eyes. I knelt, eyes raised to heaven. The words escaped in a whisper. "Merciful Creator, forgive this daughter for her anger and mistakes."

The witch laughed again. "You're barking. His people murdered me for how I was born."

"She strayed from your love—in part because of my mistakes."

"Love?" The witch scoffed. "From the God of Sodom and Gomorrah? The God who drowned the world?"

I unfurled my wings, pushing the lion's share of my essence into them until dizziness washed through me. They curled around the fire, the post and the wayward earth witch. "I claim her sin that you may greet her soul as you created it."

My wings tightened, cocooning the scene. I willed the taint into myself, drawing with it her anger.

A plague of blackness shot through me.

Poison shot through my veins.

Darkness welled in my vision.

The witch shrieked and flailed, fighting against my wings— my strongest muscles outside the heart Vilicangelus named precious.

Unholy fire burned through me, the same perverted angelic power raised against my Creator. I willed it through my skin, up my limbs and into my heart.

Water of Life, Love of God, cleanse this evil from the world.

Burning spiked to an inferno.

Pain flared like a struck match's flame, quenched in a single heartbeat by soothing waters.

Words escaped me in a rasp. "I forgive you, daughter, in His name. Go unto heaven from my embrace into Love's very arms."

I released her, absorbing my abused wings as I struggled to my feet. My first step away from the flames nearly resulted in a tumble. I strode out of the lot on wobbly legs. The old woman squinted at my feet and face in turns.

"Won't be a problem anymore," I said. "In fact, you might want to buy this lot before anyone realizes. You could probably get it for quite a bargain."

"Shrewd notion." She frowned. "You had wings."

"Yeah."

"And even kneeling you weren't actually touching the ground."

I shrugged. "It happens."

"Are you an angel?"

I shook my head. "Go with God."

Despite my fatigue, I picked up the pace. Hedingham Castle was a long walk from the town proper. Unless the Shield had moved, someone there would be able to help me reach Vilicangelus.

The castle rose in the distance, the exact same silhouette I'd watched fade into distance when Vilicangelus had relocated me to Atlanta. Nausea and nerves roiled my stomach. English wind chilled my skin, making my body shake.

One step at a time, my first home rose into the sky like a great stone brick. Stones had gone missing. Some had been replaced and repaired. Leaded glass on the high towers reflected sunlight unevenly, no lights behind them.

My feet picked up the pace, as eager as I to be home.

True, my Shield remained in Atlanta, but Vitae had never made it my home despite all the efforts of my brothers. My first Shieldheart had been so old her rebirths had produced wrinkled bodies.

She'd joked that no one mistrusted a grandmother.

Laughter bubbled out the cracks in my soul. "And a cuppa with the ladies brought truth to light better than a flaming sword."

A wooden sign hung on the front doors, acrylic bolted to it to protect the paper underneath. I stared at it, the words nonsensical despite being in English. Hedingham Castle was closed for structural repairs. The museum wouldn't reopen until next year, and parties with corporate retreats and weddings already booked at the castle were to call the posted number to coordinate alternate arrangements.

My gaze climbed the old stone walls.

I hadn't walked to the wrong castle, but my brain refused to wrap around the idea that my old Shield gave tours and housed weddings.

Standing out here staring at stone and heaven isn't getting me any answers.

The door swung in easily.

Iron sconces converted to hold electric lights hung half the height from the ceiling on walls of discolored uneven stones cemented together behind floor-to-ceiling tapestries. Electric chandeliers hung from thick wooden beams the same aged grey as the carpet-disguised floors.

To one side a spiral stair ascended up one of the towers to the garrison floor remade into some sort of reception hall. The climb brought me to the great hall floor positioned beneath a great stonework arch and upper floor gallery. On the gallery level, museum signs blocked the remaining climb, designating the space for staff only.

I hopped the rope.

A half dozen laser targeting lights swept up and down my body, drawing a dotted line across my breast.

"Halt where you are. This area is off limits."

My first shield had contained an oracle without voice, but all I'd learned about Anima told me the cultured voice threatening me belonged to another of Anima's kin. "Not to me, Watcher."

Silence.

"If you do not depart, you will be shot for violating trespass."

I climbed the next stair. "Shoot me then."

To my shock, something opened fire in a staccato of popping noises. Flesh rippled to essence just before a series of tranquilizer darts shot thru my chest. I had to believe that the Watcher expected me to dodge, because that much tranquilizer shot into a mortal would render them as dead as real bullets.

This time, the Watcher's voice didn't hesitate. "Halt and declare yourself, shield."

After Wan, I was mildly surprised he didn't accuse me of being a Fae Kissed, but perhaps he could read my essence like Anima could. "Aquaylae, Shield of the Undying Light. I hatched in this castle."

An ancient looking old woman appeared at the top of the stairs, wide grin bright enough to double as a lighthouse. "I thought I taught you manners enough to call before dropping by unannounced."

"Vita?"

"Welcome home, child."

Quayla

Vita climbed the stairs faster than I could, old body notwithstanding. It could've had something to do with the fact that I had spent days swimming across the entire Atlantic Ocean or that I'd fought off a soul clinging to Creation with an anchor of hatred for more than a dozen decades.

The stairs crested onto ancient, lovingly-preserved wood floors. A quick switchback to slow would-be invaders opened up into a massive common area. Thick, woven wool rugs lay across the hardwood like islands of color. Stained, wood framed blocky old-world furnishings I remembered to be supremely if covertly comfortable.

The hearth dominating one wall could've accommodated roasting a whole ox or even allowed me to park my Johammer. The adjacent corner offered a small, modern kitchen. A huge loom and a half-finished rug stood opposite both—the emerging carpet as brightly colored as the crystalline phoenix statues perched on stones protruding from the fireplace.

Eyes closed, I inhaled the scents of raw wool and wood smoke. *Home.*

The Watcher's voice broke my reverie. "Shieldheart?"

I opened my eyes to find an indulgent smile drop from Vita's face. "You're right, Cue. Aquaylae, child, I must see to an incursion, but you may stay here and take your ease."

"Do you need help?"

"You have no nest here, child. If something were to happen to you, you'd end up once more across the sea with your business unfinished."

The words tumbled from my lips. "I don't really have a nest there either."

Alarm deepened her wrinkles. "We'll speak when I return."

Vita hurried from the common room. I wandered the empty hall, touching things and summoning memories. I'd failed Vita. I'd curled up on the same couch, sobbing while the other shields reported the rising mortal death count.

"Does Vita leave the Shield often? She doesn't coordinate from the castle?"

"A Shield is five phoenixes, Shield Aquaylae," Cue said. "Not four and a general. How do you not know this?"

"It just isn't the way our Shieldheart does things."

"It seems strange your Shieldheart would let you travel, particularly in such dire times."

I settled onto the couch, pulling my legs up to my chest. I considered not answering the Watcher, but he would hear what I told Vita. "My Shieldheart has gone rogue. My shieldmates have been killed or captured."

"Then shouldn't you have remained to protect your shire and free your fellow shields?"

I shook my head. "Yes, and I tried, but I couldn't protect Atlanta all alone. I came seeking Vilicangelus."

"Why not seek your own Praefectus?"

"He's been captured too."

The occasional pop and shift of burning logs broke up the long silence. Emotional and physical exhaustion saw me dozing when Cue spoke once more. "Your Watcher confirms your tale. She is heartened you arrived safely."

I rubbed my nose, using the backs of my knuckles to wipe sleep from my eyes. "Did Ani pass along any message?"

"She asks that you return with haste."

I nodded, though my whole heart wasn't in it. Our shire needed protecting, but the prospect of leaving Hedingham Castle —even after only an hour—carried more dread than True Death.

A shrill shriek echoed through the room.

My eyes shot to the hearth, finding the crystalline fire phoenix bowed in defeat. Feet stomped across the floor above. A beautiful red-headed adolescent thundered into the room spitting Gaelic curses. She stopped dead at the sight of me, drawing a short, high-tech looking handle from behind her back. Flame shot up from the metallic hilt into a long, burning blade. "Who—"

Cue's firm voice drew her up short. "Hold, Flamma, this is Aquaylae of the Atlanta Shire."

Flamma's eyes narrowed. "What are you doing here? I thought the Sidhe were at war everywhere."

"I needed help."

"There weren't any nearer shires?" Flamma asked.

"I need Vilicangelus. He's still our Praefectus while Summus is training to take over the territory."

Petulance burned in every word that escaped Flamma's mouth. "And you just couldn't be bothered to work things out with this Summus? You had to tattle to Vilicangelus?"

"Summus was captured."

"Your other shields couldn't help?"

I shook my head, tired of her attitude and doubly tired of explaining myself. "I am the last free phoenix in my shire."

"That's ridiculous, certainly—"

Temper launched me to my feet. "You're absolutely right. I'm a liar. I abandoned my Shield and ran away, but rather than hiding, I headed to the Shield where I was born."

Flamma rolled her eyes, the flames retracting into her hilt. "Whatever. Cue, are the others still engaged?"

"Yes, but you are needed elsewhere," Cue said.

"Give me the deets in route." The young fire phoenix bolted for the door, stopping in the frame for a parting shot. "Don't steal anything."

So much for home.

Chapter Nine

Diverging Paths

Quayla

I tried to settle back into my seat, but couldn't tame the white-water raging of my pulse. I paced the room. I needed to find Vilicangelus. Once I kicked his ass into gear and got the help I needed, I'd return to Atlanta. At least there I'd be able to stab anything that pissed me off.

Eventually, fury and fuel waned. I sat once more, dozing in the comfortable cushions. A hand touched me. I jerked awake, whipping out a karambit hilt and extending a blade with the barest thought.

A handsome man stepped back, a quizzical smile on his lips. A rich accent warm as hot cocoa cradled his words. "Easy, Aquaylae."

"Who—"

"Mar, a pleasure to make your acquaintance. Vita asked me to look in on you and convey a message."

My brows rose.

He chuckled. "Several Sidhe escaped. It will take her some time to track them down. Is there any way I can offer you assistance?"

"I need to speak to Vilicangelus."

He frowned. "I'm afraid, that is not possible at this time."

I was on my feet once more. "You don't seem to understand. I *need* to see him. I need his help."

Mar knelt, patting the couch. "Sit. Tell me about your travails."

"It might be better to wait for Vita."

"As her second, I can weigh your words and take action as I think prudent."

"Why can't I just speak to Vilicangelus?"

Mar's calm expression flickered, his eyes tightening for an instant. "Vilicangelus cannot be disturbed at this moment, not without great cause. Tell me your tale."

"How long have you been in this Shield?"

"The first time, five centuries. I was reassigned when your egg arrived and called back when Vilicangelus was sent to relocate you."

"How old are you?"

He shrugged. "Somewhere around fifteen centuries. I've never cared to pay that much attention to time."

I couldn't help a sad smirk as a pun to delight Dylan escaped my lips. "Just go with the flow, huh?"

"Indeed." He glanced down at my Karambit. "You can probably put that away."

I followed his gaze, blood rushing to my cheeks. "Oh, sorry."

A twist of will drew my essence back from my hilts.

He rose, crossing to the kitchen. "Tea?"

"Of course," I laughed. "How bad are things here? I saw in a paper that the faeries are out."

He busied himself in the kitchen, lips pressed together. "Yes, the secret is out. Fortunately—and in no small part to your own Ignis—so far, the vast majority of issues center around serial killers and comic book geeks."

"What did Ignis do?"

"To be succinct, he put the Fear of God into many a mortal."

The kettle started to whistle. Mar handed over a smart phone. "I'm sure you can find it on YouTube if you search."

It wasn't hard to find Ignis's fight and subsequent statements. Ice knotted my belly as I watched. When the video stopped, I stared awestruck at the screen.

"You're awfully quiet," Mar settled next to me, handing over a steaming mug. "Most of the younger phoenixes cheered."

I shook my head. "I'm lucky to be alive."

Mar frowned. "Your pardon?"

A sip of tea bought me time, but not much. Mar interrupted the detailed fight between Ignis and me, repeatedly forcing me to go backwards in the telling until I'd restarted the whole tale from my morning visit to Howell Mill Humane Society.

While I spoke, other shields entered. Vita filed in last of all, forcing me in a gentile, grandmotherly way to start over at the beginning.

The Hedingham shields watched me in silence.

"Wow." Awe suffused Flamma's voice. "You're an idiot."

I bristled.

"Flamma," Vita snapped. "Go with Aether and Telli to check out the town, then do a patrol sweep."

"Don't know why you're pissed at me," Flamma grumbled. "I'm not the moron."

I'd known Hedingham's air phoenix, Aether, when I'd been part of their Shield before. She cuffed Flamma and chivvied the Pyri out of the castle.

Tellus—going by the shortened Telli—was new to me despite being twice my age. She stopped at the door, giving me an apologetic smile before following.

Vita gave Mar a significant look. "I must meditate on what I've learned. Please see to Aquaylae in the meantime."

"Of course, Shieldheart."

I gave Vita enough time to leave earshot if that was what she intended before letting a little too much anger out with my voice. "See to me? Like scolding the naughty child? I'm a full—"

Mar pressed fingers to my lips with so light a touch they might have been butterfly legs. "Peace, Aquaylae."

"Quayla."

"Quayla." Mar nodded. "Much of your tale is troubling. Enough, that Vita wished to meditate on the deeds of her fellow Shieldheart so that she can decide how to proceed."

"How would you know that?"

"You're not jesting, are you?" Mar's frown deepened. He rose, pacing the floor with his back to me. "You certainly have brought us many challenges. What are we to do with—"

I leapt up, yanking Mar around. My carefully-schooled southern accent disappeared in a flash of anger. "Neither of you has to *do* anything with me. Just let me speak to my divine and I'll get out of your hair."

Pent rage lurked behind sadness. "You're wrong, Quayla. We owe you and the Creator a duty—a duty your Shieldheart should've performed."

"Gosh, Vitae didn't do his job? What a shocker."

"Let's focus on the highest priorities and we will improve your education as we can. Cue, Id' rather not disturb Vita. Can you summon Telli back to headquarters?"

"Consider it done, Mar."

Quayla furrowed her brows. "I don't understand. Disturb Vita?"

"A Shieldheart is the heart of the shield."

"Yeah, kind of obvious."

"In order for a Shield to function in full concert, its members must be able to communicate at a distance. Once each shield reaches a certain maturity and proves themselves a full shield, they are linked into the Shield through the Shieldheart." Mar sighed. "It appears you were never linked. With your Caelum's True Death, there's no way to learn if he was linked."

"But then, shouldn't Ignis and Terrance be linked through Vitae to each other?"

Mar nodded.

That kind of connection makes sense, but why wouldn't Ignis or Terrance have said something? Why wouldn't they be using it?

A suspicion raised its ugly head. "Can a Shieldheart unlink a shield?"

"Yes, though usually that's done only during a transfer."

Heat bubbled in my core, hardening my voice. "Can a Shieldheart unlink all of his shields?"

Mar frowned. "Let's dispense with what ifs and deal with what's important, namely your nest and your egg."

"I don't have a full Shield anymore to recreate my egg."

"We have a full shield, but I am not sure a Divine One will be able to help us with—"

"What the hell now? Where is Vilicangelus? Why won't he answer?"

"Calm yourself," Mar said. "All I am allowed to reveal is that Vilicangelus is not available at this time."

A snarl escaped me. "I'm sick and tired of being treated like a child."

"Then stop acting like one."

We locked glares.

"Do you want our help or not?" Mar asked.

"I need to talk to Vilicangelus."

"You need a hell-blighted lot more than that," Mar countered. "You need an egg, enough essence set aside to survive dying and from the sounds of everything an education is long overdue."

"What's that supposed to mean?"

Mar reached down, drawing a silver hilt out of each of his suddenly liquid thighs. Curved blades almost as long as my arm slid easily from the guards. "It means you don't understand your element, let alone the others, and that ignorance is dangerous."

I stared at the long flat scimitars. They shimmered much like my own blades, but Mar showed no sign of discomfort. He was older, but I had no idea how age would make him better able to rip essence away from himself to such a degree.

"How—"

"Exactly," Mar stepped back from me, spinning the two swords in an elaborate weapon display. Part way through the display, the blades parted from the hilts, dancing around him. He threw both hands toward the hearth. The blades followed suit, banking the fire in a hiss of steam. The steam changed directions only an inch above the fire, crossing the room and reforming the blades in Mar's hilts out of solid ice.

I stared.

I gaped.

My mind reeled.

I couldn't fathom how any of what I'd just seen was possible.

"Now, Vita entrusted me to teach you while she meditates. Either you refuse my instruction or you agree to allow me to proceed as I think best. I won't negotiate."

Warmth returned, slowly bringing my blood to boil. I wasn't a fledgling. I was a full shield. Still, I couldn't do any of what Mar had just displayed.

Dylan's words shot through my memories. <Sure, Anakin's pissed. He's more powerful than most of his elders, but they won't elevate him to Jedi Master because he hasn't learned enough yet. He thinks it's some kind of personal slight...as if there's something wrong with just being a Jedi Knight.>

I hadn't really understood what Dylan meant. I'd thought Anakin had a right to be angry at his elders for treating him like a child.

But it isn't just ice or steam, infant or elder. There are stages in between.

Mar continued to watch me, leaving me to make my decision —whatever it ended up being.

"Can you do a bow?" I asked.

Mar smirked. "I can...."

He showed me his right palm. A spiked ball of ice the size of a walnut coalesced in his palm. He flipped it on the cup made by thumb and forefinger of his balled left hand then drew back a watery slingshot.

"However, I find this takes less room, is less complicated and is just as effective unless I'm dealing with extreme ranges."

Excitement and elation bubbled through me like a blending of orange and cream sodas. "I...uh...I guess I'm your padawan."

Mar's smile brightened. "Not a padawan, a knight training to be a master."

"So, what do we do first?"

Telli stepped out of the doorway's shadows. "You summoned me, Mar?"

"We need a nest basin for Quayla."

The earth phoenix brightened. "Is Quayla staying? We sure could use the help."

"For a little while," Mar said. "She doesn't have an egg or a nest though, so for now she won't be able to help."

Telli's welcoming smile warmed me, but reality rained on her contagious excitement, leaving me cold and damp. "Mar, I can't stay. Someone has to protect Atlanta."

"You agreed to do things my way," Mar said. "That means you don't go back until I say you're ready."

I opened my mouth to argue, but his stern expression stopped me.

"I am mindful that your shire needs you, so we won't keep you long, but I am not sending an undertrained shield back into a war zone with no nest and no egg."

Telli paled. "No nest *and* no egg?"

"Not at least until you head down to the marble pit and build her a nest Quayla can fill."

Telli bolted from sight.

Mar shook his head. "Young phoenixes are so excitable."

Telli was at least twice my age, so I tried not to be excitable about being included in Mar's amusement.

"Tell me," Mar sat back down on the couch. "What became of Mare's egg?"

I frowned. "I don't know, it was destroyed I guess, why?"

"If Mare's egg still exists, you can claim the vessel and link yourself to it."

Dunham

The door behind Dunham's desk parted from the wall, admitting Viviane. The scent of flowers and spring rain told him she was happy about something, but he didn't let her distract him from finishing a document notifying a competitor that Dunham had acquired controlling interest in the rival company.

Viviana slid onto his lap, blocking him from his desk.

He raised eyes and eyebrows up to her pert coral-painted smile. "Is there something I can do for you?"

Viviane's fingers ran along the edge of her blouse, buttons inexplicably becoming undone inches ahead of her fingers. "There are many things you can do for me, dear boy."

"Uh huh." Dunham leaned back, gripping his chair's arm rests. "What do you want?"

"Surely a man knows—"

"Cut the crap. What do you really want?"

"An incursion is about to turn Stone Mountain Park into an unscheduled lightshow. I want you to send Ignis to deal with them."

Why the seduction routine? What's special about this incursion?

"Ignis is not fully recovered from our last discussion about his holding back on Quayla."

"I thought you were satisfied with the drone video on that fight."

Dunham grimace. "I thought so too, until he showed network news what he was really capable of doing."

Viviane curled up, nibbling an ear lobe before whispering. "Did you ask him about the disparity?"

"I did." Dunham pushed her away from his neck, wiping her

saliva from his skin. "Apparently, what he did at Sugarloaf Mills required consuming part of his soul."

She made a pouty face. "Interesting. Did he explain why he did something so dangerous in the second case but not the first?"

"He's not willing to risk his soul on my account."

Viviane's brows rose. "Wasn't he at Sugarloaf on your orders?"

"Yes, but his actions in that case were meant to scare wafers away from making deals with the Sidhe."

"Such a sweet boy," Viviane's lips curled with genuine delight and desire. "I should reward him."

"Let's not confuse the message, Viviane."

"Why shouldn't I reward him? Ignis and Jahriss have done more for my cause this month than you have."

Dunham scowled. "Ignis didn't scare the mortals away from your sisters for your sake. Besides, unlike Jahriss's message, he warned wafers off Sidhe in general."

"Please?"

"No."

Viviane thrust her exposed breasts into his face. "Please?"

"Mister Heffernan? Your three o'clock is here."

Dunham tapped the intercom. "Thank you. Give me ninety seconds then send them in." He released the button. "No, Viviane, now if you'll excuse me, I still have a corporation to run."

Viviane's coral lips pushed together and vanished. "As you wish, Dunham Colwyn Heffernan."

A shiver ran down his spine. Viviane's hidden door clicked shut as the other door opened. Unable to give immediate chase, Dunham mastered his expression. "Good afternoon, lady and gentlemen. Please come in."

Viviane

The Lady of Water stormed up the spiral stairway to Dunham's private residence. She crossed to the control console, triggering the arm holding down Ignis's hafnium carbide cell. The heat-warped arm screamed a tortured squeal.

If she'd been in water form, the anger churning her intestines would've evaporated Viviane's torso.

I didn't go to the trouble to nullify vanguard collars for this little fight just to have Dunham be too busy.

She marched up to the diminutive fire phoenix, planting hands on her hips and glowered down with a toe resting on his egg. "Ignis."

"Hell bitch."

A muscle spasmed under one eye. "Ignis, Shield of the Undying Light. An incursion of Seelie and Unseelie threaten Creation in Stone Mountain Park. I will release you to do your duty on two conditions."

"Screw off. Your boy toy and his modifications to this cage leave me too weak for such a fight."

"Had you voluntarily given essence—you know what, there is no time for an argument." Viviane backed her voice with divine essence. "You will go to Stone Mountain Park. You will destroy all Seelie and Unseelie forces you find there. You will slay the abomination which was once your Shieldheart, and you will return here without speaking to any form of journalist."

Ignis forced words through gritted teeth. "Vitae is an ass, but he's not an abomination."

"Your Vitae has been killing himself so that he could be reborn with greater and greater amounts of Sidhe essence. He's so far gone that iron vexes him as much as it would one of our children."

Ignis's eyes narrowed. He balled his fists. "You are a lying bitch."

Viviane spoke the incantation which dropped the barrier surrounding him.

Ignis launched himself at Viviane.

Had the fire phoenix been at least average height for a modern mortal, he'd have gotten his fingers around her throat before she could will him to stop through his egg.

He writhed on the floor as she ground her toes into his egg. "A good gamble, worthy Ignis, but foolish. Go, slay the Sidhe as you are commanded and feel the truth of my words for yourself."

Quayla

Horror and cold bombarded me like I'd been plunged into a hail storm of wafer eyeballs. The older water phoenix's suggestion that I somehow take Mare's egg for my own left me speechless. Eggs were created from our essence. It took the combined essences of a full shield, molded by a Divine One to build our last defense against oblivion. Eggs were sacrosanct. I could no more steal another shield's egg than slaughter an orphanage filled with mortal children.

My jaw moved, trying over and over to tell Mar that I could not, would not commit such a blasphemy.

Even without words, Mar read my expression. "Peace, Quayla."

"I-I can't." I stared. "How could you even suggest such a thing?"

"I thought Mare was slain by a Champion blade."

I couldn't keep the outrage from my voice. "So what if she was? How could you suggest I steal the last refuge of a phoenix's soul?"

"Was she or wasn't she slain by one of the three Blades of Judgement?"

"What? How should I know?"

He frowned. "You're part of the Atlanta Shield. You're telling me you never asked after your predecessor?"

"I asked, but they wouldn't speak of it."

Mar held up a hand to silence me. "Cue?"

"A moment, Shield Mar."

My heart slammed against my ribs so hard and fast it shamed every hard rock drum solo ever attempted.

"The Atlanta Watcher confirms Mare was slain by the Unseelie Champion blade," Cue said.

"There," Mar said. "That makes using her egg all right."

"Blighted hells it does! If her egg still exists then she's trapped inside it."

"Regrowing for coming on three centuries?" Mar asked.

I bit back frustration. "I don't know. The only one I know who...who ever—"

A tsunami of grief overwhelmed me.

Mar wrapped his arms around my sob-wracked body. I wanted to push him away, but his arms proved too strong. The comfort after so long, after so much, seduced me away from repulsion until I collapsed into his embrace and let my tears flow.

My choices had resigned Caelum to True Death. I'd been responsible for the total Destruction of his soul and probably Ignis's too. A sudden desire for my own Destruction rose from my core. If I no longer existed, I'd never remember Caelum or Ignis or Dylan or Judith or any of the Hedingham mortals I'd murdered.

Cue's voice barely registered over my sobs. "Atlanta's Watcher confirms Mare's egg remains whole and in the possession of Atlanta's Shieldheart."

Telli burst through the door with words poised on smiling lips, stopped short and backed away in silent concern.

Mar held me.

I didn't deserve the comfort of his arms. Death and pain were all I deserved. I'd have asked for them if I thought he'd have delivered either. Instead, I wasted tears down his front, unsure when the fountains would dry up.

"Blighted hells," Flamma said. "That's not how new water phoenixes are made, you know that right?"

Mar spun. Even with his back to me, I heard the anger in his voice. "Depart, Flamma, go patrol, go to your chamber, I don't care, just go."

"Sheesh, sorry I interrupted your booty call," Flamma scoffed. "It's not like you put a sock over the—"

"Out!"

Using his distraction to escape, I moved to the far corner and slid down against the wall. Cold stone held more fitting caress, leaching the warmth transfusion from Mar's arms. Knees pressed tight to my chest, I wanted nothing more than to die a mortal death.

Oh, Dylan.

Mar stood over me, but didn't try to lift me back to my feet. "The Champion blades are not Sidhe, they're the Swords of Judgement, wielded by the first host to destroy whomever God decreed."

I buried my face in my arms.

"Such Judgements were seldom upon a single mortal. The swords devour judged souls, empowering Angels of Judgment to wage war on a massive scale without tiring." Mar put his hand on my head. "Mare's soul won't ever seek her egg, Quayla. There's no bringing her back."

Telli appeared again. "Mar? Is everything all right?"

"Yes, bring it in."

"You were busy," Telli said. "So, I took it to the workshop and inlaid the silver into the runes. It's ready to go except ownership and precedence runes."

"Set it down here, Telli. Thank you." Mar stepped back, giving Telli room to kneel before me and set the nest down. Mar swept his hands down his shirt, opening them at the bottom to dump a handful of my tears into the basin.

Telli stared at me until I met her eyes. "We need every phoenix, Quayla. Please, set aside what essence you can."

I nodded, hefting myself up onto my knees. Drawing a

karambit and extruding a blade, I rolled up my sleeve as I transmogrified an arm. Serrated teeth sawed into my watery flesh.

Telli went green, turning away with every indication she intended to vomit.

"Whoa, wait, blighted-hells, Quayla, what're you doing?" Mar asked.

My brows pushed together. "Severing essence."

"Who taught you to do it that way?" Mar asked.

"Vitae?"

Mar cupped his face. His jaw tightened behind the hand. "No. There's no reason for you to saw your limb off."

"But even Terrance severs essence this way." I looked at Telli. "Don't you?"

Telli transmogrified her arm then, wincing, broke the root-webbed soil away in a chunk that crumbled along the break edges. She pushed the limb back against its former stump, face screwed up until the two sealed back together. "It hurts like hell, but I can't imagine sawing at my arm like you just did."

Heat flashed through me. "Well, how in the name of hell am I supposed to do it then?"

Mar crossed to the kitchen and snatched a large metal bowl from a cupboard. He held his arm above it. The limb transmogrified to water then spread out into a dark grey cloud. Rain drops fell from the water vapor into the bowl with a pitter patter against the metal.

I gaped. "But water wants to pool together."

"In liquid form, yes it definitely does," Mar said. "In gaseous form, it wants to return to its liquid state, so it collects together until at last it leaves water vapor behind as rain drops."

"But, how do you make it go gaseous without adding energy? You know, thermodynamics?"

"How does an air phoenix generate lightning?" Mar asked. "How do life phoenixes assume their pure energy form? How does a Terra change its essence from soil to crystal to stone?"

I shook my head.

Mar stepped next to the hearth, extending the icy hand until it melted back into water while the cloud hand remained. "Every phoenix has its own gifts, Quayla. We're water—the only phoenix able to assume all three states of matter."

"I don't understand how you can just do that, or how you did what you did with the swords."

"I can see that." Mar smiled. "All things considered, maybe we should start there. Go ahead and separate what essence you can while I fix you up something to eat. No matter what, before you leave, we'll make sure you understand how rain is made."

Chapter Ten

Overthinking

Vitae

Scurith hurried into Vitae's study, ears pitched forward and tail uplifted. "Master, the oracle has shown us an incursion. A big one."

I settled a silk ribbon into the pages of an old copy of *Return of the King* and set the book aside on my side table. "How big?"

"Hundreds."

A grin grew across my lips. It was time to prove my strength to Viviane and Atlanta. "Muster all of my enforcers."

Scurith's grey and brown ears flicked toward his head. "All of them, Master?"

"I did not stutter."

"No, M-Master, I didn't mean to suggest you did, but we haven't acquired enough school or civic busses to transport them all."

I rose, taking down two of the countless elven blades taken from slain and captured Sidhe knights. Tucking a pair of batons beneath my robes, my eyes rested on the Seelie and Unseelie Champion blades.

My fingers yearned to hold them, to take them into battle and feed them the souls of my foes. I couldn't, wouldn't risk them. Technically, I could take the Seelie blade into battle with little fear, but until I freed Mare from Dolumii's sword, I'd take no chances with my prizes. I'd leave them safe along with Mare's egg within the wards of my sanctuary.

"Master?" Scurith asked.

"We shall march, like the armies of old, proclaiming our strength to our charges and giving time for fear to strangle our foes before we even arrive."

"Um, all right." Scurith disappeared before I could address whatever caused the coyll's uncertainty.

It took several minutes to bend my elven armor into a new shape to fit my muscular male body. While I regretted the loss of female wiles to manipulate mortals, my powers had grown more than sufficient to turn any extremist homophobe into an eager sodomite—not that I had occasion or desire to waste my power on such trifles.

Bradley

Bradley's magical bolts flit through the room, blasting seven empty Dr. Pepper cans from a wide selection of perches. He gasped for breath. The magical energy would regrow in time, but he'd been pushing pretty hard to expand his repertoire of magical spells.

More than once he'd lamented being a masterless apprentice —not that Bradley needed another master telling him what to do. His new spell abilities seemed mostly based on will. He'd employed an online version of a Players Handbook to help him test out his abilities. In several cases he managed spells higher than first level but failed at spells any first level wizard had the ability to cast. He'd had mixed results trying to use material components found in the spell descriptions, often learning that he needed no components outside focusing items.

A flurry of activity drew him out of his test lab. Every trollman and kyrie was fighting to get out the primary lab exit. When they finally parted, Master Vitae—now actually a male befitting the title Master—stood alone in the doorway.

Bradley hastened to bow. "Master."

"You shall stay here and continue your work, thrall."

"Yes, Master. It isn't like I can exit of my own accord in any case."

"A failing of your mortal blood, but one that will keep you safe in this time of war."

"Master's protections normally keep me safe in any case."

"This campaign will not allow me to leave behind a guard. I must mobilize all of my strength."

"I see. May the odds be ever in your favor, Master."

Vitae smiled. "Thank you, thrall, now return to your work."

Bradley's master exited the lab, closing the heavy armored door with a resounding thud. He rolled his eyes, hurrying to his test lab to the secreted cell phone.

He called Tommy. "Hey, it's me. I'll be able to slip away for a little bit. Get everyone over to my place. I just need to pick up the last of my stuff from my office and I'll be right there."

"This isn't another recruitment meeting, is it?" Tommy asked.

"No. Just friends, dice and magic."

"I'll let everyone know." Tommy hung up.

Bradley exited the lab without any trouble, his new magical energies more than sufficient to energize the lock and open the door. He hadn't had a chance to get back to Basement-E since he'd abandoned his job.

Not that I really quit so much as got fired for stealing bodies then not showing up when they wanted to discuss the missing corpses.

Bradley parked near the facility's back door and scanned his badge. The reader buzzed angrily, showing him a red light instead of the green welcome. He smirked, touching the door with his index finger. "Knock. Knock."

Magic swept from him. The door lock clicked open, and Bradley pulled the door open despite the reader's flashing red light. He almost made it to the elevator when Ashley emerged from Mercer's old office. She looked down her nose at him on reflex, eyes widening with realization a moment later. She ducked back into the office she'd exited.

Bradley shook his head.

I helped you. I could've used the same abilities that freed you from Mercer's blackmail to make you do anything I wanted, and you still only look at me with disgust. Wafers suck.

The elevator opened, two uniformed security officers waiting behind its doors. They reached for Tasers.

Bradley waved his left hand. "Sleep."

Their eyes rolled up into their heads and they collapsed where they stood. He stepped gingerly through their sprawled limbs trying not to trod on anything personal and pressed the button for Basement-E.

A mid-level bureaucratic functionary with a grey gel-cemented helmet of hair waited in front of Bradley's door, arms folded in echo of the yellow police tape sealing Bradley's office. "You've got a lot of gall, returning to the scene of the crime, as if shaving your head would disguise you from us."

"How'd you know I was here?"

"Ashley." Wallace Cross said. "I came down to cut you off just in case you slipped by security."

"I'm just here to gather the last of my personal belongings."

"You include more corpses among your," he made air quotes, "'personal belongings'?"

"No, and I'm not enthralled to a supernatural being anymore, so I have no compulsions to kill you and turn you into a brain-dead walking enforcer." Bradley marched forward intent to push the little administrator out of the way.

Cross drew a small revolver from behind his back. "I'm going to get promoted for being the one to stop you."

Bradley stopped, dropping his arms to his sides. "You actually know how to use that thing?"

He nodded, his helmet of hair not shifting at all. "Some criminals think people of my stature are easy prey."

Bradley's fingers danced as if playing tiny piano keyboards on his thighs. "Look, Wallace, I really just want to get my stuff."

"Too bad, Sky."

Bradley brought his hands up. Cross responded to the motion by bringing up his five-shot revolver. Both men fired. Weaving blue missiles shot through the hall. Had Bradley still been a wafer, he might not have had the acuity of mind to note and target the bullet speeding toward his chest. The first missile impacted the bullet and the second slammed into Cross's gun.

"You're a greasy bastard." Bradley's left fingers rubbed together before making a base runner safe gesture.

Cross's legs slipped beneath him. He danced a crazy jig trying to keep on his feet. Bradley reached him before he recovered fully, shoving lightly to send Cross sliding away on a magically slick surface. Bradley evoked an adhesion spell to glue Cross to the wall by his hair for no reason other than spite. A spell unlocked the room and let him collect his personal belongings.

It took him two more sleep spells to exit the building. Another barrage of magical bolts disarmed a pair of uniformed police and an amnesia charm helped them forget him.

He hurried across the parking lot with his personal belongings, all too aware that he had to relocate his apartment and his friends to protect them from the shit headed his way.

Quayla

Flamma glared at me from a stool next to the burning hearth. I turned her hilt over in my hands, tightening and relaxing my grip as I familiarized myself with a hilt that brought tears to my eyes.

Dylan would've loved this.

"Are you ready to proceed?" Mar asked.

I nodded, compressing my core and extruding essence up through the hilt. Pressure built up behind my eyes, knocking harder like a persistent door-to-door salesman. The essence blade managed almost eight inches.

Flamma guffawed. "Talk about size issues."

I shot her a dirty look. "Why are you here?"

"You've got one of my hilts." Flamma tilted her head toward Mar. "And he asked me to stick around—probably for the entertainment factor."

Mar darkened. "You are here to learn, Flamma. You need to understand the elements of your fellow shields, so I suggest you shut your mouth and pay attention."

Despite all expectations, Flamma looked genuinely chastened, as if Mar rarely scolded. The young fire phoenix seemed one part Ignis and two parts Caelum—frustrating and heartbreaking at the same time.

Mar turned to me. "You're not doing that in the most effective manner."

"This is how I learned."

Flamma chuckled. "She's a worse student than I am."

Heat flashed through me. "Watch it, flicker, or someone will snuff you out."

"By yourself?" Flamma sneered. "You can't even get it up."

My eyes darted toward Mar, checking to see if he intended to intervene. When my attention returned to Flamma I found her also checking for Mar's reaction.

My essence returned from Flamma's hilt. She dropped to the ground as I pulled both karambits. The young fire phoenix extended a flaming blade from another hilt.

Mar's voice cracked like thunder. "No."

Both of us jerked our heads toward him, but his attention was on me. He pointed at my feet. "You will use that hilt."

Flamma grinned and circled me.

The look I shot Mar probably wasn't very nice, but I tucked my karambits away and retrieved Flamma's spare hilt.

"Now, you have two choices, Quayla. The first will probably not be very effective against Flamma's blade but since the purpose is to teach you a better way to arm yourself, we will start with a knife blade. Do you know how hail is formed?"

"Um, clouds form rain drops but it's so cold they freeze."

Mar's jaw clinched. "Water vapor condenses in the atmosphere around some form of anchor whether that be a dust mote, a piece of grass, or what have you. Once the droplet is heavy enough that prevailing updrafts can no longer support it, it falls."

"That's called rain," Flamma said.

Mar cleared his throat.

Flamma ducked her head, eyeing him.

"In storm conditions, more powerful updrafts can move rain-drops into atmospheric layers at freezing temperatures." Mar transmogrified his hand into water vapor. A starburst of ice the size of a pea floated above his cloudy palm. "In some cases, this means the droplet will crystallize into ice. In others the droplet will merely be supercooled. The longer a frozen droplet is kept aloft, the more opportunity such crystals have to pass through their supercooled but still-liquid brethren."

As he described their meteorological phenomena aquakinesis swept the crystal in and out of the cloud, growing with every pass.

"Each time this occurs, a small amount of supercooled liquid coats the ice crystal, freezing and growing the droplet until the weight of the ice exceeds the strength of the storm updrafts."

"That's all very interesting," I said. "But I don't see how it applies to this."

The hailstone floating in Mar's palm distended, growing

longer and sharper, layer after layer of ice with excruciating slowness. He dissolved the icicle only to regenerate it twice as long and with a sharp edge in the blink of an eye.

How the hell? Where did he put the heat?

I searched Mar for any sign of the energy he'd had to of transferred to create so much ice so quickly.

"You look confused."

"She looks like a brain-dead fool," Flamma said.

"I still don't understand what you did with the energy, Mar."

"What energy?" He asked.

"In order to freeze the water, you had to remove energy from the water to move it from a liquid to a solid state. It's thermodynamics."

"Flamma, please douse your weapon." Mar crossed the distance between us, took my hand and led me to Flamma. He set my hand on her shoulder. "Does Flamma feel hot?"

"Well, she's a little warm."

"Does she feel like open flame?" Mar asked.

I shook my head.

"Did she or did she not both extrude and retract a sword formed of pure fire?"

"Yes."

"Flamma, extend your blade once more please," Mar said.

The fire phoenix did as requested, and Mar moved my hand to a blade many times hotter than a campfire. I pulled my hand free before he forced me to burn my fingers. He took my hand once more and placed it on Flamma shoulder.

"Does she feel any cooler?"

There didn't seem to be any difference in Flamma's body temperature from before, so I shook my head. "No, but..."

"But what?" Mar asked.

"Well, Flamma is living fire. It's what she is."

"Exactly," Mar said.

"No, wait. Take Wan for example. She's not made of fire, so to transmogrify into faerie fire she had to get the energy from a pretty powerful Sidhe."

"Yes?"

I hesitated, trying to find the words to explain the problem to him. Before I could form coherent sentences, Mar turned to Flamma. "Make your fire hotter."

Flamma did as requested.

"Now make it cooler that it was before," he said.

"That's exactly my problem. I'm not made of fire. I don't control heat. So how do I move the energy around without losing essence to steam?"

Flamma rolled her eyes.

Mar took a deep breath. "Quayla, why can Flamma make so hot a sword without chilling her body temperature?"

I shrugged. "She is magical fire."

"And you're magical water, stupid," Flamma snapped.

My gaze shot back and forth between them. I was still missing something, and it irritated me that at least on the surface I looked as stupid as Flamma was accusing me of being.

"This is the curse of the information age." Mar set a hand on my shoulder, his eyes entreating—willing me to understand.

"Let me try a different tack," Mar said. "How does a muscle get the energy to move?"

"From what we eat. The energy is stored in our body."

"Right," Mar said. "What does the body do if there's an excess of energy?"

"It stores it as fat," I said.

"Does a mortal have to consciously make those things happen?"

"No, their body handles it."

"Exactly." Mar held out both hands for me to see. One turned to a cloud of water vapor. The other turned to ice. "Do you think our design is any less sophisticated?"

"But—"

Irritations heated Mar's reply. "Forget mortal physics, okay?"

"But—"

"Yes, the laws of physics exist, but we are not mortals. We are the second angelic host, creatures of miracle and faith. You can change your whole body into water that still retains your shape. Can you explain that with mortal physics?"

The word escaped me in a whisper. "No."

"Then how do you manage it?"

I shrugged. "I just do."

"You just do? There's nothing more to it?"

"Will, I guess?"

"Yes, exactly. Will." Mar lifted my hand still holding the hilt. "Make an ice blade one layer at a time held together and sharpened by your will."

I tried.

It didn't work.

"She is still thinking too much," Flamma said.

Mar nodded. "But she'll get it in time. However, if you two still wish to fight each other, Quayla needs a weapon."

Flamma perused her nails. "Nah, I've lost interest."

Heat removed from essence to create ice undercut my tone. "I'd still like to shut her mouth."

"Ooooo, I'm so scared, Mister Limp Sword. Or should I just call you Stumpy?"

"Mar? What's the second way to make a sword?"

He smirked. "The way you are making knife blades contradicts everything about our element. You are forcing water to stand still while defying gravity—something you're probably over-thinking as well. Water flows. Stagnant water dies."

"That explains the smell," Flamma said.

Mar flicked her a disapproving gesture that quieted the fire phoenix. "From what you told us you are a student of Hep-Silat, so in a fight you are moving your body in ways to imitate the flowing motions of water."

"So?"

Exasperation filled his response. "You *are* water."

Once more I was missing something. "Right?"

"Blighted hells you're dense," Flamma said.

My body shook until I wondered that it didn't disintegrate into a thousand raindrops flying every direction. I threw the hilt to the floor, turned my back on them and stormed up the stairs from the ceremony floor.

Mar was just trying to help, and Flamma was probably trying to encourage me through reverse psychology.

Or she's an ass like Vitae.

Vita sat behind her loom, the shutter clicking back and forth as fingers guided colored threads in and out of service. "You do not look happy, child."

"Why would I be happy? My Shield is a shambles, my shire is under assault without me there to protect it, the wafers know about the Sidhe and apparently everything I ever learned is wrong." I pointed a finger. "Including what I was taught here."

Vita's fingers didn't stop. "That is a vast oversimplification, Aquaylae, and an unfair one."

I threw my hands into the air, pacing the floor. "According to Mar and Flamma I'm an unteachable moron."

Vita smiled. "I seriously doubt Mar would suggest such a thing. Though it seems I owe you an apology. I should've overseen the training you received from London's young Aqua just after your hatching. I will see to it Mar corrects those mistakes."

"Well, I don't have time for any of his lessons anyway. I need to reach Vilicangelus, get a new egg made and get home."

"Mar told me he suggested you link Mare's egg."

I spun, eyes boring into her as if I could give her some of the horror overflowing from me at such a suggestion. "I can't just steal another phoenix's egg."

"Mare is True Dead, Aquaylae. If she could speak to you, she'd be the first to suggest you use her egg to avoid her fate."

There was more to my aversion than I let on. Vitae had compared me to Mare since the moment I'd set foot in the Atlanta Shield. Even though he'd tried to kill me and had killed

Dylan, I just couldn't validate his accusation by using Mare's egg.

"Look, Vita—"

She held up a hand, eyes shifting out of focus. They returned to me a moment later. "My apologies. Shall we have some tea?"

"What happened?"

"Aether just dealt with an incursion and is heading to a second. She was giving me an update."

Alarm shot through me. "Where? We need to help her."

Vita's brows shot up.

"I won't say the idea of venting my frustrations on the Sidhe isn't a factor, but I need to reform my egg. I'm not willing to risk losing Aether—"

"Aether has plenty of essence set aside." Vita closed the distance between us, looking up into my eyes. "Why are you so eager to throw yourself into the fray without essence or egg?"

"I don't have a death wish, okay? I just want to speak to Vilicangelus, get an egg built—"

"Vilicangelus is True Dead." Vita said. "Destroyed."

All air sucked out of my lungs, the room, and the castle. My legs collapsed as if they'd been made of steam. My tail bone cracked against carpeted hard wood.

"We cannot make you a new egg." Vita ran her fingers through my hair, caressing the back of my head. "If you truly don't have a death wish, then your only way to regain the protection of an egg is to link Mare's to yourself."

"No," I croaked. "That's not possible. Vilicangelus can't die. I need his help."

"He's gone, child. He was forced into a rematch with the Lady of Fire before he'd fully recovered. It took all of his essence to beat her back and save the London Shield."

Vilicangelus had fallen.

I knew it was possible, how else had a shield named Lympha become Summuseraphi. Even so, I couldn't wrap my mind around the idea of his death.

"But how? Why? I thought they were restricted from Creation...the...the Articles of Ararat."

Vita sighed. "Something changed. Someone summoned her directly. I don't know. Vilicangelus isn't the only fallen divine. The Sidhe are out for blood."

"What? Why?"

She shrugged.

"Are there any left?"

"Some."

Some? Only some? Blighted hells, what do I do now?

"Can't they make more?"

"Three Divine Ones can come together to elevate another phoenix. It exhausts them and consumes a third of their total essence to empower the new divine. It takes time for all four to recover."

"All right, that's not quick, but we're not totally screwed. Anima can get one transferred in, and—"

Vita's voice hardened to a treacherous edge. "Aquaylae of the Undying Light, the Divine Ones are needed for more important things than to salve your squeamishness. If you want an egg, you will link Mare's."

"But—"

"But nothing, child. You will return to Mar and apply yourself to whatever training he thinks you require. Do you understand me?"

Gravity dragged both my chin and voice to the floor. "Yes, Shieldheart."

"Well?" Vita asked. "Why are you still standing here?"

"I need to speak with Anima. May I use one of your nests?"

Vita frowned. "The old oracle remains on the roof. Cue should be able to connect you to your Watcher."

"Thank you, Shieldheart." I trudged for the spiral stair leading up one tower to the roof.

Vita stopped me, pulling me down by my dress shirt until she was able to place a warm kiss on one cheek. "All will be well, child. Have faith."

Ripples creased the waters of the oracle, spreading in all directions as if from a cast pebble rather than with the wind's direction.

"Quayla?" Anima asked.

The sound of her voice—the reassuring sound of my dysfunctional home—brought tears to my eyes. "Ani."

"Are you all right? Why are you crying?"

"I need your help," I took a deep breath. "Where can I find Mare's egg?"

"Why?"

"I'm to link it to myself."

Anima's voice trembled. "Shield Aquaylae, that is a very, very bad idea. Vitae will not take kindly to such an action. Can't you form a new one where you are?"

"I haven't any choice. Vilicangelus is dead and we can't form a new egg without him."

"This cannot be so."

My head shook of its own volition. "If you can prove their claims faulty, I'm more than happy to bless you for the correction, Ani."

"Quayla, you have no idea what you are asking."

"Do you know where Mare's egg is? Is it safe?"

"Vitae has Mare's egg sequestered in the center of his fortress."

Of course, he does.

"To reach it you would either have to place yourself in his power or fight through the countless Sidhe in his service."

Of course, I will...no, wait.

"Ani, contact Sabrina. Ask her to locate Bradley Sky and ask if he can recon Mare's egg."

"I do not think putting more mortals in Vitae's sights is an advisable course of action."

"The three of you are all I have, Ani. Please ask Sabrina to try."

"Vitae will not be kind if they are caught."

I nodded at the rippling pool. "Make sure you warn them of the possible consequences. I'm never going to leave anyone I love in the dark ever again."

Chapter Eleven

Getting the Job Done

Detective Foxner

Sabrina set the disgruntled bronze statuette on the computer desk in her dining room. A high-end microphone Miri had called some kind of bird ran to a digital audio receiver and then into Sabrina's laptop. She took hold of a wireless mouse, but before she could open up the icon for her discord server, a new mouse mover program twirled the cursor through a small spiral.

She started the server, immediately deafened by a feedback squeal. Sabrina fumbled the new phone from the desk and muted the wirelessly-connected tactical microphone wrapped around her throat.

"Anima?"

"I am here, Detective."

"All right, you should be able to zero in on this statuette, right?"

"Yes," Anima said.

"Good, so, if you speak so that this microphone can hear you, you'll be able to talk to me through this." Sabrina tapped the earbud wrapped around her outer ear and inserted into her left ear canal. "As long as nothing knocks out the power of my router and I keep the new phone charged, we should be able to communicate."

"This is quite ingenious."

"Yeah, Miri's really good with tech."

Though her solution is going to be hell on my data plan.

Sabrina adjusted her collar, not for the first time wishing she had a better way to hide the microphone from the rest of the precinct.

"Is Quayla okay?" A thrill shot through Sabrina only a little ahead of a tingling caress across Sabrina's more sensitive bits.

Damn it, why is that happening? And why only some of the time?

<*All right, maybe I am attracted to her, him, whatever. We're alike in a lot of ways. She's definitely someone I can respect.*>

Sabrina grudgingly admitted there were good reasons to like Quayla, and even that she felt a connection with the lone warrior trying to protect Atlanta. Outside fighting each other and alongside one another, they hadn't spent enough time for such an attraction to exist. She supposed the sporadic nature of the arousal could have to do with how busy her thoughts were otherwise.

Either way, I'm mortal. She's going to live forever. How could we ever build a relationship knowing I'll grow old and die while she doesn't?

<*Maybe I should talk to Miri about it. If all the rest of this magic stuff is real, maybe she'll have a line on some kind of longevity magic.*>

Sabrina nodded to herself. Approaching Miri made sense, and she owed the other woman thanks for putting together the new method for staying in contact with Anima outside the angel network.

Anima's voice came from near the computer, following a moment later in Sabrina's earpiece. "Quayla arrived in England safely. She has a task for you."

"Hold on just a second." Sabrina crossed the apartment and

entered her bedroom to minimize her voice echoing through the sensitive microphone. "Yes?"

Anima's reply whispered in the other room, coming through Sabrina's earpiece with echoed hesitance. "You should know, I don't think you should do as she asks."

"Why not?"

"It may cause trouble," Anima said.

"Noted, what's the task?"

"She stipulated that she intends you to have all the information instead of working in the dark."

"Sounds good to me. Go ahead and spit it out, Ani."

"This task will likely anger Vitae."

"Again, noted. What's the task already?"

"Quayla wishes you to contact Bradley Sky who is currently functioning as something you call a double agent in Vitae's employ. She wishes Bradley to locate Mare's egg and determine what will be needed to remove it from Vitae's safekeeping."

Sabrina's mouth quirked to one side. "Hmm. I don't think Quayla's mentioned Mare before. Why does she want this egg?"

"She's been given instructions to make the egg her own."

Sabrina's brows rose. "Doesn't it belong to another phoenix, this Mare?"

"Mare's soul was...eaten? I think that's the right word. Her soul was eaten by the Unseelie Champion sword."

"So, she can't use the egg anymore."

"Correct."

"But Quayla," A shiver went through Sabrina. She cleared her throat. "But Quayla could use the spare to protect herself from True Death, right?"

"Also correct."

"I'll get right on it. When is she due back?"

"Normally I would tell you that she hopes to return soon, but based on her instructions I feel you should know the reasons for the delay. The Divine One she sought has been slain."

"So, she's on her own—supernaturally speaking."

Hurt flared through the earpiece. "Quayla has me, Detective."

"Sorry, I meant outside yourself."

"The Shield she chose for contacting Vilicangelus is providing her advanced training in her abilities."

"That's good then—unless you're going to tell me it's going to last a few centuries."

"No, Detective, though she will still have to traverse the Atlantic."

"Couldn't she take a plane, or hell, piggyback on a plane?"

"I will pass along your suggestions. If you'll excuse me, I must draw Vitae's attention to an incursion."

Sabrina's pulse shot into high gear. "Where?"

"Have a good day, Detective."

Sabrina cursed. She brightened almost at once.

If Vitae is out fighting an incursion, maybe we can get this egg before he notices.

Sabrina cursed once more. "You didn't tell me what the egg looks like...Anima?"

Anima didn't reply.

The discord program was still working on the laptop when Sabrina checked. The bronze angel pointed at her, a laugh hidden behind its other hand. Sabrina flicked its head, knocking it over before she hurried from her apartment.

Vitae

The hotel foyer crowded with armed trollmen, the open ceiling filled with flapping smaller minions. I grabbed two large trollmen, ordering them to guard my door. It might've been overkill due to the lethal nature of my new wards, but prudence required me to guard my prizes from any fool willing to try my defenses.

Outside, my vast forces filled the hotel parking lot and blocked traffic on both frontages. Horns blared. Angry trollmen bellowed, slamming fists through engine compartments to slay or lock immortal the annoying noises.

I considered both of my Mercedes, but decided marching at the head of my forces would strike the proper chord. Atlantan wafers would see their protector on the march, defending their small, insignificant lives from the horrors of the Sidhe so many of them had befriended.

I will deal with them in time...in fact, there is no time like the present.

"Scurith!"

The small coyll appeared by my side. "Yes, Master?"

"Once I've sounded the march, instruct my kyrie to spread out searching the buildings we pass for Fae Kissed."

"What shall your winged defenders do if they discover any?"

"Destroy them immediately, leaving no remains."

A corner of Scurith's lip curled, showing teeth. "As you wish, Great Master."

We marched from my sanctuary. Our numbers filled Atlanta's streets like the Roman Legions of old. Wafers emerged to witness my greatness, some screaming vulgarities, some screaming adulation, and others screaming from the claws of my vengeful kyrie.

It would have served me better to march the heart of my legions along a superhighway, alas Atlanta's construction wasn't well conceived enough to allow me a straight thoroughfare to my prey.

Perhaps I should have my dwarves rearrange the city's infrastructure. Creation's greatest Shield deserves Creation's greatest city.

A screech of tires drew my attention to a collision several blocks to my right. Finally roused to defend themselves, wafer guardsmen had stopped short to offer my trollmen right of way.

It's about time.

When they witnessed the scope of my forces, they chose an alternate route to whatever destination we'd blocked. Kyries not engaged in the search for Fae Kissed scouted ahead of us, relaying street layouts to Scurith. The coyll trotted sideways to my left, two trollmen holding a massive paper map of the region.

He scurried over to me. "Master, may I advise you turn aside three blocks to the right before continuing in this direction?"

"Why? Is this not a major road which runs also to our destination?"

"Yes, Master, save for some eldritch reason, it ceases for a mile before resuming."

"Scurith, make a note. I want Atlanta's infrastructure wiped out and redesigned once the Sidhe have been thwarted."

"I shall do as you command, Master."

Our detour brought us near to Aquaylae's ill-advised distraction: Ponds de Leon Flowers. I dispatched a cohort to level the building. Scurith brought word of a rotund wafer from the adjacent building trying to drive away my trollmen. I passed orders to subdue the mortal and level his business in penance for interfering with my righteous justice.

"Master, what shall we do with the domesticated animals housed within his property?"

"Feed them to the troops," I answered. "Spoils of war."

The coyll showed his teeth. "As you command, Master."

Our march across Atlanta came to a halt, progress blocked by a large contingent of mortal soldiers. An older man strode forward with an air of command. He stopped at a middle distance, holding up his hand to halt us. Two younger wafers flanked him.

A gesture ordered kyrie to relay an order up and down the ranks to stop the force. Rather than approach him, I waited for the wafer to come to me.

He did so eventually.

I didn't wait for him to speak. "You are in my way, mortal. There are Sidhe to vanquish."

A question exploded from his throat with the force of a Great Dane's bark. "You Vitae?"

"I am Vitae, Shield of the Undying Light, Supreme Defender of the Atlanta Shire."

"Right. You can't just march an army through Atlanta."

I swept a hand toward my trollmen. "If you have eyes to see, behold I can do exactly what you naysay."

The men with him tensed.

He growled. "You don't seem to understand. This is American soil. No foreign power is allowed to move troops through our territory without leave from the President of these United States."

"I would have your name, sir."

"Colonel Ronald O'Curran, why?"

"Colonel O'Curran, my jurisdiction over this territory dates back before your United States existed. You will stand aside."

"I will do no such thing." Colonel O'Curran said. "You will stand down and disband this force."

Scurith's ears pressed against his head. "Perhaps you should show the master a little more respect, Colonel, if you wish to walk away."

Colonel O'Curran barked laughter. "I am respecting this prehistoric dandy by letting him return to that hotel of his."

The word dandy raised my ire.

"I'm respecting him by allowing those blocks to stand as sovereign embassy ground despite no formal treaty." Colonel O'Curran shoved a finger into my chest. "Get this motley bunch off my streets while you can still walk away unscathed, you outdated fop."

"Colonel," I licked my lips. "It is only because my Creator insists that you are worth protecting that your disrespectful lips remain on your skull. Move aside. You stand in a contest with a Host of Heaven that you and your men cannot survive."

Colonel O'Curran whipped his side arm from its holster and put it to my forehead. "I think we'll survive just fine, especially with you dead at my feet for invading these United States."

I considered.

On the one hand, this impudent mortal stood between me

and doing my duty. His actions delayed us reaching and eliminating the faerie incursion. On the other hand, killing him likely meant a violent response from the assembled mortal forces. While I had no doubt I could win such a fight without too much loss of strength, the delay could also cost us our quarry.

If I still possessed a female body, I might've been able to manipulate his body chemicals to get my way.

"Colonel. Under normal circumstances, I'd kill you where you stand on account of your impudence."

"Except I'm not alone," Colonel O'Curran said smugly.

"No, your men do not frighten me. What stays my hand, beyond the Creator's insistence in your existence, is that I scent no faerie influence on you to give me cause to exterminate you. Your stupidity is entirely mortal."

Colonel O'Curran purpled. His fingers tensed. The gun went off, sending a bullet through the thin layer of skin stretched over pre-prepared essence.

My hand shot out, wrapping his neck and drawing him close enough that our noses touched.

His men grabbed their sidearms. A wave of my off hand sent them to the ground in slumber. Orders to attack ran the line, and the colonel's soldiers brought up their assault weapons.

Magic coursed along my whispers. "Call your men off, now!"

Colonel O'Curran waved back to his people. "Stand down. That's an order!"

My eyes flit along the disgruntled, rebellious wafers. Once I was assured I wouldn't have to slay them all, I returned my focus to the mortal in my clutches. "You are a moron, wafer. You deserve to die, but perhaps your soldiers do not. You will order your men to stand aside and allow us to pass."

Colonel O'Curran's eyes glazed. "I'm a moron. I deserve to die. My men will let you pass."

"Yes." The word escaped in a sibilant whisper. "If you ever stand in my way again, I will not hesitate to slay you. Remember that."

"I will remember."

Colonel O'Curran ordered his people from our way. We marched through disgusted, confused and angry expressions. I didn't school the young soldiers brought to their death by an arrogant commander. With the Creator's mercy, they'd realize how close to the scythe they'd stood, and correct their attitudes.

Detective Foxner

A number of people lurked in the hall outside Bradley Sky's apartment. She edged her way through the crowd to his door and lifted her fist to knock.

"He's not there, honey," A smarmy, long-haired man grinned at her like she was today's special on the menu.

"Do you know where I can find him?"

A short, plump man frowned suspiciously at her. "Who's asking?"

She extended a card. "Detective Sabrina Foxner. We have a mutual acquaintance."

"Who?" The smaller man asked.

"Quayla Buckler."

Tension she'd been too preoccupied to notice relaxed away from several sets of shoulders. "He's swinging by his office to catch up on paperwork, then we're expecting him here."

"Assuming that slave driver lets him leave at all," Eric said.

"Slave driver?" Sabrina asked. "Vitae?"

"What a bitch," Smarmy said. "Am I right?"

"You could wait here for him." A raven-haired beauty only just showing her first strands of grey offered Sabrina a kind smile. "Even out the hall's testosterone a little?"

"I'm afraid what I need to tell him may prove time-sensitive," Sabrina eyed the crowd. "Besides, I've got bigger balls than any of these boys."

The dark-haired woman snorted.

Sabrina drove as fast as Atlanta traffic allowed. She needed to get him the information from Quayla faster rather than slower. She hadn't asked Sky's friends to pass along a message because she didn't know what they knew. It looked like the group intended some sort of geekdom hootenanny. As such, if Sabrina missed him at the county medical examiner's office, she could double back confident Sky's evening plans would keep him in place.

She pulled up as the doctor crossed the parking lot to a vintage Mercedes limousine and a—Sabrina blinked and rubbed her eyes. A goblin in a tailcoat and chauffer's hat opened up the back door for the junior medical examiner. She hadn't recognized him at first because he'd shaved his head.

And thankfully that awful mustache.

"Sky!" Sabrina shouted out her window before it finished rolling down. He hesitated, glancing back and forth from escape in the limo and Sabrina's sedan. The goblin drew a wicked, curved knife.

Sky waved the goblin off and jogged over to her car, shoulders tense. Something about him moved differently than she remembered. Besides the bald head, he seemed taller, stronger, more confident.

Looks like a rookie the day after a big bust.

Sky stopped a few paces away from her window, rubbing his fingers together. "Please tell me you aren't here to arrest me again. I'd really, *really* hate to have to let him gut you."

Sabrina lowered her voice, unsure how well goblins could hear. "I have a message from our wet friend."

Sky brightened. "Is she all right?"

"She's run into a few difficulties, but she needs you to determine the whereabouts and security around some kind of egg that Vitae is protecting."

Sky frowned.

"I wanted to get you the info while Vitae is out dealing with a large incursion."

His frown bent further. "How would you know something like that?"

Sabrina tapped her earpiece. "I've got an angel in my ear."

"Technically, Detective, I'm not an angel," Anima said.

The detective hushed her.

"Do you know when Quayla needs this egg?" Sky asked. "I don't get out of the hotel often, and I really need to talk to my gaming group tonight."

"She's got a bunch of stuff to wrap up, then she has to swim across the Atlantic again."

Sky frowned. "Why doesn't she just use an Arch portal?"

"Anima?" Sabrina asked.

"Arch portals are Sidhe magic. Phoenixes don't have access to such constructs—excepting situations like the one that allowed you to traverse into Faery."

"She doesn't have access to that sort of thing," Sabrina said.

"Do you have her address? I can FedEx her one."

Sabrina found herself at a loss for words. When they arrived, they brought along the same kind of emotions talking with Miri usually created. "How do you have access to Sidhe magic?"

Sky straightened. "I'm not just a pretty face."

"Never thought you were," Sabrina sniped.

"Hey!" Sky grinned. "How about that address."

Anima related information through Sabrina's earpiece. "Just send it to Hedingham Castle in Essex. Apparently, the phoenixes there have a website."

Sky's question was rhetorical "World's gone nuts, hasn't it?"

Before she could answer anyway, dispatch came over her car radio with a possible burglary in progress. "I've got to run, but you should be able to get ahold of Miri in tech ops during business hours. She seldom leaves the precinct."

"Um, they just tried to arrest me in there."

Sabrina frowned, her hand moved toward her hip. "Why aren't you in cuffs then? Please tell me you didn't kill them."

"Sleep and amnesia magic, but even so I am not sure meeting your friend inside a police precinct is the wisest idea."

"You can do Sidhe magic?"

"Um, not exactly." Sky's expression transformed into that of a teenager caught sneaking back into the house. "I kind of altered my DNA to make myself magical."

"What? How—you know what, tell me later, all right? Right now, you need to see about that egg while your boss is away." Another thought struck Sabrina. "Can't you use some kind of camouflage magic like the phoenixes to get inside the building?"

"Don't know." Sky brightened. "I haven't tried yet."

Great, ideas are the last thing this queer little man needs.

"Does your friend know about all this...stuff?" Bradley asked.

"Not all of it, but imagine she'd love to play twenty-billion questions with someone who does."

Sabrina pulled out, acknowledging dispatch's second attempt to assign her to the robbery as she raced out of the parking lot. She'd made it only a few blocks when a sudden foreboding washed through her gut.

He made himself magical...and I sent him to meet Miri. Oh, shit. What have I done?

Chapter Twelve

Clash of Wills

Vitae

Word came back from my kyrie that the Sidhe battled one another beneath the frieze of Confederate Generals immortalized in granite. I transmogrified, intent to get a bird's eye view that I could trust. Beneath the carved mountain face, Orcs and ogres, gnolls and goblins filled a large clearing with a wild, brutal melee. Violet and emerald blood coated everything, as faerie feet trod the countless fallen bodies. Elven knights fought within the fray, trading hurled magic with spell slingers and other magical Sidhe like they only had a few hours before the magic's expiration date. Overhead, hergies, pixies, fairies, sprites and several flavors of imp filled the heavens with fairy dust contrails, magical blasts and hurled iron nails.

No Fae Kissed. Interesting.

The timbre of the battle changed as the lead elements of my force marched into view. Some Sidhe fought on, unwilling to allow their opposite an instant's rest. Others backed away from their rivals, clustering together in preparation to meet us.

Magical barrages launched from the Sidhe in waves, slamming into my forces. Neither of my enforcer types had the ability to wield magics, defensive or otherwise. The Sidhe assault mowed down scores of my forces, evoking a combined cheer.

My army waded into the faerie.

My slain rose once more to bring up the rear ranks.

Kyrie tore other flyers and harried those stuck on the ground.

I was not some pitiful mortal general to stand by and let my troops meet the enemy on my behalf. I edged my blades with essence, transmogrified into plasma and waded into the heart of the battle.

Magic slammed into me. It lit me aflame. It burned me with arctic cold. Blades slashed me. Claws raked me. Everywhere I fought, all turned to take from me a pound of essence.

They met blade and talon, spellfire and death. I waded through their number, seeking the spell casters. I subdued the more magical Sidhe where I was able but otherwise slaughtered my foes. I was Master of the Battlefield, the Hand of God in Atlanta.

Nothing can stop me.

A fiery comet slammed into our midst, shaking the earth. Ignis rose from the flame, a blazing winged inferno of might.

Sidhe nearest turned their weapons against him. Swaths of whirling flame fluttered around the diminutive female shape floating just above head height to scan the field.

"Quickly, Shield Ignis, smite the spell slingers behind you."

Ignis didn't reply.

I fought my way nearer, intent to make sure he heard me so we could coordinate our strengths. "Ignis, there's a bevy of—"

"These things smell of mortal flesh, death and Sidhe taint."

"Ignore them, they are not your enemy."

Coal bright eyes blazed my direction. "They are Sidhe constructs, perversions of His will."

"The trollmen serve me, Ignis. Turn your might against the Sidhe spell casters."

"Serve you?" Ignis's hands shot out, seizing handfuls of my pulsing essence.

In any other form, he might have yanked me to him or I might've burned, but his attack resulted in only a small loss of essence. Ignis brought my essence to his nose.

His eyes narrowed. "The Sidhe spoke true."

"The Sidhe never speak true," I countered.

Ignis locked my eyes with his. "You are Fallen."

"Help me eliminate the Sidhe, and I will show you reason."

Ignis's whisper cracked. "My Shieldheart is Fallen."

"Snap out of it." My hand cracked across his face. "We're in the middle of battle here. Do your duty!"

"Yes."

I almost didn't hear the word.

Ignis spun, the ribbons of fire sweeping outward, burning Sidhe and trollmen alike. The inferno blazed hotter and bigger for mere instants before Ignis drew the conflagration into himself. He rose, a two-story burning angel floating several feet off the ground, and leveled a finger at me.

"In the name of the Undying Light, I command you to surrender the boon of Sidhe power. Repent or face Destruction."

I transmogrified, seizing Sidhe in my talons and drinking in their essence. I swelled in size to match Ignis's own, re-linking Ignis to me as he had been centuries before.

I am not Fae Kissed, but the evolution of our kind. I am the most powerful shield ever born, the Hand of God in Creation.

<You are deceived, Vitae. Surrender this power, expunge the taint from your soul and return to your true purpose.>

Not until Mare is safe.

<Mare is gone.>

She's not. She's trapped in the sword, but once I have enough power, I'll free her so that she and I may reign over the greatest Shield in history.

<You will never have such power. Mare is gone, Vitae, and now I know you also are beyond redemption.>

Ignis attacked.

Phoenix against phoenix, we flapped and whirled. Talons

shredded essence. Beaks gouged chunks from one another. Both comprised of pure essence, we were able to do little to one another as birds of prey. Fire—especially Ignis's fire—was created to purify all that dwelt under Creation—even life plasma.

Ignis gave no thought to the Sidhe battling my forces. He gave no chase to the faeries fleeing our battle. If he noticed them, he gave no notice to the cameras filming our fight.

Is it true you fell to Aquaylae?

<It is, Vitae, but I shall not fall to you.>

I fought him with magic. I fought him with talons. I fought in phoenix and human shape, in essence and in flesh. Even armored with magical protections, even as strong as I'd grown, the phoenix lowly Aquaylae had defeated beat me at every turn.

"How could that worthless whore beat you?" I demanded.

"She is smarter and stronger than you ever gave her credit." Ignis brought forward his wings with all his strength. They detached from his back, two whirling scythes of flaming death. "And her wisdom far exceeds your own."

My attempt to dodge from the path of his blows failed. Shame, but not fear gripped me. His wings cut me into three, remaining to burn my essence so I could not grow it back together.

"This is not the end, Ignis. I will be reborn, and now I know the depths of your treacherousness."

He stepped up to me, extending a blade from his hilt. "Come at me, Vitae, and I shall slay you again and again until you dwell within your egg, no longer polluted by Sidhe taint."

"I will be stronger next time, too strong for even you."

"Spoken like a Fae Kissed." Ignis sliced the sword down through the top of my head, through my heart, his own wings and all the way down my body. White hot inferno followed the blade's path, burning away all of my body in divine flame.

Viviane

Viviane basked in the mermaid grotto beneath the crayon drawing of an amazingly powerful but long dead seventh son of a seventh son. She soaked in the power and freedom of Faery.

Creation was a world of potential, but Faery—a spirit realm created to mimic Infinity—existed as possibility. Any entity of sufficient power could bend Faery to her desires.

Once, as Lucifer's captain, she'd molded an entire kingdom.

But now I'm relegated to a pocket carved out of someone else's reality.

A smile held off the rise of outrage. Her exile wouldn't last much longer. Mab had already come to her. Dunham's dog and pony show—despite Viviane's ridicule—had doubled the influx of Fae Kissed conversions with the added bonus of stealing the souls from the Creator Himself.

Titania will come soon enough.

As if on cue, the Lady of Fire strolled down the spiral stairs descending the watery esophagus of the creature Viviane created and used as a sanctuary. Her presence burned away the creature's fluids, filling it with gas.

Viviane took her place upon the tongue of a giant clam that hid an exit beyond the stomach turned mermaid grotto.

"Viviane," an acidic fire backed Titania's sweet lilt like a subharmonic. "You are forbidden from being within Faery."

You're both so predictable. All to the good for my plan.

"So Mab mentioned, right before she offered to overlook my little island in exchange for throwing in with her to defeat you."

Titania scowled, flames wreathing her sheer, silken gown.

"I told her I would consider her offer," Viviane smiled. "After all, you might make a better one."

"How about I offer not to destroy you?"

Viviane gestured around them. "You're a little out of your element here, Titania. Next, you'll boast you can overpower me because of my lack of subjects. Really though, do you think that will make me well disposed to helping you gain supremacy against Mab?"

Titania frowned. "More likely, it'd push you into her camp."

Viviane smiled.

"I see," Titania said. "What's your price?"

"I want my throne back."

The Lady of Fire scoffed. "I don't need another scorpion at my throat. I'm better off destroying you and taking my chances."

"If you think you can."

Fury fell over her like a visible aura. "I have destroyed dozens of divine phoenixes, you are nothing to me!"

Viviane debated. Her empowerment with Divine essence made her more than Titania's match, but cowing the other Fallen wasn't as likely to produce the results she wanted.

Flattery and fear will bend her into the current.

"Oh, H-h," Viviane widened her eyes, taking what appeared to be an involuntary step backward and clearing her throat. "How did you manage that without leaving Faery?"

Supremacy replaced on Titania's face. "I lured them near a veiled Arch. When their attention focused on my children, I took them from behind."

You sacrificed your strength to destroy the divine? For what? Bragging rights?

To be fair, Viviane had sacrificed plenty of her children to achieve her plans, but unlike Titania, Viviane's plan involved reclaiming a throne and empowering herself at Summuseraphi's —and Dunham's—expense.

"I suppose I owe you an apology," Viviane said without apologizing.

Flames licked Titania's skin, but her reply carried more condescension than anger. "You owe me more than that. You're lucky I don't destroy you right here and now."

"What did killing the Divine Ones win you...other than the opportunity to eliminate unruly children?"

Her rage returned in a roar to shame movie tyrannosaurus

rexes in I-Max theaters everywhere. "It taught the phoenixes that slaying my children will not be tolerated."

It took a lot of effort not to smile. "Pity you do not have the loyalty of someone truly powerful within Creation."

"Like you?"

I shrugged.

Disgust washed over her expression in so thick a layer it might as well have been makeup for a Miss Trailer Park contest. "I will consider your offer, but don't hold your breath."

She turned her back to me, a tempting target offered in hopes I'd take the bait. "I suppose you can keep your pathetic little shelter here...for now."

I relaxed once she'd exited the boundaries of my cul-de-sac of Faery. A second figure descended the stairs, but Jahriss was the reason I'd been enjoying the grotto.

His time imitating a nymph had provided wondrous side benefits. Dedicated to his roleplay, my knight had immersed himself in the skill and abilities of the playful faerie race. More, unlike Dunham, he served my pleasure first and often.

Jahriss bowed before my clam. "Milady."

"Have you found Quayla?"

He took in a deep breath, letting it out slowly and shutting his eyes. He let his face fall forward, but spoke in firm voice. "I have not, but I am watching her mortal contacts."

"I thought she rewrote them all."

"She's sharing one with Vitae, not that he seems aware of the fact. She's also somehow removed the rewrite performed on the police detective."

A shock of icy current blew through me. "How?"

Jahriss shook his head. "I do not know. It happened after she allied with Vitae's thrall but just before she defeated Ignis."

"Did you observe that fight as I requested."

"I did."

"Did Ignis pull his punches?"

"Nay, my queen."

"Dunham punished the fire phoenix for helping her as well as not employing soul fire."

"Tactically speaking, consuming his soul to defeat her would've been overkill, an unwise use of his strength."

"Except she defeated him."

Jahriss shrugged. "She ended him outside my line of sight, but I daresay it was a photo finish."

Viviane paced the clam's tongue. Water essence was getting harder and harder to acquire. Dunham's rash Destruction of Caelum had cost her stockpiled reserves dearly. Had she left Summus caged with only the essence Dunham had on hand, they'd have lost the phoenix already.

I need more phoenixes bound to this Shield.

"Vitae has not yet taken the bait," Viviane said. "Until he changes his mind, we must do whatever we can to lure Quayla."

Jahriss smirked. "Already taken care of, Majesty. I've infiltrated the detective's thoughts, whispering suggestions and triggering physical pleasure when her thoughts stray to Quayla."

Viviane nodded. "You mean to condition her, train her like Pavlov's dog."

"Indeed." He waggled his brows. "She'll soon pant for Quayla, and I imagine that loneliness and need will drive Quayla into the mortal's arms."

"Isn't the detective homosexual and Quayla male right now?"

"Quayla's current body is male, but the mortal's appetite for males is merely burn-scarred."

"And love heals all wounds."

Jahriss shrugged. "Desire should prove close enough."

"I am pleased, Jahriss. What do you desire?"

Jahriss rose. "Only to be of service to my queen."

"Come here, Sir Knight, and be of service."

Quayla

I trudged back down to the great hall, not looking at Vita as I passed. Everything I'd hoped in coming to Vilicangelus's new Praefecture was gone.

Dylan's reasonable voice prickled my thoughts and restarted my tears. *<You came for help. Seems to me that you're getting it.>*

I needed Vilicangelus.

<Instead, an earth phoenix made you a new nest and a water phoenix is teaching you how to be a better you.>

And how exactly is Flamma helping me?

The Dylan in my imagination wiggled his fingers. *<OoOOoo. He works in Mysss-terious ways.>*

I rolled my eyes.

Goofball.

Mar didn't seem surprised by my return. Then again, since Vita probably told him when I headed down, his awareness was hardly magical or mysterious.

"I'm sorry for losing my temper, Mar. Thank you for trying to help me."

Mar beamed. "It is my pleasure to train so capable a student."

Flamma scoffed.

"Ignore her," Mar smirked. "She just jealous you know how to recognize your mistakes and make amends."

"Hardly," Flamma mumbled.

Mar ignored her mumbling. "Are you familiar at all with the crafting of swords by the Asian master Masamune?"

"Yes. If not the exact particulars, I understand the basics of how he crafted his masterpieces."

"He folded the metal," Mar stretched a ribbon of water in the air between his two hands. He left it floating there to cross the room, pick up a brochure for wedding receptions, and return. He ripped off a corner of paper and dropped it at one end of the ribbon. The scrap floated along the ribbon until it eventually fell off the far edge.

Mar caught the scrap, placing it back at the beginning of the ribbon as the center of the floating stream bent upward. Torn paper bobbed slowly up the rise and sped down the opposite side to fall off once more.

"How does the water flow uphill?"

"Aquakinesis?"

"Technically, yes, but I was referring to current." Mar drew a hilt from within his right thigh. The upstream end slid into the haft. The ribbon extended, curving into a scimitar blade then folded over top of itself to slide back into the haft. He met my eyes. "Water flows."

Bradley

Bradley called Tommy to let him know he'd be a little late. He got an earful about the Detective's visit and leaving them waiting in the hallway. "All right, fine, I'll come let you in, but I really am in a hurry."

His friends eyed the new Bradley with mixed delight and apprehension. He waved off their questions for later, opening the door for them to go inside his apartment but didn't enter himself.

Bradley hurried back to the hotel. A National Guard roadblock stopped him halfway there, but they seemed undisturbed by the goblin driving the vintage Mercedes limousine. It was possible that the goblin had somehow used glamour to disguise himself, or the mortal simply thought of him as an ugly little lamb. The limousine pulled into the hotel parking lot, driving under cover. Bradley hurried into the hotel across the foyer rounding the large fountain and heading up one of the curved grand staircases. He stopped in front of a mirror on the overlooking balcony, concentrating on his image as he tried the spell he'd never attempted before. A moment later Bradley's lack of reflection grinned back from the mirror.

The double open doorways to Vitae's study were normally guarded by grendlings. The presence of two large trollmen brought Bradley up short. They look straight ahead—uninterested or unable to see him. Bradley wasn't sure how they would take to the door opening and closing all by itself, but he figured if nothing else, he was allowed to pass the doors in search of his master.

The trollmen didn't stop him.

A holy water basin like Bradley'd seen in church stood sentry near the door. A stone fireplace dominated one wall opposite floor-to-ceiling book shelves. Luxurious leather chairs and side tables the same dark oak as the shelves filled the room without cluttering it.

Oak doors offered him access to the next room.

Bradley had read many fantasy books in which a character with invisibility often found themselves paying less attention to their surroundings, trusting in the magic to keep them safe. His heart was still pounding from slipping by the trollmen, but even so, he could still see how easy it would be to trust the magic.

Bradley made a conscious effort to circuit the room and make sure that there were no witnesses to what was about to come next.

He moved into the antechamber.

He'd never seen the egg Detective Foxner had talked about, but he'd heard the name Mare. He knew the left-hand suite was designated for whoever this Mare was. Despite no visible witnesses, Bradley crept toward the ornate wooden doors and the new yet antique brass handles. He pushed open the door and peered into darkness. "Hello?"

No one answered. He took a hesitant step into the room peering around the door. The room appeared to be unoccupied, in fact it appeared as if no one had ever occupied it—at least since it had been renovated. Antique side tables and a large wooden chest with an odd lamp atop it framed a large space against one wall.

Left open for a bed?

Bradley shook away his curiosity. This wasn't a dungeon he could take his time exploring to ensure that there were no traps.

The room faced off opposite his master's own suites. Detective Foxner relayed the concerns of the angel she said was in her ear about the danger he'd be in. Bradley had seen Vitae's temper in action.

The angel is underestimating the danger.

He faced the very real possibility that he needed to turn on a light to locate the egg Quayla needed him to find. He cursed the lack of forethought that left the Elven genetics for lowlight vision off of his list of DNA modifications.

He stepped deeper into the suite, suddenly realizing that the strange lamp atop the wooden chest was in fact a marble pillar partially covered in draped fabrics. An elaborate sapphire egg framed and decorated in silver nestled in a cavity atop plush cushions.

That's got to be it.

Bradley reached for the egg.

"That ungrateful bastard!" A strange masculine voice thundered beyond the door across the antechamber. "Has everyone lost their minds? Do I have to slaughter them all?"

Bradley jerked back from the egg and yanked the door shut. He stopped at the very last moment to prevent it making more than the slightest sound as the latch clicked shut.

The door behind him opened. "Thrall, what are you doing?"

He spun toward the voice, stopping to gape at the Viking standing in the doorway to Vitae's suites. "M-Master?"

"Yes, now answer my question. What do you think you're doing going in there?"

Bradley noted the angry glow in Vitae's eyes. He didn't have enough brainpower left unused by the primal terror strangling his voice to wonder how Vitae could see through his invisibility magic. "I was looking for you, Master. You were not in your suite or the library so I thought to check this door."

Vitae all but teleported across the room. The backhand sent Bradley flying into a pillar, both careening into the wall as an ancient vase fell to the floor in shattered shards.

Before Bradley could wipe the blood from his face, Vitae's powerful hands jerked him off the ground. He raised Bradley high enough to force the mortal to meet his eyes. Magic washed over Bradley, starting in his chest as well as in the itching spot behind his eyes. "Tell me the truth, slave. What were you doing in Mare's rooms?"

A tsunami of compulsion demanded Bradley confess his every secret. His mouth opened to do just that without his permission, but a tiny voice deep in his chest answered first.

I am not your slave.

Vitae blinked. "What did you say?"

"I-I haven't spoken, Master."

"Then speak already. Answer my question."

More compulsion flooded Bradley offering the same dopamine high he'd enjoyed when enthralled. He rejected the pleasure chemicals. "I was looking for you, Master. You were not here or in the library or in your suite, so I checked behind that door."

"I want the truth."

Bradley met Vitae's eyes. A small part of him knew that it was dangerous to match gazes, that it risked Vitae realizing Bradley had escaped his thrall. He did it anyway, answering with complete confidence. "What I said was the truth...Master."

Another wave of magic washed over Bradley, but rather than drown him, it swept around as if he were but a boulder in a stream. When Bradley neither coward nor recanted, Vitae set him down.

"Whatever you wanted is no longer important. I have need of your modern mortal knowledge. Find me a way in which I may extinguish an extremely hot fire."

Bradley dropped his chin, inclining his head. "I shall add that to the tasks I perform in your service, Master."

After several more moments Vitae dropped Bradley without warning. "Then be about it."

Chapter Thirteen

Keeping it Together

Quayla

"No, Quayla, concentrate!"

Flamma came at me with a flurry of cuts. I beat her back the best I could. Chunks of my essence short sword flashed away in puffs of steam. Hep-Silat kept me just ahead of the aggressive fire phoenix. She overextended, and I swept her legs. Rather than take advantage, I retreated, shooting the older water phoenix a glare. "I am concentrating."

"She's chipping away your essence," Mar said.

"I know that!"

"Don't let her," Mar said.

"What does it look like I'm doing?!"

Flamma rose to her feet. "Looks like you're boiling mad."

"Cut the jokes, Flamma. Hit her with the flame gout."

Flamma brightened, drawing back her offhand.

"What are you doing!?"

Fire streamed across the intervening distance. I dove out of the way, but it followed me, slamming into my legs beneath the knees and vaporizing the essence with searing pain.

Mar pointed at Flamma. "Get up, Quayla, or she's going to finish you."

"I don't have any legs." I gathered my essence to transmog from water human to phoenix and back so that I could rebalance.

"Yes, you do."

A buck at the waist threw my thighs over my head out of the path of a downward slice. Wings lifted me out of the tumble, through the second transmog, and dropped me into a battle stance somehow still in possession of the watery short sword.

Mar stopped, with an upraised hand. "Aquaylae, you cannot afford to simply discard essence."

"I didn't discard anything."

"You left your legs behind," Mar said.

"They were already gone before I moved."

Mar extended a hand. Steam coalesced into water vapor and then into liquid lower legs. "You have the worst sense of self identity of any young phoenix I've ever dealt with. Usually we have to train the egocentrism out of them."

"What are you talking about?" I demanded.

Mar pointed at the legs. "That is your essence."

He jerked the sword out of my hand. "This is your essence."

Mar thrust the blade into my body. "And this is your essence. It is all you. The moment your clothes are transmogrified into a watery form they are your essence."

I stared at him. He'd been cramming ideas into my head for hours. I was exhausted from trying to figure out what I was missing over and over again. Getting to attack Flamma had lessened my pent-up frustration but it returned double force.

My words were nearly a phoenix's screech. "I know they are my essence. I don't understand what you're trying to tell me."

Mar pointed at the legs, held up the short sword, and looked me dead in the face. "How many Atlanta Aquaylae are in this room?"

"One. Me."

He pointed to my legs. "What about those?"

"They're just essence."

"Wrong! They are you."

"They aren't me, they're just essence."

"Wrong!" Mar gestured. "I reformed them for you for the purposes of this lesson, but at no time did that essence right there stop being Quayla. This sword, those legs, that body—they all share the magical DNA that is you."

My mind reeled. What he was saying didn't make any sense. Flamma had burned away that essence. It flashed to steam, leaving my body.

Mar turned his back on me, extending his left arm holding my short sword. "Flamma, a flame gout at my left arm if you please."

Flamma grinned and shot fire at Mar. His arm flashed to steam.

The sword didn't drop.

The steam didn't waft away.

He turned, arm condensing as he faced me. "I control me. All of me. Always. Even the essence in my nest is me. Now, pull yourself together."

I flashed back to the Marriott Marquis battle. Injured and weakening, I had reached out to all of my nearest seeds, drawing them into myself for strength. I had known what I was doing. I hadn't known whether or not it was possible. I'd just done it.

I did it again.

Without any warning Flamma slammed a jet of flame into my legs. The watery essence heated to boiling. I clamped my will down, managing a wobbly stance on legs of pure steam.

Mar beamed. "Better."

Bradley

Bradley returned to his apartment only too eager to leave the phoenix headquarters and Vitae's madness. A surge of paranoia urged him to knock rather than let himself in.

Rebecca answered the door. Over her shoulder he could see the rest of his group playing an encounter under Billy's direction. The sound of dice rolling across the dining room table soothed his nerves.

At least there are some places where things are right in the world.

Tommy looked up from his character sheet, giving Bradley an uncertain look. His attention shifted to Dave's and Eric's eyes.

"Well, if it isn't our resident Mr. Clean," Eric laughed.

"I think you look nice," Rebecca said. "I mean, you still kind of look like yourself, but there's something different too. Almost..."

Bradley raised a single eyebrow, something he'd never managed to do before, despite hours of practice. "Otherworldly?"

Rebecca beamed, her voice becoming breathy. "Yes."

"You guys going to close the door and come inside?" Billy asked.

He entered closing and locking his door. He gave Rebecca an apologetic smile. "Excuse me."

She nodded, her eyes following him across the apartment.

Billy cleared his throat. "Are you here to play or run?"

"Really?!" Tommy blurted. "That's it? He's obviously done something to himself and nobody is going to ask about it?"

Eric shrugged. "He shaved his head, so what?"

Bradley couldn't help the smirk. He still had things to get done before he could enjoy the company of his friends. He ducked into the coat closet near the door, bringing down a small wooden chest and a still-unopened FedEx box.

Billy's eyes locked on the treasure chest. "What's in the box?"

"The still-living severed head of the cat I reanimated with troll marrow." Bradley said deadpan. He opened the FedEx box and removed the instruction sheet as well as the collar he tagged as being filled with Vitae's essence. He handed the instruction sheet to Rebecca. "Can you take a picture of this and messenger it over to me please?"

While she did that, he opened the chest. Eric, Dave, and Billy leaned over the lid and almost immediately started swearing as Bradley lifted out a hissing cat's head by one ear.

Eric threw himself backward, tumbling over his chair.

Billy smirked. "That must've caused you physical pain."

Eric pointed. "That fucking thing is alive!"

"What are you going to do with it?" Rebecca asked.

"How can that thing hiss? It doesn't have any lungs?" Eric asked.

"I'm going to wrap this collar around its face to hold its mouth closed and ship it to England," Bradley said.

Dave scowled. "That's never going to make it through customs."

Bradley shrugged. "You have any other suggestions? Quayla needs this."

"She needs a fucking zombie cat's head?" Eric demanded.

"This is madness," Tommy said. "It can't be happening."

Bradley pointed at his television. "Haven't you been watching the news? All of this is real. Real magic. Real fairies. A lot of really bad shit going on. How can you still be denying it?"

Tommy stood leaning both fists on the table. "I'm a doctor, a real doctor. None of this is medically possible."

A primal heat filled Bradley's lungs, but instead of letting it out, he flashed his fingers through several gestures. Blue magical bolts sprang from his hands as he demanded Tommy answer his questions. "Is that medically possible? Is that? What about that?"

The bolts danced around Billy and Rebecca and Dave to zero in one by one on Tommy's dice, leaving each a pile of powdered plastic.

"Holy shit," Billy stared. "You can cast magic missile...at objects. That totally violates the rules."

"Maybe I've had too much fun on tour," Dave swallowed

hard. "But I think the important part of what we just saw was that he threw magical spells at all."

Rebecca's eyes narrowed. "Did you make a deal with one of those Sidhe?"

"No," Bradley said. "I modified my genes."

"You total asshat!" Tommy grabbed his surviving dice and threw them at Bradley. "Do you have any idea how fast you could lose your license for experimenting on yourself, to say nothing of the dangers and consequences of unknown gene manipulation? Hell, I could lose my license for even knowing you."

Bradley caught each die, setting them down one by one. "The authorities already want to arrest me, I don't think my license has a prayer. What does it matter anyway? There's magic in the streets."

"And right here," Dave said. "What else can you do?"

Bradley used his invisibility spell.

Everyone gasped.

He picked up his couch, got it balanced on one forearm, then dispelled his invisibility.

Slack jaws and bulging eyes anchored on Bradley's sheepish grin.

Eric hurried from the table, motioning to Dave to join him. "Take the other end."

"What are you doing?" Bradley asked.

"We're going to take this thing from you," Eric said. "I figure we can tell whether or not you've done something to make it lighter."

"Got it?" Bradley asked.

When both of his friends said yes, Bradley let go and walked away. Both grunted but managed to keep the couch from falling all the way to the floor.

Billy sidled up close to Bradley, ignoring personal space boundaries. Excitement nearly crackled sparks from his whisper. "What else can you do?"

Bradley shrugged. "I haven't had a lot of time to test, look we need to get out of here before the cops come." He eyed Tommy. "I wouldn't want anything to happen to the rest of you."

"Wait, wait, wait." Billy held his hands up. His grin twisted beneath eyes gleaming of mischief. "Can you do this for us?"

"Are you out of your damned mind?" Tommy pointed at Bradley's bald head. "We don't really know why his hair fell out. Maybe he gave himself cancer."

Bradley sighed, crossed to the kitchen, and pulled a steak knife out of the butcher block. He winced ahead of the cut but sliced his palm anyway.

Rebecca and Eric both winced, Eric with a small squeak.

Bradley held up his bleeding hand and smiled despite the pain. A mad itching swarmed his skin like a hatching spider egg sac. "Wait for it..."

His hand healed before them. As soon as the bleeding stopped, Bradley wiped up all the blood with paper towels, threw the towels into the sink, and set them on fire.

"Why'd you do that?" Eric asked.

Bradley pointed at the cat's head. "If I hadn't cauterized her neck, the head would've grown back an entirely new body. I'd really rather not find out whether or not a few drops of blood can grow another me."

Billy grinned and nodded. "Like Deadpool. Can I stab you?"

"No, you can't stab him," Rebecca said. "He's your friend."

Billy shrugged. "It would be a friendly stab, you know, in the name of science and all that sort of thing."

"You just want to stab someone," Bradley said.

Billy's grin widened as his head flashed up and down. "Yeah."

Tommy stuffed his things into his bag. He brandished a finger at Bradley. "You crossed the line, and I won't have anything to do with it." He marched toward the door. "You owe me a new set of dice, but other than that we're done. Don't visit me. Don't call. Don't send me a birthday card. Just ship the dice, you know the address."

Tommy slammed the door behind him.

Bradley stared at the cheap wood. He and Tommy had been friends for as long as Bradley could remember. Their shared weird had been a comfort before the world accepted that weird was okay.

"Um, my mother still has a bronze-it-yourself baby shoe kit," Rebecca said. "Maybe you could bronze the cat's head? That might keep it from moving so it makes it through customs."

Eric scoffed. "Wouldn't work, he wouldn't be able to breathe."

Dave gestured at the glaring head. "It can't breathe now."

Vitae

Bloody essence rose out of my basin, redrawing my body one layer of cells at a time. The increased power of the newest body left my head reeling. I waited for my soul to settle and the world to calm.

My body finished forming. While I wasn't teetering over, my balance felt off. Magic pulsed throughout me, but whatever had tamed the two warring natures had faded. I crouched and swept fingers through my basin. Violet and emerald swirled through the red like three paint colors unwilling to mix.

I'd ceased killing myself as often as the mix of phoenix and Sidhe became a more known quantity. When I no longer died so often that I had to refill my basin regularly, I'd relocated my nest into my suites.

I'd died twice in quick succession.

My nest needed refilled.

Nothing stopped me from severing essence to begin the refill, but I had plenty of essence stored in my basement laboratory. I need only summon a slave to bring more of my essence blended with the most powerful knights and spell slingers of the Sidhe—not to mention Vusolaryn and Mariena.

My mouth opened to summon replacement essence, when my tongue fell quiet. A thrill shot through me.

What if this disharmony is keeping Dolumii's sword from answering to me? What if Seelie and perhaps even my own essence is creating an antagonistic response in the Unseelie weapon?

The answer to my quandary could not have been more obvious. I needed to be reborn with the most powerful Unseelie essence I could lay hands on and little else.

Before I'd learned to balance Seelie and Unseelie in the mixture that replaced a lost body, the imbalance of a pixie one way or another had afflicted me with the negative aspects of that given court. I shared my kingdom with only slaves, and they would do as ordered without regard to my next body's magical origins.

This is merely an experiment. A temporary condition easily remedied with a bit of preparation and planning.

A summoned trollman carried my nest into the basement. Down to a single rebirth, even his unsteady gait wasn't sufficient to tip the basin and spill my essence. We made our way into the secure laboratory to find my thrall absent. A rush of irritation seized me, but continued elation over a possible answer to the sword's reluctance kept me focused.

Once in the back areas beyond the lab, I emptied the basin into an unoccupied vat. Severing enough essence from my current body to ensure I was reborn a phoenix took longer than I expected. Once I'd concentrated it, my trollman trudged along in my wake, collecting the Unseelie I indicated.

I bled them one by one, concentrating their essence with my own until I had a quarter more than normally needed for rebirth. The extra ensured the near totality of Unseelie blood in my nest didn't prove too little to sustain a rebirth.

I handed the vat to my trollman. "As soon as I am reborn, empty this vat into my nest. Nod if you understand?"

The trollman nodded.

A bathtub with a water-tight drain waited to catch the results of slitting my veins and arteries. I put it to work, fading fast. In moments I was reborn a woman. The trollman dumped a vat of essence over me.

Rage roared from my throat.

Power crackled at my fingertips.

Violet electricity arched from my fingers, spitting the trollman on a lightning bolt that cooked his insides. "You worthless buffoon!"

A bar allowed me to bring my feet up and drip.

Dislodging the essence bathing me took far too long. I seethed, shaking my feet to remove whatever I could. I needed to get upstairs to the Unseelie Champion blade and Mare's egg.

The thought filled me with excitement. My genius had solved the riddle for freeing Mare.

She would join at my side.

Aquaylae would be superfluous.

I could Destroy a thorn in my side, then rule with my lady love.

Before I realized it, I was sprinting up through the sanctum, thoughts of bloody prints and wasted essence gone from my head. I burst into the adjoining study, fetched the sword, stormed the antechamber and threw open Mare's doors. Laying the sword across the egg and placing a palm across the cool expanse of sapphire, I threw all of my will and magical strength at Dolumii's sword.

Free Mare!

Something shifted within the sword. A far-off sound rose in the distance. It resolved into Mare's screams and Vusolaryn's laughter.

Dunham

Dunham stormed into his private chambers and over to the Pyri's cage. "How dare you!?"

"Pardon me," Ignis said. "I did light a match."

He stomped down onto Ignis's egg, pulling the punch almost too late to keep from breaking it. Cracks snaked across the ruby while inside the cage Ignis screamed like he'd never screamed before.

"You killed Vitae after I explicitly ordered you to capture him."

"When you sent him on a mission," Viviane said.

He whirled to find her cresting the spiral stair.

"Since you were too busy to be bothered, I ordered Ignis to Stone Mountain just as I ordered him to slay Vitae."

Fury nearly pushed Dunham to madness, but he resisted. Even with divine essence, attacking Viviane teetered between suicide and insanity. "I want him captured. It does no good to kill Vitae if he has a nest elsewhere."

Viviane yawned

Dunham spluttered, fists so tight pain burned his knuckles.

"You've enacted your petty vengeance," Viviane said. "It's time to focus on weakening Mab and Titania."

"My vengeance was never petty, and I'm not done with the church—not by a long shot."

She closed the distance, whispering an oceanic roar. "You're done, Dunham. They're tearing each other apart. Some of them are even converting to my service."

"Their hypocrisy must be punished!"

"You've destroyed their houses of worship and exposed them for what they are. Beyond that, all your efforts fall under the category of diminishing returns." Viviane's outstretched fingers swept the city's panorama. "These mortals aren't even the ones who wronged you."

Dunham opened his mouth to tell her he didn't care. Problem was, she cared even less about his opinion. She'd kept her bargain. If he failed to keep the last of his, the penalty would be world ending—his world at least.

His teeth clicked shut.

"Good. Now that reason has backhanded you, you will send Terrance and Ignis into the city after incursions."

"You already sent Ignis out on your own. Why not continue that practice?" he asked.

"You prefer feeling like you're in charge."

His expression hardened. "I imagine you have particular incursions you wish them to deal with?"

"I do."

"Are you planning on telling me where they are, or do you expect me to guess?"

He followed her gesture to a pair of sticky notes on the cage control panel. He turned back to snap at her, but she'd vanished.

You're not the only one who can do that you know.

Her voice in his head made him start. <*Oh, I know.*>

Chapter Fourteen

Conflicting Interests

Bradley

Bradley left Whisker's head with Rebecca to bronze after cautioning her to stay away from the cat's teeth. He'd failed to steal the egg, but Quayla's request had been to locate it and determine how hard it would be to take.

With intel in hand, he headed for an impromptu meeting with Foxner's friend Miri. It was already late for catching the forensic tech. Guilt ate at him. Some of his friends had taken time off to meet up for another gaming session yet he was running around Atlanta. For both reasons, Bradley didn't want to run into anything else that might delay him. Considering the conspicuous nature of the vintage limo, Bradley took Uber.

"You're going to the police department?" the driver asked.

"Yeah. Why?"

The driver shrugged. "Just checking."

Bradley frowned. The Uber and Lyft drivers he'd met had varied between untalkative to obsessive chatterboxes. However, none of them had ever asked about his destination. The phone they used to accept a ride told them where to go, guiding street by street to provide guests the most efficient ride.

He flashed back to the reception he'd gotten at the medical examiner's office. Since Detective Foxner hadn't provided any other means of contacting her outside the work location of Miri, he'd had every intention of using his invisibility spell to meet with her.

Maybe it was his short tenure working double agent for Quayla or perhaps the balancing act of keeping his job while stealing corpses, but a bad feeling whispered omens of Imperial ambush.

<*It's a trap!*>

I'm being paranoid. I requested the police precinct as my destination.

The prickle of hairs he no longer had along his neck left Bradley wondering if something odd about the destination information had caused his Uber driver to ask about it.

"I'm uh, going to shut my eyes a moment," Bradley said.

"We'll be there in fifteen."

He forced a chuckle, unbuckling his seatbelt and sliding across into the seat behind the driver. "Powernaps are awesome."

His driver shrugged. "You do you."

Bradley did close his eyes, but he didn't try to sleep. He leaned his head back and against the window, squinting at the rear-view mirror through the bottom of his lashes. After the driver checked him once or twice, Bradley reached for his magic. Having bailed out Eric on a few occasions, he knew when they were getting close.

Bradley silently removed his seat belt and cast invisibility.

The Uber pulled up in front of the building. Police leapt from hiding places amidst the parked cars, shouting orders.

The driver swore, putting his hands high on the steering wheel. His eyes flashed to the rear-view mirror. He whipped around, eyes wide. "How the hell?"

Police swarmed the car, opening all four of the sedan's doors. "Where'd he go?"

"I-I don't know. He...he said he was going to take a nap."

"Step out of the car, hands where we can see them."

The Uber driver did as instructed.

Another officer called across the car to the officer in the back passenger door. "Go get someone from SNat."

The cop standing between Bradley and the precinct bolted for the door. There was no way for Bradley to take advantage of the unguarded door and the front door yanked open by the officer, so he shifted across the back seat as quietly as he could.

He exited before the officer returned with a tall slender woman with her blonde hair styled in a cute pixie cut.

"What do you want? I was on a call with Colonel O'Curran," she asked.

The bossy cop gestured. "We rerouted this Uber to bring a suspect here, but he disappeared en route."

"And?" She said.

"Can't you detect for magic or something?"

She rolled her eyes and marched back into the building.

Bradley took advantage, squeezing in behind her. Unfortunately, she yanked the door closed in a fit of pique. He bit his hand to keep from crying out. She stormed away, leaving Bradley to limp invisibly over to a directory.

The pain faded by time he found a door with a T and a partial E in the right general area. He pulled the door open and ducked his head in.

A curly-haired brunette with thick spectacles turned toward the door.

"Hi," Bradley said. "Is this Tech Ops?"

The woman blinked at him, eyes flicking up and down

Shit, I'm still invisible.

He ducked outside, checked the hall empty and dismissed his spell. He opened the door again to find the woman already reaching for the handle.

Bradley smiled at her, meeting intelligent eyes. He offered a sheepish smile. "Sorry, I meant to pop my head in and ask if this was Tech Ops, but someone came into the hall, and I got distracted asking them."

"You were invisible."

Bradley's brows pushed together. He'd understood her very confident assertion. He just wasn't sure how she'd come to the conclusion.

My excuse covered the situation plausibly. She must be able to see magic.

"Um, why do you say that?"

"You're an unconvincing liar and there was no shadow." She gestured at a new florescent bulb across the ceiling.

Bradley cringed. "Are you Miri?"

"Yes."

He slid past her into the room, hoping to make the conversation a bit more private. "Great, I'm Bradley. Detective Foxner told me to contact her through you."

"Why were you invisible?"

He shrugged. "The cops seem to think I'm a corpse-stealing criminal."

"Did you steal any corpses?"

"Yes, but it wasn't my idea."

"Whose idea was it then?"

Bradley opened his mouth and closed it several times as the timid truth refused to exit into the harsh light of scrutiny. He squeezed his eyes closed. "A phoenix made me do it?"

"What kind of phoenix?"

"Blood?"

Miri grabbed Bradley by the arm, dragging him through the room to the workstation she'd occupied originally. She took a drink out of a large coffee mug, scooped up a yellow legal pad and crossed one leg over the other. "Describe him."

"Um, he's had a lot of bodies."

"Is his name Quayla Buckler?"

"What? No. Why would you ask that?"

"Sabrina was hot and heavy about a Quayla Buckler whom

she says introduced herself to me as a water phoenix." Miri took another drink, pushing up her glasses with a free pinkie. "I have no recollection of such an encounter."

"Um, well, I'm supposed to report back to Dete—Sabrina?"

Miri nodded.

Bradley forged on. "With the results of a recon Quayla had Sabrina send me to perform in the blood phoenix's—his name's Vitae by the by—in his bedroom."

Miri's brows rose. "By the by? Not by the way?"

"I felt telling you his name was more tangential than a simple aside."

"Interesting."

That's what she's worried about? My word choice?

Miri took another drink of coffee before poising her pen over the pad. "Start at the beginning. Don't leave anything out."

Detective Foxner

Sabrina crouched behind the building's crown, unable to see the street below. She hated not being able to see what was going on, but the thief had detected and disabled all of the motion triggers she'd rigged to catch him in the act.

Two off-duty SWAT officers crouched nearby, each woman just as blind as Sabrina was. Her eyes flit to the repelling gear laid out, ready to allow her a lightning-fast descent that didn't end in a concrete facial. Teresa and Ming Vu had walked Sabrina through their training tower until they judged her ready to repel in live action, but refused to let her first real descent go unsupervised.

The long summer day stretched daylight, despite the jewelry store beneath her closing hours before. The scent of tar clung in her nostrils as the blacktopped roof reflected heat into her body like she was cookie dough on a baking sheet.

"Prepare," Anima said.

Sabrina signaled to SWAT.

Both women tensed for action.

"Now," Anima said.

Sabrina jolted onto her feet, sweeping the ten-pound bag of flour out like casting a fishing net. She lobbed two more, grabbed her repelling line, and followed the flour to the alley.

A light dusting of flour floated in the air. The vaguely human shape bolted from beside the alarm console, running straight into the exploding flour from ten-pound bags hitting concrete from four stories up.

Sabrina's feet botched the landing, sending a jolt of pain up her leg. Ming Vu snapped up her gun. "Freeze."

"Gun," Anima said.

"Gun!" Sabrina repeated.

All three women hit the street. The gunshot creased Ming Vu's helmet. She went down.

Sabrina leapt at the shooter, a silent prayer for Ming VU and herself flashing through her consciousness. She hit the thief hard, but there was no way to tell if the invisible gun remained in the shooter's fist. Sabrina grabbed at the downed thief, trying to find arms to bind or a head to slam against the concrete.

A cannon exploded.

Something slammed into Sabrina's left breast like a semi-truck.

She rolled wildly, arms over her head.

Scraping concrete and fleeing flour fled toward a crowd of pedestrians at the near end of the alley.

Theresa aimed. "Stop where you are."

Sabrina scrabbled to her feet. Her chest felt like a horse had kicked her—bruised but not bleeding.

"I'll shoot," Theresa said.

She won't. She can't risk the bullet hitting a bystander.

Sabrina forced herself to a sprint.

Before she could catch the thief, a flaming humanoid floated down into the alley mouth above the onlookers. For a moment,

Sabrina thought it was the fire phoenix, until the enveloping flames faded to reveal spandex and primary colors.

Sabrina opened her mouth, but the vigilante dumped two handfuls of inferno down onto the fleeing ghost. Bystanders shouted, scurrying away from the vigilante's attack. The thief shrieked, dropping to the concrete without the benefit of his invisibility. Greasy hair and sallow skin melted in the heat.

"Stop!" Sabrina yelled. "We need him alive."

The floating man posed, fists on his hips. "The Sun burns darkness away."

The scent of burning human choked the alley. "Great catch-phrase, now put him out so I can arrest him and get him medical help."

The so-called hero adopted another pose. "The Sun burns away the darkness."

Sabrina raised her gun. "Put him out then get on the ground or I'll shoot."

The Sun threw his head back and laughed.

Sabrina, Theresa and Ming Vu each shot twice.

Bullet ricocheted off the spandex with exaggerated sound effects. The Sun darkened. Flame-wreathed hands extended their way.

Two more gunshots halted the Sun's attack, spinning him toward a trio of National Guard soldiers.

Hands shot fire at the soldiers like two flamethrowers. Soldiers dove for cover behind an SUV. The Sun poured on the fire at the vehicle.

Probably thinks it will explode.

Sabrina rushed back to Ming Vu. "You okay?"

Ming Vu eyed the Sun. "So far."

"Give me your Taser."

Ming Vu didn't question. Sabrina shifted from cover to cover, closing on the frowning Sun still pouring fire on the SUV in hopes of a big movie kaboom.

She shot the Sun.

The settings of the Taser could've dropped a bodybuilder on LSD. The Sun turned around, eyes aflame.

Sabrina's distraction offered the National Guard soldiers a quick retreat. One of them started gibbering into a radio kind of like the terrified little voice in Sabrina's head proclaiming imminent barbecue.

"Stand down, now." Sabrina pointed the impotent Taser. "You're under arrest for murder."

"Detective?" Anima said. "What are you doing?"

She lowered her voice so only the microphone around her neck could hear. "I'm hoping the National Guard has an idea, because there's no way my 9mm is going to decapitate a fire hydrant to put this bozo out of commission."

"He's Fae Kissed, so—"

"Yeah, figured that out on my own, Ani."

"So—as I was saying—his magic is from an external source," Anima said.

Sabrina backed down the street sidestepping near cars in case she needed impromptu cover.

"Less encyclopedia, more answer key."

"Do you have any salt?"

"No, I don't have any damned salt!"

The Sun grinned. "Guess you're going to be a bit bland then."

Heavy throbbing reached her feet before the pressure and sound assaulted her ears. A combat helicopter turned onto the street.

Sabrina exhaled. They'd handle the Fae Kissed for her.

The Sun's hands patty-caked together a huge fireball.

She glanced at the helicopter, then over her shoulder, wondering why the National Guard hadn't opened fire yet. A second helicopter banked hard onto the street several blocks the other way. It flew higher than the first.

The Sun reared back to hurl the fireball.

Sabrina shot him.

It didn't do anything, but it did distract him.

The new helicopter raced up the street, moving far faster than the first. What looked like twin exhaust pipes started expelling a cloud of noxious gas along either side of the chopper.

They're going to poison us all?

The Sun whirled to face the faster helicopter, jets of flame lancing out toward it. The water hit the flame, sizzling and flashing to steam midair. The amount of fire spewing out of the Sun's hands fell short against the water spraying from the helicopter.

The Sun faltered, flames banking and hover bobbing unsteadily.

A warm, salty mist washed over Sabrina.

Throbbing pressure and hammering noise brought Sabrina's attention back to the first chopper. It crisscrossed with its brother, deploying some kind of net rather than more water.

Despite its thin makeup, the net slammed into the Sun like a tank. The so-called hero went down with what Sabrina charitably called a girl scout war cry. She ran over to the fallen vigilante, cuffs in one hand and gun in another. What she'd thought was a net seemed to be made of metal rather than rope.

Guess metal won't burn.

"Iron," Anima said. "Keep it from his skin or it'll sear him"

Sabrina struggled with the net until she managed to free his face and neck. She couldn't remove the net from over his hands without risking setting him free.

"What will the cuffs do to him?"

"They will burn him in the same manner."

Sabrina cursed.

A trio of Humvee's raced into the street from both ends. Soldiers poured out of them, one being the handsome colonel that had put Mary in her place.

"We'll take it from here, Detective." Colonel O'Curran said. "Rest assured he'll be handed over to SNat at our earliest convenience."

Sabrina didn't hide her sarcasm. "I'm sure Mary will thank

you, but before that happens, I need to read him his rights...by the book."

The colonel inclined his head, folding hands behind his back in the parade rest position.

Sabrina finished reading the Sun his rights, sliding the card into the neck of his spandex. "All right, he's all yours, Colonel."

"I take it from your tone that you are not part of SNat?"

"No," she smirked. "I'm not part of Snot."

"Yet you knew to roll the net off his face."

Sabrina shrugged.

"You also told Captain Gamete that she had no idea what she was dealing with," Colonel O'Curran said.

"Wouldn't be the first time she was clueless."

"More importantly, it suggested you know about these creatures."

"I'm not a walking encyclo—" Sabrina's thoughts flashed to Mrs. Cox's huge book.

"Encyclopedia?" Colonel O'Curran asked.

"Correct."

"Do you understand how we were able to stop this...fellow?"

Sabrina nodded.

Anima's voice whispered the answers into Sabrina's ears, all but one she'd already figured out. She gestured. "Confronted with a faerie-powered wafer."

His brow rose. "Wafer?"

A blush rose to her cheeks. "Sorry, you attacked a faerie powered human with salt water, employing both salt and running water to disrupt the magic. Once weakened, you snagged him with a cold iron net to weaken and to a small extent injure the vigilante."

Colonel O'Curran's expression brightened. "You're far better informed than most of SNat. You one of those fantasy geeks?"

"No, just had a crash course in folklore recently."

"And paid attention, apparently."

Sabrina didn't hold back the vitriol in her voice. "I'm on the streets, Colonel, not lounging indoors playing politics."

"We could use someone like you to liaise with Atlanta PD."

Sabrina snorted. "Not a chance."

"Did I say something wrong?"

"You suggested I be your go between so you didn't have to deal with Mary." Sabrina drowned mixed feelings in facts. "If you're in any way a threat to Mary's reputation, she'll go to the ends of the Earth to make life impossible for you. As problems go, I've got enough of my own. You're welcome to keep her."

"What if instead of being her liaison, I arrange for you to replace her?" Colonel O'Curran asked.

Younger Sabrina jumped for joy in her chest, but she set a hand on her exuberance. "Thank you, but no."

"I want to be able to consult you," Colonel O'Curran said. "The salt water and iron thing got passed to us. We wouldn't have known about it all if Interpol hadn't been fighting similar problems and been nice enough to share. You apparently needed neither."

"You do have a Watcher in your ear," Anima said.

She faked a yawn, hiding mouth movement behind her hand. "I know, but we don't want to be part of this."

"Aren't they protecting Atlanta?"

"Yeah, but who's to say Quayla isn't as much of a vigilante to them as this guy is?"

"You make a good point, Detective," Anima said. "Though iron wouldn't have hurt her and salt water would've made her stronger."

Sabrina pulled her department business card, extending it to the National Guard leader. "Here. You can call me, just so long as you understand I am only volunteering what I know when I have a moment to provide it."

He took the card. "Understood. Any of your group require a medic?"

Sabrina glanced at Ming Vu. She shook her head, lifting Sabrina's repelling gear to show Ming Vu and Theresa had already cleaned up.

"Looks like we're all set, Colonel. Good day."

Sabrina walked away, knowing that she wouldn't be returning directly to the precinct to report the extermination of her jewel thief. There were fences that needed mending with a particular little old lady.

Chapter Fifteen

Throwing the Dice

Bradley

A text message jarred Bradley out of his conversation with Miri. The time on the angry text revealed he'd spent almost three hours talking to the intelligent police woman.

"Listen, this has been great."

Miri flapped her heavily scrawled-over legal pad. "Indeed."

Bradley chuckled.

Miri hadn't run out of questions yet, they'd simply side-tracked far off the topic and meandered around without any pressing need to find their way back.

"Look, I'm sorry, but I'm supposed to be running a D&D game, and I'm...," Bradley stopped at the sudden energy in Miri's expression. "You don't play, do you?"

She rolled her eyes. "Doesn't anyone with an INT over sixteen?"

Great Gygax.

"Um, despite my low charisma and in spite of a successful wisdom check, I feel the need to ask you—"

Miri rolled her eyes as she drank from her coffee mug. "Of

course, I want to come. You can answer questions while I drive. Besides, I haven't been able to play in years."

"Um, your middle name wouldn't happen to be Joanne by any chance?" Bradley asked.

"No. Why?"

Bradley checked his shoes tied. "No reason."

"You don't happen to have one of the magic detectors at your apartment? I'd love to get a look at it. We could really use something like that." Miri led him to an eye-searingly neon orange vintage Volkswagen Thing wallpapered in fandom decals and bumper stickers. A chrome Decepticon ornament replaced the Volkswagen symbol on its grill. Her license plate read: KHANGRL.

Bradley swallowed, getting into the car and taking advantage of his invisibility to glance at her left hand. An IDIC ring distracted him from the bare finger he'd been most interested in.

"Are you in, Mister Invisible?" Miri asked.

"What? Oh, yes."

"So, now that you have magic, can you detect magic without your rattler?"

Bradley blinked. "I don't know. I never thought to try."

She smiled. "You can always try it on Whiskers."

"Who?"

She rolled her eyes. "Your cat head?"

"Oh, right." Bradley tittered. "I hope everyone will still be there."

"Me too, though if they aren't it won't be a huge loss."

Bradley breath caught in his throat. He gaped.

"If you aren't running a game, you can answer more questions and we can cast a few test spells."

"Oh, right."

"Though I'm really looking forward to playing with you. Mind if I stop for coffee?"

Bradley stared and shook his head.

She pulled into a Starbucks drive thru, ordering four espresso-spiked venti coffees. "Oh, did you want anything?"

"I'm good."

She pulled up a car length. "Have you thought about offering your knowledge to the National Guard?"

"Vitae doesn't let me get out much. Besides, I think I'm on the wanted list."

"You are." She traded her credit card for a drink carrier, handing it over. She flashed him smile. "I checked earlier. Hold these?"

He took her coffee.

She pulled out, twisting the closest coffee from the holder and raising it to her lips. "To the Nectar of Hermes."

"Hermes?" Bradley asked.

"Yeah, messenger of the gods?"

"I know who Hermes is, but why are we toasting him and why is coffee his nectar?"

"He's always running here and there with nary a break, so coffee must be one of his inventions." Her explanation made sense, but didn't answer the whole question. Before he could follow up, she smirked. "Besides, any Olympian who can captain a space ship in such tight pants deserves a little adoration."

Bradly hid his grin by looking out the passenger window. When they arrived, the others—save Tommy—waited.

Miri played a badass death cleric assassin multiclass.

Billy blathered on about becoming a superhero. It wasn't a problem until he put Bradley on the spot. "So, when do we get the serum, brother?"

Miri raised her eyebrows.

"I, uh," Bradley swallowed. "Might have skipped the possibility I can give others the same abilities I have."

Miri sipped from her coffee. "Intriguing. Dave, it's your initiative."

Colonel O'Curran

O'Curran drew a hand across his face, eyelids reluctant to open back up once his fingers had passed. He massaged the sore and tingling bridge of his nose. He put his augmented reality glasses back on, returning his attention to the AR map of Atlanta afloat over the table.

His men were spread too thin. Cordoning off so many highways and roadways had them stretched to the limits. Add to that TCPs within the city's perimeter, maintaining a visible presence to discourage lawlessness and trying to capture the dozen 'super' pains in the ass plaguing the city, his lack of sleep or time to eat wasn't so farfetched.

And don't get me started on the protests and requests from SNat or dealing with that vigilante 'protector' Vitae.

He'd requested a second battalion to help of course, but there weren't any idle National Guard units to be had...anywhere.

I'll just put in another request. Maybe I'll have some good luck for once.

A headline on the nearby television caught his eye, foretelling fortunes from the other side of the scale. He turned it up to hear the latter half of Valerie whatshername's provocative teaser. "...accusations that Atlanta's so-called shields are stealing the corpses of our children."

O'Curran cursed.

A video filled the screen, showing an old woman in her seventies holding up a yellowing black and white photograph. "It was my twin flying around and ransacking houses, I tell you."

"How do you know this undead creature was your sister, Mrs. Havelock?"

"You may think me daft with dementia, but I know my own face, and that flying thing was wearing my face."

"How close a look did you get?"

"She stormed into my home, breaking family heirlooms and searching for god knows what. How close do you think I got?"

"Is there any way that this creature working for Atlanta's Shield isn't your sister?"

The old woman looked into the camera. "My twin Tawni died when we were nine." Her voice broke. "We buried her in Oakland Cemetery, now the grave's been dug up. That wretched buzzard stole my sister's body."

The screen cut back to a studio shot of Valerie. "Are our protectors stealing the dead? See the whole interview on our streaming channel. In other news, local church congregations—already plagued by freak natural disasters—fall under federal scrutiny as...," Valerie's cheeks flushed, "...as their sins come to light in a flurry of criminal accusations. Learn more—"

O'Curran turned off the television and fell into a chair. This was the last thing he needed. Based on reports from their last encounter, O'Curran was nearly certain the phoenix Vitae had used some kind of magical persuasion to make O'Curran back down.

Sure, O'Curran wanted another chance to put a bullet in the bitch's face, but considering she was a phoenix, his vengeance would only put his already-beleaguered men into a war they didn't need. With the press digging up accusations like robbing children's' graves, he'd get front row seats to mob justice turned lose against Vitae and his vigilante army.

What else can go wrong today?

"Colonel?"

"Yes, Lieutenant?"

"There's a man here to see you. A civilian of some sort."

"Can't you handle whatever he wants?"

"He's being escorted by two of the thug creatures that Vitae uses." The Lieutenant handed over an envelope. "He asked me to give you this."

O'Curran hesitated. He didn't want to touch the envelope in case it held some kind of boobytrap. He was a simple soldier. He didn't know anything about magic or faeries or whatever, but he knew his battalion was getting in Vitae's way whenever legally possible.

He took the envelope. Inside he found an introduction letter, not from the phoenix but from Atlanta police detective Sabrina Foxner.

"Bring him in, but ask him to leave his escort outside."

The lieutenant nodded, hurrying out of the mobile command center. He returned a moment later with a wiry bald man in his mid-twenties carrying a duffel bag.

O'Curran held up the envelope. "How do you know Detective Foxner, Mister Sky?"

"She tried to arrest me for grave robbing." Sky put the duffel in the middle of O'Curran's map—not that the man could see the AR without the special glasses.

"Did you?"

"Did I what?"

"Rob graves?"

Sky's mouth quirked. "Sort of, but it wasn't my fault."

"Tinkerbelle made you do it?" O'Curran's temper rose.

"Vitae enthralled me," Sky said. "I broke free eventually. A mutual friend introduced me to the detective, and through a chain of odd-yet fortunate events brought me to your door."

"Why?"

Sky pointed. "Those are magic detectors, design schematics and a user manual I cobbled together to help you. They're handwritten, and I'm sorry about that, but Vitae doesn't allow me many free moments."

O'Curran stepped forward, stopping before his fingers touched the bag. "If this is bullshit—"

"Allow me." Sky drew out a device that had once been a television remote. A huge block of AA batteries weight down the ass end opposite several glass globes with tubes leading from their housings. "This rattler uses gasses to detect radiation types specific to magical energy. I've discovered four kinds of magic so far. Red, blue, green and gold. The first three account for the three Courts of Faerie."

"Three Courts of Faerie?"

The little man caught himself halfway through rolling his eyes. "Sorry, but I assumed they'd assign someone who'd done his reading. I'll get you copies of my notes on the various faeries I've interacted with. Long story short, Red, blue and green aren't the good guys."

"Gold is good?"

"Mostly," Sky bit his lip. "I've met two, and at this point it's been fifty-fifty, so statistically speaking mostly isn't the right word."

O'Curran depressed the button.

All four globes lit.

"You're not looking like one of the good guys, Mister Sky."

Sky nodded. "I understand. You shouldn't hold the button down, it eats the batteries too fast."

"Why does your detector say you have all four types of magic?"

"Partially because I work around them all, but mostly because I injected an experimental gene modification serum into myself to save a dog."

"A dog?"

"His name's Duke."

"So, you didn't inject Duke, you injected yourself."

"Well, not exactly. I have injected Duke, but only after I tested the serum on myself."

"How did you save him?"

"He got a more stable version instead of being the guinea pig for what I got."

"Mister Sky, I'm pretty sure you've given me no end of reasons to lock you up and lose the key."

Sky's face fell. "I understand. I don't want a confrontation with you, Colonel. I need to be free to help Quayla defend

Atlanta, so I hope you'll understand that I will have to leave no matter how strenuously you object."

O'Curran's temper rose once more. "I can object pretty damned strenuously."

"I figured. Look, I brought you the detectors because someone in the Atlanta PD asked me to lend you the intel. I'll provide you my notes on faerie types, weaknesses and other vital statistics, but I'm not going to be able to let you imprison me."

O'Curran's brows rose. "Let me?"

Sky sighed. "I'm going to go now."

O'Curran seized Sky's arm. "The hell you are."

Sky frowned. His hand rose, fingers doing some sort of twitch.

O'Curran grabbed the hand to stop Sky from whatever he was doing. He woke up on the command center floor.

"Colonel? Are you all right?"

"Where's Sky?"

"He left a few minutes ago."

"Find him and bring him back,"

The lieutenant saluted and raced from the command center.

O'Curran rubbed the knot on the back of his head. He knew Sky hadn't hit him there. The angle didn't work. He tried to remember what had happened.

He failed, yawning in defeat.

Vitae

I stood in my parking lot, assessing my preparations. The kudzu elemental assault and subsequent cleanup of the Marriot Marquis told me a lot about my enemy.

Dunham Heffernan hid behind a corporate façade and a shield of wafers. He had an army of Sidhe at his disposal, considerable magical ability and nearly unlimited mortal resources. More, he had the service or at least an alliance with one of the Dark Trinity.

Even the most peripheral student of historical combat knew the difficulty in attacking an entrenched enemy. Penetrating defensive barriers and troops meant losses for the attacking force due to attrition and morale.

My army doesn't suffer from such problems.

The druid had proven himself resourceful. It was for that very reason that I had held off my attack until all of my defenses were in place.

Three high security cells held nests I'd prepared for each of my brothers. The reinforced cells had been warded to cut off the control spell–presumably cast on their eggs—the moment their nests activated. More, the cells had been built strong enough to contain my former shields in case the wards failed. Unable to acquire much of their native essence, I'd filled nests with my own essence seeded with carefully selected Sidhe blood. I'd marked each with a primacy rune while my forces assembled.

Slay them quickly to remove them from his control, deal with him and make that fallen bitch restore Mare's freedom. Simple.

I'd put great effort ordering Scurith and my thrall to dismember my trollmen and kyrie to restore the force lost in Stone Mountain Park. It'd taken far too long to regrow fully functional combatants. Not only would I storm the mortal's fortress, but we'd descend upon it from above in true bird of prey fashion.

Bus after bus filled with trollman—the seats removed to allow them standing room only. A metal ladder and railing had been added to load the roof with like number. The buses would prevent the annoying mortal soldiers from being able to move into position to stop us on the march.

Across the street in lots my dwarves had leveled, hot air balloons anchored beyond the police tape atop rubble. Kyrie clung to the balloons in looped rope stirrups that allowed them to cover the triple sized fabric sheath like scales on a dragon.

A grin grew across my lips. Victory would be sure and brutal.

After which, I'd have Mare and my brothers—the perfect Shield. Once I'd accomplished the feat, Vilicangelus could elevate me to divine. I'd hand pick a new Shieldheart and replace Caelum with an air phoenix of a proper, undamaged generation.

"Master," Scurith appeared at my right hand, ears twitched forward in excitement. "We're ready."

"Proceed."

"Are you sure you don't wish to take any of your Sidhe servants?"

"I am certain," I glanced at the balloons' baskets. "The sylphs piloting the balloons will suffice. I dare not bring Wyldfae along into a fight with the former Anseelie Queen."

"Is that the reason you ordered the slyphs to remain in the baskets?"

"Indeed." I turned more fully to my coyll slave. "Order the assault, then see to dismembering the enforcers left behind."

"Y-you're sure I cannot come and fight by your side, Master?"

"I think not. Whether I desired it or not, Scurith, you did betray me to Sidhe royalty once already."

Scurith's ears flicked back against his head for a moment before returning to a neutral position. He turned, a triple yip leading into a long low howl similar to his coyote kin. Buses rumbled off the property, headed for Circlestone corporate campus. Balloons struggled to rise at first, but the sylphs' air magic saw them into the sky and headed in the correct direction.

An uneasiness remained as my army disappeared into Atlanta. It had no basis in fact. The feeling grew from lingering fear. My last battle with the druid had cost me the Champion blades once more sheathed across my back.

This time Aquaylae will not be present to thwart my victory.

Scurith waited in the hotel entrance, probably to ensure he heard any call I cared to give. I drew both of my swords, looking at the tormented faces and pained eyes in their enchanted hilts. Viviane had claimed them Swords of Judgement, given to His avenging angels. Looking at what had been done to those captured within, I doubted her veracity. I didn't need the Seelie blade per se, but Dolumii's sword held Mare. I had to carry it into battle to ensure Viviane released Mare from the sword's imprisonment.

And it would be unseemly to wear an unbalanced pair of weapons into battle.

I transmogrified.

Elven armor obtained by Scurith transformed with me, armoring me and my vast wings with red and gold edged black to compliment my essence. The Swords of Judgement sheathed my talons, glistening golden and bluish-silver as I rose into the sky.

Before Creation learned of our true natures, I might've waited for sunset—if for no reason other than the poetic aspect sunset's banner would lend the retelling of the coming battle. Even so, I'd held the attack until most of Circlestone's employees had retired for the day. I had no way to tell if the wafers knew the type of monster signing their paychecks. I'd leave their judgement to fate.

I passed my army on the wing. Despite the delay in getting aloft, the balloons dotted the horizon when I flew over the buses. A National Guard unit accompanied by several fire trucks blocked the buses' pathway forward.

I don't have time for this nonsense.

I circled lower to investigate.

A blast of water knocked me almost from the air. Whatever chemicals they'd polluted the liquid with burned against may skin. Despite shedding the water by the simple expedient of burning it away with life plasma, my wings remained heavier than they had been moments before. An irritating residue clung to my feathers.

I transmogrified into winged human form, trying to transform the gritting chemicals, but found it resistant to my magic. The crystals dusting me fought my attempts to dislodge them, preoccupying me enough that I didn't initially see the soldiers lob several footballs—real footballs, not the oblong, American counterfeits—into the air.

I dodged them easily, letting them soar overhead.

A series of small explosions disintegrated the projectiles.

Before I could react, a cloud of tiny grey particles settled onto my skin and set my nerves aflame. My wings shriveled with the painful onslaught. I lost altitude.

Since part of our flight abilities are magical rather than purely muscle, I gritted my teeth against the flame and willed my descent to a stop.

I continued to fall.

A shockwave of impact force shot up my body, shattering leg bones, spine, ribs and my wings. I crumpled to the ground only to have a net of agony thrown over me. I fought the intricate inter-weaving of iron cord knotted by silver-coated housings.

"That's got him," a soldier said.

"What is he?" Another asked, holding something my pain-blinded eyes couldn't see. "The meter's off the charts on all four types of magic."

"He's trouble," the first snapped up a weapon of some sort. "Incoming."

A staccato of gunfire filled the air with acrid, polluted insult to my considerable injuries. The shots seemed spaced out too far to represent automatic weapon fire, but they were too close and far too loud for simple revolvers or single shot rifles.

I transmogrified once more, using my essence form to mend my injuries. The pain intensified instead. The mesh netting me, combined with the pain assaulting my senses, prevented any attempt to force either essence level through the gaps in the net.

A huge whoosh and blast of heat lit the area around me. The stink of burning, necrotic flesh suggested the soldiers had unleashed some kind of fire weapon. Since I wasn't aflame, I had to assume my trollmen had taken exception to my incarcerations.

Though not as great as the vengeance I shall level on these impu-dent wafers.

Several of my enforcers fought their way through the mortal attackers, yanking the net off of me while their body parts burned.

My thrall should've provided them some kind of fire resistance. Punishment will encourage him to be more mindful of his duties.

I rose a tempest of anger, surrounded by a halo of sea salt employed for some reason in the vile net they'd cast over me.

"How dare you prevent a Shield of the Undying Light from serving the Most High?!"

A nearby soldier unleashed several rapid shot gun blasts. Iron, silver and salt tore holes in my essence, igniting the fires of my temper into a conflagration of righteous fury.

Mortal soldiers had stopped my enforcers.

They'd prevented my forces from saving Mare and my former shields.

They'd attacked me.

By these sins, they'd proven themselves corrupt pawns of the Sidhe, essentially Fae Kissed in need of destruction.

I judged them all to the very last man.

Chapter Sixteen

Solo Encounter

Bradley

The alarm sounded before Bradley made it through to the fence line of the repurposed parking lot. He cursed. He'd hoped the sleep spell would keep O'Curran out long enough for him to escape.

He turned to the trollman and kyrie. "Soldiers are about to attack us."

The trollman snarled and flexed its claws, but the kyrie watched Bradley with wide eyes, waiting for instructions. The two types or trollkin proved incredibly different. While individuals varied within a given group, the resurrected adult corpses seemed in a constant state of road rage. Most of the child corpses Bradley had been forced to modify looked up at him with guilt-stabbing eyes like orphans pleading for more gruel.

Bradley'd chosen only to bring one kyrie so as not to be too threatening. They'd also been along to protect him in case the soldiers decided to attack him before he could deliver his gift.

Must be how the A-Team always felt dealing with the cops.

No matter what, he couldn't allow the soldiers to get too

good a look at either. Without the essence attuning that made them pliable for Vitae and himself, there was no telling the kind of havoc that would ensure—particularly if someone thought blowing them into a hundred little bits was a good idea.

More like gremlins thrown into a swimming pool.

If he'd brought two kyrie, he'd have been able to escape without an issue. Instead, he'd be forced to put his abilities to the test so that neither undead fell into O'Curran's hands.

"I don't want you to kill any of them, just slow them down so I can escape. As soon as I am clear, lead them that way for thirty seconds, then you will fly the two of you out of here and back to Vitae. Do you understand?"

National Guard soldiers surrounded them, shouting demands at gunpoint before Bradley got his answer. The trollman went Sabretooth on the soldiers. Bradley caught the frightened expression in the kyrie's eyes just before she joined the fight.

Bradley ducked between both, launching several dazzling bursts of harmless light at the soldiers. He used the prestidigitation to cover a quick invisibility spell and slipped away while mayhem distracted the National Guard.

His elven thinness and poor access to meals allowed him to slip through several close calls. Several vehicles with maintenance hatches open—a tank most notably—drew him like an iron filing to a magnet. Bradley pushed down his curiosity with both hands and an extra-large cartoon anvil. A scuffed shoe drew the attention of a soldier not involved in the fight, spurring Bradley to cast silence around himself.

Silent and unseen, Bradley crossed the camp in heart-pounding short order, arriving hot, sweaty and miserable at the camp's outer perimeter. A personnel gate offered him exit, guarded by a soldier who kept trying to get permission to abandon her position and join the fight. Orders to remain on guard evoked a sigh and a few creative names for her sergeant.

Bradley edged around her, disappointed by all the inconvenience which accompanied invisibility. The good thing about the ability lay in people not being able to see him. The problems arose from people not being able to see him. On the streets, people knocked into him, sometimes hard enough to cost him control over the spell. When he did manage to keep the spell going, angry people tried to find him.

Problematic when they have guns and IR goggles.

Bradley'd often argued against the presupposition that invisibility was a villainous power envied by peeping toms and pickpockets. In roleplaying games, invisibility meant getting into position for sneak attacks and avoiding notice of harder to beat monsters—like the attractive solider with the assault rifle huffing and puffing between Bradley and a clean escape.

His heart raced, beating hard enough that he thanked the scuffed footfall for forcing him to cast silence lest the sentry hear him. He contorted himself around her, desperate to slip away without alerting her to his presence.

His grin broke out before he'd completely escaped the guard. Miri had put the idea of helping the National Guard into his head. She seemed to think after all he'd done creating the enforcers that he owed Atlanta some recompense. He didn't disagree. His guilt fueled his desire to help Quayla, though it wasn't enough that he wanted to get caught sneaking into a military base—temporary or not—while wanted for graverobbing.

The sentry backed up.

Bradley sucked in his gut, eyes wide.

He fell sideways, barely ahead of her rump, as she leaned up against the door frame of the chain-link fence. He twisted as he fell, trying to jerk his legs out of the way. His left foot caught on the vertical bar framing the door, shaking the gate just as she leaned against it and lifted one foot to plant it against the bar.

Bradley swore in his head in time with her muttered curses. He planted his higher foot against the bar and eased the other leg from behind her. Moving slower than a marathon for snails, he slid the captured leg along the metal.

"Corporal!"

The gate guard lurched forward to attention, her lifted boot heel clipping his Achilles tendon as she slapped it down. She whipped her head around, forehead wrinkled.

Bradley stifled a yelp.

"Corporal!"

"Yes, Captain?"

Bradley put the discussion out of his mind, jerking his foot free before she finished being reamed and had time to investigate.

Thank God this spell is more like improved invisibility or I'd be screwed.

He crawled a few feet away, eyes watering before worsening the pain by getting to his feet. Bradley limped away as fast as he could, glancing over his shoulder again and again until he slipped behind a building. The healing ability he'd gotten from the gene therapy went to work quickly. Unfortunately, his brain insisted the pain couldn't depart so quickly, leaving him phantom agony.

Checks over his shoulder became less frequent, though his breath didn't ease. He had to get back to the hotel before Vitae remembered to need him. Vitae visited punishments each time Bradley took longer to answer a summons than the life phoenix thought proper, threatening to revoke what few freedoms he'd earned.

And I can't lose the ability to come and go right now. There's too much at stake...plus, I have a date.

Inner joy caused a little skip he couldn't help. Miri was perfect on so many levels, the best of which—outside of actually talking to him—was the brilliant woman not only challenged his intellect, but his actions and preconceptions.

A low growl sent some primal instinct in Bradley's core into a panicked search for a high tree. Additional throaty threats slashed a claw through his little bubble of happiness.

A hurried glance showed four huge wolves in the alley behind him. Their coats were so black they seemed to suck in the sunlight, using it to light the glow in their malevolent eyes.

Bottom canines bracketed each maw like an upside-down sabre-tooth tiger jaw.

He whipped back around, intent to put his enhanced fey speed to the test. A larger wolf and a second blocked his way forward. Something about them made his hindbrain scream in terror and his mid brain gibber certainty that the creatures about to eat him were werewolves.

All this time living with fantasy creatures and with all those reports of a werewolf pack near the zoo, why didn't I get myself at least a silver dagger?

Bradley focused on the magic within his blood and cast sleep.

The growls deepened.

He glanced around for some kind of escape. A manhole cover delved into unknown depths and a well-maintained fire escape led to a certain plummet to his death.

The largest wolf blurred, magic or his brain's weak attempt to defend Bradley's sanity hiding the particulars of the transformation. The resultant creature was furred in such a way that he could have passed for one of the Wall's Black Watch at a distance. Clawed, gnarled hands and a piggish-bulldog face belied any other possible similarities.

Something about the thing tugged at his mind. Figuring out a way to remain outside the thing's digestive track left him too busy to pay the niggling any attention.

The wild boar wolfman thing sniffed the air. His eyes glowed brighter, and he spoke with a snarl just as menacing as his other form. "You're Fae touched, but not of my queen."

"I'm not aligned with any queen."

He snorted, gobs of snot splattering the thick furry mane around his throat. "Only three courts to give you power. One dissolved but both my prey."

"Actually, I gave myself the power by—"

The creatures snarled, stepped forward and crouched to spring.

Right. You don't care.

Bradley hooked his thumbs, swinging his hands at the wolves behind. Power washed from him as a wide arc of flame filled the alley. He whipped his thumbs apart at the last moment, spraying fire from both palms.

The wolf on his left hit him before he got the fire around to light its fur. It drove him to the ground, stealing his breath. Claws shredded Bradley's clothes and tore into his chest. Burning, filthy fur filled the alley with choking stench, further hampering his attempt to refill his lungs.

"Don't kill him...," the wild boar wolfman growled. "...quickly. He must suffer for his attack."

Hey! That's not fair. I didn't start this fight...well, okay, I did win initiative, so maybe it is fair to say I struck first, but I didn't—what the hell am I doing?! I need to fight, not go all rules lawyer.

Bradley punched one side of the wolf's head. Its claws tore more skin as it half spun, half flew off of him into the nearby alley wall. A second wolf with burnt fur and crisped skin leapt at Bradley.

Bradley rolled away from the first wolf. Fast reflexes spared him from most of the attack.

Wolf teeth sank into his leg

He cried out, lashing out with the other foot. The impact threw the wolf from him, but tore the fangs through the bitten flesh.

Bradley's still-whole leg pushed him up against one alley wall. He threw a hemisphere of magical energy around himself and gulped breath. His leg burned like it had been on fire, but he wasn't sure if it was from some kind of toxin, the filthy mouths of the creatures or if having your calf shredded just hurt that much.

Wolfman stalked forward, the lone hale enemy among the five injured wolves encircling Bradley's shield. Wolfman threw a fist into the shield. The magical wall flared like a force shield struck by a blaster bolt. Strength washed out of Bradley, but without a

HUD with a mana bar display, he had no idea how much magic remained at his disposal.

Think!

His mind remained blank except for horrible pain and a tiny mammalian brain screaming about impending death.

Why didn't I give the others the serum? I'm not strong enough to solo yet.

A calmed section of mind with an oddly British accent explained why his death made sense in a cinematic sense. Bradley was a mortal in a war of magical creatures. He'd also recently met a viable love interest. He wasn't the film's main man. For the love of Gygax, he'd aspired to help the hero, firmly placing himself in the role of support character or sidekick. He might've qualified as comic relief, but as Daniel Madigan discovered, stories didn't cut the comical sidekick the kind of slack movie heroes enjoyed.

"Are you a musical wafer?" Wolfman asked.

Bradley blinked at him. "What?"

Wolfman showed his teeth, throwing an even harder fist into Bradley's shield. "Are your bones going to make gentle music once I've sucked them of marrow and turned them into flutes?"

Music, wolf, ugly humanoid shapeshifter...barghest! They're barghest—not the folklore kind, but the kind from the Monster Manual.

Bradley's elation died.

He knew what to call the six creatures about to eat him—for all the good that did, but that information failed to give him any idea how to save himself. Barghest weren't werewolves, so they weren't particularly susceptible to silver in game terms. He scanned the burned barghest, noting their skin still blackened and burned.

They don't seem to be regenerating like they should.

He looked down, noting that while his shirt was still torn, only angry red lines remained where his skin had been ripped.

I can try more fire, maybe something big like fireball.

Bradley's chuckle evoked the barghests' temper. Wolves threw themselves at his shield again and again.

At least a fireball might get someone's attention, maybe they'll call the...police!

Bradley dug his cell phone from his pocket and dialed 911. He got a few eternities of hold music while the computer connected him to overworked operators. He ignored the Muzak, focusing instead on the magic fueling his shield and not thinking about being eaten.

"911, what's your emergency?"

Bradley sucked in a lung full to make himself heard over the snarling barghest, but hesitated. He was about to tell an emergency services operator that he was under attack by six magical creatures.

"Hello?"

Maybe they're busy because this isn't that unusual anymore.

"Yes, hi, are you still there?"

"Yes, sir. What is the nature of your emergency?"

"I'm under attack by six...," Bradley hesitated, deciding to err on the side of something she would've heard of. "...werewolves."

"Understood, are you in immediate danger?"

That's kind of a stupid question, isn't it?"

"Yes, well, I'm okay so long as my shield spell holds out."

"Your shield spell?" she asked.

"Queer world, isn't it?" Bradley's chuckle pitched a bit too high.

Boss barghest slammed a fist into the brick beside Bradley, apparently intent to dig around his shield.

"We have your phone's location and I have requested units converge on your location. Do you want to stay on the line with me while you wait?"

"Thanks, no. I might need both hands to cast something else."

He slipped his phone into his pocket and sucked in breath, readying himself for a nice big fireball. He wasn't sure he could pull off the advanced spell, but he also wasn't sure his shield would keep the determined creatures from his throat long enough for the cops to arrive.

He spoke the first few syllables of the spell only to stop.

Wait, if I throw a full fireball, isn't it going to set these buildings on fire? There's no way to tell who's living in them. There might be a paraplegic, or an old grandmother or kids that don't shapeshift into hell worms.

A quick check showed the lead barghest quickly tunneling through to Bradley's unsecure flank.

Bradley's experimentation with spells had proven that the players handbook didn't know all. Spells he'd always thought inappropriately high in level worked for him even though they probably shouldn't. Other spells outside the reach of low-level wizards weren't too high like they should've been.

Not that I'm going to try something like limited wish.

Bradley moved down the wall, maintaining the shield, which officially shouldn't move with him. It did anyway. Boss barghest snarled, punching the building extra hard as Bradley escaped his tunneling.

Spells worked differently from their namesake from one version of Dungeons and Dragons to another as well as among video game versions like DDO. The barghest had really not liked the fire spells he'd used earlier, but a few of them had avoided most of the attack.

Bradley smirked.

He conjured an ode to the Exxon Valdez beneath his attackers. Barghest lost footing almost immediately, pads on their paws finding limited purchase for lunging and snapping. They slipped and fell, soiling their coats with an oily substance each time lost footing tumbled them through the muck. As much fun as watching the wolves try to survive their very first ice capade might've been, he didn't want them moving off of the bespelled area before his follow through.

Bradley set the thick layer of magical petroleum on fire.

He'd been so excited to pull a move that hadn't been allowed in more recent spell versions, that he hadn't bothered to check the Idiot's Guide to Avoiding Self Immolation.

Heat slammed into him, knocking wind from his lungs as the flames consumed all of the nearby oxygen. Being outside, he wouldn't suffocate for lack of air, but the searing pain in his lungs suggested his sudden lack of breath might have something to do with destroyed alveoli in his lungs.

He eyed possible escape routes.

The only pathway likely to offer long-term solace was up. He cursed the Wright Brothers on general principle. Up represented the worst idea ever conceived. It included death from midair collision, death from rapid deceleration trauma, death from concrete poisoning, death from hypoxia and of course death from terror.

Based upon the spells he'd already tried, there seemed no reasonable cause to prevent Bradley from casting a flight spell.

He cursed the Wright Brothers again.

While invisibility often took a bad rap, flight was touted as the power of true superheroes.

Peter Parker and Remy LeBeau survive just fine without it, thank you very much.

Howls transformed into death screams as three of the attacking barghest transformed into their furry and highly flammable human shapes. The surviving barghest fled the area of effect, struggling to put out flaming, oil-soaked fur.

Bradley dropped his hemispheric shield, cutting around the dying flames to get a clear shot at the barghest. Taking more of Peter's example to heart, he threw a blanket of thick, sticky spider webbing at the survivors.

Ha!

Bradley launched a volley of weaving blue bolts into the bound creature, each hitting unerringly between the tightening web strands.

Boss barghest struggled to escaped the tangle, only tightening his restraints. With the straightjacket of spider silk ratcheted down almost as tight as it could go, he rolled into the nearby flame.

Great Gygax, monsters aren't supposed to be that smart.

The silk disintegrated in the short-lived conflagration, boss barghest's scream turning into a snarling omen of Bradley's end.

Think! You're too smart to end up as wolf feces.

The creature closed the distance, claws raking through Bradley's belly. He lurched away from the creature, balance thrown off by the intestines spilling out of his eviscerated gut. His heel caught on a dead body.

Shit. Why did I send the trollkin away?

A live barghest chomped down on Bradley's left forearm, snapping the small bones beneath iron jaws.

Another broke his right ankle, teeth shredding flesh as they tore away his shoe.

A tiny voice in the back of Bradley's head catalogued the injuries, noting how he'd explain them on an autopsy report to prevent getting reprimanded.

Blood loss sapped the warmth from Bradley's body.

A dark purple haze clouded his vision.

His tiny voice let loose a sardonic chuckle. There'd be no autopsy report from what little the barghest left behind after digestion.

A raspy whisper escaped him. "Help. Someone. Please help."

"No one's coming to save you, wafer."

Bradley lacked the strength to nod. Moments separated him from death.

Checkmate.

Boss barghest's expression promised torment to fill those remaining moments.

Kobayashi Maru.

After all his time single, he'd found a girl worth spending time with just in time to die.

Death...blossom?

Bradley's eyes widened. "The genesis maneuver."

The head barghest frowned. "What?"

Bradley locked mind and will on the magic within him and willed it to save him. Magic exploded in all directions.

"Nice try." Boss barghest chuckled, tightening his claws around Bradley's throat. "You failed. Good bye, wizard."

Should've asked Quayla if there was life after death.

Chapter Seventeen

Damned Victory

Vitae

Once I eliminated the obstacles slowing my ground forces and had them back under way, I took to wing once more. I'd surrendered a lot of strength to the distraction, but the ground assault remained key to my plan.

Committing will and muscle to my speed, I retook the balloons just as a siren echoed from every corner of the corporate campus.

A woman's voice sounded a call to action. "Tornado Plan 1. All employees evacuate to your designated safety areas."

Metallic shutters slid out of the building infrastructure, covering every inch in armor. A grid of copper and gold lines drew an elaborate mesh across the iron plates which almost hid runes and sigils.

A thrum vibrated the air around the building.

Why would you electrify a building in the case of tornado?

A glance around the horizon showed no such storms.

I put the strange reaction out of my mind. While the armor left no room for assaults on intermediary levels, it did little to thwart an attack focused on first and topmost floors.

A battle cry echoed through the heavens, cutting through the alarm sirens. Kyrie responded to my screeched commands, dropping free from the balloons like artichoke leaves falling away from the heart and choke hidden inside.

Roars drew my eye to the nearest corner. A massive stone gargoyle unfolded itself atop a corner of the hexagonal level. It seemed to bend backward in a lazy stretch, wings unfolding and arms outstretched. Eighteen in all followed suit along the top three levels.

Before I could call challenge, their wings mantled the creature, unusual notches allowing their limbs to extend just beyond the wings' exterior.

Thunder filled the heavens.

Smoke billowed from gargoyle hands.

They pivoted left and right, red eyes glaring across the sky to leave glowing marks on my kyrie.

Flachette fragments exploded in massive clouds from the launched ordinance, shredding my aerial forces. My kyrie had the same regenerative abilities as my trollmen, but bereft of their wings they tumbled to splat marks around the building's sidewalks.

Despite coming from the eyes, the marks painted across my wings spread out along the flight joints. Two walnut-sized balls rocketed at me.

A pinion twitch slipped me sideways and down, but the exploding fragments dug into one wing. Others tracked with my motion, exploding over and over to the ruin of my wings.

I transmogrified from phoenix into the same but of living plasma. I dove at the nearest gargoyle. Exploding flachettes tore into me, filling me with agonizing starbursts and robbing me of essence with each impaling hit.

Talons ripped into a gargoyle, shredding metal painted a mottled matte grey that gave the impression of rock. While my talons tore away the wings armoring the weapon, the metal proved too hard for my beak to bite its head off. Despite my assault or perhaps because I'd closed the distance between us, the arms retracted closer to the body and continued to pepper me with exploding ordinance.

I held myself together by sheer stubborn will, sure of victory until the chest cavity opened up to unleash a gout of fire into my face.

Had I been in my physical form, the flamethrower might've slain me. As it was, the fire barely hurt more than the countless iron flachettes peppering my essence.

I destroyed the gargoyle and hurled its remains from the building top. I leapt just beneath the gargoyle's corner, latching talons onto the building to use its bulk as cover while I reassembled my body.

I'd forgotten about the runes.

Lightning lanced out of the iron plates from every angle—an angry web of electrocution. Something about the cords of sky fire tried to constrict my muscles so I couldn't let go, but I was more than some mortal creature.

I'm more than just another phoenix. By the Undying Light I am the *Phoenix—perfection of His second host.*

Releasing the building and allowing myself to free fall, I focused on reconstituting my body.

Beneath me, my trollmen engaged the building's lower defenses. More flamethrowers lit my enforcers. Sprinkler systems of some kind filled the air with airborne acids. Rune-shrouded armor treated the trollmen as it had me. Magical constructs scribed across concrete squares and only visible from my high vantage seemed to flare whenever a trollman entered, leaving behind rapidly-disintegrating necrotic flesh dispelled of magic.

I turned the speed into a dive, soaring and circling back to the uppermost floor. My kyrie had been decimated thrice over, but the remaining seventy-some percent managed to destroy enough gargoyles to create a foothold.

Even as I rose to join them, the same defenses destroying their ground-bound allies went to work against them. I perched on the smoking carcass of a lowermost gargoyle and unleashed all of the magic I could summon against Dunham's own.

The resulting explosions disintegrated all of my remaining kyrie.

Will and will alone kept my essence connected in the backlash, but no mortal's magical defenses could defeat me. It took long, vulnerable minutes to reform, almost as if I were being reborn from a tiny trickle of essence. When I succeeded and looked upon the magically-nullified balconies, I couldn't help the triumphant grin.

Retrieving my Champion blades from the concrete at my feet, I strode across the rooftop toward glass doors. A defensive mesh, much like the net the dead soldiers had used against me, covered both doors and the expansive windows. Intricate Celtic knotwork obscured the interior like a thick window screen, but I saw a cluster of standing stones to my right.

Summuseraphi—beaten and physically exhausted—pounded at a magical barrier, eyes alight with hope.

Heavens above, how incompetent can you get?

Dunham stood beyond the door when I returned my attention to entering. He smirked like a trickster god and waggled a finger at me in warning.

I sheathed Dolumii's blade, taking the Seelie sword in both hands. If the defensive magic proved sufficient to stop my assault, or worse, strong enough to damage a Sword of Judgement, I daren't risk Mare.

Dunham stepped back, a flash of concern on his face.

I grinned, plunging the blade into the mesh with all my strength.

Just as my thrust extended beyond the point of no return, Dunham's concern transformed into mockery. A blast of divine power exploded, plunging me into a nova of agony for a single moment that burned an eternity.

Summuseraphi

The divine phoenix reeled, collapsing back to the bottom of his prison. For a moment, freedom had been in sight. Atlanta's Shieldheart had come for them at last.

Elation had turned to horror as the state of Vitae's soul resolved itself in his vision. When Summus had been a mere water phoenix, he'd had no ability to see what his new form showed him.

His first glimpse of the darkness in Aquaylae's aura had troubled him until Vilicangelus showed him how to see the guilt and self-loathing from past mistakes yet haunting her. The older divine had taught him how to use his sight, separated by a veil of light so that none of Atlanta's phoenixes knew they were objects for his lessons.

Summus hadn't been able to see Aquaylae's soul through her aura until Vilicangelus taught him to part it. Beneath she had gleamed in a way that took Summus's breath away.

The reverse proved true where it came to Vitae.

Thin swirls of inky taint stained a bright aura radiating love, confidence and righteousness. Beneath the aura, Vitae's soul might as well have been farming barb maggots. He'd corrupted himself so thoroughly, that the sight brought tears to Summus's eyes. They weren't Summus's tears.

He'd never appreciated Vitae's condescension or the way he'd treated his fellow shields—technically right or not.

The tears on Summuseraphi's cheeks were God's.

I'll have to Destroy a life phoenix if I get out of here. That blasphemy will haunt me forever, always wondering if my own mistakes haven't brought him to this fate.

Second thoughts rose almost at once. His drained power, the spells containing them, even the building defenses could be obscuring Summus's vision. What he'd seen could be one more trick by Dunham or his Fallen confederate.

All hope for both rescue and reprieve from the onerous duty

of Destroying Vitae vanished in a flash of Summus's own divine magic. Even taken against his will and contaminated by the druid's other magics, Summus's power had reacted badly to Vitae —passing sentence where Summus himself was loathe to judge.

Vitae must be Destroyed.

Summus's heart twisted, wringing words from his lips. Whispers carried his reluctant decree toward Infinity. "Atlanta Vitae, be thee Shieldheart no longer."

Bradley

Bradley woke in burning torment.

Every inch of his body seemed aflame though ice clutched his core.

Figures loomed over him, backs to him. From their burned fur, three barghest in human form stood sentry above him.

What does that boss intend? Why doesn't he just finish me?

Bradley struggled onto his elbows. His left arm hurt, but he managed. A few curls of intestine draped across a narrow hole of reddened flesh. The sight brought on more cold, but after years cutting people open, the sight—even of his own guts—wasn't enough to make him nauseous. Or, it wasn't until he saw two inches of guts slither into the hole.

Bradley's eyes shot to their widest possible extents. "Holy shit, he implanted something in me."

All three guards turned toward him.

His breath caught on another barb.

Two of them were missing faces, grey muscle and blood-stained skull visible. A flap of face hung just off square from the third's face. His torso gaped empty, rib cage torn open with heart and half a lung missing.

"What's going on?"

The guards made some kind of gurgling noise, but their garbled speech meant nothing to him.

A thrill shot through Bradley.

"Um, help me up?"

All three guards bent, grabbing him painfully and yanking him onto his feet. Boss barghest and two other furry boar-bulldog men lay dead around him.

Bradley pointed at a faceless barghest. "Hop up and down."

The creature made several awkward hops, landing unsteadily but on its feet each time.

Bradley shot a look down. He cradled his exposed innards and helped them up toward the tear in his body cavity. He stuffed himself back together, watching with awe as the hole slowly eased itself closed.

Let's hope regeneration can take care of sepsis.

He assessed his appearance and that of his undead minions. "You can stop hopping now."

There wasn't anything he could do to make any of them look presentable. He didn't think invisibility could cover all four of them reliably, beside he didn't have more than a few tiny motes of magic remaining.

And I need to dismiss these things while I still have enough. I don't want them turning against me in this state.

"Um...quitting time, guys."

They stared.

"You can go wherever you want now."

None of them moved.

Bradley cringed. "You're fired?"

Nothing.

"You are dismissed?"

Still nothing.

Bradley focused on the little bit of magic within him. He willed the emanating force to abandon the undead. They collapsed to the ground in three piles of muscled limbs.

A National Guard Humvee and a police car screeched to a stop at each end of the alley.

Bradley didn't have the energy to curse. He used what he had left to make himself invisible instead.

Colonel O'Curran got out of the far vehicle, a rattler in hand.

Oh, shit, talk about no good deed going unpunished.

Ultimately, since O'Curran only brought one rattler, Bradley was able to slog out the opposite alley mouth as the police erected a barricade. He left bloody, oily shoe prints that they'd eventually follow, but he didn't have the energy to do anything about it.

The marks faded too slowly, forcing him to take a moment to remove his shoes. He found the long walk to his apartment among the most painful experiences in his life. Urban sidewalks were no place for barefoot junior assistant medical examiners.

His old gaming group lurked in the hallway, Tommy surprisingly among them while Miri remained absent. The other doctor had skipped several sessions, allowing Miri to take his seat. Beyond the door, a powerful bark rattled Bradley's apartment door.

He tried to slip by and open the door, but none of them moved out of his way. It took a few moments to realize he was still invisible. He dispelled the magic, evoking several startled gasps, a chorus of cursing and Rebecca's "Oh my god, what happened to you?"

"Got attacked. Let me get inside and get a Mountain Dew or two in me, and I'll tell you all about it."

The moment he pushed in the door, Duke bound out and knocked him over just as the barghest wolves had. Instead of breaking his limbs and tearing out his guts, Duke licked his face then turned to cleaning up the blood.

"That's not right," Dave said.

"Better hope he doesn't get a taste for you," Eric said.

Bradley tried to push the exuberant old dog off, but just didn't have the strength. Billy and Dave struggled to pull the super-strong canine away.

"Jesus, Bradley," Tommy asked. "Do that dog's ears have a point to them?"

"Huh, Tommy's right. It's an elven dog," Dave said.

"Duke's not elven exactly," Bradley said.

Outrage saturated Tommy's accusations. "You experimented on a living animal?"

"No," Bradley struggled to his hands and knees, answering before crawling into his apartment in hopes his couch would help him back to his feet since his friends seemed uninterested in anything beyond Duke. "I experimented on me. I gave Duke a newer serum to regenerate his youth and alleviate his suffering."

"At least the new stuff let him keep his hair," Eric said.

"His fur's so soft and fluffy," Rebecca's fingers seemed unable to stop stroking Duke's pelt. "It's like he's a humongous puppy."

"With pointed ears," Billy added. "So, when do we get the super juice?"

Tommy darkened.

Rebecca frowned, not at Billy but at Bradley. "If you're stuck in that hotel most of the time, who takes care of Duke?"

Bradley managed his feet and stumbled to the fridge. He downed two cans of Mountain Dew, resisting the odd urge to bite off a chunk of recycled aluminum. He popped the top on a third. His eyes flit to the still empty seat. "Um, I asked Miri to look in on him."

"Wait, wait, wait," Eric held up his hands. "You're essentially a wanted fugitive, but you've given a key to your apartment to a woman you barely know who works for the police? Dude! That mousy little girl's got to be pure magic in bed to risk all that."

"I-I wouldn't know." Bradley turned, hiding his embarrassment by fetching another drink. "She did erase my apartment from the system so we could still game here, so...maybe we should get started?"

"No super serum?" Billy asked.

"No," Bradley said.

Billy frowned. "Okay, well first things first, you have got to tell us what happened to you."

"Fine."

Bradley ran through his day.

"You actually animated the dead? With magic?" Dave asked.

"Yeah, I guess so," Bradley said.

Eric came around from his spot on the table, lifted a hand into receiving position for a high five. "My man Bradley, necromancer extraordinaire."

"No," Bradley snapped, stacking dice behind his dungeon master screen. "I'm not a necromancer."

Dave looked up from updating his character sheet. "You animated those dead barghest."

"All right, sure, but using that spell doesn't make me a necromancer any more than throwing a flame arc makes me a pyromancer."

Dave held up the book. "It's a limited access spell."

"This is real life, Dave," Rebecca looked up from where she was, still enthralled by petting Duke's coat. "Based on everything else he told us, it doesn't sound like the magic works the same way."

Dave cleared his throat. "Well, um, Bradley has been running around town digging up corpses and turning them into zombie thugs."

Bradley threw up his arms. "That's my job, Dave. That's got nothing to do with who I am."

Tommy snorted. "Says the guy who chose to work in the morgue."

"Medical examiner's office—performing forensic medicine!"

"Uh huh," Tommy scowled.

Bradley's voice filled with dread. "Great Gygax, I'm a necromancer."

"That's epic," Eric said.

"No, it's not," Bradley fell into his seat, scattering neatly stacked dice. "I don't want to be evil."

"I like to think of you as gleefully amoral," Billy smirked. "Like your boss."

"He did kill my character," Eric said.

"Your stupid doesn't make your character's death Bradley's fault," Dave said. "Though as dungeon masters go, you are downright mean."

"Fuck. Maybe I am evil." Bradley sat in silence, gaze shifting from one friend to the next. His eyes shifted to the empty chair awaiting Miri's arrival. His whisper lacked all of his normal exuberance, drained of life by the realization. "The bad guy never gets the girl."

"Look on the bright side," Billy's smile widened. "You could always make yourself one."

Rebecca shot Billy a glare. "Don't enable him."

"If enabling him is what gets me my own dose of super stud serum, you might as well dress me up in a cheerleader outfit and call me Debbie."

Vitae

I rose from my nest, shrieking with the first breath in my new lungs. "No!"

It wasn't possible. I'd been thwarted by a mere mortal. It didn't matter that Dunham was a seventh son or Fae Kissed. He was still mortal, and he'd cost me Dolumii's blade...again.

Scurith appeared, a pair of loose pants in his paws.

I shoved him from my way, taking no care for my nakedness despite the proprieties of gentlemanly behavior. Dunham had slain my entire army, stealing Mare's prison and laying me low.

I have to fix this.

After my last encounter with Viviane, I'd had no illusions about being able to abduct the Lady of Water. Gaining the upper hand enough to force her complicity was one thing.

Imprisoning and returning her to my sanctum were quite another.

I'd taken the sword so that I could force her to release Mare. Once Mare's soul was free to go where it would, she'd return to her egg.

And in a century, she'll be reborn into a perfect Shield, the new world created for us.

The sanctum flew by, noticed only when a Sidhe slowed my progress. I left them broken behind me, mind replaying the battle and my failure.

The druid had somehow harnessed Summuseraphi's power. More disturbing, he'd somehow corrupted holy power so that it harmed a shield of the Undying Light.

I had to hit Dunham's tower hard enough to overwhelm his defenses. Somehow, I had to reach Vilicangelus. Our powers combined could wreak havoc on the impudent mortal and his Fallen witch. We'd unleash Heaven's wrath upon Dunham and all he built until not two stones remained atop one another.

The huge armored door to the lab slowed me. I threw life magic into the mechanism, speaking my ancient Babylonian passphrase into the energized lock. Once the immensely thick door moved sufficiently from my way, I stormed inside.

"Thrall!"

He wasn't immediately apparent in the primary laboratory space. To one side, the enforcers I'd left behind had been cut into threes to replicate their numbers. I needed more, far more and far faster. My thrall would have an idea for speeding their growth. In the meantime, regrowing them in threes was insufficient.

"Split those enforcers into smaller pieces, a score or better each. We need more and quickly."

Before I'd rewarded him with his own living quarters, he'd rested on a cot in one of the small chambers he used for enforcer experiments. The cot and its wrappings were empty. I found no sign of him in the mixing room. He didn't lurk down any of the paths between caged Sidhe or in any of the cages themselves. None of the secure areas to which he had access hid him.

My voice echoed like an Olympian god when I returned to the laboratory. "Who let my thrall free from this room?"

No one answered.

Few trollmen and kyrie remained in my sanctum, but there were plenty of Sidhe still in attendance. Reason and desperate need for a force to retake my sword kept me from meting out immediate punishment. I checked my thrall's third-floor residence, curbing my desire to destroy every vile Sidhe I encountered along the way.

His chambers were empty.

Despite my orders, none of his affects had been relocated from his former residence.

"Scurith!"

The coyll appeared as if he'd been stalking me, natural and magical camouflage releasing him to my view. His posture and the cant of his ears emphasized the shake of his limbs.

"Find my mortal slave and bring him to me at once."

"Yes, Master."

I stood in the empty bedroom, seething yet unsure what to do with my pent energies. Regenerating enforcers at the numbers I needed would take days unassisted. I could employ my stored essence, but was loath to risk creating overpowered trollmen able to break my control.

Though perhaps that would be the solution, mindless alpha trollmen released on the druid's ground to rampage as they saw fit.

I discounted the notion. Unchecked, they represented a threat to my goals. Eyes on me grew wearisome. I had no orders for the waiting servants so I returned to my chambers. I took the time to dress in proper Edwardian attire, using the entire span of my ablutions to plan my response.

Viviane offered to release Mare from the sword. More, she'd said she could expedite Mare's hatching, returning my love to me sooner. Aquaylae had made a colossal mess of my shire.

But are things desperate enough that I should ally myself with a sworn enemy to regain an asset I so direly needed to help restore order?

The answer vexed me. Arguments for and against offered reason, but I chose not to cast my lot in with a Fallen before all my other resources were exhausted.

An idea brought a brow up in salute of the intriguing thought.

It took too long to enter the cell holding Dolumii and Gherrian. Despite continuous milking of their essence, the intravenous feeding system my thrall set up kept them in reasonably good shape. Emaciated and reeking from their own filth, they no longer resembled the effete warriors I'd defeated time and again, but a little of my essence could return them to fighting trim.

"Good evening, gentlemen." I folded my hands behind my back so that they could not witness their desperate shaking. "I wonder if one of you might be in the mood to barter for your freedom?"

Chapter Eighteen

A Faerie Trade

Detective Foxner

Sabrina pulled up outside Quayla's apartment complex. She wasn't searching for the water phoenix, though a sudden urge to luxuriate in Quayla's bed made her skin tingle.

She shook the feeling away. The confusing physical reactions came too often. Despite firming Quayla's position in her head-space to one of platonic partner, something about the woman become man aroused her.

It's probably just the danger she represents.

<Not to mention how much having the supernatural power to kick criminal ass appeals to me.>

Sure would be awesome.

Sabrina pushed away pointless thoughts. She was a mortal cop, but even so she could do a lot to help both Quayla and Atlanta. Part of that solution waited inside the three-story walkup. She exited her car and climbed the front steps. She hadn't met with the landlady since she'd had her memory rewritten. An uneasiness wrapped around Sabrina's spine. The upcoming encounter could be difficult.

But necessary.

She'd worked through multiple scenarios. None of them were as easy as just walking in and confiscating the old lady's book. Doing so wouldn't help. For one thing, no one could read it but her. Making a copy suffered the same problems.

I need the old lady working with me of her own free will, leaving me no choice but to kidnap her.

Sabrina chuckled.

Kidnapping wasn't plan A. In fact, the plan had plenty of potential downfalls, not least of which her resultant attitude toward Sabrina. Still, unless Sabrina missed her guess, old Hadley Sage Cox would prioritize helping save Atlanta over any reprisal.

I hope so anyway.

She knocked on apartment 1A.

The landlady had her frail old woman face on when she opened the door. She took two quick steps backward, removing herself from arm's length. "Yes?"

It took Sabrina a lot of effort to avoid rolling her eyes. "Mrs. Hadley Cox?"

"Do I know you, dear?"

Sabrina showed her badge. "Detective Sabrina Foxner, Atlanta Police Department."

"Oh, my," Mrs. Cox lifted a shuddering, clutched hand to her chest. "Is everything all right, Detective?"

"I'd like you to come with me...to identify someone."

"J-Just a moment." Mrs. Cox warbled, reaching to a side table. "Just let me grab my clutch."

Sabrina's instincts jangled.

Quick as a striking anaconda, Mrs. Cox lifted her clutched hand to her lips and blew. A cloud of Kosher salt sprayed Sabrina's face. She stepped back, blinking away the assault just in time to see a heavy cast iron pan coming down at her head. "You're not fooling anyone with your glamour, cursed faerie!"

Sabrina ducked in, blocking the downward swing forearm to forearm. She threw her body into the little old lady and hooked a foot behind the other woman's heel. Mrs. Cox stumbled backward, yanking a cascade of elderberry springs, silver and more salt off the door's lintel.

Sabrina pursued through the deluge, getting a kick to the shin from a very heavy boot heel. "Damn it, you old bag, I'm not a faerie."

"Don't try your tricksie lies on me," Mrs. Cox rolled to one side, swinging the cast iron pan toward Sabrina's knee. "I can smell the magic on you."

Sabrina kicked the pan out of the old woman's hand, taking a nasty bruise to her ankle in the process. She grabbed the fallen pan and brandished it at Mrs. Cox, breathing hard. "See. I'm holding cold iron. Stop attacking me, all right?"

"Then you made a deal with the Sidhe."

"No, I've been fighting faerie-powered crooks. Right now, I need your help on one of my cases." Sabrina threw the pan into the foyer, yanked up her shirt and turned her back on the old woman. "See, none of the Court marks."

"Court marks?" Mrs. Cox asked.

"Yes, when a human makes a deal with one of the Sidhe Courts, they end up marked in one of these places."

"Like an ownership brand?"

"Yes."

"What's to keep them from hiding the mark elsewhere?"

Sabrina wanted to pick up the pan and hit the old landlady with it. "Do you want me to strip naked? Would that make you happy?"

"I should say not," Mrs. Cox said. "That would hardly be appropriate."

"Tell me what I need to do to prove to you that I am not a threat."

"Have a cup of tea with me."

Sabrina blinked. A tirade perched on her lips, but she pushed it off until later. "Fine. I would love some tea, but we're in a hurry."

"There's always time for tea, dear."

"Uh huh, well, you brew it, I'll drink it and then we can go, right?"

"Of course," Mrs. Cox busied herself in the kitchen.

Sabrina watched everything she did, on high alert for flying cutlery or other surprise attacks. After several attack-free minutes, a kettle's whistle signaled the water's readiness. Sabrina tensed for a boiling water assault that never came. The tea Mrs. Cox made required five minutes steeping, leaving the two of them to eye one another suspiciously.

Mrs. Cox set a china cup in front of Sabrina without asking about how she took it. All Sabrina cared about was drinking the hot concoction and getting on the road. She blew on it a few times before hazarding a sip.

Horrid, awful, disgusting liquid squatted a skunk in her mouth and used her tongue as a bathroom. Sabrina fought her disgust and rising gorge.

Mrs. Cox watched her like an owl waiting for the field mouse to bolt into the open

Sabrina took another drink, purposefully burning her tongue to limit the torture.

Mrs. Cox's eyes narrowed.

Sabrina's stomach roiled, just as upset by the tea's presence as her taste buds. She bolted another few swallows, fighting her gag reflex.

The old lady's eyes widened.

Sabrina stirred the remaining half cup, blowing on it in preparation to shoot the rest.

Mrs. Cox put a hand on hers. "Stop. You're not faerie."

"I thought we already established that."

Mrs. Cox eyed the tea. "We certainly have now."

"You made me drink this horrid dreck as a test? What was it?"

"Poison."

"What?!"

Mrs. Cox shrugged, a soft laugh escaping her. "Poison for the Sidhe anyway, and almost certainly detrimental to their servants."

Sabrina glowered.

"Shall we go?" Mrs. Cox asked.

Just you wait, old lady. You're not the only one with nasty little surprises up your sleeve.

They drove out of the neighborhood, Sabrina turning them west rather than east toward the precinct. Mrs. Cox asked about the direction irregularity.

"I'm taking you to a crime scene."

Mrs. Cox's brows rose. "You're taking me to *see* a crime scene, right?"

Sabrina let the question hang in silence, interrupted only by Sabrina's gurgling stomach. It was the least Mrs. Cox deserved after that tea.

"Detective?"

"I am taking you to identify someone at a crime scene."

"You want me to ID a dead body?" Mrs. Cox asked. "Why wouldn't we do that at the morgue?"

"This person isn't dead."

"But you think I might know them? Is this some kind of line up?"

"No."

"Detective, I'm not sure how I feel about this."

"I can tell you how I feel about that tea."

Mrs. Cox tsked. "I was just making sure you weren't a danger to me."

"By serving me a drink guaranteed to turn me into a mortal enemy?" Sabrina asked.

"I think you're being overly sensitive about the whole thing."

"When my stomach gets over it, we'll talk."

We rode a few minutes in sullen silence before Mrs. Cox announced her unwillingness to cooperate until she'd gotten a few answers.

Sabrina refused to give them.

On some internal measurement that identified the situation as having gone too far, she barked an order. "Take me back to my building."

Sabrina ignored her.

Mrs. Cox railed at Sabrina, quoting her rights.

She drove on.

"This is kidnapping."

"Yes."

Mrs. Cox grabbed the wheel and jerked it toward the curb. Sabrina braked to avoid going into an irrigation ditch. Mrs. Cox sprang out the opposite door, leapt the ditch and sprinted toward a field full of grazing horses.

Sabrina gave chase.

To Sabrina's shock, Mrs. Cox leapt onto a bareback horse and whispered a few words from where she lay on its back. The horse threw its head, turned from Sabrina and started to run.

Sabrina cursed, pulled her gun and shot the ground in front of the beast twice. The animal reared up, threw the old lady backward head over heels and put on the speed in earnest.

Mrs. Cox was struggling to untangle herself from her skirts and regain her footing when Sabrina cuffed one of her wrists. They argued as Sabrina got her into the second cuff.

"Help! I'm being kidnapped! Police brutality!"

"Shut up already. This is for your own good."

"Liar."

"It's moments like this when I wish cuffs came with a gag."

Despite the noise, they made it back to her car without drawing an audience. Sabrina stuffed Mrs. Cox into the back so she couldn't let herself out once more and drove the rest of the way to the earth phoenix's Dallas home. It was a long shot, one that could cost Sabrina her entire career if it went wrong, but Sabrina didn't feel she had any choice.

Sabrina dragged Mrs. Cox through the back doors and into the foyer surrounding the interior atrium. The creature she'd hoped to find didn't seem to be present, but Sabrina hadn't forgotten his instructions to Quayla.

"Yarque. Yarque. Yarque."

Dunham

The blueish-silver sword slithered in Dunham's hand. The hilt refused him at first, but eventually settled down into an uneasy grip. He swished it around, frowning at the off-balance weapon.

Viviane rolled her eyes. "Your magic is wrong. It won't serve you."

"It's mine now, so it damn well better learn to serve me."

"Dunham," the crack of her voice whipped his head up and with it his temper. She softened her voice. "Could we focus on more important things?"

"I am. I sent Ignis to destroy all of Pastor Terral's properties. I still can't believe he escaped those charges."

"He had help," Viviane said. "That's not what I meant and you know it."

"Well, there'll be no question of helping him now. Whatever Sidhe is in his corner, Ignis will make short work of them."

"My sisters are consolidating power in Atlanta. They're not even buying portals from me anymore. You need to send Ignis and Terrance out to deal with them."

"Once I've tamed this weapon."

An aborted snarl escaped her lips. She marched across the distance, scooping up the Seelie Champion blade. Dunham tensed, readying for an attack. She shoved the sword into his off hand, wrapped her fingers around his wrist and unleashed power into him.

The elegant golden sword fitted itself to his grip perfectly, reforming into a radiant scythe. She snatched the Unseelie sword from his hand, freeing him to catch the scythe before it teetered.

It took him a moment to realize that while he'd suspected the heavy weapon would require a second hand, it hadn't actually done so. He swept it around one and two handed, marveling at how it felt. A shift of will changed its shape from scythe to sickle to a kukri.

He couldn't help the grin.

"Now," Viviane sheathed the Unseelie sword in a scabbard conjured over her shoulder. "You've mastered your new toy, can we please focus on weakening my sisters?"

"I'm sending Terrance to bring us Vitae," Dunham said. "He'll be weak after his attack. Now's the time."

"No!"

Dunham raised his brows.

"We cannot waste this opportunity. Wait for Ignis's return. In the meantime, have Terrance see to the rising Sidhe numbers."

He considered.

Two will almost certainly ensure Vitae finally ends up in my cage.

"Agreed," Dunham crossed to the control console. "Terra, I have a mission for you."

Quayla

Flamma sent another jet of fire at me. I dodged, glad we'd moved to the first floor and taken down the tapestries.

A firm knock on the castle's door stopped us mid training bout—not that Flamma didn't take the opportunity to sneak in a final blow. I gathered the essence she'd turned to steam while Mar approached the door.

A young man in the strangest delivery uniform I'd ever seen stood just beyond with a FedEx box. His burgundy pants and vestment, silver shirt and black boots looked more like something for a science fiction convention than a delivery uniform.

Better than dressing in a diaper and toga to mimic Hermes, I guess.

"I am sorry, sir." The boy gave an apologetic smile. "But this box must be placed directly into Quayla Buckler's hands."

I crossed the distance, hesitating a few steps from the door when I realized I didn't look like a Quayla. He slipped by Mar despite the water phoenix's position blocking the door.

"This is for you, Miss. I must advise you that while the method may offend your sensibilities, it would be wisest to do as the sender suggests."

I took the box, noting the sender's name and address. I lifted my head to thank him only to find him gone. I dropped the package, drawing my hilts and scanning for a faerie Arch of some kind.

"He didn't smell Fae Kissed," Mar said.

"How else could he have left so fast?"

"Heavens, I hope I'm not so freakishly paranoid when I get ancient," Flamma groused.

"If you intend to survive that long, you'd best develop that kind of paranoia." Mar raised his chin. "Cue, can you see anything about this package that should concern us?"

"The contents are disturbing, but not immediately dangerous."

I frowned at the ceiling and the box. Before I could decide what to do, Flamma's blade burned away one side of cardboard.

Fire flared inside the box.

I jerked the burning paper from inside, extinguishing it with my essence. A bronze gargoyle head rolled out behind it, bringing the stench of new bronze and taint.

I did a double take.

The sculpture seemed more cat than classical gargoyle and it reeked of Unseelie taint, but my attention riveted on a leather collar wrapped around the head like the ones Ignis had found.

I turned to the paper, reading what had survived three times between glares at Flamma. I handed it off to Mar and lifted the head, keeping my fingers away from the mouth as instructed.

Bradley Sky had reanimated a cat with troll bone marrow. He'd discovered a way to create short term arches between places in Creation. He'd sent both to me, asking that I return as soon as I could, sped by the magic he offered.

This could be a trap.

"This is faerie magic." Mar's dark expression loomed over an accusing finger. "That is a hell-blighted perversion of one of God's creatures."

"It was just a cat," Flamma said.

Mar whirled on her. "Go out and patrol the shire, and while you're at it, meditate on what you're supposed to be protecting."

Flamma stomped out of the castle, shooting me a dirty look as if I'd been the one to get her in trouble.

I didn't disagree with Mar. I'd been appalled when I'd learned about Whiskers, but Bradley had given the impression the cat had been slain. Of course, the reanimating of mortal bodies which followed had been far worse, but those atrocities rested firmly on Vitae's account.

Bradley's instructions indicated that the cat's head might survive fueling an Arch back to Vitae's warehouse. He cautioned me that if I chose to destroy the head, I had to be certain to completely cremate it to prevent it regenerating.

Mar crossed the distance, snatching the head and dropping it between his feet. Duel waterspouts whirled into existence on either side. I grabbed the head before he eroded it.

"That abomination needs to be destroyed," Mar said.

"I don't disagree with you, but the collar still might be useful."

"You can't think using Faerie magic to cross the Atlantic is a good idea."

It wouldn't have been my first choice. It smacked a little too close to the things Vitae was doing. Still, the messenger had seemed to know how I would respond to the contents of the sealed container. He'd advised me to follow Bradley's instructions.

Could he have ended up enthralled again? Is this Vitae's idea?

Despite the bronze, the cat bit me. I dropped it by reflex,

allowing Mar to attempt its destruction once more. I reached out, on the verge of stopping him, but my voice failed me.

"Stop," Vita said.

Mar and I looked up to where Vita stood partway down the stone steps. Despite not doing anything wrong, I couldn't help a sudden surge of guilt.

"Vita, this thing should be destroyed," Mar said.

"So you told me already, but Cue's telling of the last hour's events leads me to delay that eventuality."

Vita intended to destroy the head, but not immediately. As one of the oldest phoenixes in Creation, she'd seen many things. Her eyes fixed on me and I wondered just how many things she could see that I didn't want to share with her.

"Do you know this messenger?" Vita asked.

"No."

Her eyes turned to Mar.

He shook his head.

Her attention returned to me. "Yet he knew you on sight."

"I don't know why, Vita. I don't know him."

"The Isaac says the messenger can be trusted."

The suggestion gobsmacked me. Sure, the Isaac saw all...or rather Saw All, but for him to know a single mortal by a mere description seemed unlikely.

Of course, he could've been watching us at the time.

"How long until Aquaylae is ready?" Vita asked.

"She needs more practice," Mar said out loud for both of our benefits. "However, I've introduced her to most of the basic and a few advanced techniques that she should've known."

Vita crossed to the bronze head. A sweeping hilt appeared in her hand, glowing essence forming a khopesh blade a moment later. She lifted the blade.

"Wait! I thought you said we were supposed to trust the messenger."

"I did, child, but I cannot countenance this poor creature encased in bronze and starving eternally." Her blade came down in a flash, stopping short of cutting the head. The blade edge slid into the gouge, spreading out until it ultimately shattered the bronze egg. A second slide removed a cauterized section of neck. Flesh started to grow from the wound at once, albeit slowly.

Vita picked up the head and headed back up the stairs. "I'll see to the cat. You two finish Aquaylae's training."

"Be careful," I called after her. "It bites."

Mar pushed me harder all that night. Every time I could go no further or no longer lift my limbs, Vita appeared with slightly more cat and infused me with her essence. Telli and Aether joined into the session, helping Mar illustrate how each element functioned and how they could work together. The moment Flamma returned from patrol, she was pressganged into the lessons.

"What about life?" I gasped. "Shouldn't I learn how to work with a life phoenix?"

Mar's brows rose. "Do you think you can forgive Vitae and work with him?"

An undersea volcanic vent erupted in my stomach. Mar inclined his head a little too smugly for my preference, but I could see why he hadn't taught me how to work with Vita.

"Exactly. Once you've restored your Shield and all is back to normal, then I will see about adding to your training," Mar said.

"How could things ever go back to normal?" I demanded. "Humanity knows about the Sidhe."

"Things are a bit more widespread now, but they knew in Sodom and Gomorrah and during the time of Noah too." Mar said. "Not that I know this from personal experience, but Vita promises there will be a way to bring things back to the way they once were."

The idea staggered me.

That we could somehow reset everything back to the way it once was seemed too much to hope. My eyes rose to the heavens, brows bent in question.

Aether chuckled. "Ye of little faith."

Her good humor filled my eyes with tears. Aether had cradled me after my mistake. She'd watched over me as reports of dead 'witches' came to my ears. Terrance had taken her place once I'd been relocated, but Caelum had been the first phoenix in Atlanta to truly befriend me. Facing the physical reminder of who Caelum would've become tore my heart from my chest and stomped on it with cleats.

I loved Hedingham Castle.

I loved the Shield around me.

But no matter how much I would rather Hedingham Castle were my home, it wasn't any more. Maybe I'd thought it was. Maybe that had been why I'd chosen their Shield from which to contact Vilicangelus.

Hedingham wasn't, couldn't be my home.

I knew that because my heart yearned to return to a home somewhere other than where I stood.

Vita joined us, stroking the violently mutated cat. "It's time for Quayla to go. Telli?"

The earth phoenix nodded. The castle rumbled, flagstones reaching up from the floor into a beautifully wrought Arch.

Flamma clapped her hands, grinned mischievously, and bolted up the stairs. She returned moments later with four stone amphoras suspended from a pole over her shoulders.

Mar stepped forward, helping Flamma settle them near the Arch. Mar lifted an amphora. "Before you go, we have gifts for you, little sister."

He handed me a stone jar thrumming with the power of essence, turning back to the pile to lift a second. "These two are for you, gifts from Vita and myself to help keep you among us."

Tears collected in my eyes.

Telli picked up the next amphora, holding it rather than offering. "This is for your Terrance so that you are no longer alone."

My heart nearly broke at her words.

"This is for your Ignis," Flamma scooped up the last amphora. "Cause let's be honest, you need the help."

I laughed. I couldn't help it.

"Whiskers and I will fuel this Arch so we can ensure your safe arrival and help move your gifts," Vita's words dropped to a whisper. "Go with God, Quayla."

Aether took the amphora from my hands, setting it down so she could take my hands into hers. Her words shattered my heart. "Nothing I can give will free your little brother from his fate. So, when the time comes to free the others, have your Watcher call on me. I will fight in his stead, protect you as he would have. I offer my life to aid you in reclaiming your Shield."

There were no words. I couldn't have choked them out past my sobs even if I had wanted. If I hadn't already realized all I'd lost when I'd fled that angry mob two centuries before, I could not have escaped the truth now.

My mistake had cost more than hundreds of mortal lives and the guilt that came with it. I'd cost myself centuries of love and support.

My voice broke. "I am not worthy."

"Yes, you are." Vita caressed my cheek. "Now go prove it to yourself."

She invoked the Arch, allowing me to cry my way back to Atlanta surrounded by love and amphoras full of hope.

Chapter Nineteen

Home Gone Crazy

Quayla

The blur that was Mar set down the amphora. He shook his head at the pentagram Vitae'd drawn in blood on the warehouse floor.

Mar fished a cell phone out of his pocket. He handed it over, embracing me once more before stepping back through the Arch to Hedingham. Telli and Aether repeated his gesture. Flamma rolled her eyes before sauntering back to England.

It took a minute to locate the phone's surprisingly local number. Lifting the silver feather from my neckline, I pinched it between fingers and thumb. Vilicangelus was dead, but I had to hope the token would still connect me to my Watcher. "Anima?"

"Quayla!" Anima's exuberance sent a thrill through me.

"Stop." Discussions with Mar left me wary of Vitae listening in through the angel network. I couldn't take a chance of meeting him prematurely. I read her the new phone number. "Please give that to the bearer of my statue."

True, Vitae could call the number, but he wasn't tech savvy enough to track the GPS and locate me.

The phone rang.

I hesitated, a knot in my gut.

"Answer," Anima said.

I did. "Hello?"

"Quayla?" A tremble shook Sabrina's voice. "Where are you?"

"Where you tried to arrest me and my companion for grave robbery."

It only took her a moment to respond. "Understood. I have to finish what I'm doing here, but I'll be there shortly."

I nodded—not that she could see the motion—and hung up.

While I no longer felt quite so alone, I remained the only free phoenix still serving the Undying Light in Atlanta. Taking chances wasn't an option any more—at least not until my nest was filled.

Not an hour later the warehouse door eased open. I placed thumb and index finger tips against the nails of their opposite, drawing back and pinching a line of essence. It felt too loose— nowhere near as elastic as I thought it should, but I grew a four-sided pyramid of ice in the slingshot's crook.

Mrs. Cox's voice nearly made me cry. "In or out, Detective. We're not air conditioning the whole of Georgia."

Sabrina slid into sight, gun gripped low in both hands. She wore tactical head gear like what I'd reclaimed from the Fae Kissed guarding our headquarters building, but otherwise wore professional clothes with her air of exasperation. Her gaze flit to the sling shot. A smile flashed up her flush cheeks to fill her eyes. "It's her...him."

Mrs. Cox pushed by, stopping short just inside the doorway. "That's not my Quayla. That's her brother Kale."

Sabrina rolled her eyes, holstered her weapon and crossed the intervening distance.

"What is Mrs. Cox doing here?" I asked.

"Well, isn't that a fine how do you do? Particularly since you slept on my cot without finishing the cleaning you promised." Mrs. Cox huffed. "First you offer me no greeting, then talk about me like I'm not here in some cooked up cockamamie accent."

"I needed a faerie expert that I could explain to the National Guard colonel," Sabrina said. "I took Mrs. Cox out to Dallas for a little help from your friend."

"Yarque isn't my friend," I said.

Sabrina shrugged, stepping closer than necessary to look me up and down. Her tongue moistened bowtie lips. "You look none the worse for wear, but I'm with Mrs. Cox. What's with the fake accent?"

"Actually, the southern accent is the fake," I said. "I was born in England."

Sabrina frowned. "Did you reach Vilicangelus?"

"He's dead."

Mrs. Cox patted my shoulder. "My condolences, boy. Now, where's your sister? I daresay more phoenixes will be better than one."

I arched an eyebrow.

Sabrina opened her mouth, only to shift her attention into the middle distance. "All right, I'll hand you over. Just let me take it off."

The police detective answered my unasked question by ripping the velcroed microphone from her neck and unhooking an earpiece.

"Ani wants to talk to you," Sabrina offered both.

I took the gear, but instead of donning it, I faced Mrs. Cox. Gathering my essence, I transmogrified into pure essence. I didn't remember the last body she might remember very well, but I reshaped my outward appearance the best I could on the fly.

I transmog'd into naked flesh and offered Mrs. Cox a smile. "See, I am Quayla."

Mrs. Cox rolled her eyes. "Parlor tricks aren't going to pull the wool over these old eyes."

I shook my head, resigning myself to dealing with Mrs. Cox later as I donned the earpiece.

"Quayla!" Amina's voice had a slight echo like she was on speakerphone. "I am so glad you're back. Things are bad."

Excited fingers wrapped the microphone around my throat. "Ani? How? Why?"

"She didn't want me using the angel network," Sabrina said.

"Probably for the best," I said. "Don't worry, Ani, things will be fine. I have a plan just as soon as I find someplace to serve as a safe headquarters."

"My building?" Mrs. Cox asked.

"Dallas?" Sabrina asked.

"Too obvious," I shook my head.

"May I make a suggestion?" Anima asked.

I held up a hand to forestall the other two. "Go ahead."

"I have had a great deal of time to think on this very need," Anima said. "I am hesitant to make the suggestion, but I am fairly certain there is no fear of Vitae guessing your whereabouts or visiting the locale independently."

"Okay, where?" I asked.

"Mare's house."

Two simple words should not carry the weight of an aircraft carrier. Nonetheless, Anima's answer filled me with unease.

"Mare died centuries ago."

"Yes, but her house remains," Anima said. "Vitae refused to call on her there when she lived, and he doesn't know that Terrance kept it as she left it—more or less"

"Ani?"

Sabrina lifted her phone between us all, touching the screen several times until Anima's voice moved from my ear to the phone's speaker.

"Terrance moved the house from the area called Brookhaven several years before you were assigned to our Shield."

"Why did he move it?" I asked.

"The city government threatened to destroy it if the owner didn't cut down the overgrown foliage," Anima said. "Terrance didn't want to remove the barrier he'd erected to protect the house from vandals, vagabonds and Sidhe, so he moved it outside what was then the city limits."

"And it's still intact?" Sabrina asked. "No one's foreclosed or condemned the property?"

"It's on a lot of heavily wooded land," Anima said. "Impassible without Terrance's permission. He sees to the taxes and the Isaac has eliminated all legal gambits to seize the land."

"Ani, how are we going to get permission to enter with Terrance imprisoned?" I asked.

"That is a problem, but only for your friends," Anima said. "Nothing would stop a phoenix from flying over the barrier to the house."

My eyes shifted to the stone amphoras. I shifted my gaze to Mrs. Cox and Sabrina. Lifting them one by one and flying them to Mare's house was possible. They'd be trapped there without my help, but an otherwise impenetrable fortress to keep them protected wasn't the worst idea I'd heard—even if it did mean a lot more work on my part.

At least until I can somehow get Terrance's permission.

An idea formed. "What about the property surrounding Mare's house?"

"The neighborhood has gone considerably downhill since the house was relocated," Anima said.

"Can you buy anything nearby to serve as a staging area?"

"It seems likely Vitae's funds contain sufficient to convince someone to move," Anima said.

"No, not Vitae's funds. I don't want anything drawing his eye to that area. If mine aren't enough, we can borrow from Ignis or Terrance."

"I will arrange it."

"Sounds like a plan," I said.

"Kale, you do realize a two-hundred-year-old house won't include electricity, air conditioning or any other modern amenities, don't you dear?" Mrs. Cox asked.

"That means we can't relocate the laptop I'm using for Anima's communications either," Sabrina said.

I looked at them both. "I'll just have to save Terrance sooner rather than later so he can dig cable lines."

"And modern plumbing," Mrs. Cox said.

Sabrina cringed.

O'Curran

The lieutenant stood stiffly, watching O'Curran tear apart the message he'd brought from communications. O'Curran's eyes flashed up at the man, seeing nothing in the carefully expressionless face.

I wish this was that twice-cursed Vitae's neck.

He hadn't asked whether they had confirmation of the squad's death. His people knew better than to bring death reports without doing their due diligence.

I have to respond to this, but how?

He let his imagination roll through the possibilities, indulging images of tanks tearing through the hotel the phoenix used as a base of operations. O'Curran wished he could turn fantasy into reality. Two problems stood between him and an all-out attack. The area had been designated foreign soil—made an embassy for a countryless people by the religious right who bought Vitae's bull of being sent by God.

O'Curran had no problem leveling the area and dealing with the fallout later. It was actually the other problem that kept him from indulging in a little invasion. Vitae presented him a complicated, compound issue. He was a phoenix and his soldiers seemed nearly as immortal. Altercations with the so-called shields ground and air forces had seen them regrow into fighting trim after anything short of total cremation.

It wouldn't be enough to kill him. I have to find a way to kill him once and for all.

He lurched out of his chair, growling at the lieutenant as he started to pace. "Dismissed."

His thoughts moved to Bradley Sky, the wanted medical examiner working with Vitae. He'd indicated there were good phoenixes. O'Curran didn't put much stock in the showboat fire phoenix being one of the good guys. O'Curran suspected the fire phoenix might be behind some of the spontaneous fires cropping up throughout the city.

An earth phoenix had been caught on camera, but had thus far declined to speak to the press. He wished there was some other way to gauge the earth phoenix as a good one or another asshole. There was a poor-quality video of the showboat fighting a phoenix that seemed to be somehow made of water, but none of his men or drones had seen that one since.

O'Curran stopped, fists tightening.

I need to do something. Vitae can't just be allowed to slaughter soldiers and get away with it.

He closed his eyes, listing the roadblock points he'd set up around Atlanta one by one. When logistical minutia focused him on the big picture, he forced himself to admit that in the absence of better intel, he had no idea who to go to for the help he would need against Vitae.

I'll call up the chain for orders and more intel.

He pulled his phone, settling into the mindset required to survive a conversation with top brass.

Viviane

Despite the risk, Viviane carried the Unseelie Champion blade through Crayola Island down to her grotto. If Mab sought it, Viviane's sister could find and reclaim the sword. Even so, she could not trust it where Dunham might find it.

Letting him have a single Champion blade had been upsetting. He'd grown less and less pliant as he grew more powerful. Having a Sword of Judgement, even without him having full access to its abilities verged on treacherous.

Unlike the children she and her siblings spawned with mortals, she had no soul for the blade to consume. Still, he could kill even her with that blade. If he decided to do just that, she'd be left to the Morning Star's mercies.

That is not the way I'd like to test my standing in his favor.

A subtle ripple in the water forewarned her of a guest. She turned, expecting Mab on the descending stair. Instead, Gherrian eased himself down the spiral steps with exaggerated care.

Viviane assessed his injuries, eyes flicking to the elven sword in his scabbard. He raised his hands before stepping off the lip to fall into her grotto. He hit wrong, legs buckling.

Even his voice carried no strength. "Peace, Great Lady."

"What brings you to me, Knight Gherrian?"

"I am oathed to see the Unseelie Champion blade returned to Atlanta's Shieldheart. I have followed its power to you."

"As it happens, I wish Vitae to have use of the sword and without doubt for the very reason he wishes to possess it."

Gherrian's posture relaxed. "I am grateful you did not make me fight you."

"No." She weighed her options. She hadn't forsworn, but she was not interested in surrendering the sword to Vitae directly. "However, I cannot give you this blade."

Gherrian lifted his eyes, pain in their set.

"You are oathed to see the blade returned to Vitae, so I discharge you of this oath with one in exchange. Take message to Atlanta's Shieldheart that I will surrender the blade to him and free his beloved from its grip as I have already promised, but only once he has brought her egg close enough to catch her soul.

"Deliver this message, Knight Gherrian, and return to me to await his arrival. Hence will you bear witness to that which you have oathed."

"He may not spare me to return, and my queen may not return me to life if he should slay me."

Viviane crossed the space, putting a hand on Gherrian's chest. Power washed out of her as her power mingled into his aura. "I choose you, nephew. You shall rise before me if you fall."

"What of Jahriss?" Gherrian asked.

She smirked. "I'll let him know he's untethered...for now."

Quayla

Briar and forest surrounded Mare's house much like Sleeping Beauty's castle. Anima's warnings of an impassible boundary proved mostly true. I was pretty sure Mar's lessons included a way for me to penetrate the protection, but Terrance wasn't a fledgling.

Challenging his protections without a good reason just seems like a bad idea.

Transmogrifying into my phoenix form in the back yard of the nearest adjoining property, I launched myself airborne over the barrier, skimmed the trees and banked around a small and forlorn unmoving windmill. I landed on a series of stepping stones that led from a carriage house to an early plantation style home.

I transmog'd back into human shape on a lawn grown too long for most HOAs. The grass remained uniform and it didn't overgrow the stepping stones that led to a wraparound porch. Rose bushes and manicured flower beds bloomed like they were in late spring rather than under summer heat without any kind of sprinkler system to keep them watered.

Terrance's abilities seemed the only reasonable explanation for their condition, though I had no idea how he managed the feat while imprisoned.

The whitewashed, wood plank exterior remained clean

despite its age. Up six stairs, old wooden rockers lined the front porch flanking a blue front door with no visible lock.

This house is definitely from another era.

My foot hesitated over the first step.

Mare was long dead.

Otherwise I wouldn't be here.

Vitae's descriptions left the impression she'd have hated me, or at least been severely disappointed in her replacement. It took an effort to force my foot down. Doubt for the two-hundred-year-old step's integrity flashed through me only after I shifted my weight onto the first plank.

They all held my weight—doubts, guilt and all.

The door opened with my lightest touch. An ancient ceiling fan spun despite being disconnected from the series of belts and pullies designed to transfer motive force from the windmill atop the house.

Reaching fingers near the apparatus brought my hand into contact with a tingle reminiscent of Caelum's magic.

A sob took three tries to choke back.

An ancient rug of interwoven blues suggested ocean waves without shouting them outright. Two archways opened up to spaces. The larger was furnished much like Hedingham Castle's living areas—if older, and the smaller contained a stone fountain of some kind. Fine antique tables abutted two staircases that offered sweeping access to the upper level.

This place is huge. It could've housed our whole Shield.

The thought brought doubts to Vitae's claims. With Ignis and Terrance still imprisoned, there wasn't a way for me to ask, but something about the place made me think Mare had wanted the whole Shield within her walls.

Maybe they lived here until her passing made it too painful. That explains why Terrance took such good care of it.

Following the foyer deeper into the house offered a door and two more archways. A kitchen waited opposite a huge dining room. The door led onto the back porch where another meandering line of stepping stones led to a freestanding outhouse.

Five bedrooms awaited me upstairs—four furnished and a fifth entirely empty. The décor in the furnished rooms supported the theory that Mare meant the house for the whole Shield, and the empty room shouted Vitae's stubbornness.

This will work.

Before Americans surcame to greed and an obsession to have more than their neighbors, old houses had been tiny. As such, I'd worried Mare's house might prove too small to function as a base big enough to house Mrs. Cox, Sabrina and Bradley. I hadn't broached the subject of their relocation, but I intended to keep them close for their own protection.

And I am not sure I'll take no for an answer either.

I'd surveyed enough of the house to know that it would serve, though I wasn't sure how my modern human allies would take to living without their normal amenities. As a matter of curiosity, I tried to walk out through Terrance's barrier. It didn't let me leave any more than it let me enter. Once my allies got dropped onto the property, they wouldn't be able to depart.

Guilt and the prospect of loss warred over the idea. I let them go at each other. My first priority was getting my nest set up so a single death wouldn't be the end. After that, I had an egg to retrieve.

Quayla

Sabrina agreed to contact Bradley and request he meet me in Vitae's old warehouse. I'd chosen the warehouse to give Bradley some deniability. Even so and even though I'd used the warehouse to return, being in the heart of Vitae's atrocities left me uneasy.

A tickle of taint edged into my consciousness, feeding on my discomfort to rattle my nerves. I drew my hilts, building long knives twice their normal length with half the discomfort.

The warehouse door eased open.

A taint filled my nostrils unlike any I'd ever scented.

I tensed to spring.

An elf entered, head sweeping back and forth as he blinked away sun blinding.

I sprang, bringing the long knife to the elf's throat.

He froze. "Whoa, stop, stop. Quayla, it's me Bradley."

The warning on my lips hesitated on the edge of my tongue. He resembled the junior medical examiner I'd had rewritten a few times, but the taint wafting off him meant he'd made a deal.

"Um, can you ease off the knife and let me in out of view?"

I jerked him into the warehouse but didn't lower my blade. "Surrender your boon and tell me what Sidhe you traded with to gain supernatural powers."

"I—what? I didn't make a deal, I mean I understand why you might think so, but really, I didn't."

"Bullshit, I can smell that you're generating taint, not just stained from hanging around it."

"I want to help you protect Atlanta. Before I was totally squishy, so I worked out a way to splice Sidhe genes with my own to give me abilities, but I'm not stupid. I didn't trade my soul or sign on as a slave in exchange for supernatural powers."

A hard shove sent him out of my arms, giving me enough space to really study him. Bradley Sky remained under the bald head and pointed ears. The idea that he had experimented with and spliced Sidhe genes into his own body shocked me, but that he'd done so wasn't so surprising.

I had no idea how to deal with the situation.

Is he Fae Kissed? Is he not? What do I do with him now?

I eased my essence back into my body, pointing the empty hilt at him. "I don't like this, and we're not done discussing it, but in the meantime tell me everything I need to know so I can reclaim Mare's egg."

Chapter Twenty

Invasive Choices

Quayla

Anima's success at obtaining an adjoining property allowed me to stage everything that I wanted secured in Mare's house. Mrs. Cox made plenty of noise about the propriety of being lifted over the trees into Mare's yard while wearing a dress, but I nonetheless caught her grinning at wind in her hair.

Sabrina closed her eyes for her trip—forewarned about being scooped up in my talons as Mrs. Cox hadn't been. A serenity washed over her features, vanishing only once her feet touched ground once more.

Bradley ran.

I'd expected the geeky doctor to gibber excitedly about a phoenix taking him into the heavens. Instead, he made me chase him into the ramshackle house in my human form, tear him out of a closet and transmogrify without letting go to keep him in my talons for the transfer.

For a moment, it felt as if he were transmoging with me, but panic locked his wrongness away from my essence. Our contact reinforced my sense that he was Fae Kissed but not. Examination supported his explanations, but didn't ease my unhappiness with the situation.

He isn't Fae Kissed. The rest is free will and His to judge.

I dropped Bradley into Mare's yard. He collapsed onto the grass, unable to catch his breath. He tangled fingers into the grass, refusing to open his eyes or let go.

When I approached, he shied away like a once beaten dog.

"Allow me, dear." Mrs. Cox bent next to Bradley, stroking his back and whispering reassurances. She looked up. "Go inside. We'll follow in a few minutes."

Sabrina followed me inside, expression guarded. I exited into the back to the nests stacked next to the outhouse. She eyed the small out building, lips pushing together, but picked up another of the basins. We climbed the stairs and deposited the nests in the empty bedroom. Several trips brought up all the basins and amphoras. We arranged the nests in the corners with an amphora beside each and two beside mine.

"Nothing for this nest?" Sabrina asked.

My gaze settled onto the fourth nest, a frown walling off the other roiling emotions. I'd meant it for Caelum, but that wasn't possible any more.

"No," I shook my head. "Vita didn't give me any essence for Vitae."

"Why is that?"

I shrugged. "He's not on our side anymore."

"He's a phoenix. He's still trying to protect the city."

All of the anguish over Caelum's absence transmogrified into fury. "Vitae murdered Dylan. He tried to murder me. He's a villain."

"Why?"

"What do you mean why?"

"Quayla, no one wakes up and just decides to be a dirty cop. Sometimes they slip down that slope in a series of tiny compromises, but even as they do, they never think of themselves as the bad guy."

"He's corrupted himself with Sidhe taint," I snapped. "He's no different than any other Fae Kissed."

"Don't you offer Fae Kissed the possibility of redemption?"

A roar of fury and frustration escaped me, bringing Mrs. Cox and Bradley running.

"He has to have a reason for the things he's done," Sabrina said.

"He's a selfish, arrogant, judgmental asshole," I snarled.

A girlish angel appeared, ghostly but simultaneously too real. Wings flapped along her calves and behind her back. An inner light illuminated a swirling rainbow fog around her. Everything around her became the perfect, pristine version of itself. She watched us from a hundred eyes that populated every surface on her body including gemstone eyes that glowed a rainbow across her forehead.

The mortals gaped at the angelic Watcher showing herself in violation of the rules which governed her kind.

Maybe the rules have changed now that humanity knows about the Sidhe.

Only when Anima took my hands into her eyeball-studded fingers did I realize how hard I was shaking. "Quayla, be at peace."

I yanked my hands from her grip, whipping around so none of them could see how upset I was.

"Vitae frightens me," Anima said.

"You and me both," Bradley added. "Oh, sorry."

I couldn't see the look she'd given him for interrupting, but a corner of my lips tried to quirk upward.

"Even so, his motives are pure," Anima said.

I whipped around, crackling icicles spearing out along my skin and sending my friends back several steps. "He murdered Dylan, a mortal he was supposed to protect."

Anima didn't retreat. "So, because he has failed in his duty, you have reason to fail in yours?"

"I'm doing my duty. I came back to protect the city and free my brothers."

"Is not Vitae one of your brothers?" Anima said. "Does he not need freed too?"

"He chose this!"

"And you've never made a choice you later regretted?" Sabrina asked.

I ignored the stab of guilt. "He doesn't regret what he did to Dylan, he claimed murdering a mortal was for the best."

"His choices have imprisoned him in a taint he cannot cleanse," Anima said.

"I think she's right," Bradley said. "Each time Vitae is reborn, his attitude changes. He's continuously mixing in different amounts of Sidhe essence trying to find the right combination."

"For what? More power?" I demanded. "Vitae's a lost cause."

"No," Anima said. "But he needs his Shield to save him."

"From himself!"

Mrs. Cox set a hand on my shoulder. "You're the only one left to help him, dear."

I tore my shoulder from her reach and opened my mouth to yell at the little old lady. Her determined expression froze the words in my mouth. No doubt she'd worn the same expression when she'd charged into Faery to save me from a trap—a trap I'd knowingly volunteered to go into in the good intentioned hopes of saving Judith..

I turned my glower onto Anima instead. "Vitae was an unforgiveable ass long before he started tainting himself."

"But why?" Sabrina asked.

"How in the blighted hells should I know?" I asked.

Sabrina shifted her attention to the Watcher.

An eyeball tipped tongue moistened Anima's lips. "Mare sacrificed herself to save Vitae."

I rolled my eyes.

I'd heard all about Mare's sacrifice.

"Vitae let the Shield get drawn into Court games. His mistakes led to that last battle." Anima hesitated. "He blames himself for Mare's death."

Sabrina's eyes drooped to the floor. A hollowness crept into her voice. "He had no control over what happened, but someone had to shoulder the blame."

"So, I had to suffer because he feels guilty?"

"In a way, yes," Anima said. "You are a living reminder of Mare, Quayla. You and Mare share very similar personalities."

Sabrina's head jerked up, eyes hooded. "Seeing you reminded him of her death. You wouldn't be here if Mare hadn't died."

Pain backlit Sabrina's eyes. She looked fragile, on the edge of shattering. An urge to hold her and offer comfort overpowered me. I reached my arms out to hug her, but she jerked away from my touch.

Wrong gender. I forgot how much she hates men.

"Quayla, dear." Mrs. Cox said. "Helping Vitae doesn't require excusing his wrongdoing. Forgiving him would probably be better for your soul, but even if that's impossible, you should at least try to do the right thing."

The right thing.

Vitae had decapitated the love of my life while we kissed. He'd taken advantage of my love and relief to murder a man I'd have given up everything for if I'd been able.

No. I'll never forgive him.

Still, I'd murdered people too, if not so intentionally. Vilicangelus had refused to kill me despite Vitae's prompting. He'd seen something in me worth saving, and he'd been Vitae's friend.

If Vitae can be redeemed, don't I owe it to Vilicangelus to try?

I couldn't keep my shoulders from falling under the weight of my decision. I'd hate every moment of it, but I'd do the right thing just the same.

Unless Vitae leaves me no choice but to Destroy him.

Anima saw my decision in my face. She offered a cherubic smile and vanished back to her perch between worlds.

"All right, but I'll need Bradley to bring me Vitae's essence."

"But won't that essence be polluted?" Bradley asked.

"Yeah," I sighed, thinking back on the effort used to purify

Hedingham's angry ghost. "I'll have to find a way to filter out the taint in Vitae's essence."

Bradley

Detective Foxner hurried down the porch stairs, placing a hand on Quayla's arm. "Wait, you're leaving? We just got here."

"And I need to go," Quayla said.

"I should go with you," Bradley said. "I know the hotel pretty well, and I can get you past the guards."

Mrs. Cox touched him softly. "No, dear. If you have to bring back this Vitae's essence for Quayla, you can't be part of what she's doing."

Bradley cursed to himself.

Quayla had essence in her nest now, but he couldn't get over the feeling something bad would happen if he wasn't there to help clear the way for her.

Still, I can see why she doesn't want Vitae to know I'm involved.

He imagined the hotel complex, positioning both Sidhe and enforcers. If his estimates of Vitae's true essence to Sidhe essence proved accurate, he'd somehow have to steal huge amounts of essence without getting caught even once.

A pleading note in Quayla's voice drew him back to the conversation. "Look, what I'm about to do could very well blow up in my face. I need to know you're all safe."

"You are not leaving me here," Foxner said.

"Yes, I am," Quayla said. "I have enough dead friends."

"I need to get inside that place." Foxner's expression brooked no argument. "With what Sky's said, he's breaking the law."

Bradley wanted to do something about what Vitae was doing, but Miri had laid out the situation in somehow alluring yet brutal honesty. He echoed her observations. "Yeah, but I can't come forward while being wanted."

"But I can," Foxner said. "I can take anything I see to SNat."

"How are you going to explain your illegal search?" Mrs. Cox asked.

Foxner opened her mouth, but Quayla cut her off. "This is a non-issue. You're not going. No one is."

"What do you expect me to do?" Foxner snarled, sarcasm and vitriol dripping off every word. "Vacuum, dust, have dinner on the table when the mighty hunter returns? I don't think so."

"You're staying here where you're safe, end of story."

"The hell I am," Foxner said."

"Language, Detective," Mrs. Cox said.

He watched them fight, wondering once more at the source of awkwardness in Foxner's stance whenever Quayla entered the room.

Foxner shot Quayla a dirty look. "Even if I agreed that backing you up was the wrong answer—something I am not saying at all —I have a job. I need to be out there doing it."

"She makes a fair point," Mrs. Cox said. "I wouldn't want to neglect my duties as landlady."

"I won't be gone that long," Quayla said.

"And what if you're wrong?" Bradley asked. "What if Vitae puts you into one of the cells he made for the other phoenixes?"

"If things go that wrong, Anima wouldn't leave you here to starve."

Anima's voice emerged from the nearby oracle. "Shield Quayla, the Isaac would be very displeased with that level of inter-vention."

"It won't come to that," Quayla said.

"You hope," Foxner shot back.

Quayla darkened. "I'm trying to keep you safe."

"We're not children, dear," Mrs. Cox said.

"No, you're mortal." Quayla's body shimmered, transforming into pure water. "Look, I've heard what you're saying, and I understand where you're coming from—I really do. You might all be right, but I c-can't risk something happening to you."

Foxner lurched forward as Quayla turned toward the door. Her hand passed through Quayla's arms. The phoenix turned back to them, anguish in her expression as watery wings unfolded from her back. They swept down, launching her into the air and leaving Bradley and the others behind.

"Fucking great," Foxner snarled.

"Detective!" Mrs. Cox scolded.

"Keep your innocent, holier-than-thou act to yourself, old woman," Foxner said. "I ain't buying."

Bradley wandered away as they started arguing in earnest. An idea curled his lips, but he quashed the smile before the others saw. He turned to orbit the yard in a slow, totally inconspicuous stroll. When the house prevented Foxner and Mrs. Cox from seeing, he approached the wall of briar and kudzu-tangled trees.

When he'd first heard about the wall, he'd assumed the earth phoenix maintaining it had attuned it to repel mortals. Learning that it repelled Quayla too nixed the theory. Things he'd overheard at the hotel made him suspect the Unseelie were mostly earth-based fae. If Terrance's wall was intended to repel the Unseelie, then what he was about to try wouldn't work.

This will work. Elves are forest creatures. They can slip through tangles and briars without leaving a trace.

Bradley stepped forward, pushing branches to either side. At first, his idea seemed doomed. Nothing about the barrier seemed willing to allow him penetration any more than his high school crushes had. A moment before he was about to call off the test, the woods parted from his way.

They didn't make a lot of room, and the path closed up in mere seconds.

"Sky!" Foxner shouted. "Wait, how are you doing that?"

The wood responded to Bradley's sudden tension. Branches and briars jabbed into him, tangling his path. He closed his eyes, blocking out the police detective and focusing on the elven ability to pass through thick woods without additional movement cost.

"Come back here!" Foxner shouted. "Don't you dare blow me off! Sky! Stop, damn it!"

Bradley slipped out the last few yards of foliage onto heavily overgrown sidewalk. He smiled, pushed hands into his pockets and strolled around to the house where they'd all parked.

Maybe I can use Quayla's theft to distract from one of my own.

Quayla

After a detour to Caelum's stash where I'd first met Bradley, I landed several streets away from the hotel, ducking behind a restaurant whose dumpster stank almost more than faerie taint.

Mar's teachings hadn't covered what I had in mind, but other things he'd taught me made the ploy seem possible even if it disturbed me more than the nearby rotting food. I settled a small bag from Caelum's stash on the cement.

Transmogrifying into essence, I poured my focus into redesigning my body one section at a time. My legs shifted until they were long and athletically toned. My torso came next, ordered to the lean, wiry strength and ideal proportions that delight artists. My fingers lengthened until their delicacy neared that of my female bodies. The skin I grew beneath flowing silk robes became a sun-touched porcelain with the slighted hint of olive.

Chestnut hair flowed straight yet lustrous around pointed ears and smooth, elongated facial features. Elegant, sweeping eyebrows crowned eyes as emerald as a leprechaun's clovers.

A shimmering cloud of essence extruded for the bottoms of my slender feet, rising to give me mirror reflections to tweak my new elven persona. I dug into the paper bag that I'd retrieved from the cache and removed Wan's amulet. The gold necklace with a golden flame-set ruby pendent hung heavily around my neck.

Wan's necklace against my throat felt like gargling sewage. The potent amount of tainted power flowing through the talisman from its Seelie benefactor suggested the Sidhe either didn't know or didn't care about Wan's destruction.

But it radiates so much Seelie taint, it'll mask me as one of the Sidhe.

An elf sword liberated en route went over one shoulder, completing the disguise.

Adjusting to the new balance and adding the proper swagger took half a block, but by time I approached Vitae's hotel I walked across the parking lot like I owned the place. My electric jelly bean enticed my gaze to its smooth lines. I held off its allure, keeping focus on the two enforcers lurking either side of the door in artificial shadows.

My shoulders bunched, requiring me to maintain lazy river thoughts just under the essence held ready to create a blade.

No, if anything happens, I have to use the sword.

Releasing the readied essence made relaxing my shoulders that much easier, though I couldn't rid myself of all the tension.

They let me through without any objection.

I had time for half a relieved breath before the overwhelming taint of Vitae's hotel nearly cost me the concentration keeping my elven shape.

How can he not sense this and see it for the red flag it is?

Working through Vitae's state of mind had to wait until I wasn't behind enemy lines—the only way to describe what Vitae built to be the new Shield sanctum.

I turned aside to an ascending stair, eyes locked on the doors that led to the lavish audience chamber where Dylan had been executed. A lump formed in my throat, but I clamped down on my control. I couldn't afford to lose it just then.

A little voice, never wholly squashed, used my distress to bolster arguments against using Mare's egg.

I pushed forward, focused on my disguise, the arrogance in each stride, and claiming the egg that could keep me from True Death.

A pair of grendlings guarded the doors to Vitae's private chambers. When I reached out for the handle, one drew a troll-bone knife. "What do you think you are doing?"

In the all-pervading taint, the scent of a long-stagnant low tide coming off of him barely registered. I backhanded the grendling, outlining a section of his blueberry mold colony into a new purplish blotch. "You do not have leave to address me, filth."

The other one drew his weapon. "We are empowered by the Master to—"

"Stop people he has summoned? Interfere with his wishes?"

They gave each other uneasy looks.

I curled a lip and gave them an arrogant sneer. "By all means, filth, divert his ire at me onto yourselves."

"Shut up and get inside, Elf," the first said. "Master requires your attendance."

"Of course, *filth*." An arrogant chuckle covered the sudden pressure of an insistent nervous titter.

The study inside mimicked the one Vitae held in headquarters save his fireplace had no crystal figurines tied to our essence. Expensive paintings and old tapestries covered the walls, interrupted only by two empty sword mounts. Antique wood and old leather clothed the room in a costume centuries out of date.

Doors at the far side of the room emptied into a small antechamber. A great circle glowed to life the moment my foot stepped into the room. Taint stench had hidden the Sidhe trap from my notice, but the sudden surge of magic gave me a moment's warning. Transmogrifying flesh to essence, I beat the assault by mere instants.

Power seized me and tore me, working to rip my every molecule apart. Before Essex and Mar's lessons, the disintegration ward would've meant my death.

I let the magic tear me apart, riding agony with my will focused on not losing the atomized molecules of water that made up my person. When the magic waned, I brought my body back together and took care to watch for more traps.

Three sets of doors closed off unknown worlds. Bradley's information claimed the left door led to Mare's suites. I held my breath and pulled upon the doors.

Dunham

Building security notified Dunham the moment Ignis approached from his latest mission. Dunham collected the burning heart he'd hired Dolumii to rip from Ignis's chest and waited for the fire phoenix to enter.

It took quite a bit longer than Dunham would've preferred, draining the hourglass of his patience to the last few grains.

This isn't meant to be some kind of vacation.

Dunham smelled the burning wood and carpet before Ignis rounded into view climbing the spiral stair. He could've landed on the outside balcony and been let inside, but instead he'd insisted on accidentally burning his way up from the lobby.

I'd punish him, but I can't keep the divine much longer without another phoenix.

"Stop there and cease burning the floor."

Ignis took two extra steps.

Dunham's jaw tightened. His grip on the flaming heart tightened as did Ignis's expression. Dunham didn't apply enough pressure to cause a lot of pain, but he couldn't hold all of his temper in check.

"You aren't going back into your cage just yet. Stand there and do not move." Dunham crossed to the control console, keying the sequence that released Terrance from his cage.

With his essence resources so low, there was a lot of risk in sending all of the phoenixes fueling the containment spell out on mission. Even so, Viviane had been correct. Sending both to fetch Vitae was the best way to ensure success.

Once Terrance stood next to Ignis, Dunham went through

the commands to keep them under control. Ignis didn't fight him, setting Dunham's nerve to jangling. The fire phoenix seemed pleased to be sent out with his earth counterpart.

Let's see how he likes the mission.

"You two will go to an address I provide, capture your Shieldheart and fly him back here."

Both phoenixes darkened.

"You will not kill him. You will not get distracted by anything else. You will travel in full phoenix form and use every ability at your disposal to subdue Vitae, bring him here and place him in his cage. Acknowledge command and your compliance."

The both spoke their acknowledgements.

"Good. Begin now. Do not fail."

Chapter Twenty-One

Tangled Talons

Quayla

Just as Bradley described, pillows atop of a marble pillar cradled Mare's egg. It didn't pulse like my egg had, though a small glow lit its interior. I crossed to the egg, easing my fingers between the lines of celestial silver to the sapphire shell beneath. A soft thrum tingled up from where I touched the surface, but nowhere near what my own egg had produced.

And without the echoing touch on my skin.

"What the hell are you doing in there, slave?"

I whirled to come face to face with Vitae.

Maybe my attention should've focused on the taint he radiated or the state of his soul, but all I could see was the sudden red mist of blood from Dylan's decapitation.

"Aquaylae," Vitae snarled. His hands reached behind him into his suite. The Unseelie champion blade came to his call, faces moaning in torment as his fingers wrapped into position around the hilt. "How dare you soil Mare's egg? You will not postpone your destruction by eliminating my Shield's true aqua!"

My initial impulse was to remind him that Mare was gone, but the madness in his eyes seemed quite clear. He wouldn't believe even Vita, maybe not even Vilicangelus—God cradle his soul against Destruction. There was no way for me to know how he'd known me through the disguise, but with the cat out of the bag there seemed no reason to maintain the farce. I drew my hilts, letting my elven disguise fall away.

"In the name of the Undying Light, I command you to surrender the boon of faerie magic and atone for your sins against the Creator."

Vitae purpled. "You?! Have the audacity to accuse me of sins? And dare command me?"

I couldn't keep the heat from my voice. "I *want* to kill you, Vitae, more than you can possibly know, but I have a duty—"

"Duty?" Vitae snorted, rolling his shoulders to loosen them. "You know nothing of duty. You're nothing but a wafer-lusting whore long overdue for True Death."

My fingers tightened on the Karambit hilts strangled in my grip. "Will you surrender the Sidhe power you've stolen and surrender yourself in hope of absolution?"

His answer was a screaming charge.

The Champion blade went straight for my heart without elegance or guile—an attack which surprised me from the skilled warrior. The tip of the sword rocketed for my heart in gradually lengthening moments.

I had a nest with essence enough for several rebirths, but if Mar and Vita were to be believed, the sword in his hand could devour my soul—possibly even without having to deal an otherwise fatal blow.

A center-grip shield washed out from the finger guard of my left hilt in a swirling wave. A counter clockwise current given the large disk shoved the tip of Vitae's sword out of line.

The shield, its flash flood speed and the current took Vitae off guard, though only for a moment. A bladed knuckle guard extended from the other hilt. I twisted my wrist and reformed the hand in a reverse grip that shifted the guard ring from index finger to pinky.

A surge of taint and the rise of hair along my arm offered the only warning of the arcing magic that slammed into me.

Muscles convulsed, bringing limbs in close to my body.

Faeries rushed into the room.

A coyll brandished a bronze kukri. "Master?"

"Get out," Vitae grinned, realigning his soul-devouring sword for the next thrust. "She's all mine."

Hep-Silat was a fluid martial art. The style required flexible movements that the sudden electrical strike made impossible.

Probably why the bastard used it.

A cross body slap moved my shield out of his path.

He thrust.

My transmogrified legs dropped me beneath his strike. Using his slap for extra momentum, the whirlpool of my liquid legs spun the rest of me to bring the shield around into a leg sweep.

He leapt back, but without the arrogant smirk.

Will brought my legs back under me with one in place to kick the lunging Vitae straight in the jaw. He disengaged, eyeing me with a look of consternation.

"This is a farce, an illusion on the part of Lucifer's whore. You cannot be Aquaylae."

Heat built in my core, but Mar's lesson allowed me to believe it away. "Why's that, Vitae?"

"Aquaylae is an ignorant, lazy incompetent with nowhere near this level of skill."

The heat returned.

I shifted my hilt into the top of my right forearm and opened an oval in the shield just above my left fist. "Just because you refused to teach doesn't mean I can't learn."

"Aquaylae would've died as pathetically as her filthy mortal."

The volcanic undersea vent opened up within me.

Maybe Vitae really was so arrogant he couldn't believe I might learn from someone else.

Maybe he was just baiting me, trying to anger me enough to undermine my focus.

He needn't have bothered.

I'd known I might have to face him. I'd known I might have to look into the face of the bastard that had murdered Dylan and still offer him redemption.

Dylan loved me. He'd have wanted me safe from True Death. He'd never have asked me to avenge him at the cost of my own life. That realization had allowed me to encase grief and fury and indignation in ice.

Left to their own devices, they'd have been my undoing.

Walling the festering emotions away had unshackled me—if only temporarily—to face the older, more experienced jackass on roughly even footing. That liberty allowed me to maintain the elven disguise and penetrate his defenses. That freedom allowed me to keep my focus and even surprise my former Shieldheart.

I'm not about to surrender that to his paltry bait.

"This is your last warning, Vitae. Surrender your boons and seek absolution."

His voice pitched upward. "Or what? You'll Destroy me? The likes of you haven't the skill no matter what lessons you've learned."

"So be it," I said. "I'll try not to enjoy this."

He attacked.

His sword danced from hand to hand in a whirling attack I could barely see. He moved even faster than Aether, but because of her training I slipped away from his onslaught.

Stilettos of ice shot through the shield's gap. I kept on the move as they impaled him, aquakinesis bending their flight into Vitae's flesh.

He slowed, reaching to pull one from a shoulder.

It grew barbs as he pulled, tearing away flesh. He yanked another barbed spike out, his sneer not disguising his purple-faced rage.

Vitae transmogrified, liquid essence filling in the holes.

Finally.

Wings shot out of my back. The shield narrowed to a wedge

and a short blade slid out of the hilt atop my forearm. I cartwheeled into Vitae, slicing him into chunks starting with the wrist holding the sword.

In our liquid forms, few things could truly hurt us. If Vitae knew the things I'd been taught about self-identity—something I suspected hadn't ever been one of Vitae's weaknesses—he'd be able to move his body parts as if still connected.

For that reason, I transmogrified into pure essence and wrapped around him. He pulled himself back together and I used his intent to encase him within a box of viscous essence.

I'd braced myself for the nausea of touching his tainted essence. A wave of exhaustion ambushed me, washing through me behind a battering ram of vertigo. Images of kudzu shriveling around Vitae in the Marriott flashed across my mind's eye.

He's draining my life.

The repulsion of a cockroach running across my fingers almost made me flinch. Rage bullied it to one side, burning a red haze across my vision. I shifted the essence touching him into a wall of ice.

He tried to concentrate his essence. Had I still been under the misapprehension that I had to manage heat energy transfer, he might've been able to form some kind of attack. Instead, I trusted my Creator with the details, willing my ice to constrict with him. I thanked Dylan and some writer named Terry to grow legs beneath my square body.

Vitae gave up on compacting himself and tried instead to expand as my makeshift turtle legs did their best scurry into Mare's bedroom.

The coyll reappeared, assessed the situation and leapt atop me. He drove his knife into my top, forcing me to sacrifice a leg to prevent him offering Vitae a crack through which to escape.

The light Anseelie slowed me, but not enough. I made it to Mare's bathroom and stretched a pseudopod up to the nearest tap. Claiming the water as it emerged, I prepared to reform enough of my normal body to deal with the Sidhe.

I'm going to win.

The far wall exploded.

Flaming debris rocketed through Mare's room. Miniature comets ignited bedcovers and carpets, smashed pillars and sent Mare's egg wobbling across the burning floor.

Ignis and Terrance stood in the hole when the firestorm cleared,

Regret filled Terrance's words. "I'm sorry about this, little sister."

Bradley

Bradley pulled the rented cargo van to a stop near the hotel's entrance. He turned around, suppressing a sigh. "Did you really have to wear your SCA garb, Billy?"

"We're storming a fortress filled with fantasy characters." Billy beamed. "Of course, I did."

To an extent, Bradley's four friends would've stood out inside Vitae's domain no matter what they wore. Billy had lost his hair like Bradley, but incongruously not his beard. Tattooed symbols glowed across his arms and bare chest.

Dave's garb filled the other end of the spectrum, a high court bard to Billy's barbarian chic. An ancient-looking lyre somehow conjured for their heist hung cross body over one shoulder opposite a half cloak.

Eric looked his normal smarmy self, but that wouldn't stay the case. Billy's relentless teasing had exposed the changes gifted Eric by the gene splicing. When angered, Eric's skin had shifted to a dark grey. His long hair went from brown to a metallic silver and a haze of smoke hung around him.

Rebecca's change had been the most drastic. Bradley had concealed his long-time crush on the tall woman, but even smitten with Miri, he couldn't look at the new Rebecca without yearning for her. She'd lost a few inches of height, becoming lithe and willowy. The extra mass had shifted into two angelic wings tipped with rainbow pinions that matched her painted fingers.

She'll never hold down a day job again—okay, well maybe remote office work, but it wouldn't take much for her to use her new powers to make a living as an artist now.

A comet slammed into the second floor of the hotel. The impact rocked the van. Faeries ran toward the tumult.

Huh.

Bradley gestured to the line of brand-new plastic gas cans. "Grab those. We're never going to get a better chance at this."

Dave grabbed the red containers, passing one to Bradley and two to Eric before picking up the last.

Billy hopped out of the van's rear doors, grinning like a mad berserker. His nine remaining fingers wrapped the hilts of the two short, heavy blades at his waist. Bradley wasn't sure why Billy's transformation had cost him a finger when everyone else had gained rather than lost elements—especially considering the troll regeneration spliced into their DNA.

Rebecca followed, scanning the area, more self-conscious than afraid. Eric and Dave stepped down, the latter shutting the back doors. Bradley turned in time to see Miri take over the driver's seat. "You sure about this?"

She sipped her coffee, setting the mug down on the island between seats. "You need to guide them. It's far more efficient to have someone functioning as a wheel man. With your friend Tommy unwilling, that only leaves you one friend."

Bradley chewed his lip. "I really wish you'd taken the injection."

She arched an eyebrow. "I'm not good enough for you as is?"

His gut knotted.

Billy banged on the van door. "Date on your own time, Sky."

"I know what you meant." Miri smirked, grabbed him behind the neck and pulled them into their first, quick kiss. "For luck."

"Did you just quote Star Wars?"

She shooed him. "Go on, you'd better hurry."

Bradley led the way toward a side door. A pair of grendlings stuck to their post despite expectations.

"You're sure you can't turn us invisible?" Dave asked. "We look like we're about to burn the place."

"I can turn me invisible, but I'm not the problem," Bradley marched up to a side door out of view of the road. "Open up."

The nearest of the little blueberry creatures sneered at him. "Use another door, human."

Bradley scanned the lot for one of the patrolling enforcers. "Do you know who I am? I'm performing a service for the Master. Let me inside this moment."

"Master's busy, wafer. Buzz off." The grendling put a hand on his weapon. "Or els—"

Writhing tentacles rose from a bog of smoke, wrapping around the two grendlings. Mouths screamed silent torment as purple bodies shriveled away

Malevolent giggling turned Bradley around.

All-encompassing miasma obscured Eric, allowing only the coal bright of his eyes to leak through. "Oh, baby. What a rush."

Rebecca gasped. "Oh my god, did you just suck away their life?"

Eric giggled again. "Well, it all drained through me, but I don't think I got to keep it all."

"Where'd the rest go?" Dave asked.

Eric shrugged and giggled again.

Bradley kicked the grendling remains off to one side and tried the door. He unlocked it with a spell and hurried them down a small side stairway. The huge metal door brought them all up short. Getting out hadn't been too big a problem, but getting in was another story. Bradley had managed to piggyback other Sidhe up until that moment, but he couldn't wait for a witness.

Luckily Vitae is ignorant when it comes to modern tech.

Bradley produced his phone and played back Vitae's throat-gargling password. He pushed a pulse of magic at the door to complete the unlock sequence and stood to one side to let it open.

A line of five trollmen blocked the entrance.

"Over there," Bradley said. "Stand along the wall."

The trollmen turned, shambling out of Bradley's path.

"What are you simpletons doing?" An elven spell slinger emerged from the back room. "You need to protect our Master. We're under assault."

Bradley narrowed his eyes. "What were you doing back there?"

"None of your business, wafer. Who are these other mortals?"

Bradley ignored the question. "We're about Master's business. You're not allowed back there, Seelie."

A battle cry heralded a rush of Seelie. They slammed open the door otherwise held closed by the elf. Bradley and the elf worked spells simultaneously. Two bedraggled elven knights charged their little group while other Seelie helped the weakest of them from Vitae's prison.

A twinge of guilt shot through Bradley on the heels of his spell. He felt for all the creatures Vitae had imprisoned, but battle was engaged. What happened next came down to survival.

Quayla

A stony cestus shattered my sudden elation. Half reformed but still connected to the box containing Vitae like a genie to his lamp, the blow sent me careening into the wall.

Terrance landed beside me with a double battle glove slam to the rigid ice box. Any other ice would've shattered, but not with my will focused on holding the ice together against Vitae's struggle to escape.

"We are ordered to capture and bring Vitae to Dunham at the exclusion of all other priorities, Quayla," Ignis said. "Escape Vitae now before Dunham learns of your presence and changes our orders. You cannot hope to prevail against both of us."

What? Vitae hasn't captured me.

On the one hand, Ignis wasn't wrong. Defeating him and Terrance together wasn't within my abilities. I hadn't come to capture or kill Vitae. I'd come for the egg laying in the room's corner.

On the other hand, if Dunham got his hands on Vitae and placed him under his control, I'd be hard pressed to survive what followed. Also, there was no way to know if Terrance or Ignis would try to capture me once their priority mission had been completed.

Apparently, I took too long thinking it over.

Ignis threw a jet of superheated flames at the box, melting the frozen essence keeping Vitae contained. He exploded out of my grip in a wave of scarlet and gold plasma.

The fallen Champion blade rocketed into his grip from the other room. He lunged the moment it met his fingers.

A handspring escaped the strike. Kicking the coyll into his path fouled his assault enough to allow me to complete reforming.

Vitae's blow knocked the coyll airborne. The grey and tan canid broke a dent in the dry wall, but Vitae's berserker charge left me no time to follow whatever the coyll did next.

Both hands wove circles in front of me, creating an inter-twining swirl of shifting ice to foul his flurry of blows.

Rogue debris stole my footing.

I hit the floor, my defense evaporating.

Vitae surged forward for the kill.

Terrance's body slammed into Vitae, sending the life phoenix into Mare's bathroom without using the door.

Ignis sprinted into the door with a snarl.

Almost-black, crimson tendrils whipped out of the bathroom, spearing the fire phoenix's flesh in a dozen places. Ignis transmo-grified to flame, but Vitae's tendrils didn't release him.

269

I was on my feet and charging to Ignis's rescue without giving it much thought. Tendrils impaled me.

Vertigo and sudden weakness stole my strength. Ice wrapped Vitae's barbed tentacles as I forced myself into vapor and backed away.

Ignis didn't have my defense.

Vitae sucked away the life and fire of Ignis's essence, drawing back with the Champion blade to finish Ignis once and for all.

I threw a storm of ice shards at the life phoenix, using all but the last shreds of my essence. The assault did little to his plasma body, but the barrage knocked the sword from his grip.

Vitae vamped away the last of Ignis's essence and leveled his hatred at me with burning green eyes.

He recovered his sword, but Terrance's charge bought me time to recover myself.

Far below our feet, a savage roar shook the building.

Chapter Twenty-Two

At Each Other's Throats

Bradley

A half dozen blue bolts swarmed the Seelie spell slinger. The elf released a wave of golden magic just before Bradley's missiles tore into him. Bradley turned from the downed elf and his apparently unfinished spell to the approaching knight.

Billy stepped between the two casters just before the first knight reached Bradley. Blood ran down Billy's beard from a bitten lip. His two heavy swords flashed through the air, crude iron matched by the elf knight's elegant blade.

Tentacles swarmed the other knight, but his sword cut them away before any could get a firm grip. Dave stepped forward, pulling his lyre over his head. His first strum slammed a wave of sound into the struggling knight. Blood trickled from the elf's ears, but he kept his feet—until the tentacles got him.

"What do I do?" Rebecca asked

"Um," Bradley danced left and right, trying to get a direct line of sight on the elf knight fighting Billy. "Can you stop the others from escaping?"

Her pitch rose. "How?"

Try as he might, Bradley couldn't get a clear shot into the

frenetic melee. Billy wasn't fairing badly. He'd taken a couple of attacks, but they didn't seem to bother him.

"Put something between them and the door," Dave strummed his lyre, magic dancing out of his fingers to encompass the instrument. Its neck grew, the body widened and flattened into a bass guitar—one edge growing a long metal blade.

"Talk about playing an axe," Eric hurled bolts of swirling darkness at the other Seelie. A huge fist slammed down onto Eric, cutting off the mad cackling.

Bradley glanced toward the sudden silence.

A trollman bent, picked up Eric by an arm and leg and started to pull.

"No," Bradley abandoned helping Billy, rushing to Eric's side. "Put him down."

The next nearest trollman threw a spiked fist at Bradley. He hit the deck, eluding the strike by virtue of enhanced speed and countless schoolyard bullies.

Dave's axe chopped through the arm of Eric's attacker, hampering the creature's ability to tear Eric in two—if only temporarily.

Bradley rolled away from the trollman's attempt to stomp any part of him he could.

Rebecca screamed.

Another two trollmen trudged toward her and her partially-complete painting. Rough stone blocked most of the doorway, a finished waterfall spilling water across the linoleum tiles.

Bradley threw an arc of flame into the trollman's face. All creatures fear fire, more so the trollmen who were only slightly less allergic to the element than desiccated undead.

Rebecca screamed. "Billy!"

The nine-fingered berserker winked out of existence.

Billy decapitated the elven knight from behind and winked again.

He appeared behind the two trollmen grabbing his wife, sweeping his swords through their knees.

He winked out and back in between them, cackling like a bloody hatter and lopping off their arms. Roaring with blood lust, he dismembered the two trollmen into regrowing chunks the size of chicken nuggets.

Despite shadow magic and musical sorcery, Dave and Eric had their hands full with the other two trollmen.

The burning trollman attacking Bradley decided smothering the flames against Bradley seemed the best way to make the pain stop. Pinned, burning and under the massive weight, he did the only thing he could think to do.

He released the power pent up within him.

Muffled sounds of battle and repeated washes of magic reached him as Eric's aura edged in to swallow Bradley's consciousness. Blackness took all but a last north star.

The star exploded with a nova of light. Lukewarm goop flooded over him as a headless elven knight kicked a thick trunk of severed trollman torso off Bradley's face. He struggled an arm free, wiping viscous fluids from his mouth and nose. "Get this thing off of me and help my friends.

The weight vanished, letting Bradley choke down several lungfuls of rot and decay-filled air.

The undead knight joined his equal in aiding Dave. Eric cowered behind the musician, holding a writhing wall between himself and the trollmen.

To one side, Billy waded through almost-helpless Sidhe, cutting them down with bloody-grinned glee.

Rebecca's fingers flashed through the air, painting little still flames on the regrowing trollmen chunks. Each picture's fire burst into real flame as soon as she deemed the image complete.

Water cascaded around her feet. The endlessly falling water extinguished smaller fires and washed away paints, making her start over again and again.

Bradley had no stomach for killing weak prisoners, but he knew their safety made it a necessity. He left the slaughter to Billy and sent two, thin flame lances through the trollmen facing Dave.

He trudged to the spell slinger.

The Seelie elf lay unconscious at Bradley's feet, unable to defend himself. Bradley glanced at Billy.

Do I call him over to do the deed?

Bradley pushed the cowardly thought away. This was his mission. He'd brought them here. If anyone deserved to stain his soul by murdering the beautiful elf, it was him.

I'm already a monster. Why make them share my fate?

Bradley bent, collected the elf's long knife and went at the Seelie's throat. Cutting off his head, even with the magically sharp blade, was an arduous, bloody affair that coated his forearms and splattered his chest.

A roar from the rearmost lab shot terror through Bradley's guts, nearly turning them to water. He bolted upright to find the others standing at a distance around him.

"Rebecca, how long will it take to move that rock face?"

"I-I don't know," she squeaked, glancing nervously at the lab's rear doors. "I don't have a finger with paint thinner."

Bradley squared his shoulders and collected a gas can. "Paint us an exit to the surface along that wall. I'll be right back."

Ignis

Ignis reformed in a swirl of putrid flames. Tiled walls and a tiny window walled him and a single bunk in the small cage.

That insufferable bastard sucked away my life!

Red rage a thousand times stronger than any he'd ever felt burned like a nova at his center.

He'll die! Dunham will die! They'll all die!

Ignis let his rage escape in a roar that painted the walls in fire. He threw his essence at floor and ceiling, walls and door. The bastard druid's cage had held his fury, but Vitae's paltry walls melted and burned.

His essence returned in an eyeblink, launched from cupped hands in a column as thick as his waist at the doors and walls before him.

Movement flashed in his peripheral vision.

He sent torrents of flame at the slightest motion without a thought as to their nature. His brain had room for only one thought.

Vitae must burn!

O'Curran

The first lieutenant in charge of communications burst into O'Curran's office without so much as a knock. "Colonel, our scouts are reporting a major altercation at Vitae's embassy. Four phoenixes are going at one another."

O'Curran leapt to his feet. "How do you—forget it. Recall everyone not securing the perimeter. Order them to converge on the facility."

"What's our objective, sir?"

"Tell the men to stand by until I arrive, but we're going to get a little payback."

"How?"

"By helping whoever is attacking Vitae."

Vitae

Power surged into me as I drank in Ignis's essence. It was only right that Ignis should fuel Aquaylae's execution. He'd interfered with my triumphant cleansing of the corrupted young phoenix.

And now Ignis is free to join by my side, protected from the druid's spell by the Sidhe essence in his new body.

I snapped up my sword, turning to find the whore-bitch.

Terrance charged at me, once more stopping me from dealing the justice Aquaylae deserved. He threw a fist at me, intent to hammer plasma with stone.

Ignorant thug.

I let the blow land, willing my essence to capture his arms. Once I'd consumed his essence and given him rebirth in the prepared nest, he'd join Ignis in my service. We'd storm the druid's fortress, slay the Fae Kissed wafer and force the Anseelie queen to free Mare.

Agony knifed into my plasma body.

Shockwaves of pain crippled my thoughts. Sickness flooded me, driving my magic from reach.

The follow-up blow worsened my anguish a thousand times over.

My brain split and split again as I struggled to focus will. Terrance's fists in my essence connected us, but either his stone or the druid-bespelled battle gloves prevented my giving him rebirth by stealing the life from his enslaved body.

"Terrance!" Aquaylae yelped.

Three trollman grabbed Terrance, tearing him off of me. Even separate, the viciousness of the surrogate-delivered druid's assault left me gasping and weak.

Aquaylae leapt to Terrance's rescue, wielding thin, short swords of glowing essences. Her atypical weapons hacked limbs from my enforcers, only worsening my coming retribution.

An Unseelie spell slinger unleashed a lightning storm into Aquaylae's back. She staggered, somehow staying on her feet despite the onslaught. She stumbled away from Terrance's aid, fell to hands and knees and crawled from the fight.

I managed my feet in time to realize her target.

Aquaylae seized Mare's egg, defiling the holy vessel with her filthy hands. Whether she thought to stop Mare for supplanting her or thought to stave off True Death by mere proximity to an egg, I didn't care. I crossed Mare's suite, throwing my forces from my path.

My tendrils sank their fangs into her essence.

I drank deep, empowered by the potency of her life force.

Ice crystalized the essence beneath my touch, cutting me off from her life force. It didn't matter. I'd drawn enough to repair the damage from Dunham's foul spell and slay her.

Fingers wrapped Dolumii's hilt, the grip writhing to fit my hand.

Terrance threw off his attackers in time to watch me Destroy Aquaylae once and for all.

I thrust the blade, will focused on devouring her soul.

What if she poisons Mare against me like she has the others?

The sudden fear brought me up short.

The doorway disintegrated in a blast of fire too hot for even my plasma form to survive.

Ignis burned me to death, but I smiled through the pain.

Aquaylae is finally gone...True Dead.

Quayla

My new body reformed with an alacrity I'd never experienced, practically glowing with vitality. Lustrous, dark hair fell down across olive-brown breasts and muscular arms.

"Quayla, what happened?"

Before I could answer Ani, Sabrina charged into the room.

"Who the hell do you think—" The now-shorter woman stopped dead, jaw slack with shock and pupils wide. "—you...are?"

"'What's the problem?"

Anima answered for Sabrina. "The mortal Bradley escaped the property and followed you to Vitae's."

I cursed.

Sabrina marched forward, flushed and red-faced. "Who the hell do you think you are imprisoning me here?"

"I'm keeping you safe," I said. "And I don't have time to argue with you right now. Apparently, I need to go rescue Bradley."

"Quayla?" Mrs. Cox stopped dead in the door. "Heavens above, look at you."

"You two can gawk later. Right now, I need to go."

Sabrina grabbed me by the arm. "You will deliver me back outside the briars or I swear to Jesus I'll set the whole thing on fire."

I let her hear my exasperation. "You'd just be trapping yourself in an inferno."

"Maybe, or maybe I'd get free or maybe I can convince some firefighter to air lift us out of here."

"Fine." I snarled. "Ani, where did Mare keep her hilts?"

I fetched two hilts from behind a sliding panel beneath the stairs. They weren't anything like mine, but they'd serve until I reclaimed my own. I transmogrified and carried both women outside Mare's property.

I hated freeing them with Atlanta so unsafe, but I didn't have time for an extended argument. I dropped them without saying a word and turned wing toward Vitae's fortress.

Detective Foxner

Sabrina screamed.

She'd gotten Quayla to let her out of Sleeping Beauty's prison yard, but being unceremoniously dropped and discarded hadn't been what she wanted.

She needs my help.

<*She wouldn't treat me like this if I was supernaturally gifted like Sky.*>

Sky's mad science offered her a way to face SNat criminals on even footing. It also robbed Quayla of any excuse she might use to leave Sabrina behind.

Just not sure I want to trust Sky's miracle science for random powers.

<Of course, there are other ways to enhance myself.>

"Detective?"

Sabrina turned, reply sharper than intended. "Yes, Mrs. Cox?"

"You have the look about you of someone about to make a destructive choice."

"Only for the bad guys."

Vitae

I willed myself forward even as my body finished forming. Aquaylae had been Destroyed, but Dunham's creatures stood between me and Mare. I snapped up a combat baton, filled it with essence, and grabbed an elf sword on my headlong charge into Mare's nearly-destroyed suite.

An Unseelie spell slammed an ice storm into Ignis and the Sidhe fighting his new female body. I hurled my essence axe at Terrance, slid beneath a follow up blow and scooped Dolumii's sword from the floor.

Terrance fell on me before I'd fully spun to meet him. Swords met diamond and iron battle gloves. His stone skin shrugged off my blows like a duck's back shed water. Before I found weaknesses I could exploit, Ignis assaulted Terrance with volcanic fury.

The blast of fire tore through Mare's wall and ceiling, disintegrating part of the third floor and setting my library alight. The afront of assaulting my ancient tomes turned my fury from Terrance to Ignis.

Terrance also shifted his attack onto the turncoat fire phoenix.

More Sidhe poured into the room.

Ignis bathed the suite in fire.

A torrent of bathroom marble and tile shards disintegrated as they shot into Ignis's true fiery form. Melted stone and globs of glowing glass peppered the floors, starting small fires.

I threw my essence into Ignis, hesitating barely an instant before drawing in his life. A nimbus of white fire destroyed my assault. Hurled bolts of the same gouged chunks from Terrance.

A pillar of earth shot up three floors like a red clay geyser, creating a temporary palisade between Terrance and Ignis. Looser earth fell across the fire phoenix in a wave, but he rolled out from beneath it before it could smother his fire.

Terrance exposed his back to me.

Both fought against me, but Terrance fared better against Ignis than my own attacks. Loath as I was to use the water flooding Mare's shattered bathroom, I combined Unseelie magic with city water against Ignis.

Earth and ice slammed into Ignis, threatening to extinguish his fire. Steam and the scent of growing things filled the room.

I needed Terrance on my side.

I wasn't sure what about Aquaylae's attack had soiled Ignis's new body, but with her True Dead, she couldn't repeat the corruption when Terrance was reborn into my service. I positioned myself to deal him a fatal blow the moment our combined assault subdued the fire phoenix.

Ignis dropped back in a quick retreat. He swept a hand through his former remains, transmogrifying into human form.

Kudzu shot out of the mud soiling Mare's carpet. Rather than attempt to ensnare Ignis, they shot around my throat like a noose. I drew the life from the plants faster than Terrance managed to feed them. They shriveled around me, but even dead the intertwined vines squeezed my throat.

In our distraction, we'd failed to notice Ignis extrude a flaming katana from his hilt until it chopped down to cleave Terrance in half. The earth phoenix dodged backward, leaving the sword to sever the vines tying me to Terrance.

Terrance decked Ignis, the stone battle glove caving in the

bottom of Ignis's face. He transmogrified, rebalanced and threw twin jets of fire at Terrance. Walls, carpet and furniture remains behind the earth phoenix ignited.

Ignis had his back to me.

I could draw away his life once more, but the nest I'd prepared only held a single rebirth.

If I kill him, he'll end up back in Dunham's cage, but will that purge him of whatever Aquaylae did to him?

The sudden wave of mud signaled my hesitation too long. It engulfed Ignis from behind. The fire phoenix transmog'd, charging Terrance with a white-hot flame lance. The will-sharpened lance slammed into Terrance's chest, the tip mushroomed against granite exterior.

Kyrie swept in through the broken walls. They seized Ignis and Terrance. Wings beat hard, dragging the struggling phoenix to the floor's edge.

Ignis burst into flame, immolating his shrieking captor.

It took two to tear Terrance away from me, but the moment they ran out of floor the three plummeted to a crowd of trollman in the parking lot.

More kyrie swooped at Ignis, trying to force the winged human inferno toward their stronger allies.

A spray of water deluged Ignis.

He transmogrified into his true form, vaporizing the water and perfuming the air with ocean scent.

I rushed to the edge of Mare's destroyed suite. Mortal soldiers surrounded us arrayed for battle. Firetrucks blasted Ignis with salted water that couldn't penetrate his intense heat.

Fury consumed me.

That the worthless mortals dared march against me ignited a fury normally reserved for Aquaylae.

And she'll have had something to do with this no doubt.

They had to be taught a lesson, but on the off chance Aquaylae had survived, I would not focus on them so the whore-bitch could steal Mare's egg while my attention was diverted. I scooped up the egg and yanked Scurith up by the scruff of his neck

"Master?"

I shoved the egg into his hands. "Take this. Make sure it remains safe on pain of my wrath."

The coyll's ears pressed against his head in fitting terror. "Yes, Master."

I shoved Scurith toward the door and turned back to the gaping hole. Power welled up from my feet, coalescing in my sparking hands. Toes on the edge, I shared Scurith's fear with the mortals by virtue of a fantastic lightning storm. Arcs of lighting wreaked havoc in a widening arch before me.

My voice rode the thunder. "I command you to stop!"

A smaller thunder barely had time to reach my ears as my head exploded.

O'Curran

Vitae's head exploded.

O'Curran had shouted orders for his sniper to take the shot, but hadn't been sure anyone could hear him over the cacophonous thunder.

The lightning vanished feet from his cowering men, only setting alight the lead vehicles used for cover.

The fire and earth phoenixes laid into one another, doing plenty of damage to Vitae's trollmen enforcers and the property at large.

O'Curran shouted into his comm until he realized he couldn't hear his own shouts. The sight of blood running down the neck of the nearest soldier made him check his own ears. Fingers came back coated.

A sergeant appeared in front of him, red faced and yelling despite the ear-ringing and silence. His gesticulating point shifted

O'Curran's attention to Sky and a small group of misfits emerging from a previously nonexistent subway exit. They rushed three gas cans to a rental van.

Sky appeared again, running back toward the subway.

The van pulled away in a rush.

O'Curran shouted for the sergeant to stop the van, but the man had blood coming out of his ears too.

Bradley

Bradley rushed through the lab, snapping up important possessions. The others had gone with as much essence as he could gather in short order. The fire phoenix had almost slaughtered them all in passing, but by some fortune, they'd escaped his wrath.

Fire was something he knew from testing could resist his regeneration abilities. Subjecting his group or the still-human Miri to such dangers wasn't something he could stomach, so he'd sent them away.

But I have to make sure Quayla has enough essence to do whatever she's planning just in case I can't come back.

He rushed into the back rooms, searching for surviving essence caches. Vitae had stored earlier mixtures with lesser amounts of Seelie and Unseelie taint, but Bradley'd sent that away with the others. The fire phoenix has slaughtered the Sidhe prisoners and destroyed much of the secured areas in his rampage.

The cells contained extra nests with essence in them but mixed with other elements. Bradley wasn't sure whether Quayla could even make such mixes work. He headed for Vitae's backup nests.

A wash of magic knocked Bradley from his feet.

Vitae stepped out of his nest, eyes aglow.

"What are you doing, slave?" The life phoenix snatched up

the partially full gas can before Bradley could answer. "Why is my essence in this container?"

Bradley rolled onto his knees and hid his face. "Master, I was concerned your backup nest might not hold enough essence. I feared if I did not add what I could find you might not be reborn."

Deafened by the slam of pulse in his ears, he didn't hear Vitae move. Instead he felt the phoenix's fingers run softly across his scalp. "Oh, my good and faithful servant, I have been betrayed by my kin, yet a worthless mortal like you serves me even in the face of danger. I have wronged you once more. I have no time to grant you a boon, but take yourself from these dangers so I needn't lose your service to accident."

"Yes, Master, anything you want, Master."

Vitae strode from the room.

Bradley gasped in relief once he could no longer hold his breath. He picked up the emptied gas can and glanced at Vitae's nest.

Quayla's just going to have to make due.

He discarded the empty container, cast invisibility and fled.

Chapter Twenty-Three

Turning Tides

Terrance

Heat washed over Terrance like he was inside a volcanic caldera. He shifted his exterior stone to obsidian. Brittle and less capable of stopping damage, it fared better against the intense heat cremating Vitae's enforcers.

"Ignis, stop. We are not enemies."

The sound of Terrance's voice focused the fire phoenix, but rather than slowing the attacks, it drew them. Ignis blasted away at Terrance with hotter and hotter flames.

The earth phoenix circled his brother, redirecting the assault away from the mortal soldiers. Doing so didn't cease the gun fire cracking and shattering the obsidian coating his back.

He couldn't blame the mortals.

They'd come under fire from Ignis and Vitae, but he still wished their panic wasn't forcing him to form and regrow layer after layer of heat-resistant rock from the inside out.

The threat of Ignis represented failure to obey Dunham's orders. That possibility allowed Terrance to team up with Vitae rather than ignore Ignis and capture their Shieldheart. While he'd been able to work with Vitae to extinguish Ignis's fire, alone he and Ignis were ill-suited for defeating one another while they remained in their essence forms.

Ignis could achieve heat levels able to melt Terrance's stone, but Terrance could transfer that heat to the ground beneath him and draw replacement mass from the same.

"Ignis, stop this! Please, brother, find your focus."

A wild madness filled Ignis's unseeing eyes.

The imperative to capture Vitae bored into the back of Terrance's mind like a diamond drill. It fought his instinct to keep Ignis occupied. Somewhere inside the madness, Ignis felt the imperative, but somehow capturing the life phoenix had fallen second to wholesale destruction.

I cannot let the compulsion force me to leave Ignis to his rampage.

Shocking as it was to admit, they needed Aquaylae. Just as she had with the faerie fire what felt like lifetimes ago, she could turn common water into something to bank Ignis's fire.

He had no idea if she'd found a way to rebuild her nest. When he'd sent her to flight from Dunham's prison, he'd hoped she'd find some way to free him and the others.

Finding her alive and bearding Vitae in his den—successfully yet—had thrilled and tortured him.

Her last death could've been in fact her very last death.

Terrance couldn't trust to her return, and he couldn't fight Dunham's command much longer.

Mortal forces added flame throwers to their bullet onslaught against Vitae and his creations.

Ignis stole their flames, willing fire golems into the fray and using the rest to grow in size.

Vitae complicated matters by appearing in yet another body wreathed in Sidhe magic. He waded into the mortals as mad as Ignis and just as deadly.

So be it.

Terrance called upon the totality of his essence and sank his will into the earth.

A shrill cry rent the sky.

Quayla

The battle had moved into the streets by time I picked up the two balls I'd taken from the fire inspection center in Dallas and made my way back to Vitae's hotel. In a far-off corner of my mind I recognized my arrival as too little and too late.

Mortals lay burnt and bleeding in the first ranks. Husks that had been human beings before Atlanta's Shieldheart reached them twisted my guts. Sidhe spell slingers threw death at the mortals with obscene glee. Ignis rampaged two stories tall and Vitae drained soldiers' lives to revitalize his own enforcers. Terrance knelt like a boulder in a river of fire.

A wrongness clung to Ignis's flames akin to the pollution in Vitae's red and gold essence. That he laid into the mortals with his element proclaimed his madness a result of a rebirth polluted by Vitae's tampering.

I had one rebirth left in my nest and my attempts to place Mare's egg between me and oblivion hadn't gone to plan.

I have to act...no matter what.

A single shriek cut through the sky. Transmogrifying to winged human, I hurled s-shaped blades at the nearest fire hose and the as yet untapped hydrant on the corner.

"Soldiers! Fall back!" I yelled.

The earth shook.

Whatever the purpose of my Creator, he'd weakened our ability to influence our elements outside true phoenix shape. Since taking the shape risked discovery, we seldom exercised our abilities to their utmost.

Mortals were dying.

Vitae slaughtered them

Like he had Dylan.

Firefighters and soldiers died trying to protect the city.

Like Sabrina.

Innocents lives were on the line.

Like Mrs. Cox.

I shifted back into my true form and reached for the water. It didn't matter if it fountained fresh from city pipes, lay salty on the ground or even clung in the air like a sweltering wet blanket.

I made it part of me.

Like Mar taught me.

Water rose in a wave across the battlefield. The edge between Vitae and the mortals iced, holding off his tendrils. Vitae's trollman smashed into it, riddling it with cracks that I willed sealed.

Ignis vaporized it with fire, only for it to reform as I willed.

Wielding aquakinesis on such a massive scale felt like flying against a hurricane in lead armor. I fought my shieldmates anyway. Anything less meant hundreds of lives lost.

Not happening, not again.

The tremors worsened.

Terrance rose.

At first, Ignis's shifted attention allowed him to stand, but he kept standing and standing, up and up, bigger and bigger. The whole facing of Vitae's hotel reached out with cracked concrete stumps. They flowed into Terrance's swelling form.

Mortal panic fire forced more repairs to my barrier until Terrance grew taller than the protective wall. The massive behemoth turned his back on me, focused on Vitae.

Distracted as I was by shielding the mortals, it took me too long to recognize Terrance's construct for what it was—massive, gargantuan armor.

Like Dylan's mecha.

Terrance stomped the broken street where Vitae stood. The life phoenix's energy form slipped around the lumbering giant. Tendrils shot into the nearest limb, coming away hungry.

Spell slingers repositioned to a perch on the third floor and resumed fire on the mortals. A few took bullets in chest or skull before magical shields arose to deflect the attacks.

Trollman swarmed Terrance, impaled by sudden spike growths.

Flying trollmen harried me, but the winged abominations had no business trying to steal the sky from one of His phoenixes.

Ignis turned his rage on Terrance.

His fire had little effect against rock and soil, but Terrance's size seemed to make him Ignis's target. The unfortunate byproduct of the assault meant interrupting Terrance's attack on Vitae.

I cleared the sky and scanned the ground. Once I'd located the army commander, I dove for him. Assault rifle fire caught my wings, forcing me to begin my transmog early. I landed on one knee mere feet from the commander with what felt like the weight of the sky on my wings. Holding up the wall of ice and water crushed me like a medieval iron maiden.

Changing back to phoenix would alleviate the effort, but I had to convince the general or whatever to pull back his forces so I could focus on something other than defending them.

A man in a camouflaged field uniform with grey creeping along his temples looked no different than the others, but an aura of presence designated him in charge. My assumption was confirmed when he waved off the other soldiers and ordered a cease fire.

I looked up from my one knee. vaguely aware I looked ridiculously like a knight kneeling before a king, but unsure I could lift the weight of holding the wall and regain my feet.

"General."

"Colonel," he corrected. "O'Curran. Who are you?"

"Quayla," I croaked. "Look, holding the wall like this is killing me."

He darkened. "You're dying?"

I'd meant it figuratively, but if it moved him to action, I'd let him keep his misunderstanding. "Pull your men back. I can't defend them and deal with Vitae and Ignis."

"Ignis is the fire phoenix?" O'Curran asked.

"Really not time for a school lesson or introductions, Colonel. Ignis is our fire shield. Vitae has done something to him."

"What about stony?"

Terrance's stomp shook the street.

"He's trying to capture Vitae like Ignis was when they arrived."

"So, they're the good guys."

The pressure squeezed a groan from my lips. "Complicated. Will you please pull back?"

Vitriol bit into me from another soldier's tone. "We're protecting the citizens of Atlanta from you freaks."

"That's enough Captain," O'Curran snapped. "We'll pull back, but you will bring the war criminal Vitae to me once he's captured."

The ramification of his request staggered me. The mortals considered me a freak and Vitae a war criminal. We'd failed to protect our Praefecture so completely as to become the enemy.

I struggled up onto my feet, risked my life by shifting essence to flesh and met his eyes. "No. Vitae's wrongdoing will be dealt with, but he is not yours to Judge."

"He killed my men," O'Curran snarled.

"Vengeance is mine; I will repay, saith the Lord." I met him tone for tone. "Vitae's sins are not up for debate, Colonel. The longer you keep your men here, the longer I have to play defense and the more of your men die."

The captain pulled his sidearm and put it to my head. "You'll do as the colonel orders."

O'Curran knocked the gun upward and sucker punched the solider before I responded.

I spat two words at him before transmogrifying back into a phoenix and rising into the air. "Pull back."

The pressure of maintaining my defensive wall eased the moment I retook my true form as if I'd replaced a weak connection to my element with a maxed-out signal.

O'Curran shouted up at me. "You'll come discuss this with me when all of this is done."

Sure, if I get a spare moment.

I turned away from the mortals to the three-way battle royale wrecking Vitae's hotel. A tiny voice worried about Mare's egg, but the Sidhe gleefully picking off mortals required my focus first.

Dead Sidhe littered the hotel's alfresco balconies by time O'Curran's men had pulled back. Terrance and Ignis went at each other like creatures from a *kaiju* movie, wrecking another of Vitae's buildings.

Where did Vitae go?

Terrance double over. The massive makeshift armor fell away revealing Vitae anchored to Terrance's true back. He raised his Champion blade for a killing strike.

I seized all of the water I'd claimed to protect the mortals and blasted Vitae with it. Even in my true form, turning the tidal wave midair to slam it into Ignis's face felt like holding up the wall while talking to O'Curran. I landed behind Terrance, drawing the resultant steam to my call.

Terrance whirled toward me, first raised.

I held up my hands. "I'm going to coat your back with ice to keep Vitae off of you."

Terrance rumbled with something I'd never seen from him— anger. "To what end, little sister?"

"I'm not here for Vitae. I don't really want Dunham to have him, but I am not sure I can beat Ignis alone. He has to be stopped to protect the mortals." I threw a flurry of ice knives at the recovering Ignis. "If you can contain Ignis in a rock cell, I can stop him. In exchange, I'll help you capture Vitae."

Terrance nodded.

"I'll need a temporary window in the cell."

Before Terrance could confirm my instructions, Vitae and Ignis attacked us from both sides.

Terrance and I fought back to back, me in phoenix form and him in his reassembled armor. Vitae was a better fighter. His Champion blade gave him a dangerous advantage, but whatever he'd done to himself unbalanced his mind. Baiting him to rage proved an effective defense until Terrance compressed Ignis into a ten by ten cage of rock. The cage glowed brighter in moments.

Strain undercut Terrance's voice. "Little sister?"

I blasted Vitae, Terrance, myself and Ignis's cell with a wave of now-filthy water. While Vitae recovered, I summoned the two water-coated balls hidden on a building roof a few blocks away.

Terrance opened the cell and I dunked both extinguisher balls without the slightest bit of rim.

"Now, smash him!" I said.

Violet lightning hit me, knocking me from the sky. I turned my head, every nerve in my body alive with agony.

Vitae stalked toward me. "Your destruction is long overdue. Filthy whore-bitches have no place in my perfect Shield."

Terrance dropped a flattened ten by ten stone house on the arrogant bastard.

Transmogrifying eased my pain. I fought through the rest, bringing all the water I could summon around Vitae in a sphere of ice. As before, Vitae's struggles forced me to shrink it, but this time I thickened the walls as I did so.

Terrance loomed into view, an expression on his face I couldn't read. A shift of will mimicked by my outstretched arms swung the ice ball around to him. "He's all yours. As promised."

The expression eased. "What of Ignis?"

"Killing him should've rid him of Vitae's taint."

"And put him back in Dunham's cage."

I smirked and opened my mouth to tell him about what I achieved in Essex. I thought better of it. Like it or not he was still Dunham's servant. I chose instead to offer him a hint of hope. "That is one possibility."

I transmogrified and leapt skyward, leaving Terrance to deliver Vitae or not. I had a house guest to check on.

Ignis

Ignis reformed in an empty room filled with nests. The rage that had consumed him was gone.

Winter filled him.

I murdered mortals.

He didn't know how many he'd killed, but the thought of returning to Vitae's hotel to capture the life phoenix knotted Ignis's insides. He couldn't stomach the idea of burning more mortals to death in Dunham's service.

Wait, I don't feel any imperative to capture Vitae now.

The need to capture Vitae hadn't been present when he'd been reborn in the life phoenix's basement, only a need to vent his boundless rage. He'd also shed Dunham's orders to return.

Winter turned Antarctic.

Until he uses my egg to order me.

"Welcome back, Shield Ignis."

A lump filled my throat. "Anima?! What's going on? How is this possible? Why aren't I back at Dunham's?"

"Quayla set this up, gaining essence to fill these nests when she sought Vilicangelus."

The name of his former divine shot panic through him. "Anima, I can't be here. Dunham will learn what she's done and where she is. He can't be allowed to capture all of—"

The view out the window brought him up short. His voice fell to whispers. "This is Mare's."

"It was my idea. It seemed unlikely Vitae or anyone else would seek Quayla here," Anima said.

"That was true, except now that I know...," Heat built back up in his core. "She has no other choice. She has to attack Dunham now. The only way for her to stay free is to free the rest of us."

The sound of Quayla's landing drew him outside. Ignis rushed to meet her, almost sprinting through ghosts that tore at his heart. She met him on the front porch.

Concern narrowed her eyes. "You're better? Free of the Sidhe taint?"

"Yes, rebirth freed me of the taint and Dunham's orders."

She beamed.

"But, Quayla, you're in danger. As soon as Dunham uses my egg to order me back, he'll learn you're here."

Her smile wavered.

"You have to attack him, now while you have the element of surprise on your side."

She searched his face for a long moment. After a long silence she gave him a single nod. "Anima, notify Aether it's time. Ignis, tell me everything I need to know about Dunham's defenses."

Quayla

Ignis paced the backyard, seething and glaring at Bradley and the friends he'd just introduced. I'd landed in the staging house behind Mare's when hailed by the former medical examiner. Ignis had gone for Bradley's throat before the queer little man could finish explaining why he couldn't surrender his faerie boon.

The resultant faceoff hadn't been pleasant, but I'd saved the mortals without Ignis and me coming to blows.

Fortunate after my failure with Emma.

Several gas cans filled with Vitae's polluted essence rested on the back patio between us.

"That's all I could get." Bradley's hangdog expression backed up his story. "He thought I was trying to refill his last nest, so I should be able to go back for more."

I shook my head. "I wanted Vitae reborn from his own essence, but I don't think there'll be enough left for a single rebirth after I purify it."

"What do you want me to do?" Bradley asked.

Mrs. Cox descended from the back porch with a tray of muffins and a glass milk bottle.

"Time's wasting, Aquaylae," Ignis said.

A bald and bearded man with glowing tattoos stepped forward. "What's going on?"

Ignis practically snarled. "None of your business...mortal."

"Here you go, dear," Mrs. Cox offered Ignis the tray. "Surefire cure for a case of the hangries."

Ignis looked like he might incinerate her on the spot.

"Just give me a minute longer, Ignis." I put a hand on him. "We're going to break out the other phoenixes."

"Where are they being held?" Bradley asked.

"Circlestone," I said. "Look, I appreciate your help this far, but things are about to escalate. You need to lay low. I can lift you over the barrier. You'll be safe on Mare's prop—"

"Absolutely not!" Candle flames flickered to life along Ignis's shoulders. "We need to go."

He put action to his words, launching skyward in a blast of heat.

I took a proffered muffin and shifted my wings into existence. "Thank you, Mrs. Cox. Look after them for me, will you?"

"Of course, dear."

I launched myself into the sky, turning away from Circlestone and shouting at the fire phoenix circling above me. "We have to pick someone up first."

Mrs. Cox

Hadley extended the tray to the strange humans congregated beneath the phoenixes flying away. More than half of them displayed a youthful glint of mischief and rebellion. "Eat up, dears. You're going to need your strength."

The angelic woman took a muffin and milk, murmuring thanks as the first bite hit her lips. She moaned indecently for a public gathering and snatched another muffin from the tray. "Oh, god, Billy you have to try one of these."

Billy offered Hadley a grin that during her youth had often portended her older brothers perpetrating barroom shenanigans. "So, we're going to help them, right? Rebecca? Dave?"

A young woman wearing thick spectacles but otherwise normal in appearance took a muffin and a cup of milk. "This does not sound very well thought out."

She bit into a muffin. Her eyebrow arched toward Hadley.

"This is why we took Sky's injections," Billy argued.

"You took the injection so you could have powers," Dave said.

Billy shrugged.

"How do you intend to 'help?'" Miri asked.

"I don't know," Bradley said. "But he's right that I did this to myself so I could help protect Atlanta."

"Quayla didn't think we should get involved," Miri said.

"They're going to invade an evil lair and free other phoenixes," Billy grinned. "They could use some support. You with me, Eric?"

Detective Foxner pushed open the screen door from the back porch. Her badge glinted from a cord around her neck.

"Ix-Nay," Eric whispered. "Op-Kay."

Foxner rolled her eyes. "Did you know most pigs are fluent in pig Latin?"

"And she's not the only police officer here," Miri said.

Eric scowled. "You had a cop drive the getaway car?"

Bradley shrugged. "Why are you here, Detective?"

Foxner reached for a muffin, but hesitated. "May I?"

Hadley smiled. "Of course, dear."

"I was hoping to catch Quayla," Foxner said.

"Why?" Rebecca asked.

"She's headed into a shi—"

"Detective," Warning filled Hadley's tone and she pulled the tray from Foxner's reach.

"Shoot storm," Foxner amended. "I wanted to help."

"That's all we want to do," Billy said.

"That's what you want to do," Rebecca said. "I'm not sure it's a good idea."

"How could we even help, BJ?" Dave asked. "No one but Rebecca can fly unless you've been holding out on us."

Foxner shook her head. "They can't go in from above. From what I overheard, the complex is designed to fend off airborne assault."

"Makes sense," Miri sipped her milk. "If they're holding phoenixes captive, they'd protect against others taking issue."

Eric laughed. "Well, they're not exactly inconspicuous."

"Neither are some of you," Foxner said.

"But I am," Hadley said. "The detective too."

"She'd need a warrant," Miri said.

Foxner shook her head. "No, I have claims of people being held against their will in immediate danger for their lives. It's enough to get me in the door."

"Won't be enough for a review board," Miri said.

Foxner shrugged. "I've got to back my partner's play."

Billy grinned. "So, we'll do it Payday heist style. The detective, Sky and the old lady—"

Hadley cleared her throat. "I beg your pardon?"

"Um, sorry, I don't know your name," Billy said.

"You can call me Mrs. Cox—widowed, not divorced."

"They go in to scout and distract the guards," Billy said. "We come in after, secure the entryway and let Quayla and Mister Temper do the rest."

Rebecca shook her head. "I don't know."

"Come on," Billy grinned. "It'll be fun."

"I'll need to fetch my frying pan," Hadley said.

Chapter Twenty-Four

Traps within Traps

Vitae

The ice encasing me reshaped into a long coffin. I reformed my body, gripping Dolumii's sword close to my leg. I'd resisted concentrating my essence too much lest Aquaylae shrink the ice too small to accommodate the blade.

Whoever released me would lose their soul.

The ice melted away from my head in time to see Terrance step onto a stone pedestal. A glass jar descended over him, thick sludge obscuring him from sight. Behind him Summuseraphi slumped inside a magical barrier atop a central stone.

"Hello again, Vitae," Viviane cooed.

"Again?" The druid asked from beside a control console.

"Later, Dunham."

"Release me at once, Sidhe, or face the repercussions."

Her brows rose. "Like what? Being cast out again?"

"In the name of the Undying Light—"

"Shut up!" The power of her voice shook the building around us. "You are not His servant any more and your wielding of the title offends me."

"I am his servant, Sidhe," I snarled. "I am the perfection of His will on Earth."

The druid snorted. "The perfect perversion maybe."

The ice kept me from dealing him a proper response, but my eyes told him to make peace with the trees or whatever he worshipped.

"Now," Viviane circled me. "You're here with the Unseelie Champion blade as I requested."

"If you think I came willingly or that I'd give you Mare's e—"

Scurith crested the stair. A smirk twisted his maw under ears flicked forward—not at all the cowering cur I'd come to expect. The ice sank its fangs into me.

The coyll handed over Mare's egg.

I threw myself at the ice, but the thin layer held like iron. I transmogrified and willed myself up through the opening. An invisible barrier kept me from escape.

The druid tsked. "You really believe we wouldn't prepare for that? Can I punish his disrespect yet?"

Viviane held up a hand. "True, I am a fallen angel, but I still value my word. I will keep my promise and release Mare from the sword if you will allow me."

My breath caught. "You're lying."

"I am not."

They'd captured me, using my treacherous shieldmates to deliver me into captivity. The magical barrier constraining me and the quick way she'd slain me suggested she had the power to do whatever she intended with me.

So why the charade...unless it isn't a lie after all.

My eyes tracked to the softly-lit sapphire egg.

Fingers tightened and relaxed around the Unseelie sword's hilt.

Logic and experience guaranteed that the Anseelie had no intention of keeping her bargain. She wanted the sword, plain and simple—except she already had it. With no evidence of Aquaylae's presence, it had been the Lady of Water who'd changed the shape of the ice ensnaring me. She could've just as easily shrank it until the sword protruded.

There's more than enough magic in it for her to sense even inside the ice.

I faced Viviane but stared into the days leading up to my capture. I'd tried everything in my power to release Mare from the sword. The percentage of Sidhe essence to my own in my rebirths bordered on ninety percent. I'd exhausted the supply taken from Vusolaryn and Mariena. Nothing short of a Sidhe queen's blood could raise my power level.

"You oath on your power to release Mare from this sword?"

She smiled. "I do."

Summuseraphi shook his head, panic on his face.

"And you will quicken her hatching?"

"With your help."

"How is it that I am to help?" I asked.

"Life essence combined with my power will regenerate her faster."

"If that were possible, Shieldhearts would've quickened hatching before now."

"I'm not a Shieldheart," Viviane said. "I'm an angel."

"Fallen," The single word carried an acerbic edge.

"Do you want Mare back or not?"

"I do." My gaze shifted to the eager expression on the druid's face. "If you send the mortal away. He is unworthy to see."

Dunham purpled. "This is my—"

"Relax, Dunham dear."

White replaced the mortal world. I stood free of the ice and magical restraint in the spirit realm.

"This isn't possible," I gasped. "Only a divine—"

"Angels are divine." She extended her hands, one holding Mare's egg. "Please take Mare's egg and place the sword hilt in my hand."

My eyes narrowed, but I did as she asked, ready for a betrayal.

"Now, hold the egg in your cupped hands." Viviane said. "I will lay the tip atop her egg to ease her journey."

"That doesn't make any sense. She should be able to find her way back to her egg from any distance."

Viviane shook her head. "Swords of Judgement sever the soul from everything. If she were truly still connected to her egg, wouldn't the essence within glow in time to her heartbeat?"

"In the sword she has no heart to beat."

"True, but that doesn't change what I've told you."

I took a moment to consider, but only a moment. I needed Mare back. I needed to undo the mistake that had taken her from me. I needed her to replace Aquaylae and help me build Creation's greatest Shield.

I've come this far to free her, what is a little farther?

I lifted the egg in both hands and did not take it away when Viviane lowered the sword so that the blade tip rested on Mare's egg, mere inches from my heart.

Viviane's seductress appearance fell away. Two pairs of black wings unfurled from her suddenly-naked body. She hovered off the white ground beneath us, wings beating slowly but not keeping her aloft. A nimbus of glowing white power surrounded her, then filled the space between us.

The sword writhed in her hand. The blade warped and shifted shapes, but the tip never lost contact with Mare's egg.

An instant or an eternity later, the glow around her faded.

The glow inside Mare's egg brightened and faded in slow rhythm.

A sob escaped me.

Life glowed inside the egg. I felt Mare within the shell. Potential filled the egg. In one hundred years—less based on the eagerness of the magic contained within—Mare would hatch to rejoin me.

My breath quickened. I met Viviane's eyes. "How do we quicken her hatching?"

"Surround the egg in your essence," Viviane said. "Keep it surrounded and I will do the rest."

I did so.

Viviane pored divine energy into the egg.

At first nothing happened. Without warning, the egg drank in my essence. I fed it more and more, but the egg's thirst seemed unquenchable. I gave Mare's egg everything she desired, willing to give all of me if it returned her to my world.

The egg cracked.

Terror shot through me for an eye blink. Had we fed it too much energy? Had we burned Mare out inside the egg by forcing too much energy into her? What will the Sidhe essence mixed in my blood do to my beloved?

The egg shattered.

Unlike normal hatchings, the concentrated mass of water essence unfurled, taking shape quickly into the Mare that had been stolen from me by the sword in Viviane's grip.

I fell backward, my legs unwilling to hold me upright any more.

Mare stared at me, tears running down her cheeks and head shaking back and forth. "By the Creator, Vitae, what have you done?"

"It is done. She is returned to you. Our bargain is complete." Viviane clapped her hands.

The spirit world vanished around us, dropping me atop a stone basin, surrounded by a curtain of beads inside a magical barrier. To my left, Mare pounded on the inside of a glass bell jar.

"Thanks for bringing us a water phoenix." Dunham grinned at me from the other side, a garnet egg in his hand. A pressure tightened around me, cracking my ribs. "Allow me to give you a quick tour of your new home, slave."

Quayla

I landed outside Vitae's warehouse to find Aether waiting for me. Seeing the air phoenix brought back all the emotion of our last parting. Ignis circled above us, his looming shadow encouragement to put my feelings on the backburner.

"So, what's the plan?" Aether asked.

"It's going to be rough," I said. "The place is armored, warded and trapped with lightning. I'm hoping you can help there."

Anima's voice emerged from my pendant. "Begging your pardon, Shield Quayla?"

"Yeah, Ani?"

"Detective Foxner, Bradley Sky and his friends are en route to Circlestone now, intent to secure ground floor access."

I cursed.

Aether gave me a questioning look.

"Mortals, well, mostly mortals. It's a long story, just please don't execute anyone who seems Fae Kissed, all right?"

"You seem blessed with friends compared to our last meeting."

A Jurassic sabretooth of worry sank fangs into my nerves. "Blessed or cursed. We've got to hurry."

When we finally neared the facility, a siren rang from every corner of Circlestone's campus. A woman's voice blasted out of nearby speakers. "Tornado Plan 1. All employees evacuate to your designated safety areas."

A fantasy castle drawbridge door appeared in an armored length of window. The wooden bridge fell away, flattening a flower bed and slapping the concrete. The rainbow-winged mortal stood in the entry, waving me through.

I dove, screeching to signal the others to follow. Rebecca managed to clear out of my way, but I still came in too fast and almost lost my footing on the marble flooring.

Huge spiderwebs pinned security guards to walls and in one case the ceiling. Billy held a heavy iron blade to the throat of a beefy guard next to an elevator control board.

Sabrina marched over to me.

Heat flashed through me. "What are you doing here?"

"Backing my partner," she said.

"We're not partners," I snapped. "You're mortal. You could've been hurt, besides this could cost you your job."

"So glad you care," Sabrina snarked.

"I do care, dammit. I can't take losing anyone else dear to me."

"Aquaylae," Ignis marched toward the elevator banks in dark, brooding human shape. "Now."

"So really, you only care about your own hurt," Sabrina said.

"What? No, I—"

Sabrina rolled her eyes, yanked me forward and pressed her lips against mine. Firm but yielding lips caressed mine, the tip of her tongue teasing but never invading my mouth. Her body melted against mine, bringing the scent of pheromones and her sex to my nostrils. My new body responded, but more, something deep inside me wanted her too. Her touch tantalized every nerve, setting them alight with desire like the night I'd shared my first new body with Dylan.

The thought of Dylan sent the wrong kind of lightning bolt through me. Another thought quenched my desire in icy water.

Grynnberry.

I pulled away from Sabrina, spinning on the spot.

"Ignis, Aether, there's a Sidhe here somewhere."

Sabrina's iron tone snapped like a bear trap. "What are you talking about?"

I faced her. "I care about you, Sabrina, really, but something about that kiss—"

"Wasn't enough? Too mortal?" Sabrina asked.

I didn't have time for the hard warrior to fall apart on me. I had to get upstairs and free the others.

"I think someone tampered with us magically, a nymph Sidhe named Grynnberry."

Scandal filled Mrs. Cox's tone. "That little fairy in your apartment was a nymph?"

A growl escaped me. "Ugh, I don't have time for this. Mrs.

Cox, there's a nymph here playing games. Deal with him, would you? I've got to go."

Sabrina yanked me back around. "My feelings have nothing to do with faeries, Buckler."

I opened my mouth to refute her claims, but didn't have the time. As soon as Dunham worked out Ignis had returned to attack him, he'd neutralize the fire phoenix or worse. I kissed her quickly on the lips. "I believe you, but I've got to go."

The elevator opened for us and the security guard scanned a badge to take us up to Dunham's offices. I heard Sabrina barking orders to find Grynnberry as the doors closed.

"I'd have thought you'd learn your lesson," Ignis said.

I glowered. "We'll discuss this after everyone is free."

The armor covering the double doors which led from the elevator bank into Dunham's lushly-appointed reception area weren't runed or crackling with spell magic like the exterior.

Ignis chose not to melt them.

"We're not running through his maze," Ignis threw a gout of superhot fire through the ceiling at an angle, setting off fire suppression sprinklers.

He and Aether leapt through, leaving me to bring up the rear. I landed in the burned carcass of an expensive couch. Viviane held both Ignis and Aether by their throats. Both phoenixes transmogrified several times, but couldn't shake her grip.

I extended a shortsword from each hilt. "Release your captives, Sidhe."

A sword went through my back and out my chest. Cold seeped into me from the blade, sinking barbs into my spirit.

Dread filled me.

A terrible magic with even more terrible potential loomed around me, its final judgement held back by something I couldn't name.

Grynnberry's thick, nasal accent whispered as he twisted the blade. "Always wanted to take you from behind, love. We don't need another water phoenix, so this is our last fling."

Viviane vanished with Ignis and Aether in a flash of white. She reappeared beside my once-cage—Aether and Ignis appearing within the cages by some magic.

"At least I gave you one last kiss to remember me by—even if it was with the mortal's lips. Good bye."

It worked with Vitae.

I incased the blade in ice, flashing the rest of me to vapor. The sword's magic tore at me, trying to drag me into itself. I disowned the water gripped in its hold, replacing it with more from the sprinkler system.

My body reformed behind him, thrusting one sword into Grynnberry's—no Jahriss's—heart while the other speared his brain. I kicked the Sidhe off of my blades. The Champion blade tumbled to the floor. I faced Viviane. "Free them."

Her fine brow rose. "Or what?"

Dunham descended a stair in the same druid's attire he'd worn at the Marriott. Fury bent his features. "She's mine."

"Of course, Dunham dear," Viviane smiled. "But next time."

White light and oblivion slammed into me, killing me before the pain could even register.

Viviane

"You killed her," Dunham snarled. "She was mine."

Viviane rolled her eyes. The boy was becoming more and more of a problem, but it wouldn't matter soon enough. "She'll be back, now shut off those sprinklers."

He turned his back to obey, allowing Viviane to ascend onto the single stone linked to the center stone caging Summuseraphi.

"Wait, what are you doing?" Dunham asked.

She gave him a smile to haunt his nightmares. "I have five phoenixes, child. I'm going to reclaim my throne."

"Wait, no, the divine's power is mine. You can't do this!"

"I most certainly can, and you agreed to it," Viviane said. "This was our deal. I help you have your vengeance and you let me use the phoenixes to reclaim my throne."

"I never agreed to you using the divine."

She shook her head and invoked the circle. He could rage all he wanted, he'd never penetrate the barrier before she could finish. She'd summoned Jahriss to take care of Dunham if he tried something rash, but she hadn't decided whether or not to restore her knight to life.

Once more she worked the whole incantation rather than the one she'd led Dunham to find. With the power of all five elements to hold Summuseraphi, she drew the divine phoenix's essence into herself—all but the very last mote.

Who knows, maybe I'll come back for more once he's recovered.

Chapter Twenty-Five

For the Shield

Quayla

I was moving before my body fully formed. I dumped what little remained in my nest into Ignis's and sprinted out the door, transmogrifying back into water on the run. I hit the second-floor balcony and launched into the air as a phoenix.

I'd failed...again.

I'd cost Aether his freedom and lost Ignis with barely a fight. Somewhere in the background that little voice told me I wasn't enough. It warned that against Viviane, I was just a young phoenix without the means to save my Shield. The nasty little whispers reminded me that I had no egg and no essence left in my nest.

What had survived my last rebirth wouldn't have sustained another, but combined with the remainder in Ignis's nest it might amount to enough to save him if what I intended went wrong.

I'm not enough, but I'm not alone and I have a plan.

A hard dive swept me from sky to Circlestone's ground floor. I transmog'd again as I streaked through the drawbridge door. I hit the floor on hands and knees, essence allowing me to slide across the foyer like a bullet as I regained my feet.

"Quayla?" Sabrina said.

"Died. Can't talk."

"We can help!" Bradley shouted.

I whirled at the elevator entrance. "No. Clear out. Win or lose, I want you all safe."

"What happened to the other phoenixes?" Sabrina asked.

I shoved razor-edged wings into the elevator doors and yanked them out of my way without answering. A leap, foreshortened wings and my will propelled me up the shaft. I dodged a descending car part way up, sliced the cable of a descending car in the other shaft to be sure it didn't sneak up on me and hit the exit like a permafrozen cannon ball.

Ignis's entrance gaped above me. There'd been nothing stealthy about my entrance and there seemed every reason to believe they'd lay in wait for hot-headed young me.

Transmogrified to vapor, I pushed through gaps in the armored door and took the long way around.

Only three things seemed to have changed since my death. The sprinklers had stopped, Viviane wasn't present and poor Summus looked halfway across death's door. Dunham turned from his ambush point over the hole Ignis had made, somehow sensing me even as a silent cloud of vapor.

I can probably take him.

I didn't try.

I didn't waste what might be my one opportunity on hubris.

I didn't risk underestimating him.

I didn't give him a chance at a first strike with the wicked-looking sickles he held in each fist.

I seized what water I could from the room and hurled it as a gigantic s-shaped blade overtop the stone cages. Before he could react, I threw all of the remaining water weight I could muster behind my momentum and slid underneath the cages.

Even though I didn't really have a heart to beat, a roar of surf against stone throbbed in ears I didn't have. Dunham yelled something obscured by the waves.

Soothing, soft and inviting, water can shatter stone. Water can carve canyons and wear down mountains and uproot trees. The blade I'd hurled should've decapitated the robotic arms holding the cages in place, but I threw absolutely every last iota of strength and will upward.

The cages rose, tipped and tumbled over.

Our nests fell from the cavities beneath the stone basins, cracking and shattering. Deprived of our essence to power them, magical barriers collapsed. Floor and force knocked bell jars askew.

Before anything else could go wrong I speared the eggs I could see—Terrance's and Vitae's. Neither Aether nor the woman who occupied my cage had eggs for Dunham to control them.

Everyone's free except Ignis.

I spun, searching for the last egg.

A sickle cut down through my watery shoulder. Pain shrieked from my lips and the world swam in darkness. Another sickle cut into my waist, nearly chopping me in half.

Terrance slammed into me, catapulting me into the nearby wall. My very physical and heavily-bleeding body dented the wall. I shouldn't have been physical. My body had been pure essence.

I willed a transmogrification, but my body refused to change.

The woman appeared, both arms shifted into water. "Stay still, I'll mend the tears then help you transmog."

"How?" I croaked.

"Benefits of experience." She smiled. "I'm Mare."

Shock seized me, but I pushed the revelation away until later.

Behind her, Dunham's sickle sliced through Terrance's stone armor like whipped cream. His body rippled, becoming flesh once more.

Dunham decapitated him.

Mare's essence bridged the rent flesh in short order. She shifted both hands to my center and pushed her energy into my core. The beginnings of a transmogrification sent tingles through my body. I leaned my will behind hers, desperate to shift and rebalance.

Dunham stalked toward her, sickles raised.

I opened my mouth to warn her, but Ignis hit the druid at full force, sucking the oxygen from my lungs in the process.

Vitae put a hand on Mare's shoulder. "Leave her, we must retreat."

"I'm not leaving a fellow shield injured and dying," Mare snapped.

"She's not a shield." Vitae glared at me. "She's a mistake."

Mare jerked away. "Go if all you've made of yourself in my absence is a coward."

Fury flashed across his face, but for me rather than Mare as if he found a way to blame me for her words. "Atlanta needs you."

Magic sprang from his fingers, cocooning Mare in some kind of shimmering crystal. Vitae jerked her imprisoned form from me, blasted a hole in the nearest wall and launched the two of them into the sky.

Ignis slammed into the cage, shattering already-cracked stone. Summus cried out.

Aether danced around Dunham, bladed fans whipping around her controlled maelstrom. He parried her strikes, cracking the fans with every blow.

The transmogrification energy ebbed.

I pushed my focus from the fight around me into restoring the chance Mare had gifted me. Resuming the change took every stubborn ounce of will I could muster and still failed to kindle the change.

Aether cried out.

Dunham's sickle hacked cloudy limbs from the air phoenix, leaving bleeding stumps behind in his blade's wake. He laughed at her, taunted her as she bled.

Aether had offered me a single life in proxy for Caelum. She hadn't volunteered to be tortured and tormented.

Ignis bent a torrent of flames around Aether into Dunham.

His second sickle absorbed the energy and Dunham drove the blade into Aether. She burst into flame, screaming and unable to transmogrify away from the pain.

Ignis charged, hands extended into fiery claws. He beat Dunham's strikes to the side one by one, barely avoiding the weapons' dangerous edges. A lucky blow knocked one of the sickles from Dunham's hand.

The fire phoenix stomped a fiery spike into Dunham knee.

A scream wiped the smile from Dunham's face. He fell to one knee. A wild swing lopped off fingers and a part of Ignis's hand—forcing Ignis back into a flesh shape.

Dunham scooped up the champion sword my death had left discarded on the floor. "I've had enough of you, Pyri."

Rage pushed my transmogrification over the edge.

Both wings swept forward, launching a dozen icy pinions at the lead of an angry wave. The water drove Dunham back from Ignis, blood bubbling out around ice knives to darken the water.

A flash of white stole Dunham from the room.

Summus lay unconscious where I'd last seen him.

Every instinct in my body sent up an alarm. I dove sidelong, shifting into pure water to slosh around the exterior windows like a makeshift water slide.

Dunham appeared where I'd been, sickle and sword coming down in what would've been my death.

I threw a half-shattered bell jar at him.

He vanished, reappearing behind Ignis.

Instead of murdering Ignis, he hugged him. Unable to transmogrify into flame, the fire phoenix fought Dunham's grip. I gaped as Ignis's body shriveled right before my eyes, silhouetted by a glowing, emerald gleam of magic.

Dunham dropped the emaciated fire phoenix to the floor, smirked at me and stomped Ignis's skull like a rotten pumpkin.

"Now," Dunham stalked forward. "I will finally deal with you."

The sickle in Dunham's hand had cut through our essence

forms. The injuries stole our ability to transmogrify. The sword in his other hand ripped souls from the world and imprisoned them in eternal torment.

My hilts lay across the floor where I'd died before.

Essence weapons connected to me were no defense against Dunham's sickles. Nothing seemed able to defend against them.

I took a deep breath, shifting my feet in the fluid circles of Hep-Silat. My arms followed, leading my whole body into the water-based martial art.

I am water. Water is me.

If I could stay ahead of Dunham, strike without getting struck, I might still defeat him. Ice had proved defense against Vitae's life stealing magic. Dead, frozen water not connected as essence had mostly protected me from the sword in Dunham's hand.

"I seriously doubt you've practiced your fighting style as much as I have in preparation for this day," Dunham said.

He sliced with the sword and hooked the sickle low to catch my forward foot. I abandoned the leg to splash to the carpet, drawing up another to catch my weight.

I smirked, focusing on every cell of my essence. "Maybe not, mortal, but there is a difference between us."

"What's that?" He swung and stabbed.

I slid around the blow, distending my center out of the way of his follow up. "You've trained your body to fight. You became a warrior."

"And what? You were created to be a weapon?" A hard flurry put me into a quick retreat. A tail of water trailed behind my sweeping arm, crystalizing to catch and slow his strike.

"I *am* water," I focused on my hands, feeling the hilts held firm in their grip. "In the name of the Undying Light, I command you to surrender your boon and lay down your arms or face Destruction."

He shook his head. "I'm not a little boy you can terrorize into obeying. You won't steal anything from me, not ever again."

Two short ice blades whipped up from the ground, severing his arms at the armpit in a flash of my third and fourth arms.

Shock registered as the ice melted away from my hilts to cap the bleeding stumps.

"Raging river or a half dozen streams, Dunham, water will carve away whatever stands in its way." A fifth hand lifted his lost sickle, gifting it to me. "This is for Caelum."

I brought the sickle down atop his head, bisecting him cleanly from crown to cock.

I stood unmoving as his halves oozed fluids around my feet.

Dunham's sins had been my fault, a result of my cowardice. My mistake cost Caelum eternity in the Creator's embrace. I deserved no less a fate than Dunham.

Later, once I've dealt with Viviane.

I used the Anseelie blade to destroy Dunham's sickles then turned to the wreckage of Dunham's cage. Summus weighed less than a child. I had no idea how Mare had gifted me her essence, but I tried to give Summus what I could. He didn't return to consciousness, but flying him back to Mare's required little effort.

Need to make sure the others went home first.

I found Ignis's egg beneath the wreckage, badly cracked—another victim of my careless sins. The glow within brightened and faded, giving me hope he'd either been caught by the egg or another nest somewhere.

Summus may know how to repair it or Vita.

Sabrina, Bradley and the others were gone when I landed back on the first floor.

I thanked God for all of his blessings, transmogrified into my true form and gently lifted Summus's frail body into the sky toward Mare's home.

Chapter Twenty-Six

Changing of the Guards

Viviane

Viviane descended the stairs toward her grotto. The hijacked crayon drawing held its breath, stillness announcing her guests.

A smirk lit her face.

Brazen of them, meeting me in the water.

Mab and Titania stood at opposite ends of Viviane's grotto, separated by sand, coral and a giant clam. Both straightened when she descended the last few steps, offering menace through poise and presence.

As if I've forgotten how to be a queen.

"Sisters."

They started their prepared speeches together, Titania blurting a hair faster than Mab. The Unseelie inclined her head to her Seelie opposite, winning through graciousness what she could not with alacrity.

"We are on to you," Titania said. "You've somehow usurped the Atlanta Shield and are employing it against us."

"Bravo by the way," Mab said.

"Yes, yes, an impressive gambit if it hadn't been a failure," Titania said.

Viviane arched a single eye brow.

"You thought we'd fall for your ruse? Turn to you for help against the other?" Titania asked.

"You did," Viviane smiled. "Both of you."

Mab frowned. "We've chosen better allies instead."

"One another?" Viviane laughed. "Then you chose poorly."

"Watch your tone, Viviane," Mab scowled.

Titania folded her arms. "We can do far worse than exile you."

"Are you sure?"

"The punishment options are deliciously infinite." Mab said.

"No," Viviane put menace behind her smile. "Are you sure you have the power to do anything to me?"

Viviane turned her back on them—an intentional slight—and relaxed upon her throne. She assessed her sisters, tapping a painted lip with one finger until the pause was pregnant on the verge of labor.

"You're both weak," Viviane said. "You've spent your forces against one another, paying me for the privilege. The increased warfare brought you to the Shields' attention, costing you even more strength."

"We've destroyed over a dozen divine phoenixes," Mab snarled.

"True."

"We still have our subjects to draw upon," Scorn filled Titania's voice. "You have only yourself."

"You both do have your depleted subjects to grant you strength." Viviane rose, standing between them without showing either her back. "My subjects are thriving, enriched and equipped in part by your subjects."

"You're not a queen," Mab snapped. "You have no subjects."

Viviane gestured to the throne she'd just vacated. "A queen in exile is still a queen. Whatever seat she chooses becomes her new throne. The subjects denied her becoming fervent in their devotion."

"No," Titania raised her hands, emerald magic throbbing between her fingers.

"I think not," Mab followed Titania's gesture, violet lightning crackling from fingertip to fingertip.

"I appreciate how you've come to my stronghold to signify that my power isn't a threat." Viviane lowered her voice, malice backlighting her eyes. "But while you were destroying Divine Ones, I was harnessing one."

Violet and emerald magic lanced across the intervening space, met by a swirling flow of sapphire and divine white. The Anseelie queen's power shot up the paths carved through the water by her opponents' spells—a moray eel swallowing lesser serpents.

Her power latched onto the two queens, lashing them in pain and weakening their bodies. They fought her, eventually stepping side by side to combine their strength.

Viviane pushed more of her stolen divine energy into the conflict. She overwhelmed them, putting both on their knees. She'd hesitated in her departure from Dunham's chambers and considered fetching her Sword of Judgement.

It would've been too tempting to test our mortality against one of the swords.

"Now, sisters. We can continue this fracas to what I think we all realize would be the eventual outcome," Viviane beamed. "Or the ruling Sidhe queens can vote to reverse my exile. What do you think, hmm?"

O'Curran

O'Curran poured over the casualty reports from their altercation with the life phoenix. He searched through the after-action reports from the platoon leaders present at the altercation, getting a feel for the portions of the battle he hadn't witnessed in preparation to send his own report up the line.

His door opened.

When no one spoke, he addressed the door without looking up. "I told you I didn't want to be disturbed unless that water phoenix turns up."

A hard basso growled a reply. "I'm not the waiting sort."

O'Curran glanced up and immediately leapt to his feet, snapping a salute to the highly decorated officer. "General!"

Brigadier General Francis "the Meatgrinder" Small glowered up at him. Shorter but built like a Bradley tank, the dark-haired man's exhale rippled a thick mustache. "My chair?"

O'Curran fought the urge to bristle, exchanging sides of the desk with the superiorly-ranked army officer.

Small sat in the too-low chair, folded beefy hands together on the desk and growled. "I've seen your reports, Colonel. I'm not one to gainsay an officer when I didn't witness him in action, but I'm hard pressed to find anything praiseworthy in your tenure here."

O'Curran didn't defend himself. The Meatgrinder wasn't known for patience, quite the opposite.

When O'Curran held his tongue long enough, a small, arrogant smirk turned up the corners of the general's mouth. "Good. Maybe you'll prove me wrong after all. Your battalion is hereby placed under my command. Report for a battalion commander's meeting in ten minutes, dressed in proper officer's attire."

O'Curran glanced at his field uniform, unsure how it was anything other than proper.

"Maybe if you're dressed like a command officer, you'll remember how US military officers are supposed to deal with terrorists."

Mare

Vitae whisked her out of the strange, impossibly tall building and away from the injured water phoenix. Taint encased her in some kind of crystal, different than the tainted landscape that had kept her prisoner. A city streaked beneath them, huge and bizarre but still somehow Atlanta.

There'd been no way to measure her tenure inside the horrible wasteland imprisoning her away from Creation and her Creator. Recent days had been plagued with new nightmares. The sword's wicked consciousness had made a game of finding new torments for each of its prisoners.

The glimpses of Vitae had been the worst yet.

She knew she was free. She knew the Vitae that had stolen her from battle was real. The moment her soul had been caught by her egg she'd felt the warm embrace of God once more.

The peace of strong father's arms had enveloped her.

The cage that sucked at her life force, the Fallen consuming the power of a divine phoenix she didn't know, none of it compared to the terror of discovering that the corrupted horror that had once been her friend wasn't just the stuff of nightmare.

Vitae landed them in the wreckage of a dilapidated, half-demolished building. His muffled voice called to someone, but no one came. He rested her newest prison beside a wide pool in what remained of an elegant foyer.

The crystal melted away.

Taint slammed into her so thick she felt within Faery itself. Her breath fled before the stench. She collapsed to her knees, still weak from trying to help the other water phoenix.

The waters pushed back the taint.

She lurched forward to the fountain's edge, sucking in the less polluted air like crawling through an inferno.

A childish female voice whispered from the water almost too quiet to hear. "Shield Mare?"

"Ani?" Mare shot a look toward Vitae who paced the foyer calling out to people who didn't answer. Mare had met the Watcher when she and Terrance had built their own oracle. The two had built their fellow shields a home close to the mortals in the hope that it could become the new Shield sanctum.

Anima had asked them not to reveal her, and Mare had never broken that promise.

"Does Vitae know of you?"

"Yes, but I cannot believe you are alive, returned."

"Who are you talking to?" Vitae demanded.

Mare splashed the oracle's waters onto her face and looked up. Vitae towered over her. "We have work to do."

Mare rose, shifting a thin veil over her nose to filter the taint. "What happened here?"

Vitae darkened, hatred and venom infused one word. "Aquaylae."

"The water phoenix trying to save us?" Mare asked.

"That selfish, incompetent whore wasn't trying to save us. She's responsible for all of Atlanta's ills. She willfully exposed Faery to the mortals, consorted with demons, murdered hundreds of mortals, tried to keep me from freeing you and destroyed not one but two Shield sanctums."

An angelic creature of eyes and wings burst into reality, ramming into Vitae and slamming him into the still-remaining stairs. "Lies! Slander!" The being pointed an eyeball-tipped finger like judgement itself. "You're the corrupt one. Quayla has sacrificed everything time and again trying to protect this city and you will not poison Mare to the...phoenix......responsible—oh, Creator, what have I done?"

Anima vanished in a flash.

"Ani?" Mare asked.

Sobs broke Anima's reply. "I'm sorry. I shouldn't have attacked Vitae. I shouldn't have intervened in Creation."

"It's all right, Ani," Mare said. "None of us are perfect."

Vitae climbed to his feet, emerald flames flickering around him. "Where is that putrid creature?"

"Vitae stop. She's sorry, but she obviously felt strongly that you were maligning this Quayla."

"Aquaylae is a demon, a turncoat sent to plague me. Look what she did to my sanctum!"

Plague me? My sanctum?

Mare extruded a necklace of essence beads and closed the distance between her and Vitae. She felt the beads like she would if she were tracking a Sidhe.

Oh, Vitae.

The life phoenix before her reeked more powerfully than a Sidhe Knight. Whatever he'd done to himself, he was more Sidhe than phoenix. Not declaring him Fae Kissed and demanding he surrender took all of her will.

I must have time to seek answers and a Divine One.

She surveyed the building.

But I will not do so here in this hell-blighted place.

Mare turned back to the street.

"Where do you think you're going?" Vitae demanded.

"Sanctuary," Mare said. "I must meditate on all I've learned."

"Stay," A pleading note undercut Vitae's anger. "This is our Sanctum, yours and mine. Here we will build the greatest Shield ever to grace Creation."

She looked at her Shieldheart, her own heart broken. She shook her head. "No. This will not be my new home."

"It'll be fine, Heaven on Earth once my dwarves repair all the damage Aquaylae did to the place."

"No, Vitae. I'm leaving."

"You have no idea what I've sacrificed so we can be together." Emerald flame and violet lightning danced around him in a dark corona. "You are not leaving!

Mare stared at him for a long moment, fighting the urge to let her true feelings reach her face. "I think I know what you sacrificed, Vitae."

Your soul and my respect.

"But...I love you, Mare."

Mare hid her repulsion. "If you truly care about me, you will give me time to collect myself."

Vitae's emotions warred for dominance on his face. Vulnerability won over fury in the end. "Where will you go?"

"Like I said, Sanctuary. I need to seek God's face."

"Your house is long gone."

Mare shrugged and marched away without looking back.

THE STORY CONTINUES...

Keep reading for the excerpt from
***Blood Phoenix Chronicles 5:
Razing the Last Bastion***

Thank you for reading *Rise of the Exiled Lady*.

Word of mouth recommendations and book reviews are insanely helpful, not just to other readers, but to an author's success. Moreover, we use these reviews to know what *you* want to read more of. Please consider leaving a short, honest review—nothing special required, just a sentence or two about how you felt about this book. I can't thank you enough.

If you loved this story and would like to stay up to date on the latest book releases, promotions, giveaways, and a free story, please be sure to become a member of the Delirious Scribbles Readers Group. [Your email address will never be shared, and you can opt out at any time.]

Begin your journey, just scan this image with your phone camera!

Keep reading for a sneak peek....

Sneak Peek:

Razing the Last Bastion

Vitae

I stared from the broken hotel facing as Mare walked away from the world I'd built to accommodate her.

Sanctuary? What more could she want than this? Than me?

Surveying the damage objectively, the condemned hotel had been in better shape before I'd started restoring it.

A cold welled up from my feet.

Maybe it isn't much of a home right now, but she should know I'll fix it.

Her desire to seek God's face rankled, but I understood. She'd been separated from His love for centuries. At the same time, I could've given her the love she needed. I could've explained the changes to Creation.

Fear suggested her departure was about more than a need for love. She'd outright refused for our Sanctum to become her new home—much as I had when she tried to move us out of the tower.

Is this punishment for that?

A certainty grew with the spreading cold icing my insides.

This is Aquaylae's fault!

Aquaylae and her corrupted brethren had attacked me and destroyed the home I'd made for Mare. I'd thwarted Aquaylae's machinations to destroy Mare's egg, but she'd corrupted my love when Mare joined their essences.

She'd exposed us to the wafers.

She'd brought about the death of countless Atlantans.

She'd turned Mare and the others against me.

She has to die once and for all.

I would Destroy Aquaylae myself, Vilicangelus's misgivings be damned. Once her influence was removed from the world, Mare could be cleansed.

I whirled back into my sanctum. "Scurith!"

The coyll didn't answer. He'd delivered Mare's egg to Viviane. Like with luring me into Vusolaryn and Mariena's trap, it appeared as if he'd betrayed me. At the same time, his actions brought Mare back to me.

But was he helping me or serving his queen?

It didn't matter. The loss of one sniveling servant wouldn't hamper my triumph. I called out for the other Sidhe servants. Not knowing or caring about their names, I climbed to the third floor. "Dwarves to me!"

None answered.

The third floor held none of my countless servants.

The sound of ultimate rage shook the building, bringing a small smile to my lips. Terrance had fallen in the battle at Circlestone.

Now he's been delivered to my care, reborn cleansed of the druid's and Aquaylae's influence.

His anger at Aquaylae and the impertinent mortal caused another understandably furious bellow. I left him to calm and ascended to the remaining servant quarters.

They were empty.

Whatever Viviane had done before stepping through her Arch, she'd stolen away my loyal servants—probably just to spite me.

I don't need them.

The basement had been ransacked and all but destroyed. A few trollmen nibblets grew in throbbing, slowly expanding lumps of flesh. There seemed no sign of any kyrie, but my mortal thrall could recreate them.

Good that I sent him away to serve me now.

Most of the secure areas had been reduced to melted slag. The Seelie cages were empty and fire-blackened Unseelie remains choked the air with burnt flesh.

Another bellow proceeded a blow that made the tile beneath me tremble. Ignis had melted closed the entrance to my phoenix cages, forcing me to reverse course back to the main foyer.

Standing at the ravaged balcony rail over top of my oracle pool, I called out to the vile creature that had attacked me. "Anima, come here this moment."

Her attack had been part of Aquaylae's treachery, but the creature served the Shieldheart, and she would do as I commanded.

"Anima, this moment!"

Her image rippled into existence on the water's surface.

"I require a putti repair team—"

"No."

My blood heated. "I beg your pardon?"

"My pardon shall not be offered in return."

A growl accented my voice. "I gave you an order."

"You are no longer a Shieldheart," Anima said.

"I was created a Shieldheart. No one can steal that away."

"You gave away your position when you recreated yourself in the image of the Sidhe," Anima said. "In the name of the Undying Light, I command you to surrender the Sidhe powers corrupting your soul and humble yourself before the Most High in hope of absolution."

"I am Atlanta's Shieldheart! I am the Hand of God in Creation!"

"You are nothing, Vitae, but a voice lost in the wastelands of sin."

Her image disappeared.

A moment later the waters of the oracle drained away until the underlying stone was bone dry.

Though it cost me my final breath, Aquaylae will answer for her actions.

Appendix A: Cast of Characters

Phoenixes:

Aquaylae (Quayla Buckler): A water phoenix assigned to the Atlanta Shield. Recently released from house arrest. Employed running a florist shop in eastern Atlanta. Dating Dylan Snyder. Preferred weapon: karambit knife

Caelum (Caelum Kite): An air phoenix assigned to the Atlanta Shield. Employed as Head of Charitable Projects by Circlestone Corporation. Preferred weapon: handgun or battle fan.

Ignis (Ignis Round): A fire phoenix assigned to the Atlanta Shield. Employed as a firefighter and arson investigator for the City of Atlanta. Preferred weapon: duo hilt bow and katana.

Mare: A water phoenix formerly assigned to the Atlanta Shield. Lost in a battle with Unseelie forced.. Preferred weapon: short swords.

Summuseraphi: A divine phoenix assigned as new praefectus of the shields of the southeastern United States. Formerly Lympha, Summuseraphi was recently elevated to divine status and placed under Villicangelus for training. Preferred weapon: chain blade.

Terrance (Terrance Wall): An earth phoenix assigned to the

Atlanta Shield. Employed at the Department of Motor Vehicles. Preferred weapon: cestus battle gloves.

Villicangelus: A divine phoenix assigned as overseers of the shields functioning in Southern Britain. Formerly overseer of the southern United States. Training supervisor over Summuseraphi. Preferred weapon: unknown.

Vitae: A life phoenix assigned to the Atlanta Shield as Shield-heart. Responsible for overall operations. Concerned about mortal deaths in her former shield, Vitae placed Quayla on house arrest. Preferred weapon: lajatang—bladed staff and baton forms.

<hr>

HUMANS:

Detective Sabrina Foxner: Atlanta detective currently assigned to the robbery division. The former homicide detective is investigating the Howell Mill break-in.

Doctor Bradley Sky: Intelligent and enthusiastic junior assistant coroner working in Atlanta's morgue. His memory has been rewritten multiple times to remove discovery of the Fey.

Dunham Heffernan: CEO of Circlestone Corporation

Dylan Snyder: Quayla's bisexual boyfriend. Dylan is aware of Quayla's true nature. He's employed as an IT professional

Emma: Fae Kissed human who made a deal to resurrect her cat. Employed at Howell Mill Humane Society

Judith: Pessimistic and disinterested Korean college student employed at Ponds de Leon Flowers.

Mara: Employee of Camp Woof doggie daycare

Miri: Atlanta PD tech ops.

Mrs. Hadley Sage Cox: Quayla's sweet but nosey landlady. Superstitious with detailed knowledge of Fey folklore.

Nicolas: Owner of a hole in the wall grocery store near the Atlanta Sheild's HQ and Caelum's supplier for honey candy and milk used as currency in the Goblin Market

Pete: Owner of Camp Woof doggie daycare

Tommy: Doctor at Grady Memorial Hospital Long time friend of Bradley Sky.

Valerie: News anchor. Subject of lingering crush by Bradleh's friend Tommy

Viviane: Dunham Heffernan's executive assistant

FEY:

Grynnberry: A Seelie nymph. An informant that provides Quayla with intelligence.

Knight Dolumii: Knight Champion of the Unseelie Court.

Knight Gherrian: Knight Champion of the Seelie Court.

Lady Esloah: Knight of the Seelie Court

Oshyn: Half sized elf merchant in the Goblin Market. Provides brownie cleaning services.

Princess Mariene: Unseelie sovereign and royal court adjunct between the Seelie queen and the phoenixes.

Prince Vusolaryn: Seelie sovereign and royal court adjunct between the Seelie queen and the phoenixes.

Thatch: WyldFae representative for the Sidhe's Georgia Shire near Atlanta

OTHERS:

Anima: Monitoring entity assigned to the Atlanta Shield

Look for more great books like these at a book reailer near you and learn more at www.deliriousscribbles.com

Acknowledgments

We've come to the ending of the fourth Blood Phoenix novel. It's been a rollercoaster ride so far, but I hope you've enjoyed it. I can't say this one didn't come with as many surprises for me as BPC3, but I'm glad you've stayed with me so far. With only one more book left in the series, there's a lot going on and a lot more to resolve.

I'd like you to know that as one of my readers, you are always in my mind when I'm working through a story.

Hmm, how can I torture the readers this time?

Kidding...mostly. :)

As with all the other Blood Phoenix Chronicles I need to thank talented artist Andrea Fodor for her gorgeous work. I can't wait to see the final cover for the last novel. We—myself and the great crew helping me—have endured some life issues that combined with previous scheduling issues to put this one behind schedule, but they stuck with me to help bring you the book in time for the scheduled release. I love the team that helps hunt down errors and brings the best out of my words: Rebecca and Sarah, Billy, Scott and Tina are just plain awesome.

Unfortunately, the surviving characters of the Blood Phoenix Chronicles don't get a break. We're only one book away from completing this story and time's wasting. Our last adventure begins now in BPC5: *Razing the Last Bastion*.

Thanks for joining me on this adventure...

Revision addendum: I'd like to thank Clint D for saving the day on this one by offering last minute proof reading. His assistance meant giving you a better book.

About the Author

Photo credit: Jim Cawthorne

Michael J. Allen is a star-lord, goofball, and USA Today bestselling author of character-driven, multi-layer, full-spectrum science fiction and fantasy novels - pretty much whatever madness sprouts from his head... (Learn more at www.deliriousscribbles.com)

Let's Connect

I love chatting with my readers, and hope you'll join my reader groups. If you'd rather stay up to date without joining in on the fun, there are plenty of ways to follow along.

— Michael J Allen

Reader Groups:

Discord : https://discord.gg/WeM4bwq
Facebook: https://www.facebook.com/groups/dsreaders
MeWe: https://www.mewe.com/join/dsreaders

Follow the Scribbler:

www.deliriousscribbles.com

amazon.com/-/e/B0096GEILG
bookbub.com/authors/michael-j-allen
facebook.com/deliriousscribbler
goodreads.com/deliriousscribbler
instagram.com/thedscribbler
twitter.com/Thedscribbler

www.ingramcontent.com/pod-product-compliance
Lightning Source LLC
Chambersburg PA
CBHW030710190726
48286CB00001B/264